GENE RODDENBERRY'S
Andromeda™

THE BROKEN PLACES

NOVELS FROM TOR BOOKS

DESTRUCTION OF ILLUSIONS
KEITH R. A. DeCANDIDO

THE BROKEN PLACES
ETHLIE ANN VARE with DANIEL MORRIS

VISIT THE ANDROMEDA WEB SITE
AT WWW.ANDROMEDATV.COM

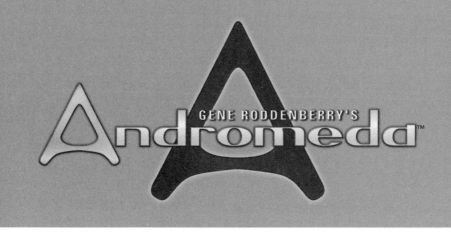

GENE RODDENBERRY'S
Andromeda™

THE BROKEN PLACES

ETHLIE ANN VARE
WITH DANIEL MORRIS

A TOM DOHERTY ASSOCIATES BOOK
NEW YORK

TOR®

GENE RODDENBERRY'S ANDROMEDA™: THE BROKEN PLACES

Copyright © 2003 by Tribune Entertainment, Inc., and Fireworks Entertainment, Inc.

Edited by James Frenkel

A Tor Book
Published by Tom Doherty Associates, LLC
175 Fifth Avenue
New York, NY 10010

www.tor.com

Tor® is a registered trademark of Tom Doherty Associates, LLC.

ISBN 0-765-30484-8

First Edition: November 2003

Printed in the United States of America

0 9 8 7 6 5 4 3 2 1

Dedicated to the memory of Virginia Heinlein,
science fiction's original kick-ass redhead

ACKNOWLEDGMENTS

First I must thank Gene Roddenberry, who not only imagined the seeds of the *Andromeda* universe but whose vision has informed the popular culture of a planet. It was Robert Hewitt Wolfe who grew those seeds into a rich, complex, and fully functioning reality. Robert's an inspiration and, I'm happy to say, a friend.

Without Kevin Sorbo, Lisa Ryder, Keith Hamilton Cobb, Laura Bertram, Gordon Michael Woolvett, and Lexa Doig, that reality would have no breath, no voice, no face. I thank them for bringing flesh and bone to the characters, and endowing them with virtues and foibles I never even thought of.

Let's not forget the people who put that reality on the screen: Tribune Entertainment executives Dick Askin and Karen Corbin, Fireworks Entertainment executives Jay Firestone and Adam Haight, and Executive Producers Allan Eastman and Majel Roddenberry. It's all fantasy until someone throws money at it.

Without the fans there would be no hit series and without a hit series, there would be no books. So—thanks, gang, for your support, always.

Which brings us to the book. Thank you, Henry Urick, for making a line of *Andromeda* novels possible. Thank you, Tor Books, for wanting to publish them. Thank you, Jim Frenkel, for asking me to write one and for supporting me through the process.

A special thanks to physicist Tom Chrien, who did his best to keep me honest. Writing may not be rocket science, but rocket science is.

I owe a huge debt of gratitude to my cowriter, Dan Morris. I couldn't have done it without you, kid.

As you may know, I was one of the original writers of the television series, and have since gone on to other things. It was a treat to live in this universe again. I hope you enjoy it as much as I did.

—ETHLIE ANN VARE
Los Angeles, 2003

I'd kiss the pain away if I could
Lord, if only I could
But it's our scars that tell us who we are
And I love you best
At the broken places
— SONG FRAGMENT, EARTH
(PREHISTORIC)

PROLOGUE • RAFE

Valentine's Rules of Engagement: Talk first. Run second.
When all else fails, shoot the bastard.

—IGNATIUS B. VALENTINE

The plan was flawless, in theory. *More than flawless*, thought Rafe
Valentine. *It was classic.* From time immemorial, the best way for one
person to make a lot of money was for a lot of people to lose a little
money. That way, no one gets hurt so bad that they come screaming
for your blood. It worked for lotteries, it worked for stock markets,
and it damn sure should have worked for the pyramid scheme known
as Gallipoli Fiduciary Holdings.

What Rafe hadn't figured on was the Petard Effect. As in, hoist by
one's own. Gallipoli, a frontier system at the ass end spiral of galaxy
M-82 and colonized some ninety years ago, wasn't going to survive a
solar flare, much less a Nietzschean strafing run, without a vested

and committed population. They needed settlers and they needed them fast, so they did what anyone in their position would do: they made some. No, they didn't violate anticloning treaties—not that those old Commonwealth treaties weren't roundly ignored anyway. Rather, they promoted multiple births among the first homesteaders, a technologically simple and socially acceptable tactic. Hell, Nightsiders and Chichins consider anything less than fifty offspring a small litter. Of course, they eat their excess young, but that's another story.

When Rafe discovered Gallipoli IV, it was a planet ripe for plucking precisely because of this anomaly. The pig-in-the-python population bump of Firsters (as the earliest arrivals called themselves) was rich, it was privileged, and it was getting old. The combination—inflated sense of entitlement meets degraded every other sense—was electric. No class of folks is easier to con than those who think the universe owes them something . . . but can't remember exactly what it is. The thing Rafe hadn't allowed for was that having become vested and wealthy and old, the Firsters were using the same equation Rafe was relying upon to secure their own future. They wrote the rules in such a way that a few people (themselves) would benefit greatly, while the many (everyone who came after) suffered so little that no one complained. Much.

Firsters got a better deal on mining rights, and a break in their FTA dues, and—this was the big "and"—crimes against Firsters were prosecuted more harshly than crimes against anyone else. The petard Rafe was hoist upon was officially known as the Elder Protection Act of AFC 275.

Bloody geriatric identical sextuplets, fumed Rafe. *How was I supposed to know that I was selling the same share of the same project to the same person for the third time? And since when is petty fraud a capital crime?*

So it was that the confluence of these forces found Rafe sprinting across the pressure-glazed rock surface of the nearest Free Trade

Alliance cargo port, ten meters ahead of a security force that was anything but geriatric. He turned, fired a sonic pistol. The blast stopped the pursuers temporarily . . . and permanently destroyed their ability to produce sperm or appreciate classical music. Rafe, having done this before, had illegal cochlear implants to protect his hearing; his sperm was safely stored on Sintii.

Rafe was safety-checking a modified courier ship that didn't exactly belong to him and analyzing his blunders on Gallipoli when the cops recovered. *I can't keep making the same mistakes and expect a different result*, he thought. Then the plasma grenade he left on the dock blew up in a lovely flume of orange and white, and he was off. It never quite occurred to Rafe that a last-minute escape from a Free Trade Alliance cargo port in a stolen ship was also something he had done many times before, invariably with a bad outcome. But at least he was beginning to identify the problem.

ONE

Any government that guarantees its citizens freedom of choice exposes itself to the risk that they will choose a different government.

—YIN PAN-WEI, *THE RISE AND FALL OF THE SYSTEMS COMMONWEALTH*, CY 11942

Deck 84 felt empty.

Of course, Deck 84 *was* empty, as were Decks 14 through 63, Medical Deck, three out of five Hangar Decks, and the unwanted-invitation-only V Deck—better known as the brig. *That's what happens*, thought Captain Dylan Hunt as he stood roughly geometric center of the *Andromeda Ascendant, when a ship massing 96,410,000 kilograms carries a crew massing* . . . Dylan let the thought trail off. He wasn't even going to estimate Beka Valentine's mass. He knew that much about women. He also knew that five people rattled around in here like so many BBs in a boxcar.

But Deck 84 was more than simply unoccupied. It was . . . uninhabited. Dylan felt like he did the time his father accidentally left him behind after work, locked in the Imperial Museum in Etashi Tarn past closing hour. He was eight, and the ceilings were ten meters high.

Where's the AI?

Dylan's wide blue eyes did a quick, accurate sweep of the corridor. Glorious Heritage-class ships like this one were built for both aesthetics and function; the *Andromeda Ascendant* was as much art as architecture. The burnished copper walls, the carved moldings, the seamless integration of technology and design, so Vedran in concept—it all looked perfectly normal. And yet . . .

"Rommie? Are you there?" Dylan spoke aloud to nothing in particular. Nothing in particular responded with nothing in return.

"Andromeda? Are you off-line? Report."

"She's with me, Boss."

The voice came from behind him. Dylan turned to see a face on the nearest comm screen: vaguely blond, undeniably human, with a cocky grin that made most people want to mop the floor with his brush-cut. The captain, however, had an uncharacteristic soft spot for Seamus Zelazny Harper's decidedly unmilitary antics. *If I grew up on a slag heap, starved and beaten like an unwanted dog, I probably would have turned out to be a brat myself.*

"Are you jealous? Be jealous!" said Harper.

"If by jealous you mean annoyed, impatient, and capable of severe retaliation, then yes, I'm jealous. Harper, what the hell are you doing to my ship?"

Dylan wasn't simply being possessive; he was being all-inclusive. *Andromeda Ascendant* is not only the name of a heavy battle cruiser—technically, her name is Shining Path to Truth and Knowledge, AI model GRA 112, serial number XMC-10-182—but also of the awesome artificial intelligence that inhabits it. Andromeda operated everything from her imaging sensors to her missile launch tubes to the Oracle attack drones to the microwave oven by autonomic reflex. Everything, that is, except the steering wheel. Only organics can actually pilot the Slipstream.

Andromeda was also Rommie, the ship's public interface avatar, which interacted with the crew in a humanoid form that artfully blended every Old Earth genotype into a visual amalgam Harper referred to as "babelicious." But that was Harper.

It also was Harper who turned the holographic avatar into a flesh and blood (well, nanosilicate and petrolubricant, at any rate) woman, making a silk purse out of a battle-damaged utility 'bot, some human DNA, and his own lusty imagination. It was this last (the avatar, not the imagination) that Harper was currently fine-tuning—if anything in his bag of spit-and-baling-wire engineering tricks could be called "fine"—and the reason Andromeda's attention was not currently on Deck 84.

I should have known, Dylan thought. Harper's mind ran to two things so consistently that you could see the grooves: girls and gadgets. Rommie was both. Whenever there was a brief, much-welcomed respite in the Things Go Boom general theme of their experiences since Dylan had arrived in this post-Fall dark age, Harper could reliably be found with a Sparky Cola in one hand and a nanowelder in the other.

Back in the machine shop, Rommie herself spoke up. It wasn't that she resented Harper's constant mechanical intercession, or even minded his puppy-dog infatuation; it was just that she enjoyed talking to her captain: he was, after all, the only living thing that shared her memory of the Systems Commonwealth. Oh, and she was desperately in love with him. Not that a good High Guard officer like Andromeda would ever admit such a gaffe. Even to herself.

"I can't be everywhere at once, Dylan," she said, with an unstudied pout on her fantasy lips and a toss of her anthracite-shiny hair.

"Yes, you can," said Dylan. "In fact, you're supposed to be. Regardless, whenever the two of you are finished, meet me on the Command Deck. I need to talk to you about this Drago-Kazov situation."

Calling the latest Drago-Kazov mess a "situation" is like calling Pythia's planet-shattering hyper-earthquakes "geological disturbances." It's accurate, but one hell of an understatement. The "situation" in question was an open revolt of the human slave worlds in the Alpha Centauri system against their Dragan overlords. Of course, this wasn't a phenomenon unique to Alpha Centauri—as of late, humans everywhere were rising up against the Nietzschean yoke, thanks in part to the efforts of the aforementioned Seamus Harper and his cousin Brendan Lahey, who orchestrated the first rebellion against the fierce Drago-Kazov Pride on Earth itself.

True to form, the Dragans responded by unleashing a litany of brutal atrocities against humans. A disproportionate number of the atrocities were aimed at a trio of planets in the Centauri colony, the foremost being the Earth-like planet Natal. There were two reasons for this choice, as Dylan saw it. One: Natal was where the Human Interplanetary Alliance had come into being, evolving from a ragtag group of freedom fighters who picked up the Bunker Hill battle cry and transformed themselves into an organized militia. Armed with little more than what they could scrounge, the HIA had nonetheless managed to severely disrupt Drago-Kazov slave-labor operations.

Which resulted in reason number two: the Nietzscheans, never ones to forgive losses at the hands of any enemy, let alone these genetically substandard kludges, seemed willing to quell the rebellion at any cost. Even if the cost was reducing an entire sector of space to rubble. It was time to bring the HIA and the Dragans to the negotiating table, whether they liked it or not.

Dylan sighed. *A nice quiet slag heap is actually beginning to sound rather appealing.*

Dylan walked to a ladderway. He activated the AG unit on his belt and stepped out over the opening, free-falling toward Command

Deck. Andromeda hated when he did that; it was, after all, a distance of two hundred meters, and what if the artificial gravity field failed? But Andromeda was in the machine shop, and Dylan delighted at the forbidden sensation of flight as he plunged weightless through space.

"I saw that." Rommie's voice came out of nowhere and everywhere. Dylan smiled wider. *Yup. I definitely would have been a brat.*

"You're watching me again, aren't you?" Tyr Anasazi didn't look up from his *kata* as he addressed the seemingly vacant space precisely two and a half meters to his left. There was no response. Tyr put down the extended force lance that served as his *bo* and stared at the hydroponics garden. The nictitating membrane of his eyes blinked; the vertical pupils contracted. Tyr's genetically enhanced vision wasn't likely to miss the sight of a pointed, purple ear peeking out from between the translucent leaves of an Infinity water rose. He waited, perfectly still. If he was breathing, no one could have heard it, be they hunter or be they prey.

Trance held out as long as she could, then she began to giggle. The colorless, fluid-filled globules that passed for flowers on Infinity Atoll jiggled as she laughed, which made her laugh more. The corners of Tyr's mouth turned up, but he stopped short of actually smiling. Unlike some Nietzscheans—the Drago-Kazov, for instance, practiced their menacing looks as children, and were punished for laughing—Tyr valued his smile. It was beautiful, and powerful. Which is precisely why he hoarded it.

Tyr's opinion of Trance was this: he liked her. She was useful and amusing and had a feel for living things. He understood that she was far more than she appeared to be, and he approved of that. He also feared it. So while Tyr Anasazi—of the Kodiak Pride, out of Victoria, by Barbarossa, etc., etc., etc.—was willing to kill for Trance Gemini, he was also prepared to kill her. Which is pretty much how he felt about every member of the crew of the *Andromeda Ascendant*.

Don't look for sentimentality in a Nietzschean. It was bred out of them, along with sickle-cell anemia and male pattern baldness.

Trance stood up behind the hydroponics vat, and the rest happened rather quickly. Her tail got caught in a feeding tube, which pulled free of the watering system, which toppled the ultraviolet bar, which short-circuited the timer, which sent Tyr diving across the room to pull her out of the vat before she electrocuted herself, just as Andromeda's face appeared on the comm screen to warn them that she detected a surge in the force lance's power pack, which at that moment exploded . . . just as Tyr put a full body length between himself and the time bomb.

Water roses splattered, klaxons blared, and a burst of undifferentiated laser light painted stark shadows on the walls. Tyr helped Trance up, but didn't let her go right away. He held on, maybe a little too firmly. Trance didn't squirm or flinch. She just looked at him with the quizzical expression Harper called her what-me-worry? face. Harper said it was an Old Earth cultural reference, which annoyed Tyr, who considered himself something of an expert in Old Earth culture. But then, Harper frequently annoyed Tyr.

"That was very lucky, for both of us," said Tyr mildly.

Trance brushed rose goo off her leotard. "But not for the poor roses." Well, save for one particular rose that, separated from the force of the explosion by Tyr's bulk, had somehow gone unharmed. *Dear, egocentric Tyr,* thought Trance, carefully ignoring the flower, *he'll think I did this all for him.*

"Still, wouldn't you call the timing of your accident . . . fortuitous? Imagine the odds."

About thirty-five thousand to one, Trance estimated. But she didn't say that. She just said, "Yeah. Imagine."

What Trance guessed—Trance is a very good guesser—and Andromeda quickly determined by forensic analysis, was that Harper had been putting tinfoil across the force lance's circuit breakers again. So to speak.

Force lances, like many High Guard artifacts, are powered by a "displacement battery," which was as close to perpetual motion as any technology is likely to get. The power pack consisted of a few billion nanobots navigating the Slipstream on a subatomic level. Of course, being nonsentient and nonorganic, they had no idea where they were going and couldn't reach their destination if they did, but that didn't matter. Charging around an enclosed space like so many microscopic bumper cars, the nanobots unleashed an enormous amount of displaced kinetic energy. In the case of a force lance, it was usually displaced as a plasma blast—although force lances also had less destructive uses. They made dandy flashlights.

Since nanobots are self-replicating and since the Slipstream exists within the interstices of matter and energy and is essentially infinite, this is a power source that lasts practically forever. It's also a power source that's too strong to put in the hands of enlisted men. That's why displacement batteries were designed by the Vedrans—the legendary, lost race who tamed The Universe As We Know It—with a staggering array of baffles, governors, and overrides built in.

Harper spent half his life circumventing these safety mechanisms. He had, in fact, only just hot-rodded the very force lance that Tyr was using for weapons practice. *Well, it worked, didn't it?* thought Harper as he surveyed the damage safely from a comm screen in the machine shop, tucked far away from any angry Nietzscheans.

Beka Valentine, at this particular moment, wasn't thinking about how big and empty the *Andromeda Ascendant* felt. She wasn't worried about the relative mass of the ship, nor was she concerned with the relative mass of her own body, whatever Dylan might think. Beka wasn't the type to worry about what her butt looked like in a pair of black leather pants. She was always more concerned about what a quick-release ankle-holster would look like in them. Besides, Beka was, as usual, ensconced in the familiar and far smaller area of the salvage ship *Eureka Maru*, the current occupant of Hangar Deck Two. Beka liked confined spaces. Something to do with spending three-quarters of her life in actual Space, no doubt. Space, as Harper liked to remind people, is Big. Infinitely, coldly, unimaginably Big. Off-duty, Beka was quite comfortable somewhere a tad more circumscribed, thanks.

What Beka Valentine was worried about at this particular moment was a silvery plastic disc that dated back to sixty-ninth-century Earth. Beka did a quick mental calculation: *AFC 306, minus CY 6990, give or take an era* . . . That makes it over three thouand years old. Wow. An artifact from a region known as "Eire-land," it was part of a museum salvage job that never quite made it back to the client. *They didn't miss it, and wouldn't have had the taste to appreciate it anyway,* Beka thought. But now the silvery disc was missing.

"Where's my goddam Pogues album, God damn it!" yelled Beka in frustration.

"Are you making a request of the Divine?" The voice came from what had been a weapons locker, since converted into a greenhouse for Trance's bonsai plants. Beka wouldn't say so to Trance, but the fact is that she missed the locker. She had a recurring dream where she grabbed for a Gauss gun, and found herself facing a Nietzschean Alpha brandishing a midget tree instead.

A face and body connected to the voice: mangy and scabrous, with fetid breath and rheumy eyes, its needle-edged fangs primed with paralytic poison. A Magog, the most feared creature in the Known Worlds. Rapacious. Remorseless. Relentless.

Wearing a monk's robe.

Beka grinned. "Hey, Rev. Didn't know you were in there. And I don't think the Divine responds to requests when they're phrased like that."

"I would caution against deciding what the actions of the Divine will or will not be. My experience is that all prayers are answered. Sometimes, the answer is—"

"*No,*" Beka finished the thought. It was an old game between them. "Yeah, I got that one."

Rev Bem arranged his features into what he hoped was a warm smile. It was more like a twisted leer, but Beka knew him long enough to read the intent as much as the grimace. Rev added, "Have you misplaced one of your sound recordings?"

"I don't misplace priceless antiques. It's been stolen."

"Now, Beka. I'm sure that Harper . . ."

Beka waved off Rev Bem's instinctive defense of the larcenous engineer. It wasn't that followers of the Way were blind to bad behavior, or even that they forgave it. They just accepted it.

"Not Harper. Rafe."

"Your brother."

"May he eat glass and die ptooey amen. Yeah, him."

Rev's impression of a grin stretched wider—which was even scarier than the first grotesquerie. Nothing amused Reverend Behemiel Far Traveler more than cosmic synchronicity. It was, he thought, the universe's way of being funny. Admittedly, the Divine played some truly sick practical jokes, but Rev appreciated the spirit of the thing. And this particular bit of coincidence was a knee-slapper.

The reason Rev Bem had come looking for Beka in the first place was to tell her that Rafael Valentine, missing and presumed incarcerated these past two years, was hailing them.

TWO

I used to get high on life. But then I built up a tolerance.

—SEAMUS ZELAZNY HARPER

Commonwealth Year 9797 sucked. And that's being generous.

After millennia of peace and prosperity—so much peace that the High Guard itself considered disbanding, so much prosperity it could build the *Andromeda Ascendant* to look like, well, the *Andromeda Ascendant*—the end came in the form of a Magog. A swarm of Magog. A locust horde of Magog that consumed everything in its path. And that was just the beginning.

The Magog are the most hated and feared race in the universe, and for good reason. Genetically engineered killing machines, Magog eat only sentient creatures . . . and eat them only while they're still alive. They reproduce by injecting first paralytic poison and then a batch of eggs into a living host and then waiting for the larvae to hatch and eat their way out of the still-screaming incubator.

It was because of the Commonwealth response to a Magog raid on Bradenburg Tor (CY 9766) that the Nietzscheans first fomented revolution, and it was because of the Nietzschean rebellion that everything turned to shit. Unsurprisingly, the Magog thrived on shit. The Long Night (CY 9784 to ten minutes ago) was a litany of planet after planet broken and pillaged by Nietzscheans and then scoured by Magog. Because as bad as the Nietzscheans might be—and Harper has a long list of Bad Things about Nietzscheans—they will kill you, but they won't eat you.

Which brings us to CY 9797. Earth is your basic dung heap, with humans playing the role of your basic dung beetle. Scrape, scrounge, survive. Humans are nothing if not survivors. That's the reason we have *Homo sapiens invictus* (a.k.a. Nietzscheans) in the first place, although the irony's lost on most *Homo sapiens*. And in Africa, still the most benighted of the continents despite countless attempts to reengineer the rain clouds, the future was about to change.

The sub-Saharan village where Father Francis Ntume worked and taught had remained remarkably untouched by the technological advances of the Commonwealth. It had even remained largely untouched by the ravages of Nietzschean . . . shall we say, entrepreneurship, since there wasn't much there worth appropriating. When travelers expressed surprise to find not only the simple village but an honest-to-God mission house in the middle of it, Father Francis would say, "If Darwinism can survive the Long Night, what makes you think Christianity can't?"

Father Francis was not to survive. His faith was.

The swarm ships came in early autumn, after Purim but before Good Friday. Their arrival was heralded by a barrage of photon bombs exploding in the heavens, unleashing light so intense it blinded anyone within a radius of several kilometers . . . and made them easy pickings for Magog. Most of the villagers were simply eaten alive in the first wave; Father Francis, far enough from ground zero that he sustained little damage to his sight, stayed awake for three days and nights giving Last Rites. Sometimes, he gave them to scraps of meat whose DNA he had to analyze before he could give them a name. He had no tears left. He had no conception of God left. He had only ritual, and love.

Father Francis was raped by a Magog whose name was an ear-splitting ultrasonic screech roughly translating as "Fleshrender." Fleshrender was of the officer class: Magog who used weapons and intellect to keep their bloodthirsty charges from killing and eating one another before they ever reached their targets. Francis was just unfolding his long frame, bent over yet another corpse, when Fleshrender's fangs sprayed him with venom, then injected him with eggs. Instantly paralyzed, Father Francis slumped against a slender acacia tree; Fleshrender sat next to him, and waited for his larvae to ripen.

There was no physiological reason why Father Francis's vocal chords weren't paralyzed by the Magog venom. But any follower of the Way knows a miracle when they see one.

It takes six Earth days for Magog eggs to gestate. On the seventh day, they hatch and eat their way out of their host. The host's last drop of blood provides the Magog babies their first meal. And so for six days, Father Francis talked to Fleshrender. There was nothing else for him to do.

Father Francis told Fleshrender of the crucifixion and resurrection of Jesus Christ. He told him about Moses and the burning bush, and Judah the Maccabee. He told him about Buddha, and Mohammed, and Joseph Smith. He told him about African ancestor worship and Haitian voodoo and an Indian god with an elephant's face. He tried to describe Zoroastrianism, which he himself didn't understand. He walked the Eightfold Path and climbed the Twelve Steps. He was, Francis realized, not so much explaining to Fleshrender but rather trying to explain to himself the Mystery he had devoted his life to.

And while it would be satisfying to report that Father Francis had a cosmic epiphany in the last moment of his life, there is no record that such a thing ever happened. Perhaps it did. Or perhaps he simply died, died the same way he had lived: in Awe. What is recorded, however, is the epiphany of Fleshrender.

Put simply, Fleshrender received a vision. Opening up before him, against the backdrop of a burnt sky, shone a path. This path was the Way—a just and good path, one that could only be traveled with love, wisdom, and a belief in the Divine. It was all-inclusive, and it was all-forgiving. And as this road stood before him, Fleshrender understood that it was now *his* road, and that it could accommodate an infinite number of travelers of any species, and all he had to do was show it to them and start them down it. It was the best he could do to atone for his sin against Father Francis, and it was the only way he could ever honor what he came to believe was his love for the man.

As the last seconds of Father Francis's life spooled away, the Magog larvae chewing their way through the skin of his stomach, Fleshrender held the man's head in his lap, wiping away his tears, comforting him with a tender, respectful hand. When his young finally emerged, Fleshrender quickly pulled them free.

He refused them the blood of their host, offering instead his own flesh.

Suffering the pain of his own offspring, Fleshrender dipped his hands into the blood that had welled in the hole in Father Francis's abdomen, cupping this precious liquid, then lifting these hands to the sky. He let the blood fall onto his head, and it dripped down and around the horns in his forehead and face. Thus baptized, Fleshrender assumed the name of the Anointed, then said a prayer over the lifeless form of Father Francis.

Eternal life grant unto him, and may perpetual light shine upon him.

Certain that the body would not be found by other Magog, the Anointed left Father Francis, leaning in the shade of the tree. He pulled his suckling sons from his bleeding fur, vowing that neither they nor he would taste the flesh of another sentient being again. It is a fact that Magog retain some of the DNA of their host, and the Anointed, knowing this, was determined that his sons should live to be worthy of Father Francis.

The Anointed returned to his people, preaching what he had learned, speaking even when his words fell on deaf ears. The Magog, hardly famed for their friendly dispositions, viewed the Anointed with a deep suspicion and his efforts were usually greeted with violence. With the aid of his disciple sons he did manage, through the example of his sheer devotion and belief, to win over a small number, but he could not win over them all. While attempting to convert the Magog of Rexos Arteris, the Anointed walked into the midst of a young swarm that was being starved in preparation for an attack upon a nearby system. It is doubtful whether any of these Magog, insane with hunger, heard the Anointed's last words as they ate him alive.

Eternal life grant unto them, and may perpetual light shine upon them.

Which brings us right back to CY 10089—as Dylan would call it, although to the rest of the crew it was AFC 306—where one finds the Way still very much alive. Although Rev Bem might argue that the Way had never really been dead. Rev Bem, like the Anointed, had been converted by a human, although this human was already a devout Wayist. By now the Way had spread to all corners of the universe, originally via the Anointed's first Magog disciples who spread about the galaxy as missionaries, and then by their respective con-verts. Until a Magog attack on the planet of Kingfisher found a young Magog called Red Plague mourning the gravesite of his human host-parent, feeling something uncharacteristic in a Magog: shame. Shame for the violent crime his Magog parent had perpe-trated, and shame for his (albeit unintentional) role in the crime. And that was when Brother Thaddeus Blake approached him, and that was when Red Plague became Reverend Behemiel, and that was when Rev found the Way.

How Rev Bem became the sudden audience to a flood of obscene epithets aimed at Beka's brother Rafe is another story entirely.

"He's a liar, a thief, a cheat, he's, he's . . ." Beka chewed at her full lower lip as she cast around for ten more reasons why Dylan shouldn't allow Rafe's ship to dock. Eventually she just gave up with an exasperated groan.

Dylan commented wryly from the *Maru*'s comm screen, "I take it that this is your way of saying you're pleasantly surprised he's here."

You would put it that way, thought Beka. *But then, you never got arrested because Rafe hid a stash of counterfeit thrones on your ship without telling you.*

"Rev, please go and greet our new arrival at Hangar Three," said Dylan.

"Of course." Rev nodded and exited the *Maru*'s Flight Deck, eager to give Beka some berth.

"His ship's a little banged up," said Dylan. "Harper says he dinged his MPD thrusters and his Slipstream drive is shot. Apparently, he was ambushed by Nietzschean pirates while en route to Zibetha."

"And let me guess," said Beka. "He just *happened* to outmaneuver these pirates in, of all things, a courier ship, and then *happened* to be just a few Slip jumps away from the *Andromeda Ascendant*, where he just *knew* he'd be safe. How convenient."

Dylan shrugged. Despite Beka's bluster, she seemed to do the

right thing in the end . . . most of the time. And surely Rafe didn't
fall too far from the Valentine tree, he imagined. He assumed. He
hoped.

"I'll leave Rafe in your charge," said Dylan. "You two can sort this
out yourselves. I've got my hands full with a trigger-happy Dragan
admiral and a system of slave planets screaming for revolution.
When you and your brother finish catching up on old times, meet me
on Command Deck." Dylan thought for a moment, then added,
"Both of you. Rafe's a smooth talker, to put it mildly, and I'm going
to need all the help I can get making this peace negotiation a reality."

Beka gave a mock salute. "Aye, aye, Cap." She shut off the comm
screen.

Convenient, Beka harumphed. *With Rafe, there was no such thing as
"convenient."* His arrival wasn't some lucky coincidence, and Beka had
long since given up hope that Rafe possessed a single honest mole-
cule. The list of Rafe's infractions was a long one: somewhere near
the top were her stolen CD collection, followed by the time he
trailed her to Asporia and then beat her to the Tablet of Kalderash.
And, lest she forget, there was the last time Rafe stepped foot on the
Andromeda—and practically got them all killed by hyper-militant
Restorians.

Beka sighed. Sometimes she couldn't decide whether having Rafe
for a brother was any better than having no family at all.

"I decided I shouldn't leave you to face the criminal charms of Rafael
Valentine alone," said Beka, joining Rev Bem at the entryway to
Hangar Three.

Normally, Rev would have pointed out the rewards of being
patient with others, even our most wayward brethren. But he took
one look at the flash of Beka's pale eyes and resolved to save the
thought for later.

There was a commotion from back at the end of the hangar access corridor, and both Beka and Rev turned to see Trance come tripping around a corner, presaged by a clatter of maintenance drones desperately maneuvering to get out of her way. "Beka, your brother's here!" she announced, out of breath, running to greet them.

"Not for long," said Beka. "Enjoy it while it lasts, because it's going to be a brief visit."

Trance came to a sliding stop, barely avoiding losing control and barreling into Beka and Rev. "What do you mean?"

"If there's a more accurate harbinger of trouble than my brother, I have yet to meet it."

"You're just saying that . . ." Trance cut herself short. The expression on Beka's face suggested that would be the most intelligent thing to do. "Sorry," Trance squeaked. Trance liked to think she knew just when to shut up. The problem was, she never stayed shut for long.

"Ooh, I almost forgot," she exclaimed. She pressed what appeared to be a data disk into Beka's palm. "You dropped this."

Beka started to hand the little disk back to Trance: "I didn't—"

But Trance cut her off. "You did. I went to find you on the *Maru*, and that's where it was. I mean, I think it was on the *Maru*. At least, that's when I found I had it. And the *Maru*'s so big it could have been anywhere now that I think about it, maybe behind one of the control banks, or I could have stepped on it, or it was in one of the storage lockers—"

"Trance, this could belong to anyone," groaned Beka. She turned the disk over between her fingers. Etched on one side was the Commonwealth insignia and a numerical designation: Alpha seventy gamma twelve. Beka nearly choked. It wasn't a data disk, it was a key.

"Trance, I'm only going to ask you once. Where did you get this?"

Trance repeated with perfect innocence: "I went to find you on the *Maru*, that's where it was. I mean, I think it was on the *Maru*—"

"Okay, Trance, I get the idea. I believe you." Which was an

absolute lie. But as Beka began thinking about the myriad uses for the key Trance had given her, she figured it was probably best not to know too much in this particular instance. And it was best that as few people knew about this as possible. Rev Bem watched with silent interest as Beka pocketed the key. She answered his unspoken query: "Looks techie. Probably Harper's. He'd lose that wise-ass grin of his if it wasn't permanently attached."

Before the matter could be pursued further, Trance again broke into hyperkinetic animation. "Rafe's here!"

The three of them watched from the safety of the airlock as the small courier ship came to an asthmatic and lopsided rest. The ship was vigorously spraying antiprotons from its undercarriage and one of the solenoid valves was belching smoke. It looked pitiful sitting in the cavernous hangar bay, like a small toy. Beka knew that back in the heyday of the Commonwealth, this hangar would be holding a full complement of thirty-six Centaur Tactical Fighters along the double-tiered racks that ran the length of the bay. She tried to picture them, but couldn't. Dylan, she realized, must see their shadows every time he steps into the hangar bay.

Andromeda's AI appeared briefly on the comm screen next to the door. "Pressurization complete."

Rev Bem unlatched the door, then made an exaggerated bow. "After you."

"And they said chivalry was out of style," Beka chided. "Maybe instead of teaching the Way, you should cross the stars, spreading good manners."

Rev snarled his amusement. "Etiquette is very spiritual," he chided. "You should try it sometime."

Beka stepped into the hangar just as the courier ship's side-mounted door unlatched with a screech. Making a lame attempt to open, the cargo door only managed to release halfway. *No doubt dam-*

aged by those pesky pirates, thought Beka, marveling that Rafe's lies weren't even good ones.

An arm appeared through the slim opening, followed by a shoulder, and then the head of Rafael Valentine himself, trying to squeeze his body through the available space, barely making it. He jumped free of his ship and stretched contentedly. Rafe is a good fifteen centimeters taller than Beka, and literally towered over Ignatius, their father. He's as dark as she is fair, lean and muscular with deep mahogany curls—what was called "tall, dark, and handsome" in simpler times. Beka noted with some amusement that he possessed something nearing a suntan, unusual for someone whom she had until now believed to be incarcerated, and who had probably spent about two percent of his life on solid dirt in range of a nonlethal sun.

When Rafe saw Beka waiting for him with her arms crossed, he gave the most charming smile in his repertoire, the look-at-you, you-gorgeous-thing-you grin. "Booster Rocket!" he boomed warmly.

Beka frowned at the sound of her old family nickname. "Why are you here, Rafe?"

"What? No hug and kiss? No 'Hey, big brother, it's good to see you'? Is this your idea of a warm welcome? Sour looks and a Magog?" Rafe quickly added, "Nothing personal, Reverend."

"Greetings to you too, Rafe," responded Rev.

Trance jockeyed for attention: "Don't forget me."

"Miss Trance Gemini, I couldn't forget you if I tried. There are just not that many purple humanoids with tails running around anymore."

Beka impatiently cleared her throat. "In case you didn't hear me the first time—what brings you to the *Andromeda*, big brother?"

Rafe motioned to his little ship. "Well, as you can see, this tin can is in some trouble. I had some debts to pay off at Zibetha and—"

Beka cut him off. "Right, Zibetha. And then you got run to

ground by pirates. Rafe, if you're going to try and con me, at least put some more imagination into it. Pirates? Might as well tell me the dog ate your flight plan."

Beka could practically see the circuits triggering behind Rafe's dangerously innocent green eyes. *Right about now you're deciding whether to keep up the charade, or whether to come clean. And I'll bet the Hegemon's Heart it's the latter. Ah, Rafe, you can be so predictable.*

As if on cue, Rafe sighed, and held his arms apart in uncharacteristic supplication . . . immediately putting Beka on guard.

"Okay, so maybe it wasn't pirates," said Rafe. "Pirates, Gallipolans, what's the difference?"

Rev sensed—rightly, as usual—that Beka would prefer he and Trance make themselves useful elsewhere. "I'm sure there is much the two of you need to discuss. Trance and I will take our leave, as we are quite busy—"

"No, we're not," insisted Trance. "Don't Beka and Rafe look happy to be together?"

Rev smiled at Rafe and Beka. "Positively carefree," he said chuckling. Then he grasped Trance firmly by the hand and led her away, allowing her one last stop to turn and wave good-bye.

As soon as they were gone, Beka began impatiently tapping her foot. "Gallipolans?"

Rafe whistled. "Looking good, little sister. How come a hot number like you is still single?"

"Because I keep meeting men like you, big brother. One more time. Gallipolans?"

Rafe squirmed. "Yeah, there was this deal, it kind of went bad. Hasty exit. You know the drill. Touchy old geezers those Gallipolans."

"Yes, imagine, people upset over . . . let me guess. Being robbed? Being duped? The nerve."

"But the setup was perfect—"

Beka stopped him with a wave of her hand. This was a speech she'd heard before. Hell, half the time it was she who'd been giving it.

"And you thought it would be a great idea to ditch what I'll just assume is a stolen ship here on the *Andromeda*. Then you'd take off again in something these supposed Gallipolans would never look for. And why do I suspect you had the *Maru* in mind? I wonder, were you planning to take me along for the ride, or were you just going to steal that ship too? And all this time, I worried that you were rotting in a cell somewhere."

"I did some of that, too." Rafe's face softened. For a moment, Beka could glimpse the pain and punishment his chosen life meted out to him. But she wasn't about to soften in return.

"Forget it. I want my CDs back, then I want you back in that junker of yours and on your merry way. I don't care if the entire Gallipolan security fleet is after you. If such a thing even exists."

"It does, and they are," Rafe added helpfully. "But I've also been doing some thinking lately. Maybe it's time for me to get out of the game. It's . . . getting old."

And so is that ploy, thought Beka. Beka had heard her brother say he was contemplating walking the straight and narrow so often that she had learned to tune it out, like white noise. She realized long ago that waiting for Rafe to clean up his act was a waste of time. Might as well wait for the Big Bang to reverse itself and the universe collapse back into a fist-sized marble of dark matter.

"I want you gone," said Beka. "There's not a single thing you could possibly say to change my mind. Go. Now. Good-bye." Beka turned and started toward the exit. "I'm telling Rommie to open that hangar bay door as soon as I'm out of here. You best get back in your ship unless you want to get sucked into the wild black yonder." She got one foot over the threshold of the Observation room. "See you in a couple of years."

"Hey, Booster Rocket," called Rafe. "There is one more thing I wanted to mention."

Beka paused. This couldn't hurt too much.

"I found our mother."

Beka hated being wrong. Especially when she was so sure she was right. But it appeared that there was something Rafe could say after all that would indeed change her mind.

As far as Beka Valentine was concerned, she didn't have a mother. Her family consisted of herself and Rafe, two small moons caught in the orbit of the contradictory, fast-burning sun that was Ignatius Valentine. Pop had always said their mother died young. Except once, while detoxing off Flash, when he said she ran off with another man. The possibility of her mother being alive was, quite frankly, incredible.

Beka stopped, turned around, and retraced her steps. She didn't let herself get too excited. This was Rafe she was dealing with, after all. Certainly not a pillar of reliability. He was probably just trying to buy himself more time.

"You have exactly one minute to explain," said Beka.

"First, let me just say that I've been meaning to see you for a while. But you know, things come up. I get sidetracked. I'm here now, and that's all that matters. Right?"

"I changed my mind. I'm giving you ten seconds." This was *not* going well.

This time Rafe presented her with his c'mon-you-can-trust-me, conspiratorial smile. He'd told her once that he categorized and graded his various smiles and smirks based on what they communicated and how effective they were. Numbered them, even. She didn't doubt him for a second.

"Okay," said Rafe. Then quickly: "The Sigrund Moon. The Nebulos Scepter. The Fist of Pac Tull."

It took less than ten seconds. Rafe shut up and waited for the words to sink in. After a moment of silence, he laughed. "You should see the look on your face, Rocket! You know, you're cute when you let your guard down. Was that surprise I detected?"

Beka turned a shade of pink. She wanted to kill Rafe, and was pretty sure she would. But first she'd find out where he'd gotten his info.

"You just bought yourself an extra five minutes."

Rafe really did know his sister better than anyone else. And it wasn't necessarily due to any keen perception on his part. It was just that she thought and acted exactly the same way he did.

"C'mon, Sis. You've been looking for these antiques ever since you figured out how to pilot the *Maru*. And what, you think I don't have an interest in them, too? We're only talking about the Vedran Runes, the biggest score since . . . hell, I can't think of anything bigger."

Neither could Beka. She'd already devoted an estimated eight-point-two years of her life searching out pieces of the Rune. She'd even found one, which was currently hidden away nearby and about which she was not going to tell Rafe. (She was also not going to tell him the other name she had come to call the Runes. . . .)

Rafe eagerly embarked on what fellow grifters call the tough sell—convincing the unconvinceable. But of course, with Rafe, the tough sell was practically the only form of communication he knew. He couldn't conduct a normal conversation if he tried.

The centerpiece of the tale involved his recent incarceration, the result of smuggling bundles of protopolymer for an independent producer into the FTA stronghold known as Prospero Post. If the FTA had its way, the rest of the universe would resemble that terraformed trading planet: strict guidelines regulated who sold what to whom and for what price, and any threat of competition was all but eradicated, allowing the established dues-paying members to reap deep and institutionally guaranteed profits. Needless to say, the Powers That Be weren't too happy to find unendorsed product sneaking into their own backyard.

Rafe got collared at a routine cargo search on Diligent Commerce Drift. Normally, Rafe wouldn't be one to take such treatment sitting down—although this time he did exactly that, having fallen asleep in the pilot's chair. Unable to procure the necessary thrones to abet his release, Rafe found himself biding time in one of Diligent's dirtiest cells, across the way from a Perseid named Sammie. At least, that's the approximation of his name that Rafe used.

Sammie and Rafe got to talking. More accurately, Rafe got to charming, bullying, and coercing—eventually learning everything of note about old Sammie. And there was one thing in particular of very big note: Sammie was an amateur archaeologist. In fact, he had an abiding interest in many of the very same valuable and prestigious artifacts that Rafe had, albeit for different reasons. Sammie loved history. Rafe loved profit.

Rafe's amusing impression of the Perseid aside, Beka was losing patience at the pace the tale was unraveling. "And what does this have to do with the Moon, Scepter, and Fist? None of which have even been verified as existing, I might add."

Rafe appeared truly shocked. "This goodwill mission you're on has really kept you out of the data loop, hasn't it? Beka, in certain circles—which we're both very aware of, and which shall remain nameless—there's talk. And lately this talk says that these three artifacts definitely exist . . . because they've been *found.*"

Savoring the sensation of having made his sister now produce *two* rarely seen blushes, Rafe got to the point. Sammie, it turned out, had gotten busted for hacking the Diligent Commerce branch of the All Systems University library. The library existed entirely in the Drift's computer network. Certain lower-tier FTA members who were based on Diligent used it as a cover, hiding their not-so-on-the-level business records in the mountains of library data. Hence they were a bit touchy about the Perseid's snooping. But Sammie wasn't after any business records; he was after information, particularly a rumored cache of literature relating to his beloved artifacts that the All Systems University had made forbidden and secreted away. In his search of the darkest, most neglected corners of the library, he instead found—tucked away beneath piles of junk code—an indiscreet program that tracked every library file ever accessed, where it was accessed from, and by whom.

"So let me guess," said Beka. "You and Sammie either broke out or bribed your way out of jail."

"Bribed. My generous employer finally came through—a gift for not revealing his identity."

"Then you had the Perseid find out who was accessing information on the artifacts, and how often. Just in case there was some money in it for you somehow. Maybe in case it meant finding the remaining pieces of the Runes."

Rafe grinned. "Correctamundo. And while the identities were never the same for long, the locations—one in particular—remained constant. The most likely suspect was downloading from Farside Drift. We tracked the ID to a hotel cubicle complex, one of those stopover body lockers. And with a little maneuvering, Sammie produced a security scan of our mystery person."

Rafe reached into the collar of his boot and pulled out a flexi, handed it to Beka. The scan was a bit grainy, but there was no questioning the identity of its subject. It was a blond woman, maybe forty-five years old, with deep-set laugh wrinkles and a familiar see-if-I-care air that translated even across the scan. It was an older Beka, with slightly higher cheekbones and a slightly smaller chin. Beka gasped. "Mom?"

Rafe smiled. "Magdalena Valentine in the very flesh. We can be at

Farside in less time than it takes to change the color of your hair. What do you say? Are Valentine Smart and Smarter back in business?"

Beka felt a momentary, terrifying doubt. Maybe this was another of Rafe's cons. But that doubt was short-lived. Rafe was good, but he wasn't *that* good.

"Grab your things," said Beka. "We're getting on the *Maru* and we're leaving. And for the record, I'll be Valentine Smarter this time."

The *Andromeda* was operating quite passably these days. That is, for a ship accustomed to a complement of 4,132 crew members now managing with a decidedly far leaner crew of six. Four of them, plus Rommie's avatar, were currently manning the Command Deck and debating the finer points of Drago-Kazov personality.

"We can try appealing to their softer, caring side," suggested Harper.

"Nietzscheans have no softer, caring side," Tyr responded automatically.

"My point exactly," said Harper. Speaking under his breath he added, "Not much of a sense of humor either."

"I heard that, boy."

Dylan decided to intervene before Tyr began using Harper as a practice bag. There were more pressing uses for their time. "Look. Even I don't expect to appeal to the Dragans' sense of moral responsibility. But if they can't be persuaded to grant Alpha Centauri its freedom for the common good, maybe they can be persuaded that *not* doing so will bankrupt them. And I get the feeling they've already begun to realize this."

Harper was having a hard time seeing the situation as anything but the wanton murder of fellow humans who want nothing more than their own freedom. "I still can't believe you want to talk with the Nietzscheans. After what they've done . . ."

"What I can't believe is that the Dragans are willing to talk, period," said Dylan. "We have to give the process a chance. And every minute they're talking is a minute they're not slaughtering civilians on Natal."

Tyr snorted. "I agree with Mr. Harper in this instance, much as it pains me. Once again, your ideals are going to get us all killed. Despite everything I've told you, and everything you know about Nietzscheans, you believe the Dragans' intentions to be honorable. Either you're bravely stupid, or stupidly brave. Neither is acceptable to me."

Dylan considered the comment, and he considered the source. Dylan knew that the Drago-Kazov murdered Tyr's parents and the rest of his Kodiak Pride. And he knew that vengeance never quit Tyr's waking mind. But he also knew that Tyr wasn't the type to embark on any suicide missions.

Dylan didn't trust the Dragans any further than he could throw one of *Andromeda*'s warbots, but for now he wasn't saying so aloud. He had been just as surprised as the rest of the crew to receive the message requesting that *Andromeda* aid negotiations in the Centauri system. The thing that convinced him to come, though, was the fact that the Drago-Kazov fleet, in all its hostile glory, wouldn't be there to breathe down the *Andromeda*'s neck. Because not only were the Dragans' resources stretched policing their now-rebellious slave worlds, but the formidable Maroon Pride had picked this of all times to declare a war against the Drago-Kazov. This meant the Dragans would be bargaining without the full resources of their preoccupied army to back them up. Of course, this wasn't to say the Alpha Centauri Dragans were weaponless—according to information obtained by Harper's contacts in the human resistance, the Dragans were traveling with a Nimitz-class flagship—a very large, very armed, very fighter-ship-carrying flagship.

Dylan's attention moved to the new arrivals on Command Deck:

Rev Bem and Trance, returning from the hangar bay. Rev Bem took his station at sensor control and Trance wandered next to Harper.

"How's the family reunion going?" asked Harper.

Rev diplomatically replied, "They seem to be making progress."

"I think Beka's mad at Rafe," said Trance.

"Entire galaxies are mad at Rafe. But they can work that out later," said Dylan. "This message from Admiral Rasputin Genovese is already two weeks old." Since Dylan also knew from Harper's intel that the HIA wasn't faring well and had been suffering large casualties, he didn't want to waste any more time. Alpha Centauri was a few Slip jumps and some PSL time away; this was going to take some traveling.

"Andromeda, please tell Beka her piloting services are required on the Command Deck."

"One moment, Captain," said the AI. Her virtual expression seemed concerned. "I'm putting her through."

Beka appeared on the large Command Deck viewscreen. She was attaching herself into the *Maru*'s pilot harness. She smiled. "Hey, Dylan. You're never going to believe this. Rafe found our mom."

Dylan did a double take. He had often heard Beka talk about her father—occasionally even in words suitable for mixed company—but had never heard mention of a mother. And having dealt with Rafe before, he wasn't sure if he *did* believe it, if "it" was something produced by Rafael Valentine.

But Beka was practically giddy. "So we're gonna go find her. I'll be back, oh, when I'm back."

"Beka, you can't just leave," said Dylan.

"Want to watch me?"

This is a bad time to regress to your anti-authoritarian defaults, thought Dylan. He didn't want to lose his best pilot on the eve of a tricky negotiating mission. "You are the acting executive officer of this vessel and our most capable pilot. You have a responsibility here. I can't let you leave on a whim."

"Whim? This is no whim. This is my *mother*."

"This crew depends on you just as much as you depend on them. Running off is a betrayal of our trust. Hell, it's grounds for court-martial."

"Court-martial? That's a good one." Beka was getting angry. Dylan kept forgetting one tiny little fact: the High Guard *no longer existed*. "Look, this New Commonwealth is *your* idea, and I'm all for *my crew* helping you out. But right now, this is more important to me than any Commonwealth. Okay?"

"Not okay." Dylan's face was set.

Harper turned to Dylan with a quizzical expression, "C'mon, Boss. It's her mom. I can Slip-pilot just fine."

"That's not the point," replied Dylan. "Beka doesn't get to run off, putting our mission at risk—maybe our lives at risk—just because she feels like it. It doesn't work that way."

Dylan looked around at the rest of the crew, and was surprised to see that their sympathies obviously lay with Beka. Even Tyr, whose expression was never easy to read, seemed to approve; family is sacred to the Nietzscheans. Only Rommie was automatically on her captain's side—protocol was in her programming.

"Dylan, I'm sorry. But my mind's made up," said Beka. "Andromeda, open the hangar bay door."

Rommie looked at Dylan for her response. He shook his head. "Override. Beka, I'm not allowing you to leave."

Rev Bem turned to Beka's image on the screen. "You know, Beka, being responsible is just that, a responsibility. It's a burden that is borne, sometimes when we'd rather not carry it. I think perhaps you should reconsider."

"Rev, I'd have thought you of all people would understand."

"He does understand," said Dylan. "He knows that as a member of this crew, you are beholden to a code of behavior."

Trance squirmed as the conversation continued. She could have said something, maybe remind Beka—but that might give too much away. No, things would turn out all right. Beka was smart, she'd remember. But still, there was always the chance the odds went against her. Trance tried to see the filmy threads of probability . . . no, it was no use. They were too pale.

Beka turned back and yelled. "Rafe, move it. We're going."

"Going where? You're locked in," said Dylan. "You certainly can't shoot your way out. And I'm not granting you permission to leave."

"Then I'll just have to do it without your permission."

Beka paused, and became more somber. "Please understand, Dylan. I'm not doing this *to* you. It's something I need to do, for me. I hope you can understand. You should understand." The viewscreen went dark; Beka had closed the communication.

Rommie suddenly turned to Dylan, surprised. "Something's wrong. The hangar doors are opening."

Trance smiled. *Good girl . . . and good luck.*

All eyes immediately went to Harper. An occupational hazard when you're a mechanical genius with a predilection for mischief. "Don't look at me," he whined. "I had nothing to do with this." And it was not lost on him that of all the times he'd said that, this was the first time he meant it.

"I don't think it is Harper," said Rommie. "It's not his style. There's no sign of internal tampering—she's using a manual access key."

For the fifth—or was it sixth?—time today, Dylan yearned for the days when he had an actual crew aboard the *Andromeda*. Back then, access keys didn't go showing up in the hands of rogue pilots. Only senior Lancer officers had the appropriate security ranking to get to those keys. But any one of this motley gang—with the possible exception of Rev—could have stolen those keys without it being a stretch of character.

Rev Bem shot a glance at Trance Gemini. He was all for coincidences—sometimes they were much needed and fortuitous signs of

Divine goodwill—but this exceeded the limits of what coincidence could accomplish. What game was Trance playing, he wondered, and why? How did the rest of the crew fit into it? How did he fit into it?

"I'm sorry, Dylan," said Rommie. "She's gone. Do you want me to pursue?" Dylan studiously kept his calm. "No. Track the *Maru's* flight path. And find out how Beka got that key." He watched on the viewscreen as the small, rusty form of the *Maru* made distance from the *Andromeda*, turning ever smaller. Blasting the ship to pieces was not a viable option, and catching Beka wouldn't make her any more cooperative.

He'd just have to make do without her, but he didn't like it. And the more he thought about it, the more he wondered if he had another reason besides military discipline for wanting Beka to stay. After all, technically the case could be made that she was a civilian and therefore couldn't be held to the same code of responsibility as an actual officer. *Don't tell me it's just my ego,* Dylan thought. *Surely I'm bigger than that.*

It took him a while to figure it out, but he wasn't too surprised when he did. The truth was, he felt safer knowing she was around.

THREE

It's never a good day to die.

—NIETZSCHEAN PROVERB

AFC 304. The Battle of Bunker Hill. It's fitting that humankind's call to arms against their Nietzschean slavelords should start here, on Earth, the birthplace of *Homo sapiens.*

Of course, Earth is also the birthplace of *Homo sapiens invictus,* but that's a technicality the Nietzscheans themselves tend to ignore. If the Dragans ever considered that they shared common ancestors with the humans they rounded up into their ghettos and work camps, they'd long gotten over it. To a Nietzschean, "weak" equals "exploitable." And Earth's humans, after wave upon wave of Magog attack, were weak.

When the Drago-Kazov made their first incursions into Earth territory, they met little resistance. Not only were the locals decimated after decades of trying to fend off the Magog—and failing miserably—but the Nietzscheans actually seemed a preferable alternative. At least they didn't spray you with poison and incubate their young in your guts. Millennia of peace had reduced the planet's standing armies to a mere formality, so it was no wonder the Dragans found enslaving the human population absurdly easy. Of course, they simply attributed this to the dull and inferior nature of kludges, never mind the psychological and physical toll that years of fear and chaos had taken on the average Earther.

By the time Seamus Zelazny Harper and his "Irish twin" cousin, Brendan Lahey, were born, the slavery of humans was a brutal fact of life on Earth. If not for the improbable series of circumstances that landed him on the *Andromeda Ascendant*, a mistreated and malnourished Harper probably would not have lived to see AFC 304 . . . or CY 1088, as Dylan called it. And when Brendan learned that his own cousin was helping the fabled Captain Dylan Hunt revive the Systems Commonwealth, he immediately sent a message. The message was simple: "Help!"

The game youths organized an offensive in their hometown of Boston, North America. The liberation movement was as optimistic as it was futile: the humans had no weaponry and no training; the Dragans had Gauss rifles and armored flivvers. But in the end, it didn't matter who was better armed. It didn't even matter who won. What mattered was the act of defiance itself.

Because the humans got slaughtered at the Battle of Bunker Hill.

The last Harper heard from his cousin, Brendan was being overwhelmed by an assault team of Nietzschean soldiers while leading an attack on one of their garrisons. With his last few breaths, Brendan broadcast these words to the galaxy:

The Dragans call us kludges, they call us mutts and mules. As if we're a genetic mistake, because we're only human. But now we've shown them what humans can do—we kludges, we mutts, we mules. And we're going to keep showing them. Today. Tomorrow. And every day. Until Earth is free.

Brendan Lahey isn't dead. He lives on at Persephone Station. He lives on at Winnipeg Drift. He lives on at NeHolland. And he damn sure lives on at Alpha Centauri.

By the time humanity entered the Systems Commonwealth in CY 7085, they had long since colonized Alpha Centauri. You don't need Slipstream technology to get to a star (okay, three stars . . .) only four and a half light-years away; you just need patience. Natal, orbiting the most Sol-like of Alpha Centauri's suns, was the planet that most reminded the early settlers of home. Natal quickly became the economic and cultural hub of the system; the more distant Sisulu and its moon Pedi, while both far less hospitable, soon drew a human population as well. Rich in natural resources, these planets helped fuel humanity's growing reach.

Things were good around Centauri for three thousand years or so. Then came the Long Night. And then came the Dragans.

For the slaves of Natal, "Today, tomorrow, and every day" became a call to action. And it was within the slave camp at Xhosa—a once-great Natal city that lay mostly abandoned, its people corralled into a walled ghetto at its center—that the Human Interplanetary Alliance came into being.

When the HIA began, the freedom fighters' weapons consisted mostly of the rubble beneath their feet. But they watched and they waited, and they grew. They collected intelligence from their comrades on Earth—like how to build shrillers (a high-pitched whistle invented by friend Harper, painful to the Nietzscheans' genetically engineered, hypersensitive ears), or where to find chinks in Nietz-schean armor. Soon, the HIA had cells throughout the Centauri system. It was decided that Xhosa would be the site of the first revolt. Meanwhile, Sisulu and Pedi would quietly stockpile weaponry and supplies until a systemwide attack could be launched. The Dragans would be caught by surprise.

As it happened, the first revolt caught the HIA by surprise, as well.

The latest outrage of Nietzschean occupation on Natal was an edict that anything spoken other than Common, the lingua franca of the Systems Commonwealth, would be punishable by death. After all, sneered the overlords, it's not our job to learn your pitiful local patois. One unseasonably cool spring day, a Dragan soldier in the Xhosa quarter overheard a female slave speaking the outlawed Natalese dialect. Naturally, he shot her.

She was fourteen years old.

As word spread and outrage among the Xhosans mounted, the HIA realized they would have to play their hand: it was time to act. The Natalese leader of the HIA, Pac Peterson, sounded a shriller, giving the signal. Whistles all over Xhosa picked up the call. As the shrillers echoed through the alleys and hovels of the quarter, the Xhosans rose. They armed themselves with rocks, with stones . . . and with caches of weapons hidden in shallow pits, in underground cellars, in hollowed-out walls. The people took to the streets brandishing homemade spears, the rare stolen Gauss gun, Molotov cocktails.

The plan was to engage the Nietzscheans at the center of the quarter, drawing the majority of troops into the city's heart. Then, HIA tactical teams would take the city gates and lock the Nietzscheans inside the very ghetto they had created.

The plan succeeded . . . for a few hours, anyway. Dragan reinforcements eventually broke through the gates and the rebels dispersed, disappearing into cracks and crevices like the animals they had become. But those hours were some of the sweetest the Natal natives had ever known. Humans had held Xhosa, and they wouldn't stop until all of Alpha Centauri was theirs again. They knew it, the Dragans knew it—and Admiral Rasputin Genovese knew it, which was why he was aboard a Nietzschean transport vessel heading for the *Andromeda Ascendant.*

Dylan and Tyr watched on the main viewscreen as Rasputin arrived on board the *Andromeda. So far, so good,* thought Dylan. True to his word, the admiral's freighter had an escort of only two fighters. Rasputin allowed his transport to be hangared, but insisted that his fighters stay in a position of readiness alongside, to which Dylan consented. Dylan doubted that the negotiating team was also, as stipulated, unarmed. But, despite Tyr's sour predictions, he decided not to body-search them. In Dylan's experience, it was a bad idea to start peace negotiations with such an obvious sign of bad faith. Rommie's sensors would pick up anything actually ticking.

Tyr conceded—silently, of course—that Rasputin Genovese was as formidable a Nietzschean specimen as he himself. Towering, broad-shouldered, with neck ligaments as thick as steel cable . . . his hair was pulled straight back from his eyes, emphasizing his hawklike nose. He wore an impeccably tailored, floor-length military coat, and seemed to take special pride in his outsized bone blades, which he brandished at every opportunity. Rasputin traced his ancestry to the Alpha Odysseus, an influential genotype in the Drago-Kazov line. *All the more reason not to trust him,* surmised Tyr.

Rasputin was accompanied by two armored guards and, Dylan noted with distaste, a human slave whom Rasputin referred to only as "you." The man kept a respectful distance of two meters between himself and his master, except when helping him off with his coat. While intellectually Dylan knew that a few hundred years had often meant the difference between slavery as a way of life and slavery as an atrocity—look at the Great British Civilization between Earth dates AD 1700 and AD 2000, for example—he hated to see the trend going the other way. *It's not just technology that regressed while I was missing in action,* Dylan thought.

A maria led Rasputin and his men onto the Observation Deck. The Nietzschean guards and the human slave took up positions near the entrance while Rasputin sauntered to the expanse of window, taking in the crystalline swirl of the planet Natal below. So far, Rasputin was finding his time aboard the *Andromeda* quite enjoyable. There was the ship herself—a magnificent work of craftsmanship, far superior to the utilitarian design of his own flagship. Nietzschean ships of the line were designed to intimidate, not to inspire. Rasputin was also looking forward to a verbal joust with the famous—and famously earnest—Captain Dylan Hunt and, of course, to meeting humankind's unlikely hero.

The idea of enlisting Seamus Harper himself in the negotiations delighted Rasputin. It was positively baroque—like outlawing the native dialects, or his idea to force Centauri schools to replace human history with Nietzschean history. *Aren't conquest and assimilation really two different words meaning the same thing—or at the very least, two different roads to the same destination? It's that kind of thinking that earned me the position of admiral in the first place,* decided Rasputin. Well, that and the well-timed murder of his predecessor.

Rasputin's thoughts were interrupted by Dylan's arrival on Obs. The Nietzschean looked the High Guard captain up and down. Yes, he decided. The human would be easily deceived. Rasputin smiled warmly, and greeted his host.

"Captain Dylan Hunt. It is an honor, sir."

"I want to thank you, Admiral, on behalf of the Systems Commonwealth, for initiating these negotiations. We can begin as soon as the HIA delegation arrives."

"I suppose one can't blame the humans for their tardiness. Their interstellar travel is a bit . . . nontraditional. They have the most fascinating fleet, you know. Rowboats, with mirrors."

"They're solar sails," came a nasal voice from behind Rasputin. The admiral turned to see Harper, barely containing his anger, storming onto the Observation Deck. "And considering the genocide your Pride's been laying on them for—"

Dylan signaled Harper to zip it. Now was not the time to bring emotion onto the bargaining table. But Rasputin's response to the feisty engineer surprised him.

"Seamus Zelazny Harper. Just the man I was hoping to see. Even the Drago-Kazov are not deaf to the tales of your exploits. You do realize, Captain Hunt, that this Earther is the only reason I'm here." Rasputin waited a moment to see the effect his revelation was having on both Dylan and Harper. They were dumbstruck. Good.

Finally, Dylan spoke. "Actually, no. I thought you were here to initiate peace talks."

Rasputin clasped his hands behind his back and took up a position watching his erstwhile slave planet.

"Peace is a romantic illusion, Captain—like love, or God. And you know what Nietzsche said about God. No, what I believe in is risk and benefit, profit and loss. What I see at Alpha Centauri is a waste of resources. Dead Dragan soldiers are wasted resources. Crippled human slaves are wasted resources. Fallow fields and blocked mines are wasted resources.

"I've tried to reason with the humans. I've offered to extend their curfews; I've offered to install their own people in posts of some localized power." The admiral shrugged as if to say, *And look what it got me!* Then he glared at Harper. "Maybe they'll listen to one of their own kind. This great hero—perhaps he can reason with them."

Somehow, Rasputin made "great hero" sound a lot like "dung beetle."

Harper's knuckles whitened; the veins on his temples engorged. His lips parted in a snarl. But just then, as if she had been poised to defuse the situation—and who knows, maybe she had been—Rommie appeared on a comm screen next to the observation window. "Captain, the human delegation has arrived."

"Thank you, Rommie." Dylan turned to Rasputin. "We'll meet on Command Deck in one hour. Harper, please make our new arrivals welcome."

"Anything to get away from his *überness*," muttered Harper.

"And, Admiral . . . ?" Dylan waited until he had Rasputin's attention. "I've known peace. I've seen it, I've felt it, I've lived it. It's not an illusion."

No one has a happy childhood. Childhood is when you're small, weak, and impotent; everyone else makes decisions for you, and you rarely get your way. Everything hurts more than it should, because the armor of experience you're developing is still more chinks than plates: you have to burn your hand a few times before you learn to avoid the fire. Childhood, for most, is one painful disappointment after another.

Dylan Hunt was the exception to the rule. He had a terrific childhood. As a youngster he felt secure, he felt loved . . . he felt peace. His mother, a Heavy Worlder built like a well-upholstered fireplug, was a pilot—nothing fancy, just a high-gee shuttle jockey ferrying cargo on and off Tarn-Vedra. His father was the landscape architect at the Imperial Museum in Etashi Tarn. Okay, he was the gardener. Bram Hunt was a quiet man, and when he did speak he said what he meant and he meant what he said. One thing he often said was that he had married his best friend, and never regretted it for a minute. Another was that he loved his son more than he loved his life—and he loved his life a lot.

They lived in the human district of Etashi Tarn, the Imperial capital—"Apetown," some called it. Young Dylan excelled at school, was a stellar athlete, and was popular with his peers. From as far back as he could remember, Dylan knew he would be a High Guard officer.

Sometimes, the boy understood on an intuitive level that his sense of well-being and comfort was unusual. That it was a gift. Sometimes, he gave himself a handicap. He would tie one hand behind his back for a week, or go blindfolded, or block his ears with wax. Not that blindness and deafness were likely occurrences in the technologically advanced Golden Age of the Systems Commonwealth; modern medicine and nanotechnology had made disease all but obsolete. Dylan wasn't testing himself; he was building his empathy muscles. Because young Dylan Hunt didn't just want to be a High Guard officer. He wanted to be a *good* High Guard officer.

And now, the High Guard was gone. His parents were three hundred years dead, and he never even got to say good-bye. Now, he was finally being tested.

Dylan distinctly remembered telling Tyr to make himself scarce during the negotiations. Dylan also remembered Tyr agreeing—at any rate, Tyr had fixed him with the unblinking stare that Dylan took to be Tyr's way of accepting an order. But with Tyr, nothing was ever really certain.

As Dylan, the admiral, and the admiral's entourage walked onto the Command Deck, Rasputin's respect for the physical plant of the *Andromeda* increased. Admiring a door upon which the Systems Commonwealth insignia was etched in silver, Rasputin confided in Dylan that perhaps the greatest blow to the Nietzschean people when they broke from the Commonwealth was the loss of any outside influence to offset their utilitarian sensibilities.

It took every ounce of Dylan's self-control to not point out that three centuries of war, famine, and universe-wide chaos could be considered a loss as well. But Dylan got the feeling that him losing control was exactly what Rasputin hoped for.

For some reason, Rasputin seemed to take genuine pleasure in Trance, whom he called "the purple creature." And he was amused by Rev Bem: "A tame Magog," is how he put it. Rev Bem's own impression of the admiral was that Rasputin Genovese embodied the worst of the Nietzschean ideal: a superhuman without a trace of humanity. Rev accepted the concept of Evil—you needed it to appreciate Good, just as you needed Sorrow to understand Joy, and Pain to value Pleasure. But he could find no trace of divinity in Rasputin's brand of total self-interest.

And then Dylan noticed Tyr, leaning nonchalantly against the weapons control module. The captain tensed. *Okay, Tyr. What's your personal agenda this time?*

Rasputin had known there was a Nietzschean crew member aboard the *Andromeda*, of course. Gossip—or "intel," as they preferred to call it—was a Nietzschean officer's stock in trade. Tyr Anasazi, the last of his Pride. Rasputin was a bit disappointed when he was greeted by only the High Guard relic, and not the disenfranchised Kodiak. Rasputin, after all, had been a key instigator behind the Dragan betrayal of the Kodiak. Knowing that—and knowing that Tyr did not know it—gave Rasputin an exquisite thrill.

Rasputin approached Tyr and smiled. His eyeteeth were sharpened, Tyr noticed. He considered it a telling affectation.

"So there is a Nietzschean already aboard this ship," said Rasputin. He glanced at Tyr. "Tell me, do you take orders from the human? Or the Magog, or whatever other species you might have on this antique floating High Guard zoo?"

Tyr's chain-mail vest rustled with a metallic clang as his muscles tensed to lunge at Rasputin. The admiral's guards snicked their bone blades erect, ready to strike. But Tyr only stretched, and grinned. He leaned closer to Rasputin: "Don't worry. Your rudeness won't get you killed. Not here. Not yet."

Rasputin spoke to Dylan, but kept his eyes on Tyr. "My apologies, Captain. That was rude of me. I can only claim stress as an excuse. My Pride has handed me the enormous task of keeping Alpha Centauri productive despite the rebellious human population. These are uneasy times, and they make one uneasy."

Dylan allowed a curt nod, but wasn't about to give Rasputin the satisfaction of accepting his apology. Tyr was amused by this. Dylan, no matter how hard he tried, was still far more soldier than statesman. Tyr relaxed and sauntered back to his station. If the admiral thought his emotions would be so easily manipulated, he was wrong. Tyr wasn't about to do anything rash when a little bit of patience would surely provide him with the perfect method for dispatching the Nietzschean.

Rasputin, meanwhile, pretended to examine the Vedran marble inlay of the Command floor as he said, nonchalantly: "I could offer the humans freedom, I suppose. But I will require . . . compensation."

That was the opening Dylan had been waiting for. But Rasputin didn't wait for a response; he immediately turned to admire the design of a navigational display. Dylan wasn't naïve enough to think that both sides were going to walk away from these negotiations feeling that they'd won. The best he could hope for was that each side left the table without feeling that they'd lost. With what, then, could the HIA buy Alpha Centauri's freedom? The only commodities the Centaurians owned, the Nietzscheans had already taken. Piling them with massive debt would only facilitate a transition from slave world to tribute world; it's not enough to simply go from slave to indentured servant.

No, Dylan had to convince Rasputin that the humans were not going to back down. That the Dragans would incur such an enormous financial drain from a war with their slave worlds that they could in fact win simply by walking away. And Dylan would have to find a way to make a Dragan stand-down look like a victory for them, else Rasputin would never hold on to his title of admiral. *Hell,* thought Dylan, *if he comes out of this looking weak, he wouldn't hold on to his title of "alive."*

And perhaps that was what the admiral had meant by "compensation."

Rasputin, for his part, was convinced that he was the pillar of reasonability in all this. Certainly, after the first revolt at Xhosa, he killed whatever rebels he could find. *But*—he left the humans their city (for the time being), and the majority of its people kept their lives. After all, the Dragans had a considerable investment in them. But despite his having run the HIA underground, despite their being constantly hounded by his troops, they had nonetheless managed to shape themselves into a hardened guerrilla unit, educating and recruiting practically the entire human populace. Rasputin devised an assortment of "persuaders" to break the humans' spirit—torture, random executions, separating children from parents, tripling work shifts, planting spies, etc. Such escalation tactics had worked quite well in the past. But apparently things had changed.

Despite the many deaths, despite the inevitable destruction of Xhosa, the HIA and the humans of Natal had yet to give up. They had even managed to take a considerable toll on Rasputin's forces—the bombing of a supply depot on Pedi had been a particular nuisance. They had actually engaged some of his fighters in those barbaric "solar sailboats" of theirs. And now, rebellions were breaking out on the worlds of Sisulu and Pedi.

In a way, all of this pleased Rasputin. One could say that the organization and cunning of the HIA were a tribute to his own organization and cunning. It was quite Darwinian, really. Given the conditions enforced by Rasputin, only the strong would survive. Against all expectation, the HIA was proving up to the task. But that didn't solve his problem: the Drago-Kazov had other wars to win, and they needed Alpha Centauri's resources to win them. Nor could the admiral afford to squander a perfectly good Nietzschean battalion on a bunch of scrofulous humans when he could be deploying them against the Maroon Pride.

That was when Rasputin got the idea of calling in the *Andromeda*. It would at least get the humans' attention, and put a temporary halt to their activities. Of course, this was an incredibly unpopular decision among his ranks. He'd had to execute a few of the more vocal critics—also wasteful, but then it never really hurt to demonstrate authority so unequivocally. Rasputin considered himself above all a practical Nietzschean, and the *Andromeda*, he believed, posed a very practical solution.

At least, he hoped it did.

Harper was underwhelmed by his first sight of the solar sails. He'd heard of them, of course, and knew how they worked, but he had never actually seen what one looked like. He'd never actually seen an abacus, either. The Nietzschean had been right: not exactly ships of the line. In fact, they looked downright dangerous.

I wouldn't fly one of those things for all the thrones on Ugroth.

There were three sails, each carrying one person. The actual cabin portion was little more than a cylinder with an enclosed seat at one end and a rocket engine at the other. The engine was used primarily for planetary takeoffs, but could also be used, albeit sparingly, for bursts of speed once spaceborne. The majority of power, however, was derived from the sails, which were actually two-square-kilometer mirrors that captured the momentum of solar photons. The sails were extended and retracted via inflatable tubes that radiated from the center of the sail, where the cockpit was, to the sails' outer edges. By deflating or inflating specific tubes, the surface of the mirror could also be warped, thus allowing the pilot to steer.

You couldn't go fast in a solar sail, but you could sure go cheap. For landing, the sections of sail had been deflated and stowed in rolls, making the craft look awkward and somehow defanged. As the humans climbed out of their rickety contraptions, Harper decided that their Environmental suits were more prehistoric even than the solar sails. The E-suits looked like mismatched canvas sacks attached to a fishbowl. Still, Harper felt immediate affection for these clumsy sack people and their hodgepodge sails. Of all the crew, only he really understood what it was like to make do with so little. Chewing gum and baling wire: it was pretty much the story of Harper's life.

Rommie examined the humans and their equipment with a slightly more critical optical sensor. Even though she'd been with Harper at the Battle of Bunker Hill and had seen what the Earthers' sheer determination could accomplish, she had a hard time believing that anyone with such antediluvian technology could be successfully harassing the most powerful of the Nietzschean prides.

The rebels helped one another remove their E-suits. The first one to ease her way free now walked toward Harper and Rommie. She had jet-black hair that had been cut short and military; her clothes, although intended for company, were patched and stitched . . . although she didn't seem the type to care. She shook Harper's hand with an incredibly firm grip.

She was the most beautiful girl Harper had ever seen.

"Arca Nelson, second in command to Pac Peterson, commander of the Human Interplanetary Alliance," she said, introducing herself, then pointed to her companions—three malnourished but defiant-looking men. "These are my counsel and cavalry."

Harper's knees turned to jelly and he grunted some kind of greeting, but it quickly devolved into a nervous laughter and an embarrassed grin. Rommie, sensing Harper was having difficulty playing diplomat, stepped in. "Welcome to the *Andromeda Ascendant*. If you'll follow us to the Observation Deck, Captain Hunt would like to meet you."

"I take it from the Nietzschean fighters buzzing around outside that Admiral Genovese is already here?"

Harper tried to look dangerous. "Yeah. What a jerk."

Woo-hoo! He'd spoken a whole sentence! *A whole totally lame sentence. Harper, you loser. Loser, loser, loser. . . .* Harper's self-flagellation was interrupted by Arca's hand on his shoulder. It felt like flame. *No, not flame, ice. No, flame . . .*

"So," said Arca with an incandescent smile, "the legendary Seamus Harper speaks after all."

Rommie looked at Harper's reddening face and hid a smirk. *Looks like Harper's finally met his match.*

By the time the HIA contingent made it to the Command Deck, Harper was back in full bombastic form, recounting his brave turn in the Battle of Bunker Hill. Arca and her associates were genuinely impressed. Harper, meanwhile, found Arca to be intelligent and capable and, better yet, not above a little playful sarcasm, which immediately earned his admiration. As soon as the HIA members saw the Nietzscheans, though, they became taciturn.

Rasputin, who had been making an unnecessarily close inspection of the firing console, rose to his full height and strode toward the delegation. He sized up Arca with cold, dark eyes . . . which squinted in amusement. The girl couldn't have been older than nineteen.

"Pity your superior couldn't have made it," Rasputin said with a curt nod. "I was hoping to make her acquaintance as well."

Arca did little to hide her distaste for the admiral. "The commander sends her regrets. But the HIA isn't ready to risk making her whereabouts known to the Dragans."

"You're quite a suspicious little band, aren't you?" Rasputin chuckled.

Harper wanted to punch the Nietzschean in the mouth, but Arca seemed unaffected by the jab. "Rest assured that I carry Pac Peterson's full authority. Any decisions made here, by me, will be honored by the HIA."

Tyr watched the exchange with interest. He leaned over to Dylan and whispered: "I hope you realize that everything the admiral says is a deception."

"Naturally," said Dylan. "But at this point, I have no choice except to trust him."

"Of course you have a choice. You can kill him."

Sometimes, Dylan envied Tyr. *It must be nice not having scruples. So . . . uncomplicated.* He patted Tyr on the chest, "Just keep an eye on him for now, okay?"

Dylan was about to call for everyone's attention when a shock wave tore through the ship, unannounced. Command shuddered and the viewscreen lit up as an explosion erupted from a point in space only kilometers away. Two fireballs slammed against the *Andromeda*'s starboard side. There was a thunderous groan as the *Andromeda*'s structural supports absorbed the force of the explosion. Dylan grabbed on to a console to steady himself. Arca, her human contingent, and the Dragans tumbled violently to the ground, while Tyr scrambled to the weapons station. Rev Bem was knocked completely off his feet, and hit the back of his head on the sensor console.

"Andromeda, report!" barked Dylan.

Andromeda's AI image flared to life on the secondary viewscreen. "The Dragan fighter ships just exploded, Captain." Now Rommie herself snapped to life and moved to Dylan's side. He turned his attention from Virtual Andromeda to the avatar.

"Give me a damage assessment. And sensor readings." Dylan's first instinct was to suspect Dragan subterfuge. Was this a distraction of some kind? Or were those explosions an attack on the *Andromeda*?

"Damage is minor, Dylan. And my sensors report nothing out of the ordinary—if there's a ship out there, it has advanced stealth capability."

Dylan cursed under his breath. Just what he needed: a new, more technologically sophisticated enemy. "Okay, launch a drone, let's get a better look around. Maybe we can extrapolate the origin of the attack. Tyr, prepare to fire offensive missiles on my command."

Tyr moved toward his station just as Rasputin pulled himself to his feet. The Nietzschean admiral had instincts of his own, and his suspicions pointed right to Dylan. Tyr didn't see Rasputin move until it was too late. The Dragan came up behind Dylan and wrapped his huge hands around Dylan's face. Dylan felt something press into his jugular. Bone blades. Rasputin turned to Tyr.

"Move away, or I rip out your captain's throat."

Tyr grabbed a railing and vaulted effortlessly onto the lower tier alongside Dylan and the admiral. The Nietzschean guards reached underneath their armor and withdrew small hidden Gauss guns. The guards quickly leveled and aimed their guns at Tyr. Harper, helping Arca to her feet, saw the Nietzscheans about to fire.

"Tyr, watch out!" he shouted, racing to grab the closest one's gun . . . and was tripped by one of the still-prone HIA members.

Tyr dove behind the captain's console as the Nietzscheans fired. Their smart bullets, not smart enough to follow Tyr's sudden direction and velocity change, buried themselves in the base of the console centimeters from Dylan's shins.

This time Arca helped Harper to his feet. Harper had barely been vertical for two seconds when Arca produced a gun—an ancient revolver—from a shoulder holster. Laser knives quickly appeared in the hands of her cohorts. The two factions faced off against one another in a three-pointed standoff.

"Captain Hunt," said Arca. "We can take the Dragans. Just give us the word."

"I overestimated you, Captain," said Rasputin through clenched teeth. "I should have realized you'd side with the kludges." Rasputin nonetheless admired Dylan's plan: get him onto his ship, ambush his fighters, and then murder him. Thus Dylan Hunt plays the hero and saves the humans of Alpha Centauri. It was a plot worthy of a Nietzschean. Rasputin wouldn't have thought the noble Commonwealth captain capable of such a thing, but he was apparently mistaken.

Dylan gasped, "I've got nothing to do with this, Rasputin. Tell your guards to lower their weapons."

Tyr, crouched behind the command console, watched the stalemate unfold. *I told him they'd be armed*, he thought. *I told him not to trust a Nietzschean*. Tyr reached into his boot and withdrew his own hidden Gauss pistol. *Not even me.*

Tyr slowly got to his feet, aiming his gun at the admiral's forehead. He knew he was in one of the Nietzschean guards' sights, but he also knew he was safe as long as he was in a position to kill the admiral.

Nobody moved.

Tyr briefly considered killing Rasputin outright. He weighed the consequences: he was certain he would make it through the ensuing melee with few serious injuries. But he couldn't predict how the others would fare—especially Dylan. Both Trance Gemini and the Magog priest were capable medics, but he doubted they could repair a severed head.

Tyr stood solid as an obsidian statue, pistol pointed unwaveringly at the admiral's temple. "Take his life, Rasputin Genovese, and you forfeit your own."

Rasputin whispered into Dylan's ear, "I may die today, Captain. But I find solace knowing that I will not be alone. I hope your humans are worth it."

FOUR

The Divine loves equally the Vedran who cossets her young, and the Nightsider who eats hers. This is the problem with the Divine.

—KEEPER OF THE WAY,
VISION OF FAITH VII, CY 9874

Lack of sleep, Beka decided, is cumulative. Lose two hours tonight, and you're two hours' short of sleep. Lose two hours tomorrow night, and you're not two hours' short of sleep again, but rather, four hours' short of sleep. Then six hours, then eight, and next thing you know you're a walking in vivo experiment in sleep deprivation.

And since Beka refused any stimulant stiffer than Harper's Java—the daughter of a Flash addict, she had already seen too much and fallen way too close to that pit—she considered the next Slip jump on Rafe's map with some trepidation. Surely, there was a shorter, more direct route. But, no. Between Sammie the Perseid's natural paranoia, and Rafe's learned version, the path to Farside was about as linear as the web of a Terran spider. More precisely, the web of a Terran spider on Harper's Java.

At least recovery from sleep deprivation isn't *cumulative*, Beka reassured herself. *All I need is one good night.* . . .

Farside Drift's hotel cubicle complex, or Farside Gardens as it insisted on being called, wasn't the worst rack Beka and Rafe had ever seen. It wasn't the best, either. A skeevy-looking Nightsider chow shop to one side and a noisy but empty discotheque to the other, it unenthusiastically wooed prospective patrons with a holo-advert depicting a human luxuriating in a room the size of a shower stall. *Reminds me of school,* thought Beka. *And not in a good way.*

With the *Eureka Maru* safely docked, the pair of Valentines crossed the Drift's not-so-bustling main thoroughfare and ducked into the poorly lit lobby. The first thing that greeted them wasn't a bellhop, as Beka had hoped against hope, but rather an almost palpable stench. The smell, along with most of the room's illumination, emanated from an assortment of transparent tanks and cages. On display were various alien life-forms that, even on their best days, didn't cry out as ideal candidates for domestication. Beka stopped to examine a bulky globe with a circumference of easily two meters, empty except for a tendrillike Wisp Worm pirouetting tirelessly in the sphere's zero-gravity environment. She placed a hand on the globe and the worm burst toward her in a ferocious, if futile, attempt to burrow through the sphere and into Beka's open palm.

Rafe, meanwhile, holding a hand over his nose, bravely peered into the open tank from which the majority of odor seemed to originate. The tank was filled with brackish water atop which a festering black alga congealed.

"Now, this is one pet that actually *deserves* to be flushed down the toilet," choked Rafe. "If it is a pet."

"That is a Myaloid Slime," came an indignant voice. "And it has been a loyal and much beloved companion to my family for several generations."

Beka and Rafe looked around. As their eyes adjusted to the poor light, they made out a Chichin sitting motionless behind a countertop, eyeing them with mixed suspicion and disdain.

Rafe leaned over the tank, flashed his dimples, and yelled at the slime. "Sorry!"

Beka roughly grabbed his arm. "Smart-ass," she whispered, pulling him toward the hotel counter.

The Chichin's leathery skin was a dull brown, with patches of large dark freckles scattered across the forehead. Beka didn't think the reptilian-humanoid-hermaphroditic Chichin looked well. His ("his" being a term more of convenience than accuracy) loosely hanging cheeks looked like a partially sculpted slab of nanosilicate, she decided. The Chichin absently reached to his shoulder and stroked the dozing Kubik curled up there, a small pet rodent with splotchy fur that changed color according to its owner's emotional state—a mood ring, with attitude.

Something strange happened when the Chichin took a closer look at Beka. For a brief moment, a surprisingly warm smile crossed his beaklike lips. But this quickly gave way to confusion, and the smile disappeared. Beka and Rafe looked at each other. Rafe had seen the smile, too, and both reached the same conclusion: that was a smile of recognition. The Chichin knew Magdalena. They had been right; she was here.

The Chichin pointed to the hotel entrance and addressed Rafe. "We don't sell rooms by the hour here. Take your breeding partner somewhere else. Try Andorf's Habitat on C Level."

Beka snorted. "Don't insult me. Anyway, we're brother and sister."

The Kubik swiveled its disproportionately large eyes toward the pair, and the pigment in its skin took on a yellow tinge. The Chichin hurriedly pressed a button beneath the counter, turning off the bright VACANCY sign that hung on the wall behind him. "Either way, all booked. No more rooms. Good-bye."

Rafe gave Beka a leave-it-to-me look and leaned over the counter to read a nametag stuck to the Chichin's shirt. "Well . . . Yevlos. We weren't interested in getting a room here, anyhow."

Beka's face fell—she really was hoping for some sleep. But she knew there were more important things on their plate. Rafe produced the security scan of Magdalena and placed it on the counter. He dropped a credit chit on top of it, and slid the two toward the Chichin. "We're after information."

Both Yevlos and the Kubik contemplated the chit. Eyeing Beka and Rafe suspiciously, Yevlos picked up the chit and fed it into the money reader.

Rafe held his breath. The chit was a fake, of course. Rafe had a dozen others just like it in his pocket. They were pretty good cheats, and most of the time they fooled the money readers—the operative phrase being "most of the time." Approximately three times out of ten they failed miserably, which was always a matter of concern.

The Chichin laughed, sending his Kubik into fits of alternating pink and orange. Apparently, the chit was good.

"As you can see," said Rafe. "I pay handsomely."

Yevlos couldn't stop laughing. "Please! I wouldn't tell you the time of day for this amount."

Rafe looked sheepishly at Beka. *Behold*, she smirked. *The great con man in action.*

Rafe gave Yevlos another chit. And another. And another. Yevlos kept demanding more, and each time Rafe handed over a chit he silently prayed it wouldn't get them arrested. Finally, the Chichin seemed satisfied by the combined total of four (apparently legitimate) credit chits. He picked up the scan and examined it. He looked from the scan to Beka, then back again.

"I seem to recall having such a customer," he said. "Stays here every so often. Never more than a few days at a time. But she hasn't been here recently. Perhaps seven, eight, cycles ago." As he spoke, he nonchalantly placed his hand over the Kubik, which had turned a queasy green. The Chichin smiled.

Rafe smiled back. "You're lying. Your little friend just gave you away." Rafe tapped the scan. "Where is she?"

"Don't be silly," said the Chichin. "Zsuma here—why, her colors mean nothing." The Kubik's fur bristled, crackling with bursts of green. Yevlos laughed nervously, then began trying to pull the Kubik off his shirt. The more he tugged, the greener the Kubik became. If Chichin could sweat, the clerk's forehead would be soaked by now. "I'm telling you, I haven't seen the human in this scan for quite some time." Again the Kubik flared. It defiantly dug its claws into Yevlos's shoulder, but the Chichin kept pulling despite the obvious discomfort. Now the Kubik began to keen unhappily.

Yevlos cursed at the little creature. "*Schtum*, Zsuma. Enough. Behave yourself for once!"

"Is she on Farside?" asked Beka.

"No," said Yevlos. The Kubik flared green.

"Is she in the hotel?" asked Rafe.

"No," whimpered Yevlos. The three of them waited tensely for the Kubik to react. This time, a muddy red slowly spread across its back. Yevlos sighed with relief. "See, you can't go by what Zsuma says. She knows nothing."

Beka took an educated guess. "Is she at the All Systems University?"

Yevlos scrunched his face in painful anticipation, and yanked on the Kubik. The creature bleated viciously and then bit Yevlos's finger.

The Chichin howled in pain. Rafe reached across the counter and grabbed Yevlos by the collar.

"Answer my sister," he said, all traces of companionable smile gone from his face.

Yevlos meekly replied, "She's not there."

Beka and Rafe waited. The Kubik didn't disappoint: Triumphantly, it unleashed a vigorous blinking green. Beka was already sprinting for the hotel entrance. "Let's go," she shouted.

Rafe followed after her, but stopped halfway. He turned back to the Chichin and threw him another credit chit. Then he ran after Beka.

Yevlos waited a few minutes to make sure they were gone, then deliberately gathered his composure. *In through the nostril, out through the beak. In through the nostrils, out through the beak. . . .* A few deep breaths, then Yevlos scowled at his pet. "Zsuma, you've been very bad," he yelled at the Kubik, wincing as the creature squeezed its claws into his shoulder by way of apology. Yevlos grabbed the commlink. He knew he wasn't supposed to contact her unless it was an emergency.

Well, he thought, *if anything counts as an emergency, surely this is it. Two humans claiming to be, of all things, Magdalena's children! Showing up here, at Farside!*

After a moment, Magdalena Valentine appeared on the link. She looked older than on Rafe's scan, and harder. Maybe it was the irritated expression on her face. "This better be good." She frowned, recognizing Yevlos.

Yevlos screwed up his courage. How Magdalena was going to take the news was anybody's guess.

Despite its remote location in the Hebrides system, at the far and tingly edge of the Triangulum galaxy, Farside was once an extremely prosperous spaceport. This is because the Drift was within easy reach of four Slip points that provided access to a variety of far-flung destinations. In the heyday of the Commonwealth, Farside was a busy and reputable hub for both travelers and commercial enterprise. But as the borders of civilization contracted AFC, Farside became a shadow of its former self. While its prime location guaranteed it at least continued survival, the kind of commerce Farside attracted these days had more to do with trafficking than tourism.

Miraculously, Farside's All Systems University campus escaped the fate that befell most other regional learning institutions. It wasn't gutted and turned into an Oblinko gambling parlor; it wasn't dismantled and sold for parts. It wasn't even converted into a Flash den. (Well, except for the dormitories.) No one in his right mind would cross the quad after dark, of course, but the library, with its huge database, was remarkably intact.

Rafe and Beka twice passed right by the library's once-proud entrance before a one-armed Umbrite, stumbling out of a whorehouse, pointed them in the right direction. There was little left to distinguish the main entrance from the avenue wall; the gates were thick with generations of graffiti. Beka dubiously tried the entry pad and was surprised when the door slid open, revealing a low-ceilinged room about seven meters deep. Three xenochairs—species-adaptable barstools-cum-hammocks—took up most of the floor space, and there were three monitors mounted to the wall on the right-hand side.

But no Magdalena.

Beka walked to the closest monitor, which was still active. Judging by the disrepair of the other screens, it was obvious somebody had taken pains to keep this one in working condition. They had even managed to install a dataport.

Beka felt the xenochair; it was still warm. "She must have just left." It was an eerie feeling, knowing that her mother could have been in this exact spot only moments ago.

"We probably passed right by her," said Rafe. He turned to head back outside, but jumped when the door quickly slammed shut on him. A brief flash of light glowed through the crack around the door's edges, and there was a small explosion. Then, Rafe saw movement: something appeared at the graffiti-obscured window. Rafe ran to it and stared outside. The vague outline of a ghostly face stared back at him. The figure quickly turned and jogged away.

Rafe was incredulous. "Beka. I think that was Magdalena." He ran to the door and pulled on it: no go. Jabbed at the exit keypad—this time, it wouldn't respond. "And she just locked us in!"

But Beka was too preoccupied with the display on the active monitor to respond. If there was one thing that could make Beka forget her mother, her current predicament, and her inherent distrust of her brother, the document on that screen was it.

"Out of curiosity," she asked, finally, forming her words slowly, "did that Perseid buddy of yours ever find those forbidden All Systems documents he was looking for?"

Rafe retried the entry pad, inputting all the standard lockbreaker codes and a few of his own devising. " 'Fraid not. I wish he had—you know how much those things would be worth?"

"Damn straight, I do. Rafe, come get a look at this. It could be that where the chinhead failed, this mother of ours actually succeeded."

On the screen was an excerpt from a Vedran text called *Avrexat Vingareth Ot*—loosely translated, *Tales of Futures Past*. Beka had heard of it, of course, but never actually read a passage from it. Nobody she knew had ever seen so much as a verifiable word of it. She wasn't, in fact, sure it even existed. Until now.

The *Ot* was a metaphorical history of Tarn-Vedra. Hidden within its riddlelike quatrains, legend had it, were parables, predictions, prophecies . . . and coded maps to the scattered remains of the most valuable artifact in the Known Universe, the Vedran Runes. Magdalena had been reading a passage about something called Ixthathos's

Crown—apparently a dismembered hunk of Rune. *And forget codes and riddles,* thought Beka. *Aside from some obnoxiously florid prose, this thing's written as straightforward as a kindergarten primer.*

"Good for Mom"—Rafe grimaced—"but if we don't get out of here, it doesn't do jack for us. And somehow, she's completely disengaged the lock." After a few bruising attempts to shift the door with his shoulder, Rafe managed to work his fingers into the scant open millimeters where the edge met the wall. He quickly surveyed the room, then fixed on one of the xenochairs. It was bolted down, but with a few vigorous kicks Rafe was able to dislodge a metal stirrup normally used as back support for a Than. He wedged it into the small crack, and levered the door open.

Beka, meanwhile, continued to scan the data on the monitor with growing glee. The page Magdalena had been reading described "the burial place of king and crown" as "a false star." Beka was sure she could figure out where this "false star" was, and odds were that's where they'd find Magdalena. *And if I get us there first, we not only find our errant mother, but we beat her to the prize.*

Suddenly, the page of prose on the monitor was replaced by a flashing red triangle and a piercing siren. Beka yelped in surprise. "Violation!" warned the triangle in Common. "Access revoked!"

Beka slammed her fist against the monitor, and began furiously tapping code onto the keypad. The monitor wailed like a Chichin being mugged. "Leave it," yelled Rafe as he screeched the door open just enough for a person to fit through. He grabbed Beka, and pulled her after him.

Outside the portal, it was easy to divine what their problem had been. Magdalena had crushed the external access pad with some sort of blunt object. Simple, but effective. "Sidesucker!" cursed Beka (a reference to Nightsider mating habits . . . don't ask). "And I was so close!"

Rafe touched a light stand to hail a conveyer cab. "Worry about that later—if we hurry we might still be able to catch her at the hotel."

Beka insisted on paying for the ride with some of her own good money. The last thing they needed was to get nailed by one of Rafe's bad chits now, when the trail was hot. When they finally arrived at the hotel, Yevlos was waiting for them out front. "She's gone," he gloated. "And I don't know where to."

Beka examined Yevlos's clothes, looking for the Kubik. But the clerk wasn't about to make the same mistake twice: The Kubik was busily occupied making a meal for a hungry Enkindu constrictor. "You'll have to take my word for it, but I'm telling you the truth. She was here. She left." Beka sagged at the news. Seeing her reaction, Yevlos's expression softened—he seemed almost sympathetic. He said simply, "She mostly keeps her own company."

Beka was inclined to believe the Chichin. She doubted Magdalena would stick around Farside Drift after her cover had been blown. Beka turned to Rafe. "Come on. Let's get to the *Maru* before she Slip jumps."

"One thing before you go," interjected Yevlos. "She asked me to give you this." The Chichin held out a small flexi. Beka snatched it from him and quickly read it. She laughed so loud that a squat Heavy Worlder passing on the walkway almost lost his footing turning to look at her.

"What's so funny?" asked Rafe. Beka handed him the flexi and, still giggling, set off for the docks.

Rafe looked at the flexi quizzically. On top were scrawled the words "Love, Mom." Below that was an itemized list detailing two nights' stay at Farside Gardens.

Magdalena had left them her bill.

Odin Borgia—out of Katherine, by Montezuma—was looking forward to an evening spent enjoying the twin pillars of Nietzschean entertainment: Greco-Roman wrestling and pornography. Of the two, Odin preferred the latter—you got more bang for the buck, as it were. After all, Nietzschean pornography not only formalized the physicality and competitiveness of wrestling, but included the epic drama of reproduction. Odin, unfortunately, had all the time in the world for such diversions. His breeding status was so low that his Pride brothers called him "Odin Omega." For a Nietzschean whose central goal was genetic (if not actual) immortality, this was a mixed blessing. On the one hand, no aspiring Alpha considered him an enemy worth assassinating. On the other hand, fertile females weren't exactly begging him to sire their offspring.

Odin belonged to the obscure Ghidra Pride, Nietzschean pirates who had been harassing the diminished Farside and its environs for the last two years or so. This kind of stability was unusual for the gypsy Ghidra, who had spent most of their history wandering from one forgotten outpost to the other, rarely staying more than six months in any one place. Clan lore had it that the ancient nomadic Pride trolled such obscure backwaters of the universe for so long that news of the Commonwealth's fall didn't reach them until ten years after the fact.

Odin's Salvager was parked close to the hull of a Thurgood-class cargo tanker. The tanker, along with tens of thousands of other cargo, courier, and transport ships—plus a couple of centuries' worth of Farside garbage—comprised the Farside spaceship grave-yard, sole reminder of the Drift's glorious past as a galactic nexus.

Over time the graveyard had wandered slightly, and was currently loitering directly over one of Farside's four Slip points, about seven light-minutes out. This circumstance proved especially beneficial to Odin and the Ghidras. Take a pilot just exiting the Slip point—one nanosecond he's in the psychedelic light storm that is the 'stream, the next he's about to blindside, say, an ancient caravan transport. He has to go from twenty PSL to essentially a squealing halt. Or take a pilot

who's heading for the Slip point—the poor fool's more than preoccupied negotiating the floating obstacle course. Either way, the graveyard distracted pilots and slowed ships, making them easy prey for
any Nietzschean pirates in the neighborhood.

But this still didn't keep Odin particularly busy. The three other
Slip points were the more desirable posts; Odin, as usual, was left
with crumbs. Aside from the occasional lone scavenger who came to
scrounge the graveyard for parts, it was mostly just Odin in his Salvager, thinking about wrestling and pornography.

Odin flipped a switch on the comm module. The cacophonous
sounds of Creeping Entropy, a juke-blast quartet out of Oceania,
filled the small cabin. Odin leaned back and began entertaining
grandiose visions of founding his own dynasty. He'd need a truly
awe-inspiring name for it, something that would strike fear in all his
enemies. Intimidation—that was key. Fang Pride, perhaps. Or Triangulum Measles Pride. Of course, first he would have to make some
enemies. *You have enemies,* he reminded himself. There was that
smuggler with the backfiring Sliprunner a few months back—he was
none too happy when Odin stole his ship. Odin smiled and made a
mental note on a blank and (because you never knew) quite large
imaginary slate titled: "Enemies to Intimidate."

1. That smuggler.

A blinking light on the console broke Odin's reverie. A sensor
drone he had attached to the prow of a cargo sled close to Farside
was picking up a ship whose trajectory would take it straight through
the graveyard. It was a call to action, but Odin didn't stir quite yet.
Maybe he'd just let this one pass, and if it ever came up later, he
could claim the sensor wasn't working. That way he'd be able to call
it quits a little early, head home to the decrepit battle cruiser his clan
had turned into home base. Then again, that would give his mother
that much more time to harp on him about the sorry state of his
reproductive status. If he heard one more dramatic sigh out of the

old woman over her lack of grandchildren . . . ! Sure, the Great Progenitor, Drago Museveni, said that a matriarchy was the only sensible social system for an enlightened civilization. But the Progenitor had never met Katherine Borgia, either.

Another signal from the sensor made Odin's mind up for him: there was a second ship behind the first. Two ships coming through the graveyard in one day was an opportunity even Odin Omega couldn't pass up. He was bound to bag at least one; if things went well, maybe he could get them both. This would give quite a boost to his breeding status. He was about to start a new mental list ("Women to Impregnate"), but realized he'd have to attend to the approaching ships first.

At its current velocity, the first ship would enter the graveyard in about fifteen minutes—plenty of time to search out a nice vantage point, using the junk ships as cover. He'd wait until a ship got in range, then fire the harpoons. Odin turned up his music and grinned. Maybe he'd even get to kill someone. *What do you think of me now, Madame Katherine Borgia?*

In exchange for a liberal amount of Rafe's phony credit, the Farside dock captain agreed to copy the *Maru* on Magdalena's flight coordinates. As the information came up on the monitor, Beka saw that Magdalena wasn't as far ahead as she had feared. Sensor readings put her five light-minutes out, tops. And since the *Eureka Maru*—technically a cargo ship, despite appearances—wasn't currently carrying any cargo, and the only mass Beka had to push around was Rafe and herself, she figured she could probably get up enough steam to reach forty PSL. If she could do that, she'd be breathing right down Magdalena's boosters.

Beka pulled back firmly on the toggle grips and engaged the drive. A warning light immediately began to flash—the *Maru* was exceeding Farside's posted departure speed. A startled courier boat had to reengage its thrusters just to get out of the way. As the *Maru* hit open space, the *Maru* received a terse message from Farside Port Authority, stating in no uncertain terms that Beka and Rafe would not be welcome should they decide to return. Rafe sent a return message, suggesting that any complaints be taken up with their local representative, Yevlos of Farside Gardens.

"That's just rude," said Beka. "What did he ever do to you?"

"He robbed me blind, the greedy Chichin," said Rafe indignantly. Beka smiled to herself. Rafe's cons were so convincing that he himself was beginning to believe his fake money was the real thing.

Beka was gaining ground on Magdalena, but not much. She calculated that the fleeing ship would hit the Slipstream portal one or two LM ahead of her. But that should be good enough. *If I can find her, I can catch her,* thought Beka, who would happily have chased this infuriating chimera of a mother to the far side of Herodotus to get some answers.

Beka kept one eye on the sensor readings and another on her course coordinates. Magdalena had been close enough to two Slip points that Beka couldn't be sure which way she was going to run. A few more light-seconds, and Beka would be able to lock a trajectory. There it was: Magdalena was definitely heading for the nearer of the points. Beka looked again at the sensor data. Strange. The Slip point seemed to be in the middle of some kind of debris field. Since Beka's calculations were predicated on running at full speed, this debris field complicated things.

Still, both ships would have to slow considerably to manage the obstacle course, so in the end it would still come down to who was a better pilot. And as much as Beka had begun to admire Magdalena's pluck, she wasn't even going to entertain the possibility that her mother could outfly her.

A new flashing sign appeared on the *Maru*'s monitor. Broadcast from a nearby warning buoy, this one was a polite message from the

Farside Drift Restoration Committee. The Committee wanted to alert ships to the hazardous debris field ahead, and recommended that, for the time being, pilots utilize a different Slip point until the floating junk could be removed. Apparently the removal process was a time-consuming one; the message was dated AFC 249—almost sixty years ago.

Magdalena slowed her velocity as she neared the graveyard, allowing the *Maru* to creep within one light-minute of her ship. Beka urged the *Maru* forward at full throttle, intent on bringing the distance down to a few light-seconds. They were close enough to get a visual on the graveyard, a nebulous clutter of ships, parts of ships, discarded equipment . . . candy wrappers . . .

Rafe watched the detritus expand to fill the viewscreen at an exponential rate, and felt a twinge of unease. "Are you sure you should be going so fast through this hash?"

Beka wanted to snap back at him, but he was right. She would be hitting the debris field too fast. It was a risk she was willing to take in order to get them closer to Magdalena. She figured the *Maru*'s gravity-field generators would repel pretty much anything smaller than the *Maru* itself, so she only had to worry about any hunks of space junk actually bigger than she was. Beka took another look at the monstrous collection of garbage. O-kay. Maybe she *was* going to have to worry a bit.

When the *Maru* moved to within fifteen LS of Magdalena's ship, Beka hit the reverse thrusters. Even decelerating, the *Eureka Maru* would be traveling fast enough to overtake Magdalena. Beka smiled with grim satisfaction. Yup, she was a better pilot than her mother, all right.

"Ten light-seconds and closing," said Beka. "Five. Four. Three. Two. One. . . ."

"There!" shouted Rafe. They had Magdalena's ship on the *Maru*'s main screen, close enough that Beka could almost make out what class of ship her mother was flying.

"Bend it!" Beka cursed. "She's pulling away." Whatever Magdalena was driving, it had some formidable acceleration going for it. Beka realized immediately that while Magdalena was picking up speed, she herself was still locked in to a deceleration maneuver. Furthermore, Magdalena seemed to have no qualms about bringing her ship into the graveyard at an increasing—and increasingly dangerous—velocity.

Beka grinned. Her mother was a better pilot than she thought. Plus, she was batshit crazy. *I'm beginning to like her more and more,* Beka smiled to herself.

Squares of fullerene plating loosed from any number of abandoned spacecraft intersected the *Maru*'s trajectory. At first the debris was fairly light, but it quickly became denser. The *Maru* bucked as the gravity-field generators deflected larger and larger pieces. Beka maneuvered around an ancient Perseid saucer . . . finally, over a labored whine from the engines, she was able to ease the *Maru* into a gentle acceleration. Beka grimaced; she hated putting excessive wear and tear on the *Maru*'s engines—doing so never failed to hasten the arrival of some esoteric repair she couldn't afford.

The sensors, overwhelmed by flotsam and jetsam, were practically useless: Magdalena's ship appeared and disappeared on the monitor, playing hide and seek with the massive pieces of space junk.

Then, *wham!* The *Maru* rocked with a sudden impact. Something hit them hard enough to decenter the ship.

"Whoa," said Rafe. "I didn't expect you to fly right into the litter."

"I didn't hit anything," growled Beka. "Something hit me." The sensors indicated a fast-approaching object. At first Beka thought it might be a missile, but as fast as it was traveling it still wasn't coming for them at ninety-PSL missile-type velocity. Beka went evasive, rolling away and dropping into a canyon between two Vedran barges.

"We're being fired on," said Beka. "That second one missed."

Rafe checked the system's status monitor. "It doesn't show any damage."

"I'm losing speed," said Beka. "We're dragging something." A light on the *Maru*'s console blinked; they were receiving a communication. Beka opened the channel and a blast of truly obnoxious music filled the cockpit. Beka winced.

A voice overrode the grating harmonies. "This is Odin Borgia, out of Katherine by Montezuma, of the Ghidra Pride. I'm commandeering your ship but, if you cooperate, I will spare your lives."

"A pirate. Even better, a Nietzschean pirate. Great," muttered Beka. She tried to accelerate, but the ship felt as if it were glued in place.

"He must have harpooned us," Rafe realized. And there wasn't a hope in Gehenna that the *Maru* could outfight a Nietzschean jolly roger.

Slowly, Beka looked at Rafe with a mischievous twinkle. Rafe knew that look. It meant trouble. He immediately began tightening the buckles on his safety harness.

She sent a return voice message to Odin Borgia. "Tell you what, big boy. If you can catch me, you can have me."

Beka picked out the biggest hunk of floating garbage on the sensors—a cargo tanker five kilometers long—and set a course straight for it. As the *Maru* pulled congruent to the hull, the ship's name, *Spirit of Trade*, flitted by in letters each as big as the *Maru* itself. Beka did a visual scan of the tanker's bulk, and saw what she needed at the aft of the ship: a breach in the hull.

Rafe stared into the massive maw of the rip in the tanker's side. "Are you going where I think you're going?"

"Hold tight," warned Beka.

The Nietzschean began ratcheting in the harpoon cable. Which is exactly what Beka was counting on. She maneuvered the little ship into the tanker's hold and engaged the *Maru*'s external lights. Vast support beams ran vertically and horizontally in a grid pattern. Beka began weaving in and out of them, crisscrossing and then doubling back. Now Beka headed toward the central support, a huge cylinder four hundred meters thick that connected the deck to the cargo-hold floor. She got as close to the beam as she dared, and began following its circumference.

"Are you sure you know what you're doing?" asked Rafe. "These circles are making me seasick."

"O ye of little faith," said Beka, deep in concentration. Her improvised plan was simple: wind as much of the harpoon cable around the beam as she could and leave the pirate the dangerous and difficult task of unwinding it. It was a good plan, save for one minor aspect—if the pirate lost it and went splat before releasing the harpoon, he'd take the *Maru* with him.

After the second pass, the Nietzschean realized what Beka was up to. The pirate began accelerating in order to pick up the slack in the cable and get as close to the *Maru*'s derriere as he could.

So far so good, thought Beka. With the slack in the cable gone the *Maru* was no longer pulling the pirate's dead weight, which meant the *Maru* could gain some crucial speed. She was daring the pirate to keep up with her, bringing the *Maru*'s pace up from fast to suicidal.

Beka gritted her teeth; it was taking all her strength to keep the *Maru* in a tight circumference around the support beam. The centrifugal force threatened to rocket them into the wall of the tanker—there'd be little left of the *Maru* besides a smoking scorch.

C'mon, baby. Just a little faster . . . The *Maru* groaned under the strain. A warning light began to blink—the stress on the *Maru* was getting close to exceeding structural limits. *Just a little longer* . . .

"Got it," shouted Beka. It was almost imperceptible, but she could feel it through her pilot grips—the drag of the harpoon cable wasn't there anymore. Beka shot the *Maru* straight away from the beam, then pulled heavy starboard to avoid the hull wall.

"Got what?" said Rafe. "You're gonna kill us—that harpoon's still wound around that beam!" It was a tense few seconds as the *Maru* got closer and closer to the hull breach. And . . . nothing happened. Rafe gave a sigh of relief. "Or not."

"Any sign of our friend?"

In his best I'm-trying-not-to-sound-embarrassed voice, Rafe replied, "Uh, nope. No sign of the buccaneer."

Beka swiftly brought the *Maru* through the hull breach in the tanker. After making it outside, she smiled at Rafe. "I think our pirate deserves a little something to remember us by."

"That's my girl." Rafe grinned. He accessed weapons command and, with a few deft flicks of his fingers, launched a missile aimed straight for the opening in the tanker. Two seconds later, the missile reached the far end of the tanker, splitting the prow open in a massive eruption of shrapnel. As Beka sped the *Maru* out of the graveyard, behind them the force of the blast had sent the tanker spinning in a slow somersault, crushing scores of other smaller ships.

"Yee-ha!" shouted Beka as the *Maru* surfed the blast wave out toward the Slip point. She held a palm up for Rafe to high-five. Instead, he impulsively grabbed her and squeezed her in a bear hug. Then, embarrassed by his spontaneous show of affection, he abruptly let go.

"Booster Rocket, you are a madwoman."

"At least I come by it honestly," said Beka, pointing to the monitor. "Look."

Indeed, Magdalena had made excellent use of the pirate's attack; there was nothing left of her little ship but ion spray. Beka and Rafe stared soberly at their quarry's fast-fading trail.

"You know, I'm beginning to get the idea that Mom's not too thrilled to see us," said Beka.

FIVE

Better to be ruled by smart evil than by stupid good.

—MUGANI PROVERB

Slipstream is, for all intents and purposes, a subreality, a dimension where the very connective tissue of the universe is made visible. These strings, also called quantum connections, link everything in the universe to everything else in the universe. Latch on to one and you've got a speed-date with a destination three galaxies (give or take a galaxy) away.

So far, Beka's date was going badly. The Slip route out of Farside had seen so little traffic these past few decades that it had reverted to a bramblelike tangle of branching interstices. It was a rough ride— the *Maru* bucked unpredictably, and nearly lost its hold on one of the more doubtful quantum strings. Not that Beka was overly concerned or anything; she had yet to find a Slipstream route she couldn't master.

Rafe knew all the horror stories about ships lost in the 'stream, unable to escape, meandering eternally through the neverwhen. But he also knew who was at the controls. The *Maru* gave an especially violent lurch before finally being spit out of Slipstream into nice smooth linear space. Beka disengaged the drive and let the engines coast, giving the *Maru* a bit of a reprieve.

"Very nice flying," said Rafe. That unanticipated display of affection had made him uncharacteristically polite. Plus, while he'd always fancied himself a handy enough space jockey, he knew he didn't come close to possessing his sister's chops. "Kudos on the smooth bye-bye to our Nietzschean privateer."

"Thank me *after* we find Magdalena," said Beka, already preparing to launch a sensor drone. According to the navigational charts, the Slip points in the area were few and far between, which meant they had a good chance of spotting Magdalena before she reached one.

"That was sooo close," mused Rafe, stretching out languidly in the copilot's chair. "Imagine if we could get our hands on the rest of the Runes. . . ."

Beka's Rafe-o-Meter blared warning alarms and waved big red flags. "Runes? I thought we were trying to catch our mother."

And more importantly, thought Beka, *what did he mean by "the rest of the Runes"?* "Rest of" implied that some of the artifacts were already in their possession. She casually glanced at her brother. *Does he know I have one of the pieces?*

Worse yet . . . *does he have a piece?*

"Sure. Yeah. I was just saying," said Rafe, realizing he'd revealed too much. But he knew the perfect way to distract Beka: put her on the defensive. "Don't try to tell me *you* agreed to drop everything and bail on the *Andromeda* just because you miss Mommy. We've done just fine without her and we're going to keep on doing fine, whether we find her or not.

"You can't con a con, Rocket—you're hot for the Runes and you know it."

"Of course I want a shot at the Runes. Who doesn't?" said Beka. "But they're not everything. Five minutes with Magdalena—I can't even tell you what that would mean. Well, maybe you of all people do understand. Even if it's just so I can scream at her for never being there, it's better than nothing."

"It's the Valentine Curse, isn't it?" mused Beka. "Everyone leaves. Mom. Dad. You."

Rafe studied Beka before answering. "I'm here now."

Beka's face quivered with unexpressed emotion. She wasn't going to cry, damn it. She was going to yell instead. "Only because you got out in time, didn't you? You freakin' ran away, right when it really started to get bad, when Ignatius was doing Flash all the time because he knew he was losing it. He was drowning, and you disappeared to who knows where and didn't even bother coming home for his funeral."

Rave swiveled his chair to face Beka, but he didn't say anything. What was there to say?

"The Last Time Rafe Saw His Father." Rafe always thought of it that way, as if it were a hologram illustration with an engraved title underneath it. The images in the hologram are of a boy—call him a youth, maybe eighteen years old—and an older man. Much older, you'd think to look at him, the boy's grandfather, perhaps. But that was only the rapid aging effect of the Flash. You can tell instantly that the older man did Flash, because his eyeballs are white. Opaque white, like frosted glass, and rimmed in an angry red.

The older man is throwing the younger man across the room. Okay, not a room. A cabin, probably, perhaps in a small spaceship. A really cheap spaceship, maybe a salvage vessel constructed out of recycled parts and fervent prayers. The older man's mouth is open. He's shouting. No way to know what he's saying.

This is what the old man is saying: *Think you're faster than me, do you?* Or maybe it was, *Think you know everything, don't you, kid?* Rafe mixed them up in his mind, commingled it all into one big misery. Sometimes it was, *I'll teach you to show me up.* And poor stupid Rafael, the only way he knew to win Ignatius's approval was to get faster and smarter and stronger. It had always worked before. It even worked now, sometimes. It worked right up until the old man's eyeballs turned white again.

When Rafe finally spoke, it was barely a whisper. "Pop wasn't an easy guy to get along with," is all he said.

Beka looked at him in utter revulsion. How dare he? How dare he dismiss Ignatius that way, the man who hauled rocks from one end of the universe to the other just to feed the two of them. The man who gave his damn life for—Beka's internal rant lost momentum as she saw the look on Rafe's face. There wasn't a bit of hardness in him anymore. It was like his cheekbones had melted. His eyes were as sad as Beka had ever known eyes to be. Maybe she even glimpsed within them the barest outline of that hologram. She shut up and waited for Rafe to speak.

"He didn't like being second best, you know? Never." Rafe spoke hesitantly. Telling the truth felt foreign to him, as if he were on some alien Drift with no map. "I grew up, and I suddenly became the competition. It was like I was a constant reminder to him that he was getting older and slower. Hell, it's probably my fault he started frying in the first place. He was so used to being the quickest . . . I had to leave, Booster Rocket. He would have burned himself out even faster, and probably taken me with him. I wanted to be there for you, but it was easier for all of us if I just disappeared."

Beka looked at her brother. *Who are you and what have you done with Rafe?* He'd never uttered anything so candid since he'd learned to lie. Beka wondered if this was a new angle her brother was trying to play, and then immediately hated herself for thinking it. Then she hated herself for hating herself. It was exasperating—she wanted to believe Rafe was being sincere, but how could she? He'd burned her way too many times in the past. This new side of Rafe was beginning to make her uncomfortable. *Time to change the subject.*

"Here's something that's been bothering me," she said. "You could have found Magdalena on your own. Why split the Runes three ways, when you could have split it two?"

"Because you're my sister, and she's our mother. And I already told you, I didn't mean it to sound like I was interested in just the Runes."

And then it hit her: *Of course!* He was also interested in losing some law enforcement officials from—where was that again?—oh, yes, Gallipoli. "Funny how I'm only your sister when it's a legal or medical emergency." *Or if you want something I have.*

Rafe didn't respond, which was just fine with Beka. The conversation wasn't getting her any answers, just bringing up more questions. And it was easier to stay angry than revisit all those old hurts. The thread was mercifully cut short when the *Maru*'s sensors hummed to life. "There she is," said Beka, pointing to a blue blip on the monitor. "That's Magdalena."

Magdalena had some distance on them, and the sensor reading from the drone was already a minute old, but at least they'd be able to get a lock on her trajectory. Beka could already guess which Slip point Magdalena was heading for.

"Hold tight," said Beka. She fired up the *Maru*'s engines and gunned it. The thrusters roared and the *Maru* made an abrupt leap, but something was wrong. The engines popped and sputtered and then the lights flickered out and the cockpit went dark.

"That can't be good," said Rafe.

The emergency lights clicked on, bathing the cockpit in a crimson glow. Other than that, the only illumination came from the flashing ERROR signals on the systems status display. As Beka sorted through the data she developed a flashing ERROR signal of her own—right behind her left eyeball, where a pounding headache was taking root.

"Engines are down," said Beka. "The AP tubes got thrown out of alignment, taking most of our internal power with them." It was actually a fairly minor problem, repairable in situ. What really irked Beka was the fact that they were going to lose valuable time that they didn't have in the first place. "Must have been those jolts in Slipstream."

With the engines powered down, all of the *Maru*'s operational systems automatically went off-line, save for life support and the relatively untaxing communications unit, which operated on the *Maru*'s reserve power. Beka overrode the defaults to divert some backup juice to the active sensors; she did *not* want to lose Magdalena. She left external communications intact (on the off chance she'd need to send an SOS), but shut down the internal. Then she iced down the empty cargo bay and redirected whatever energy she had left to the passive sensor array, just enough to keep the connection with the drone.

"Well, at least misalignment is something we can fix," said Rafe.

"But it'll take hours," grumbled Beka. The sensor array was back in business, and Magdalena's blip was getting farther from the *Maru* every millisecond.

Rafe was up and out of his chair. "Hours? Now *you* have a little faith. I'll have this pile of bolts back to speed in a matter of minutes."

Beka suspected he was right, but somehow she was uncomfortable having him tinker with the ship. She had become awfully proprietary about the old rust bucket, and letting Rafe under the hood was like watching him go off with an old flame, or something. Beka shook her head to clear it. *You're pathetic! It's a ship, f'r'empress'ake.*

As Rafe was quick to explain, displacing a ship's antiproton tubes is one of the oldest tricks in the book. It was by far the easiest way to disable a ship in a pinch—like, for instance, if that ship belonged to any would-be pursuers, jailers, debt collectors, etc. "As many times as I've done it," assured Rafe, "I should be a pro at reversing the effect."

The sirens on the Rafe-o-Meter made an unwelcome return. "You *should* be a pro?" queried Beka. "Are you telling me you've never actually realigned AP tubes before?"

"You make it sound like that's a problem."

Before Beka could respond—and a variety of colorful expletives leapt to her lips—a beep from the sensor panel got her attention. A ship, and not Magdalena's, was approaching the *Maru* from the Far-side Slip point.

Beka tapped her skull, right where that incipient migraine was setting up housekeeping. She had seen that blip once before—diving into Slip space, she glimpsed a bogey only seconds before the sensors blacked out. It could have been any number of things: one more sensor anomaly in a debris field full of sensor anomalies, space rubbish that had been knocked clear by the back-flipping cargo tanker, random feedback—it could even have been a figment of her imagination. But, her headache told her, there was one more option. It could have been a ship. And now, it had followed them.

Time for an update, thought Odin Borgia. His "Enemies to Intimidate" list had just doubled in membership: *2. That ship that got away.* No, that wasn't right. The *Eureka Maru* called for more than just intimidation. The Nietzschean absentmindedly stroked the crooked points of the bone blades on his right arm. He considered giving the

Maru a list of its own: "Enemies to Obliviate," maybe. Yes, that was much stronger. But, wait a minute. Wouldn't dividing the list compromise the very guiding principle behind the list? The more enemies, the more impressive. The more impressive, the more likely to foster procreation.

With an inward *Ha!* Odin Borgia gleefully set about completing his "Enemies to Intimidate and/or Obliviate" list.

Odin was incredibly pleased with himself. This whole "mighty warrior" gig wasn't so hard after all. *One more enemy, and I may have to commit my list to a flexi.* This triggered a spiraling flight of fancy involving said flexi being secretly passed among an ever-growing number of fans, mostly admiring Nietzschean females, throughout known space. He would be more widely read than the Great Philosopher! "Thus Spake Odin Borgia."

It was a far cry from the dour mood that had enveloped him only a short time earlier. Losing the *Maru* in the first place had hardly done wonders for his confidence. His dream of snagging one, maybe two ships and returning triumphantly to base—a solar wind dramatically blowing his long red locks, his muscles bulging (he'd do some push-ups beforehand), greeted by jealous looks from the Alpha males and sultry come-hithers from their harems—had quickly turned into a nightmare. A nightmare replete with scary clowns, appearing naked in public, and falling from very high places. Having a ship escape his grasp was definitely *not* going to help his southern placement on the Ghidra Pride pecking order, especially with a windmilling cargo tanker as spectacular evidence of his failure. He'd barely escaped with his life, finding a small rupture in the tanker's skin just in time to avoid the nasty side effects of the *Maru*'s missile. But as far as Odin was concerned, he'd probably be better off having died.

Then, it occurred to him that the spectacular evidence of his failure could also be turned to his spectacular advantage. Because not only was the *Maru* now an enemy, but it could also be considered a

worthy enemy. An enemy who not only was obviously armed, dangerous, and resourceful, but who—with a healthy dose of exaggera-
tion—could be described to the Ghidra as a nemesis of legendary
proportion. He'd paint the *Maru*'s pilot as a battle-hardened mercenary, a sinewy rogue with facial scars, a cyborg fist that shot smart
bullets, and an overcoat sewn from the hides of previously defeated
pirates.

Of course, he'd still have to catch the *Maru*, but that seemed to
Odin a minor technicality as he reclined in his pilot's chair, embel-
lishing the details of his grand conquest.

The comm module suddenly squawked to life. "Odin Borgia,
come in." Katherine Borgia appeared on-screen, her face set in a
scowl so familiar he'd always assumed the disapproving arch of her
eyebrows was a hereditary feature, like dimples. The one time he did
see his mother smile, he had been absolutely horrified.

"All the Pride is talking about an out-of-control tanker that's
destroying half the graveyard in its wake. Everyone wants to know,
'Who was on patrol?' I had no choice but to tell them it was my son,
who might as well be sterile for all the good he's done contributing to
our lineage."

"Mother . . ." groaned Odin.

"Your brother Pol Pot nabbed two scavengers last month, don't
you know. And did I tell you? He just impregnated another of his
wives. Which reminds me, I know I promised to buy you a porno-
graphic holoplay for your birth celebration, but now I have to spend
the money on a baby gift. It's not like you bring in any revenue, after
all, and—"

Odin cut her off with a click of the comm module controls. He
didn't need that kind of abuse, especially when on the trail of a
hardened mercenary, who, it suddenly occurred to him, was probably piloting a ship loaded with treasure. Stolen weapons, and cargo
bays overflowing with platinum thrones . . . Odin's imagination

took flight once again. He'd show them; he'd show all of them! *I'll go from Omega to Alpha yet.*

Odin kicked the Salvager's engines into action, bringing the ship out from under the broad stabilizer wing of a Than skimmer. The Nietzschean wasn't particularly concerned about the *Maru*'s lead. After all, he had an edge—the harpoon tip that was still attached to the *Maru* contained a sensor beacon. It was an old trick that gave pirates a second chance: any ship able to break free of the harpoon would be trailing a path of electronic bread crumbs.

Odin raced for the Slip point; it was time to put up or shut up. *Prepare yourself, Enemy, for you are about to be Omega-fied.*

"I think our Nietzschean pirate may be making an encore appearance," announced Beka, looking from the *Maru*'s sensors to the empty air that had moments ago been occupied by her brother. She thought she could hear his footsteps clanking down the central corridor. She was tempted to forget the pirate and go after her brother, lest he do something unpleasant to her ship—forcing Beka to do something unpleasant to him. But still, she had to admit, having Rafe touch her ship was far preferable to having it stolen entirely.

With the *Maru* dead in space, there would be very few traces of it to detect—no exhaust or electronic noise, just its mass. As long as she and Rafe didn't start any shouting contests on an open mike, the pirate might pass them by thinking they were a stray chunk of rock. And with the *Maru*'s weapons systems off-line, Beka considered that a consummation devoutly to be wished. So it was with some disappointment that she watched the Nietzschean make a beeline for the *Maru*'s coordinates. She debated rediverting the power from the sensors to the weapons system—but that meant she would lose the drone, and that meant losing Magdalena.

It was an easier decision than she thought it would be. The sensors were staying active. *I've gone through too much already to lose that signal.* The pirate had closed to about half a light-minute away, and was still bearing straight at her. She reached under the control console and withdrew a small Gauss pistol that had been taped to its underside. She waited as the Nietzschean closed to within range. Then Beka shuddered and the *Maru* shivered under the impact of the pirate's two harpoons.

The comm light blinked. *What does he want now?* wondered Beka as she activated the ship-to-ship. The Nietzschean was still playing his grating music at full blast.

"Once again, it is I, Odin Ome—er, Odin Borgia, your bitter arch-nemesis. Did you really think you could escape a great warrior-poet like me? I am like the mighty mintauk, and you but the annoying flea. Now I crush you! Prepare to meet me in battle, dangerous mercenary."

Beka rolled her eyes. *Mercenary? What fumes has this trashpicker been huffing?*

"Listen up, Odin Borgia," said Beka. "If you think you're just gonna breeze in here and take my ship, then you're as stupid as you sound."

Odin laughed. It was supposed to be a fiendish cackle, but it came out more like a nasal whistle punctuated by a hiccup. "It is not I who is stupid. It is *you* who are stupid. Prepare to face my indescribable fury!"

The Nietzschean began to reel in the *Maru*, the vibrations sending Beka's fuzzy dice jiggling in the front observation screen.

Beka was familiar with the pirate's Salvager. These ships extended two arms that could get around the bulk of most small- to mid-size target vessels, and which were also capable of extending flat and attaching to the surface of anything larger. The pirate would then gain access through the underside of the Salvager, which was equipped with cutting tools and a movable shaft that acted as a pressurized conduit between both ships.

Beka guessed rightly that the Nietzschean would attach to the top of the *Maru* and attempt to open the maintenance hatch. He'd either try to codebreak the outer airlock, or just cut his way in. Beka fervently hoped that it would be the former. *And if Rev Bem were here, I'd have him throw up a prayer to that effect.*

Beka climbed four levels to the *Maru*'s dimly lit top deck. There wasn't much there but storage, mostly empty metal cages intended for cargo. She looked inside a few of the holding lockers and found a motorized dolly carrying a small crate. She brought the dolly outside the maintenance bay, and set the crate down near the opposite wall. She knelt behind the crate, steadied her gun on the top of it, and waited. A simple plan, really, but less is often more when it comes to spontaneous ambushes.

Eventually, the *Maru*'s hull stopped transmitting the sounds of machinery and an eerie silence pervaded its corridors. Beka exhaled with relief as she heard the hatch being manually activated, and not ripped through with a laser saw. There was a hiss as the ceiling-mounted portal opened and swung down.

Beka waited. The pirate jumped through the opening, not bothering to use the ladder, falling some three meters and landing in a heap. Beka unloaded her clip at the inert pile almost without thinking. The Nietzschean never even moved. Beka wondered if he hadn't just snapped his neck during the fall. *Now, that would be anticlimactic.* She cautiously walked into the maintenance bay and nudged the Nietzschean's body with her foot . . . and was dismayed to find that in the *Maru*'s anemic emergency lighting, what she had taken to be a body wasn't that at all. It was a gunnysack filled with whatever it was pirates took with them to work—a sandwich and clean change of clothes, for all Beka knew.

Damn. Smarter than he sounded after all.

Beka looked up just in time to catch a quick glimpse of the airlock shaft extending all the way up into the Salvager—but this vision was preempted by the bottoms of Odin's boots. That was when Odin Borgia dropped down on top of her, knocking the gun out of her hand (accidentally, as it happens) and sending it skittering across the metal mesh of the floor. Naturally, he also lost his balance in the process, getting tangled with her as he stumbled and fell. Beka found her footing first and got in a good kick to the pirate's stomach before he was able to climb to his knees and unsteadily regain his feet.

Beka looked longingly at her pistol. She warily eyed her opponent in the gloomy confines of the access bay. The pirate was shorter than most Nietzscheans, with eyes two sizes too big, giving his face a babylike quality. Beka usually found Nietzscheans rather appealing, especially when they were like Tyr—tall, dark, and hunky. One disappointed human space jockey even accused her of being an "*uber* lover." Well, actually, he got as far as "*uber* luh—" before she cut him off with an uppercut to the larynx. Racial epithets are so impolite. Odin Borgia, however, was short, dark, and oddly polite-looking— not much of a heartthrob, nor a menace, either.

"Your ship is mine!" huffed Odin, already out of breath. He rested an arm against the access ladder to regain his wind.

Beka inched backward toward the crate—the pistol had come to rest along its side. Sure, she knew the gun was out of bullets . . . but Odin didn't.

Odin followed Beka, and as he got closer, he began appearing proportionally more perplexed. "You're a mercenary? I expected you to be at least seven feet tall. And where are your scars?"

"Sorry to break the news," said Beka, "but I'm no mercenary."

"Not a mercenary?" He sounded so disappointed Beka almost felt sorry for him. She couldn't know the elaborate fantasy construct that was even now unraveling. "Then I'll just have to take your treasure."

Beka couldn't help but laugh. "I don't know where you got your data, but there is zero treasure on this ship. I might have a losing Berzian lottery ticket around here somewhere, but that's about it."

"No treasure?" Odin pouted; his full lower lip trembled. It was the closest Beka had seen a Nietzschean come to crying. He shrugged. "I guess I'll just have to kill you, then."

Odin put a hand on the Em-lash in his ceramic polymer hip holster. Beka's eyes widened. You don't play around with a monomolecular filament whip—damn thing can cut through the hull of a ship like it was made of origami paper. You don't even want to know what it can do to a human limb.

Odin stared at Beka; Beka stared at the Em-lash. She wasn't sure if the Nietzschean was serious, or was playing some kind of elaborate practical joke. She got her answer when he activated the thin line of cable, and began recklessly flinging the whip around the cramped corridor of the *Maru*. He came close to lobbing off a bulkhead door . . . and a few of his own extremities in the process.

Beka ducked just as the lash snapped right above her, its tip shearing off the corner of a ceiling support. A smooth rolling dive, and she managed to snatch up the gun and simultaneously avoid falling architecture. The *Maru*'s main lights suddenly crackled and illuminated, while a general mechanical hum returned to the ship. The sound was pure music to Beka's ears—it was the sound of an operational *Maru*.

Odin looked around, startled by the sudden thrum of the equipment. Beka pointed her gun at him. "Put that toy away before you hurt someone."

He gave her a lopsided smile in return. "That's a Theta Five Gauss Pistol you're pointing at me, and its clip holds eleven. You're out of bullets. I counted."

Definitely smarter than he sounded. Okay. Time for the old standby. "Watch out behind you!" Beka shouted.

Odin instinctively turned to look over his shoulder, one drawback of Nietzschean paranoia. Beka ran up and hit him across the back of the head with the handle of her pistol.

Apparently, she didn't hit him hard enough. "Ow," said Odin, spinning back around. He snarled, although it made him look like a toddler who had just bit down hard on his own lip. Odin grabbed Beka by the wrist, and while he may not have been the most intimidating specimen of selective breeding, he was certainly strong enough. It felt like he was going to snap Beka's arm in two. She dropped the gun and the Nietzschean shoved her backward. Beka backpedaled for a second, then landed unceremoniously on her rear.

Odin cleared his throat. He knew that gloating over a fallen opponent was bad battle strategy, but the warrior-poet in him demanded a speech. "Now, you shall feel the pain of my weapon," sang Odin. "May you die as all my enemies have died, defeated." Odin lifted his arm, ready to bring the lethal Em-lash down on his foe.

"Behind you!" called Beka.

The pirate laughed. "You'll have to do better than that if you hope to outsmart Odin Borgia of the mighty Ghidra Pride."

Behind Odin, Rafe held a laser torch held high in the air, then gracefully brought it down, hard, on the pirate's brainpan.

Odin Borgia winced and fell into a heap on the floor.

"She warned you, Odin Borgia of the mighty Ghidra Pride." Rafe winked, standing over the pirate. Then he turned to Beka. "You did, you know. You practically gave me away!"

"I had to do something. Even I could hear you coming." Beka got up and brushed herself off. "But, all is forgiven if the *Maru* is actually back on-line."

Rafe beamed grin number eighty-four, the am-I-good-or-what model, and rested the torch nonchalantly on his shoulder. "Hi, I'm Rafe 'The Invincible' Valentine, master of all I survey. Have we met?"

"Oh, I knew you could do it," lied Beka. "But let's save the self-congratulations until after the engines fire up, okay?"

Beka pointed to the inert Nietzschean. "In the meantime, take Sleeping Beauty back to his ship. And while you're there, try figuring out how to release the *Maru* from the Salvager's claws."

"Roger that," said Rafe. He reached to retrieve Beka's pistol, but she grabbed it out of his hand so fast the air cracked. *Touchy about her toys.* Rafe shrugged, then picked up Odin Borgia by the ankles and began dragging the pirate to the maintenance bay.

Rafe had fixed the *Maru*'s engines in record time, which Beka decided was either brilliant, suspicious, or just plain lucky. She didn't know whether to admire her brother or to accuse him of some kind of subterfuge. On the way back to the cockpit Beka tried shaking off these doubts. This new Rafe had her so confused that she was beginning to second-guess him. And under these conditions, that could be dangerous . . . to both of them.

Beka plopped into the pilot's seat. *At least we can finally get on our way . . . if Rafe's handiwork holds up. Damn—there I go again*, she thought. She looked for Magdalena's ship; it was gone, of course. But on the bright side, Magdalena had used the exact Slip point Beka predicted that she would; they still had a bead on her.

Beka was just breaking into an anticipatory smile when there was a significant new development: five ships in formation only a few light-seconds away, standing between the *Maru* and the Slip point. They had been hailing the *Maru* for some time. Beka's stomach dropped as the *Maru*'s computer ID'd the ships: Gallipolan.

Guess Rafe had been telling the truth about something after all. Beka opened the comm channel just in time to hear: "Attention, *Eureka Maru*, this is the Gallipolan Police Command." On-screen flashed a mug shot of her wayward sibling, flashing the smile he had developed for the sole purpose of pissing off authority figures. Harper called it his "Bart Simpson," although Beka had no idea why.

The voice continued. "Rafael Valentine, you are wanted by the Gallipolan High Authority, convicted in absentia on twelve counts of fraud, six counts of resisting arrest, six counts of assaulting an officer, and three counts of spitting on a public thoroughfare. Your unnamed accomplice is hereby charged with aiding and abetting a fugitive. Surrender herewith, or pursuant to Intergalactic FTA code 344.8, we will fuck you up big time."

"Rafael Valentine? Never heard of him," responded Beka. *Well, it's worth a try.*

"Not according to our informants on Farside," answered the Gallipolan. "Which reminds me. You're also under arrest for counterfeiting."

Beka could hear an echo reverberating throughout the *Maru*; Rafe was disengaging the Nietzschean's ship. They only needed a few more minutes . . .

Another signal cut into the Gallipolans' threats. It was Rafe, responding from the Salvager. "Hey, rent-a-cops. For your information, Rafael Valentine works alone. The lady I was with is a clueless hostage, and I don't want her getting *any* of my credit. So don't forget to stick a kidnapping charge onto that laundry list."

Beka let the "clueless" comment slide; she was just hoping Rafe had a way out of the hole he was digging for himself. She played her part: "He made me fly him out to this Divine-forsaken system to rendezvous with his Salvager . . . shoot him before he gets away! Oh, I'd also like to add 'ravishment' to the charges, your honors."

Rafe tried, with limited success, not to laugh. "Lady, you should be so lucky. Just be grateful these Gallipolans decided to poke their pointy heads into my business, or you would have never walked out of this alive."

Shut up and get back on the Maru, *Rafe.* It sounded like he was getting carried away by his own performance. The *Maru* would be completely free from the Salvager any moment now. Beka kept her eye on the systems monitor, watching the maintenance hatch—she knew that if it closed, it meant Rafe was on board. If it didn't close and the *Maru* was set loose, top deck was going to become one with outer space. She began to seal off the area, just in case.

Rafe still wasn't finished. "You Gallipolan goons disappoint me.

You should know by now a Valentine *never* gives up without a fight. I've got a couple of missiles with your name on them primed and ready to fly, so save yourselves some trouble and just add a couple of blown-up copper choppers to my list of offenses."

Rafe! Can it already! Beka watched with concern as the computer indicated that the *Maru* was fully released, but the hatch was still open . . . and that meant no Rafe. Still, the top deck was maintaining pressure. Beka put her hands in the pilot toggles and got to work. There was only one possible way the top deck could have stayed stabilized: Rafe must have maintained the connection with the Salvager's airlock shaft. A good move, but without the steadying influence of the Salvager's arms, the only thing keeping that passage attached was a two-guilder plastic seal that the *Maru* could snap with so much as a shudder. Meaning Beka had to maintain her position to the millimeter: too far one way and she'd break the seal, too far the other and she'd crush the airlock corridor.

"Attention, *Eureka Maru*," ordered the Gallipolan police. "Move away from the Salvager immediately!"

The Salvager fired a missile. *Probably just a harpoon*, thought Beka. *Now watch things get really tricky.*

The Gallipolan ships easily neutralized the harpoon with a head-on hit from a defensive missile. "*Eureka Maru*, we repeat, move away from the Salvager or you will be destroyed along with it!"

Beka needed to stall. She raised her voice half an octave and tried to sound helpless. "Oh, dear! I'm having trouble disengaging!"

"We repeat, move *now*."

Beka glared at the red light on the monitor, the one that indicated the maintenance hatch was still open, while trying to keep the *Maru* at a very delicate and precise hover. *C'mon, Rafe, get that ass into gear!*

Finally, the hatch light turned green and she slammed the *Eureka* into action, dropping the ship as far and as fast from the Salvager and the Gallipolans as she could. It was a hell of a time to test Rafe's mechanical aptitude, but she had no choice. As she pulled away she was startled to see the Salvager continue to maneuver, firing additional sallies. A black dread enclosed her. *Rafe is still on the pirate ship!*

She didn't even think it through. She brought the *Maru* to a stop and turned back. If Rafe was going down, she was going down with him. After all they'd been through, how dare Rafe leave her now! She was furious.

"Did they fall for it?" asked Rafe as he strolled into the cockpit. Beka, shocked into silence, looked back at the screens. The Gallipolans were still firing on the Salvager, and the Salvager was still taking defensive action and returning fire. You can't do that without a pilot, yet Rafe was standing right behind her. *What the hell . . . ?*

Rafe looked concerned. "What's the matter, Rocket? You look like you've seen a ghost."

"No, I, uh . . ." stuttered Beka, then gave up. She indicated the display, which showed the Gallipolans battling the feisty, outnumbered spacecraft. "How'd you get that ship to dance?"

"Just a little something they teach you in Scoundrel School." Rafe smiled, taking the copilot chair as Beka pushed the *Maru* at full speed toward Magdalena's last Slip point. The truth was, Rafe had no idea how he had done it—or if he had done it at all. He fired the one harpoon, and that was it. But hey, if there was credit to be had . . . Rafe leaned back and folded his hands behind his head. "I'm so good, sometimes I amaze even myself."

Beka looked at him, and Rafe was caught off guard by her expression. There was something in her face that he hadn't seen since back when they were kids—back before he left, back before he gave her all those reasons to hate him. She was looking at him with admiration.

For a moment neither of them spoke while, on the monitor, the

Salvager exploded in a fireball of oxygen combustion that the Gallipolans believed heralded the death of one Rafael Valentine.

Odin Borgia awoke on the floor of the Salvager's cockpit with a splitting headache. He touched the back of his skull and felt the tender knot of a large bruise. Last thing he remembered, he had boarded the mercenaries' ship. He engaged his enemy in an epic battle, and then everything went dark. Odin groggily sat up and looked around. He was alone on his own ship, no sign of the mercs anywhere. He crawled to the control bank, and quickly forgot about the female with the Gauss pistol when he saw the blips of not one but five ships approaching. His eyes lit up, and his imagination kicked into overdrive; surely this veritable armada was his ticket to Alpha status, and a giant step on the path to his own dream pride. He pulled himself into the pilot's chair, cranked up the decibels on Creeping Entropy to earsplitting volume, and aimed everything he had at the Gallipolans.

Odin Borgia's last words were: "Prepare to be Omega-fied!"

SIX

Diplomacy is the art of telling someone to go to hell so elegantly that he packs for the trip. War is the simpler matter of bringing hell to him.

—HIGH GUARD ADMIRAL CONSTANZA STARK,
CY 9779

Someone was going to die on the Command Deck, and Dylan didn't want it to be him. True, his throat was about to be torn out on the tines of Rasputin Genovese's bone blades—but there was also Tyr, who had a gun trained on Rasputin and who in turn had a gun (in the hands of one of Rasputin's jumpy guards) trained on him. Meanwhile, the second of the admiral's goons was drawing down on the delegates from the Human Interplanetary Alliance, who of course had weapons of their own aimed at anyone and everyone, hoping to return the favor.

So much for guarantees of mutual disarmament.

Dylan checked the strength of Rasputin's grip around his neck.

About on a par with titanium alloy, he decided. He went for a more reasoned tactic. "Look, Admiral. Whoever attacked your ship is getting ready to attack mine. And since you're actually standing on that target at the moment, you might want to back off and let me do my job."

Rasputin scoffed. "Nice try, Captain. But I bought your story last time, and it cost me two fighter pilots."

Rommie moved to help Trance tend to Rev Bem, who had regained consciousness and was insisting that he didn't need medical attention. "Magog skulls are as impenetrable as your past," Rev said pointedly to Trance. "Anyway, I'm not the one in need of help." He directed Rommie's attention to her captain.

Indeed, the bulk of Andromeda's computing power was presently chewing over ways to save her captain. So far, her circuits were drawing blanks—or, at any rate, they were drawing scenarios that all included loss of life. If the admiral suspected an attack, he wouldn't hesitate to take Dylan's head off. Suddenly, Rommie's head cocked left and her hologram flickered into life and approached the sensor console. The HIA delegates flinched; it was always odd to see Rommie walk *through* Rommie.

Where the ship's sensors had been reading empty space, they were now reading spacecraft. The Rommie hologram looked at Dylan. "I'm finally reading enemy ships on my sensors. Three of them, maintaining position two-point-three-five LS away."

Rommie's human interface avatar moved toward the weapons console, but Rasputin tugged at Dylan's throat and glared at her. "Not another step."

The avatar froze, and virtual Andromeda's face appeared on the Command comm screen. "They don't seem to be making any hostile moves," she said. "But I recognize them. The ships, they're Genite in origin. And they're hailing us."

Rasputin dragged Dylan back a few feet, out of visual range of the screen, then nodded. "Put the captain's accomplices through, Ship," he said.

Rommie ignored Rasputin's command and looked at Dylan. "Shall I put them through?"

Dylan didn't know who decided it was a good idea to give an AI attitude, but right now he wasn't finding it to be a very helpful programming feature. "Just do it," he choked out.

The gorgeous features of the Andromeda Ascendant on the main screen were replaced by ones considerably more odd. It seemed to be human: it was completely bald, and had pale skin that clashed violently with a pair of dark goggles that kept the eyes completely hidden. The small, round glasses gave the odd impression that the being possessed bullet holes instead of eyes.

"My apologies to the Andromeda Ascendant," it began. The voice seemed male—it was raspy, but had a sharp edge. "That was a rude entrance, but know I mean your vessel no harm."

"Who are you, and what do you want?" asked Rasputin, safely out of sight of the intruder.

"My name is Lord Nyain Parchman, and I want to be part of these negotiations, as a representative of the Knights of Genetic Purity."

Dylan groaned inwardly. *Things just keep getting better and better.* Dylan hadn't dealt extensively with the Knights of Genetic Purity, otherwise known as Genites, but what little experience he'd had was enough to make him both dislike and distrust them. The Genite philosophy was simple: Nietzscheans were responsible for the downfall of the Commonwealth. Nietzscheans are genetically engineered humans. If it weren't for genetic engineering, they believed, everything would still be hunky-dory. They believed this with such fanatical fervor that they made it their goal to cleanse the universe of genetically modified humans. "Cleanse," in these cases, is usually just another word for mass murder.

The Nietzscheans in the room, not surprisingly, also had an opinion about the Genites. Rasputin moved himself and his hostage into view of the screen.

Lord Parchman's formal smile fell from his face as he saw the scene on *Andromeda*'s Command Deck. "Obviously, it's too late for me to warn you about Nietzschean treachery. But perhaps my timing was still fortuitous."

Dylan felt Rasputin relax slightly, easing the pressure on his neck. Rasputin had been willing to entertain the possibility that the captain would betray him for the sake of the HIA. But he knew Dylan Hunt's reputation, and he couldn't see the man in league with the Genites. The High Guard relic ascribed to archaic moral standards—it was, in fact, his greatest weakness. And the Knights of Genetic Purity were notorious genocidal maniacs.

Rasputin didn't move his bone blades completely away, but he did release his hold on the back of Dylan's head, allowing him to stand straight. "Find out what he wants," whispered Rasputin.

"You're the boss," muttered Dylan, trying to keep his sarcasm to a minimum. Then he said aloud to Parchman: "I'm Captain Dylan Hunt, and I don't recall inviting you to the table. Your unprovoked attack has put this negotiation in jeopardy, and unless I get a good explanation for your actions, I'm going to instruct my ship to return fire."

Parchman laughed. "Before the Nietzschean slits your throat, or after? The Dragan is prepared to kill you, Captain. Why am I the enemy? By destroying those fighters I saved your ship. I was expecting better treatment than this."

"Rasputin," said Tyr levelly. "The captain didn't shoot down your fighters. You have no reason to kill him."

Rasputin nodded and slowly released Dylan. "He's right," he said, and signaled his guards to lower their weapons. Tyr cautiously lowered his gun as well. An audible sigh of relief swept the deck. Dylan massaged the painful dimples in his neck left by the admiral's bone blades, and decided against demanding an apology.

"We can make our amends later, Captain," said Rasputin, anticipating him. "First, let me alert my flagship to the Genites' presence. As you can see, I am here today as an honest broker."

Lord Parchman smiled tersely. "More like a good actor, Dragan. But I'm not as trusting as Captain Hunt. Your fighters were preparing to open fire on the *Andromeda*. I simply acted to prevent it."

"He's lying," said Rasputin, matter-of-factly.

"Am I?" said Lord Parchman. "I intercepted a datalink transmission between the Nietzschean fighters that indicated as much. Listen."

An audio signal came up on the speakers. It was a brief conversation, punctuated with screeches of interference, between the Nietzschean pilots. One thing that was quite audible was a countdown. Someone was preparing to fire on someone. Still, Dylan wasn't entirely convinced. Datalink communications between fighters weren't something you casually intercepted; they were among a military's most guarded secrets. Harper himself would have a hard time tapping into Nietzschean ship-to-ship chatter.

"Even if that noise meant something, this human has destroyed two ships," insisted Rasputin. "I must at least warn my men."

Dylan glanced at Tyr, who took the cue. Tyr's Gauss gun reappeared, aimed at Rasputin. *This is working out better than I expected,* thought Dylan.

"Sorry, Admiral," said Dylan. "Not yet. First, I want to figure out what's really going on here. In the meantime, have your guards hand over their weapons."

Arca had been keeping a distrustful eye on the Nietzschean guards throughout this exchange. Ostentatiously, she pulled back the hammer on her ancient revolver as Harper moved to relieve the Nietzscheans of their guns.

"Tyr, you take the HIA's weapons," ordered Dylan.

"Come on, Boss. They didn't even do anything," argued Harper.

"No? I thought *all* parties agreed in good faith to come to these negotiations unarmed."

The delegates grudgingly handed over their weaponry. As Tyr reached for Arca's revolver, she clamped a hand on his wrist and stared him down. Not easy, considering that he had half a meter's height advantage on her. "I'd better get this back," she said fiercely.

Tyr looked at the ancient gun, at the hand on his arm, and then at Arca with amazement. "If I destroyed it, I'd only be doing you a favor. You're lucky it hasn't already blown your hand off."

Dylan turned and spoke to Lord Parchman. "This doesn't mean I trust you. And I'd better not find out you faked those transmissions. But, for now, remind me why the Genites feel it is necessary to interfere in this negotiation."

"My Knights might be able to help the human cause. Let me at least talk to their delegation."

"And what's to stop me killing him as soon as he steps aboard this ship?" said Rasputin, gripping the command console so hard that his knuckles turned white. *His self-control has its limits*, noted Dylan.

"Me, for one," said Dylan. But he made the threat with some reluctance. This peace negotiation was unraveling before it had even begun. Two Nietzschean fighters destroyed, his throat a millimeter from being slashed, subterfuge from every party involved . . . and now he was going to have to spend time with both Nietzschean slavers and Genite bigots, neither of which had ever appeared on Dylan's holiday card list.

Dylan felt a hand on his shoulder, and turned to see Arca and Harper. They wore matching expressions: hopeful, pleading, desperate. Harper stared up at the captain. "You know, Boss, the HIA really could use the Genites' help."

Arca stepped forward. "We both know the Dragans won't willingly give us our freedom, no matter what Admiral Rasputin claims. I, for one, would like to hear Lord Parchman out. That's all."

"C'mon, Dylan. What could it hurt?" said Harper.

Dylan was able to think of any number of things it could hurt, but he knew how much Harper in particular—and humanity in general—had suffered at the hands of the Drago-Kazov. He was loath to refuse him, no matter what he personally thought of Parchman and his ilk.

But there were other factors to consider. He needed time for Rommie to inspect the Nietzschean datalink transmission—he wanted to triple-check its authenticity before he did anything drastic, like throwing the admiral onto V Deck. And really, wasn't it best to have Parchman on the *Andromeda* where he could keep tabs on him? Dylan wasn't comfortable with the idea of a pissed-off Lord Parchman, armed with stealth fighters and flying around unchecked in space.

Keep your friends close and your enemies closer, Dylan smiled. *A Nietzschean must have said that.*

Dylan cleared his throat. "Lord Parchman, permission to board the *Andromeda* is granted. But you *will* be searched for weapons."

Nyain Parchman was taller than Dylan expected, almost as tall as Tyr and Rasputin. The Genite's shaved head seemed to grow directly out of his torso without benefit of a neck, while his heavily muscled upper body was precariously balanced atop long and wiry legs. He wore a simple white tunic rather than the formidable Genite armor Dylan had encountered in the past. The Genites, having shunned genetic engineering, sought to improve themselves through strictly mechanical means, and their battle armor was one of their potent creations. It utilized photoreactive plating, a superior camouflage that made its wearer practically invisible. And obviously, Dylan noted with some concern, they now possessed a similar technology that allowed their ships to avoid sensor detection. Something else for Andromeda to look into. He wanted Harper's input on all this as well, but had yet to pry his lecherous engineer from Arca's side.

Dylan greeted Lord Parchman with the towering, glowering Tyr Anasazi in tow. It was his way of making it clear from the start that he was unsympathetic to the Genite's prejudices. From the moment he stepped from his ship, Parchman refused to acknowledge the Nietzschean, although he was warm with Dylan. Tyr, to his credit, displayed only his normal disdain for the visitor. But this new arrival was tricky business; it was already putting a strain on the negotiations. *And negotiations haven't even started yet.*

"I was hoping to speak with the human delegation alone," said Parchman, walking the springy, composite-covered corridors alongside Dylan and Tyr.

"I really can't allow that. Remember, this isn't a negotiation for the benefit of the Genites." Dylan walked a while longer, then offered, "One thing I can do for you is keep Admiral Rasputin otherwise occupied while you talk."

Parchman reacted graciously. "Thank you, Captain, that's very diplomatic of you. And I do understand your position." He placed a conspiratorial arm around Dylan's shoulder and added, "You know, it's a shame there's not more like us around."

"Diplomats? Or humans?" asked Tyr, without a trace of sarcasm.

"Both," answered Parchman, without a trace of embarrassment.

Dylan's skin crawled at Parchman's touch. The Genite had been on board the *Andromeda* just five minutes, and already Dylan wanted to turn him back around and send him on his way.

"For the record, Tyr Anasazi is a loyal and capable member of my crew, and if you're going to breathe my air and eat my food, you are going to treat him as such." Dylan knew he was stretching it a little when it came to the bit about loyalty, but Parchman didn't know that.

The Genite regarded Dylan for a moment, then shrugged. "If you insist. But only out of respect for you."

Empress defend me, the man wants to bond! cringed Dylan inwardly. He recoiled as the self-appointed lord—because Dylan was sure the man didn't descend from any recognized aristocracy—again hung his arm upon his shoulder and began describing the Knights of Genetic Purity's long High Guard tradition.

"The order was founded by High Guard officers, you realize," Parchman explained. "And we have retained much of the old honor code. I think a military man like yourself would feel right at home among our ranks. And I'm sure that with your standing and reputation, you'd be a great success. Of course, we'd have to cure you of your misguided notion that these mutants can be trusted!"

Dylan pasted on a polite smile. He wanted to snap a force lance in half in Parchman's face, announcing himself as the genetic hybrid he was—half human, half bioengineered Heavy Worlder—but kept his cool. It was information better kept to himself, he decided. For now.

Harper and Arca were waiting for them on the Observation Deck. Lord Parchman made a show of bowing on one knee before Arca, taking her hand, and kissing it. Harper found the Genite's goggles unsettling; you never knew if his eyes were turned on you or if he was looking somewhere else entirely.

Parchman smiled at the two humans. "It's an honor to meet both of you. You do our race proud."

Harper exchanged a look with Dylan: *What's up with this guy?*

"I'm here today," explained Lord Parchman, "because Alpha Centauri is a colony of good people—more than that, of *true* people. The Knights of Genetic Purity do not want to see these people, our brothers, dying at the hands of a mutant army." He turned to Arca. "You fight these Dragans with sticks and rocks."

Arca bristled. "We do all right," she said defensively.

"More than all right! And it's a proud testament to what pure humans can accomplish. But the Knighthood has more at our disposal than sticks and rocks. We have ships, we have weapons, we have anything your people need. We can help you defeat your oppressors. We want to help you."

Dylan quickly stepped in. "Look, I'm all for leveling the playing field, but I didn't come here to escalate a war. The idea is to save lives."

"Fair enough, but even you have to agree that the HIA coming to the bargaining table alone is different than their coming to the bargaining table with the Knights of Genetic Purity behind them. By aligning themselves with us, the HIA improves its negotiating position from one of supplicants, to one of equals."

"Equal's good, Boss. Right?" said Harper. True, this Genite's talk about race and purity was a bit freaky at times, but it was a damned attractive offer. The only reason the HIA—heck, any human rebellion—hadn't yet won its freedom was that they were so pitifully outresourced. Add the Genites' advanced weaponry to the humans' passion, and you just might have a victory on your hands.

Arca seemed to be thinking the same thing as Harper. "It's a generous offer," she allowed. "What do you expect in return?"

Parchman shrugged. "We want only what you want: freedom for your people. In fact, I propose that with you at our side, we can free *all* humans. We can carry this crusade to every Nietzschean-held world. Imagine, no pure human will ever again know the bonds of slavery."

"And no Nietzschean will ever know the meaning of death by natural causes," said Tyr dryly. Dylan shot him a look; he had almost forgotten the big Nietzschean was there. Parchman ignored the comment—and Tyr—entirely.

"Freedom from bondage is a no-brainer," said Dylan. "But Tyr does have a point. What happens in Act Two? Is that where you wipe the universe clean of Nietzscheans altogether?" Dylan looked to

Arca and Harper. "What about Nietzscheans who aren't slavers? And what's the Genetic Purity position on humans who've been genetically engineered to live underwater, or to breathe ammonia?"

"Or to pilot a shuttle in a gravity well," said Harper enigmatically.

Dylan almost jumped. *Of course Harper would know about my mother,* he realized. *He practically lives in the VR library.* But all he said was, "Arca, are you sure you want the HIA to put its stamp of approval on genocide?"

Parchman's black glasses turned to Dylan and peered at him as if scanning his very DNA. Did he guess? If he did, he said nothing. He simply responded evenly, "Unpure is unpure. Nature will be served."

"O-kay, Mr. Lordship, but you just graduated from off-center to totally nutso," said Harper, backing away. He took Arca's arm. "I think I've heard enough. You?"

Arca wouldn't return Harper's gaze, and she didn't share his conviction. The potential of Alpha Centauri's freedom was not a carrot she could dismiss so lightly. "It's just an option, right? And options are something the HIA has precious few of. At least, let me think about what he said."

Dylan spoke to the walls: "Andromeda?" Her image appeared on the nearest comm screen. "Would you send an android to escort Admiral Rasputin to Obs Deck?"

Dylan turned to Arca. "It will take a few minutes for him to get here. Use the time to decide where you stand . . . but consider this. If you choose the Genites' support, you will most certainly lose mine."

"Listen, Boss—" began Harper, but was cut off by the appearance of an Andromeda hologram flickering to life in front of him. "Dylan, I need to see you on Command Deck."

"Immediately?"

"Sooner than that," answered the hologram, and winked out.

As Dylan turned to jog out of the Observation Deck, he realized he'd be leaving Parchman alone with Arca, Harper, and—of all people—Tyr. He considered his options: Trance was taking care of Rev on Med Deck, and Rommie's avatar would be busy on Command . . . Dylan was reminded of the usefulness of first officers. *Note to self. Talk to Beka about the difference between "personal time" and "AWOL."*

"Well," said Harper, displaying his keen gift for pointing out the painfully obvious, "this is awkward." With Dylan gone, an uncomfortable silence descended on Obs. Lord Parchman had withdrawn to the main observation window to fume. "Baldy there looks like he's about to explode."

Tyr was cemented to his favorite spot, leaning against a wall, his eyes half closed in seeming disinterest. Harper got Arca's attention, nodded in the direction of a potted Vaxos tree. "Over there," he whispered, vigorously pointing with his forehead.

"Something wrong with your neck?" asked Arca impishly.

Harper finally grabbed her by the arm and pulled her to the tree. "I just wanted to talk without being overheard. You know Parchman is crazy as a moonstruck Perseid, right? I mean, you're not seriously considering his offer, are you?"

"I don't know," said Arca noncommittally. Harper, and Dylan for that matter, were beginning to remind her of the HIA commander, Pac Peterson. Pac had seen her own children murdered by Nietzscheans, yet she still retained a sense of compassion. Arca felt the time for compassion was long since over. They were at war, and war meant you did whatever it took to win.

"Don't you see, Harper? With the Genites' support, we could defeat the Dragans once and for all: no compromises, no negotiating, no nothing. We'll have our independence, and we'll have earned it ourselves. Don't you want that? Doesn't your blood scream for revenge?"

Harper shook his head. "I'm no card-carrying member of the Slavelord Fan Club, and sure, maybe with the Genites' help you could even defeat the Nietzscheans. But are you sure you won't end up being no better than either of them? It's one thing to fight the Dragans for your freedom. It's another to exterminate them entirely—and something tells me that's exactly what Parchman has in mind. Natal's freedom isn't his goal—it's just a lucky by-product."

"I never said the HIA would throw in with them," said Arca. "We'd just accept their help. That's all."

Harper felt frustrated. Couldn't Arca see that when you lie down with genocidal fanatics, you wake up with bloody fleas on your hands? *Okay, that was bad. I wish Dylan would get back. He always knows the right thing to say.*

Arca peered at Harper's face. Yes, he was definitely like Pac—she probably wouldn't agree to an alliance with the Genites, either. Pac was the one who advocated negotiations with the Dragans in the first place, while Arca had argued vehemently against it. What Pac couldn't see, or was ignoring, was that her stand on the issue was causing dissension within the Alliance. Most of the rank and file agreed with Arca: negotiation was useless, the only bargaining table the Dragans understood was the battlefield. Many were beginning to openly criticize their commander, calling her weak.

Arca thought there was another option, an option even Pac would approve. An option that Arca advocated for a number of selfish reasons.

"There is one other alternative. A morale boost so enormous that the Human Alliance could take on the Dragans single-handedly, and win," said Arca. "What if the legendary Seamus Harper himself returned with me to Natal, and accepted a leadership position within the HIA? I know the high command would approve." Arca touched Harper's arm seductively, "*I* would approve."

For some reason, Harper felt exactly the opposite of how he thought he'd feel. No seeing stars and little birds. No cartwheeling around the room. Instead, it all started to feel painfully similar to those last moments with his cousin Brendan. Back then, the choice was either stay on Earth and fight, or return to the *Andromeda*. He made his decision, and he knew it was the right one. But not a day went by that he didn't feel guilty about it.

"I can't," said Harper. "I wish I could, believe me. But I'm a member of this crew. These are my friends—hell, they're my family. And ultimately I can do more good for humanity here on the *Andromeda Ascendant* than I can anywhere else."

"I understand," said Arca. Harper glimpsed disappointment, but she covered it.

Time to change the subject. "I've got a plan," he ventured. "How about after this first round of negotiations, we spend some quality time sharing a fine meal of reconstituted Earth hamburgers from *Andromeda*'s mess."

"Why, Harper. Are you asking me out on a date?"

"Not if 'date' means I have to pay." Harper grinned, but his smile quickly disappeared as he spotted Lord Parchman approaching. "Bogey at eleven o'clock," he warned.

Lord Parchman launched right into his agenda. "I'm wasting my time here. Arca, I suggest you simply accept my offer so we can leave immediately. Or decline, and I'll leave you to your fantasy of a negotiated peace. But do it quickly.

"And I caution you, don't listen to Captain Hunt. He comes from another time, another place. Look at the way he fraternizes with the mutants. A Nietzschean officer—it's an affront to Nature."

Laughter filtered across the expanse of the Observation Deck. It was Tyr, who was nonchalantly approaching the group. "An affront to Nature. I like that." Then, looking directly at Parchman's goggles but speaking to Harper and Arca, "You'd think by now he would know about Nietzschean hearing."

Parchman's features hardened. "I wasn't talking to you, mutant." He said this just as Admiral Rasputin strode onto the Observation Deck. "I'm sorry," said the admiral, flouncing onto a gel couch. "But did that kludge just call the *Andromeda*'s weapons officer a mutant?"

"Stay out of this, *uber*," seethed Parchman.

Harper broke in, "Okay, enough with the name calling."

Tyr moved close to Parchman. "Call me that again," he said quietly, "and it may be the last word you speak."

Rasputin watched the brewing confrontation from his seat with glee. "Are you going to take that from a mutant, Parchman?" he called saucily.

Like just about every Nietzschean, Rasputin Genovese's idea of a perfect day was this: one awakens, and one does one's part in propagating the species with any of one's several mistresses. Meanwhile, one's greatest enemy is elsewhere being destroyed in a well-orchestrated—and entirely untraceable—manner. With no mistresses close at hand, Rasputin was happy to settle for watching Tyr Anasazi eliminate this Genite for him.

"Go ahead, Tyr. Tell him how you're the last of the mighty Kodiak Pride. Surely he'll respect that."

Tyr looked at Rasputin, bewildered. *What game is he playing?* But the internal warning bell sounded too late.

A sinister chuckle slowly climbed out of the Genite's throat. "The last of the Kodiak? Then let me finish the job. One less Pride brings us that much closer to a pure universe."

That did it. A pale red haze obscured Tyr's acute vision and his intellect conceded command to his building anger. His banded arms shot out, ready to grab the Genite's neck and throttle the life from those already lifeless eyes. But Lord Parchman's reflexes were surprisingly quick. He ducked beneath Tyr's arms, then retaliated with a roundhouse. Tyr caught the punch with a quick twist, just enough to deflect it and render it mostly harmless. A ring on Parchman's finger, however, caught Tyr on the cheek, drawing blood. Tyr's nictitating membrane flashed across his eyes.

Suddenly, there was a burst of movement. Rasputin appeared in the midst of the fray, pulling the combatants apart. One incredibly strong hand gripped Tyr's long dreadlocks, the other pinched the back of Parchman's neck. "Don't be stupid," Rasputin hissed, pointing at the *Andromeda* Maria that had just escorted him to Obs Deck. It stood silently, watching the scene from the doorway. "Settle this somewhere where Captain Hunt can't see you."

Rasputin released them both, but his sonorous voice echoed in their ears. "Unless you're afraid to prove yourself against a lowly Nietzschean . . ." he continued, leering at Parchman. He turned his mischievous eyes on Tyr, ". . . or are too weak to stand up for the honor of your Pride."

With a jerk, Tyr pushed Rasputin away. He ran his hand along his cheek and examined the blood glistening across his fingers. The injury was already near healing (another perk of genetic engineering), but his anger hadn't abated in the slightest.

"Hydroponics," said Tyr with a quiet menace. "We'll settle this there. And we'll fight with these." Slowly, Tyr raised his fists and held them, motionless, in the Genite's face.

SEVEN

A corpse cannot seek revenge.

—*THE WIT AND WISDOM OF*
DRAGO MUSEVENI, CY 8691

Magdalena Valentine brought her ship, the *Hypatia*, out of Slipstream. She wasn't sure how long a lead she had on Rebecca and
Rafael (she never could get used to calling the kids "Beka" and
"Rafe"), but since they weren't riding her tail she figured they must
have gotten waylaid in the ships' graveyard. She smiled to herself.
Well done, munchkins. But you'll have to do better. Magdalena was on the
teetering brink of seeing her wildest dreams realized, and you don't
put that on hold for anything, not even a couple of long-lost children.

Magdalena locked in a course and stepped into what the engineer
who reconfigured her ship obliquely called "the convenience room."

Perseids. So bendin' prissy, sighed Magdalena. She checked her reflection in the mirror over the sink. *If I let those circles under my eyes get any bigger, I'll have to pay excess baggage charges for them.* Magdalena was forty-eight Standard Years old—or maybe fifty-one, she forgot which—but she presented about age thirty-five. A few nanobots constantly repairing your telomeres and some subtle genetic engineering can make a huge difference in a girl's appearance. Magdalena appreciated her vitality and she certainly utilized her good looks, but she wasn't one of those who wanted to be eighteen forever. *Teenagers get no respect,* she thought.

The *Hypatia* was an overhauled research vessel, not a racer, and Magdalena was already pushing it to its limits. The ship was useful when it counted, capable of short bursts of extreme speed for fast getaways, but over parsecs of open space it tended to get short-winded. It was a good dozen light-minutes to the next Slip point, and she knew she was going to need every bit of her head start if she hoped to maintain a lead.

Magdalena extrapolated the course she had set in the ship's navigational computer, to see if it sent her through any parts of space where she might encounter hostility. Angry locals who wanted to, say, arrest her. After all, you don't get to be the best archaeologist in three galaxies by playing nice and doing things like agreeing *not* to steal ancient Kalderan armor from the ganglord who had looted it in the first place.

Nope. Looks like things should be pretty quiet, noted Magdalena with almost a hint of regret. She'd be traveling through mostly unpopulated space, which meant she wouldn't need the protection of her many aliases. Callista Bray, Ludanni Thompson, Nelly Constantine . . . these were just a few of the alter egos that had gotten Magdalena out of (and occasionally into) one scrape or another.

Her destination was the Bodega system and its unimaginatively named fourth planet, Bodega Blue (not that "Bodega IV" was any more lyrical). The planet had shed its numeric designation, given to the bulk of the universe's mostly unnoteworthy planets, and received an actual moniker in CY 9606, after it was purchased for commercial development as a resort destination. Magdalena's research indicated that the planet's population was currently zero; presumably, the planned resort had failed.

Magdalena periodically checked *Hypatia*'s sensors for signs of her pesky kids. In theory, a family reunion was a delightful prospect. Here and now, though, it was just a bad idea. *The Divine knows where they got such lousy timing,* she thought. *Certainly not from my side of the family.* Still nothing on the sensors—so far, her luck was holding out. These days, it seemed that was all her luck ever did. Hell, it wasn't just holding out, it had unpacked and moved in. Evidence A: her landmark discovery of *Avrexat Vingareth Ot.*

Magdalena had long ago dismissed talk of "forbidden" books as just that—talk. But lo and behold, there she was strolling among the virtual stacks of the All Systems Library when she found an apparent error in the VR matrix—a doorway, blinking into and out of existence like a faulty lightbulb. Always one to let curiosity get the better of her (bad for cats, good for archaeologists), she strolled on through. There weren't many books, but what was there packed enough cumulative punch to rock what was left of civilization to its core. When she found chapters of the actual *Ot,* her heart stopped. She grabbed it and fled the matrix—well, she did pause just long enough to skim a top secret Commonwealth report that had some pretty interesting things to say about who *really* assassinated Empress Sucharitkul XII, but that's another story.

The mythical (or so she had always thought) *Avrexat Vingareth Ot* was the Rosetta Stone of Vedran history. It supposedly told the story of the Great Sage Rochinda and her discovery of Slipstream technology in 112 BIE, and of the Teacher Rovona, whom Rochinda entrusted with the Vedran Runes—an artifact of unimaginable age and, naturally, value. It was a story archaeologists had spent the past ten thousand years painstakingly reassembling. The *Ot* allegedly contained not only the reason for the dispersal of the Runes, but the location of all the pieces. If the *Ot* existed, it would make perfect sense of all the disparate tales, songs, and fables that seekers like Magdalena had spent a lifetime sifting through. If it existed . . .

The *Avrexat Vingareth Ot* was Magdalena's obsession, and she never for a minute thought she would really find it. Now she not only had a fragment of the true *Ot*, but a fragment that clearly stated the location of the legendary Crown of Ixthathos.

That's more than just good luck. That's galactic lottery luck. That's sidesucking Divine intervention.

But, like most uninvited houseguests, Magdalena's phenomenal good fortune also made her uncomfortable. She shook it off: *No. You deserve this. You put your soul into it. Look at everything you've given up. . . .*

For Magdalena, finding the first Rune, the Nebulos Scepter, had been the most difficult. It also came at a price far steeper than she had ever wanted to pay.

Magdalena's best friend and mentor was a treasure hunter named Estrella Alejandro. They met at the ruins of Susheel; Estrella was charmed by the brash Magdalena, and Magdalena was awed by the free-spirited Estrella. Estrella Alejandro was the picture in the Dictionary of Slang next to the phrase "been there, done that." She was the only human ever formally adopted into a Than-Thre-Kull breeding nest and she was worshiped on at least two planets as a minor deity. Estrella had blown fortunes larger than Magdalena had ever hoped to earn . . . and she didn't care.

"In the end," said Estrella, "it ain't worth squat if it don't breathe."

It was their mutual fascination with the Vedran Runes that brought them to an asteroid in the Zeta Centauri Globular Cluster. It was a scorched chunk of coal that didn't even have a name, a godforsaken rock baked by the glare of a dozen stars. The location was pinpointed by a map in Estrella's possession—a map Magdalena never got to see. Any requests to examine the document itself were met with an evasive wink: "Random access storage device," Estrella would say in that smoky voice of hers, and tap her forehead importantly. "Password protected."

The asteroid's surface was riddled with sinkholes and faults, tectonic freaks of nature that lay dormant under sheets of dust sometimes only centimeters thick. E-suit or no E suit, Magdalena felt as if she were being braised to a tasty medium rare. She was convinced that the sweat pooling in her boots was two degrees this side of boiling.

The two women waited for the twin suns to align; this was supposed to point them in the proper direction. Twenty-eight hours of waiting, and Magdalena began to lose hope that there was treasure anywhere on the asteroid. She was hot, she was bored, she was getting irritated. She asked Estrella if maybe this mental map wasn't simply a product of Estrella's imagination.

Magdalena didn't have many regrets in life. That harsh accusation made to Estrella was at the head of a very short list. Not the top spot, of course. The top spot was reserved for the names "Rebecca" and "Rafael."

Estrella patiently assured Magdalena that they would indeed reach the Scepter, and that they'd know it when they got there. She smiled, took a step forward . . . and the asteroid ate her. The ground broke open beneath her feet and just swallowed her up. Magdalena flattened, leaned over the ten-meter-long crack in the asteroid's crust. Beneath the opening, the crevasse led into a larger chamber carpeted with sharp outcroppings of flint. She could see Estrella's broken body there, splayed out on an obsidian escarpment so black and so shiny that Estrella's hair seemed to disappear into the rock.

Magdalena leaned over the crevasse, reaching for her partner. There was no way Estrella could have survived the fall, but Magdalena didn't care. She braced her right ankle under a boulder and stretched as far as she could . . . and then stretched farther still. It was hopeless. Her ankle snapped right about the time Estrella's eyes popped open. Magdalena gasped; Estrella was still breathing. She was still alive.

Her back was bent at a violent angle, her legs twisted and crooked. A rivulet of blood spilled out of the corner of her mouth and a widening crimson pool spread beneath her. Estrella whimpered softly. "It hurts, Magpie."

"I know it does, 'Strel. I'm sorry."

"You have to help me. Please."

Magdalena wanted to say something, anything, but her mouth felt as if it were filled with sand. The blistering sun dried her tears, and the hot wind blew the ashes away.

"I . . . I can't."

Estrella stared at the sun. She couldn't really see anything—Madgalena looked to her like nothing so much as the pupil of a huge, glowing eye. The words floated up from the bottom of the chasm, a fragile whisper that echoed along its walls: "You promised."

Magdalena stared at her friend. After all the promises she had broken in her life, why did she have to keep this one? Slowly, Madgalena unsnapped the Gauss pistol at her waist, steadied her arm, and aimed at Estrella's forehead. She took a last look into her partner's eyes, then turned away as she pulled the trigger.

The shot sounded like a Nova bomb. But the whimpering had stopped.

For a long time, Magdalena just hung there, impotently. Five minutes, five hours . . . she wasn't sure. Finally, she became horribly aware of the agonizing pain inching up her right leg. Dry-eyed, she climbed to her feet. She clenched her teeth as she settled her weight on the broken ankle, then she started walking. For a day, maybe two, Magdalena just kept moving, following a trail whose end only

Estrella knew. Somehow, turning around and going back now seemed like an insult. Like there was no point in Estrella's death at all.

Just as Estrella predicted, Magdalena knew the Scepter when she found it. In the middle of a barren plain was a waist-high pile of rocks, each stone roughly the size of her fist. They looked rather like potatoes except they were dark gray. As she picked up the stones and moved them away, Magdalena was struck by a feeling not unlike the one Beka would experience some thirty years later, sitting at a library monitor vacated just seconds ago by her mother. It was like . . . a connection. Magdalena *knew* she was touching the very rocks Rovona the Teacher had stacked. It was more than a hundred centuries ago, but to Magdalena it felt as if it could have been the day before yesterday.

Sitting under the rocks, miraculously untouched for millennia, was the Nebulos Scepter. It was an intricate wand of delicate transparent strands—at one end, they bloomed to hold a tripartite stone the likes of which Magdalena had never seen. She held it up to the brutal light in triumph, but the victory was a hollow one. Estrella's death haunted Magdalena, and she didn't have the heart to profit from the Scepter while her mentor's body was still warm. She finally stashed the artifact on Winnipeg Drift, and swore she'd honor Estrella's memory by finding something that breathed.

Ignatius Valentine did more than breathe; he sucked up all the air in a room. He was handsome and arrogant and the best damn pilot Magdalena had ever seen, and he set out to conquer Magdalena just like he set out to conquer space itself. He brought her water roses from Infinity Atoll. He brought her purple oranges from Rigel. In honor of her touchy ankle, he brought her a walking stick from Scheherazade, its head a gargoyle of silvery filigree that warmed to her touch.

Unfortunately, like a lot of conquistadors, once Ignatius acquired the desired territory, he was abysmal at administering it. It was a restless and discontented Magdalena who received the fatal envelope from the courier pilot. The pilot, a jittery Than who had been spending an unhealthy amount of time in Slip space—and had the facial ticks to show for it—had tracked her to Ignatius's rattletrap cargo ship, the *Eureka Maru*, which was then docked at a trading outpost near Diphda V for repairs. The Than pilot, one of the independent couriers that the Free Trade Alliance was trying so hard to put out of business, had been attempting to find Magdalena for five years.

As a note accompanying the envelope explained, the contents were to have been given to Magdalena upon Estrella's death. Inside the envelope, creased and withered, was a map. More specifically, it was a joke map from a souvenir shop, a novelty purporting to be the "Treasure Map of the Lost World of Tarn-Vedra," complete with cartoon Vedrans hiding pots of gold.

Magdalena laughed. Then she looked closer, and laughed even louder. This was just like Estrella, she thought. Because it really *was* a treasure map—Estrella's mental map to the Vedran Runes, pieced together from decades of research and exploration.

A week later, Magdalena was gone. Ignatius would never forgive her for it, and spent the next twenty years trying to get rich enough, strong enough, and fast enough to win her back. The last one was what killed him. And the children . . . well, they were so young they'd hardly remember her. At least, that's what Magdalena told herself. She told it to herself so often she even started to believe it.

Magdalena located the second Rune, the Sigrund Eye, on an ocean world called Minos. Estrella's map warned of a formidable protector—Magdalena discovered that this outsized cross between a shrimp and a jellyfish had protected the Eye by swallowing it. Magdalena found herself inside a submerged volcano, facing off against a nightmarish, highly annoyed undersea alien. It was no wonder the creature had such a poor disposition: the Sigrund Eye, a sort of collar ringed with sharp pins each no thicker than a human hair, must have given it a colossal stomachache.

Once she had two pieces of the Rune in her possession, Magdalena's hunt seemed to gather momentum. Evidence she'd been seeking in vain for years suddenly revealed itself. Leads she had dismissed as cold became vital. Finding the third piece, Empress Fashateel's Wisdom, had been practically boring. After tracking a clue to a retirement slum on Morgun II, the Wisdom was literally handed to her by a blind Nightsider. He was using it to crack open a pile of steamed Orza—a Nightsider dietary staple, kind of like a snail.

And now Magdalena was about to make a Slip jump that would bring her within reach of the Crown of Ixthathos. She stuck her hands firmly in the pilot's toggles, and braced herself for Slipstream.

Bodega Blue was a by-product of the Pleasure Colony boom of the late CY 9600s. Earth was all the rage right about then—Earth customs, Earth culture, Earth cuisine—and dozens of planets, or systems of planets, were terraformed to give the well-heeled recreation seeker a truly Earth-like vacation experience. Given a few decades and a sufficient budget, even a celestial dud covered in craters and space lice could be made over into a temperate paradise with kilometers of pristine beaches, acres of gravity-controlled golf courses, and game preserves of rare and exotically beautiful cloned animals for the paying customer to hunt down and kill.

The first Pleasure Colonies were an enormous success, and entrepreneurs lined up to follow suit. There were plenty of systems out there ripe for the taking . . . and Bodega Blue Enterprises sure got taken.

As the *Hypatia* traced a leisurely orbit around Bodega Blue, Magdalena began to think that maybe her much vaunted luck had just run out. While the *Avrexat Vingareth Ot* didn't give exact coordinates

for the location of the Crown, it did provide a number of planetary
characteristics that would guide one in the right direction. Only
problem was, whatever planetary characteristics Bodega Blue once
possessed had been terraformed into oblivion. All Magdalena saw
below her was a friendly looking but featureless planet, boasting the
carcass of a half-completed Casino Drift for a moon.

Magdalena searched the *Hypatia's* not-inconsiderable onboard
library for information relative to the planet's transformation. Her
efforts yielded a few press clippings and a brochure entitled *An Invi-
tation to Investors.* Magdalena put her feet up on the console, hitched
the tooled handle of her cane over the arm of the pilot's chair, and
played the brochure on the main viewscreen.

Gentle chimes preceded the Bodega Inc. logo, but any feeling of
peace that stirred in Magdalena was immediately obliterated by the
jarring sight of the Bodega CEO. He was a middle-aged human
wearing an absurd hat Magdalena associated with the ancient Earth
occupation of transporting meat animals. *Hang on, it'll come to me in
a second . . . Cowboy! He's wearing a cowboy hat!* Making matters worse,
the hat was loaded down with gewgaws, including one piece of
unbelievably gaudy jewelry in the middle. The wearer of this absurd
chapeau looked like he hadn't slept or shaved in a week, and sweat
stains had taken up permanent residence in the armpits of his shirt.
There was an easily detectable layer of hopelessness beneath the
man's forced good humor. This was one desperate entrepreneur.

"Congratulations, savvy investor, on discovering the most exiting—
and profitable—new development in the Milky Way: the Bodega
Pleasure System," said the cowboy, looking sincerely into the cam-
era. "As you can see, terraforming of the primary destination planet,
Bodega Blue, is already under way. Soon, construction begins on our
five-star orbiting casino, Lady Luck. All forms of gambling are legal
on Bodega, thanks to its unique location just outside a number of
interplanetary borders. Why, even Nietzschean bloodsport tourna-

ments are legal here, and we are not limited by age restrictions or drug regulations of any kind."

The image of the cowboy gave way to a picture taken on the surface of Bodega Blue. The terraforming effort was obviously in its very early stages: massive amounts of carbon dioxide were being pumped into the atmosphere, creating a greenhouse effect. The planet looked like a soggy ball of mud.

"By our projected completion date of 9728, Bodega Pleasure System will no doubt—"

Oh, Cowboy. You've gone and changed the planet on me. Magdalena put the brochure on mute, leaving the hapless human and his silent dance of impending insolvency in the background while she let her mind fall into a light meditation. She got her best ideas that way, just being still and waiting for the intuition to bubble to the surface.

The cowboy must have been coming to the crucial portion of the pitch. His eyes got bigger, his smile turned sincerer, and he clasped his hands in front of him as if he were about to pray. Sure enough, a string of numerals appeared. Magdalena turned up the volume in time to learn that two million thrones would make you—yes, you!— a proud part-owner of Bodega Pleasure Systems. And what kind of profit return could the potential investor expect? "Why, the sky's the limit!" trumpeted the brochure. "The blue skies of Bodega Blue."

The brochure soon ended, but Magdalena kept watching, letting it endlessly loop. She was fascinated by the huckster and his goofy hat. Apparently, the man's instincts in financial investments were about as bad as his taste in clothes. That jewel on his hat . . . ugh! It was quite possibly the most atrocious thing she'd ever seen. Where did Mr. Cowboy find himself such an ugly piece of rock?

Suddenly, Magdalena stopped. She instructed the monitor to pause and zoom in on the jewel. Her instinct was right; that ugly gob of kitsch was like no tchotchke she had ever seen. In fact, up close, she could clearly see the way it was cut in a familiar trisected pattern. . . .

Exactly like the stone on the Nebulos Scepter. Magdalena shook her head. *I'm an idiot! It was staring me in the face the whole time. That jerk is wearing the Crown of Ixthathos on his head!*

And why not? The cowboy could easily have found the Crown during an early planetary survey, or it could have been dug up by ter-raforming machinery—a Land Eater, say. Magdalena got a sinking feeling in the pit of her stomach. She had absolutely no idea what finally happened to the cowboy or the Crown. A further search of *Hypatia*'s database revealed not a clue to the cowboy's real name, nor any sign of his eventual whereabouts. People didn't just pick up and disappear—well, she herself had on occasion, but she was a trained professional. Another intuition surfaced: *What if he never left in the first place?*

Magdalena returned to the brochure, the one piece of significant information she had, and sifted through the rest of its contents. It was subdivided into chapters, each outlining plans for a different continent on Bodega Blue. There were two main land masses planned, a sport continent and a beach continent, as well as various air and sea resorts and species specific subdivisions, including a lux-ury burrow complex for the Than and an arboretum for Umbrites. Bodega Blue was to be opened in stages, with the anticipated wind-fall profits fueling each subsequent expansion. The first sector slated for completion was the beach continent, Blue Island, and the brochure contained schematics of hotels, restaurants, and a detailed map of the proposed beachfront. The island was shaped like a wheel, with a large ocean pool at its center and countless peninsulas flaring from its edges, in order to maximize the continent's exposure to water.

Magdalena studied the plans for the port of entry Welcome Cen-ter, which also included a nearby interplanetary destination hub. Her eye stopped at the blueprint for the facility housing the reservations and concierge operations. It was the building's name that caught her eye; it was called the Temple. *Funny name for a business office*, thought Magdalena. She recalled the passage from *Avrexat Vingareth Ot*, "a resting place for king and crown." Somehow, the Temple sounded like as good a place as any to begin her search for a bankrupt cowboy prince.

Magdalena had to admit, Bodega Blue was a nice place . . . for a planet. If there was any long-term benefit to living on an orbit-locked globe, Magdalena had yet to find it. She'd much rather spend her time on a nice clean Drift or, better yet, an actual space-faring vessel. At least, she noted with grudging admiration, Bodega Blue had been engineered for a minimum of dreary weather. Despite the cowboy's disastrous financial fate, the self-guided terraforming technology had continued to operate unimpeded, shaping the planet according to the parameters of its programming. A few hundred centuries later, the place was a blue-skied, teal-oceaned, lush-landscaped orb.

Before disembarking the *Hypatia*, Magdalena poked her cane experimentally into the planet's turf. (Medibots had long ago reknit her ankle, but a gift is a gift.) A soft blue-tinged grass carpeted most of the island, the blades precisely spaced apart and each exactly the same size. She stepped gingerly onto the ground, and then with increasing gusto. Magdalena had never experienced soil so pleasing to the foot. Each step felt as if she were walking on a cushion.

The *Hypatia*'s ad hoc landing pad was within sight of the Temple. The edifice had been built to mimic the Hanging Gardens of Tarn-Vedra: a multistoried structure with open terraces from which tongues of greenery and flowers overflowed. Immaculately groomed vegetation surrounded the Temple, including man-sized Dyhedran flowers and tropical palms. The mellow clap of breaking waves in the background provided a calming soundtrack. It was all so alluring, Magdalena was ready to rethink her long-standing aversion to sand and saltwater.

Magdalena walked toward the Temple across an open expanse of lawn. Slowly, an uncomfortable awareness grew. She was being followed, no doubt about it. She tightened her grip on her cane, preparing for a quick strike to the sensory organs of any would-be pursuer. She turned, raising her weapon . . .

There was no one there. Well, no one living anyway. What faced her were two small terrabots, motionlessly appraising this intruder. Identical and about ankle-high, the pair of robots had spherical bodies suspended on spiderlike legs. Magdalena waved her cane in front of one, but it didn't respond. Then she inadvertently shifted her weight, moving her left foot back half a step. The closest terrabot scurried into action. Startled, Magdalena took a few more defensive steps . . . and the other terrabot joined the pursuit. She soon realized they weren't coming after her. They were after her footprints.

The 'bots worked quickly and efficiently, repairing any damage she had done to the precious blades of grass. Each possessed a "mouth"—a small bubble on the underside of its body that apparently contained photosynthetic nanobots programmed to generate new blades of grass. A top-mounted spindly leg pulled the blades of grass free as the mouth spit them out, and then plunged them into the turf. Meanwhile, a small comb restored any grass that had been bent or flattened, and a tiny vacuum in the robot's underbelly sucked up any damaged greenery. The robots hovered around Magdalena's heels, and didn't move unless she walked.

Magdalena was familiar with standard-issue terraforming equipment, and these 'bots weren't any part of it. Probably the landscape AI got bored, she decided, and began taking liberties. A couple of hundred years of mowing the same lawn would have that effect on anyone.

Closer to the Temple, Magdalena realized she'd made a mistake; the building's design wasn't based on the Hanging Gardens of Tarn-Vedra after all. It seems the AI gardener couldn't help but expand its jurisdiction to the bungalow, and had turned what was supposed to be a traditional Earth-style building into an explosion of blooming vegetation. The exterior was covered with a stone-colored wiry moss, and the windows had been replaced with enormous papery leaves crisscrossed with slender red veins. It was a landscape artist's wet dream.

There were several entrances—the building had been designed to be as open to the engineered elements as possible. As Magdalena stepped through one of the wide collapsible entryways, she saw that both the floor and the walls were covered with shimmering blue grass. Magdalena peered around the remarkable room—the ceiling was a dense tangle of purple Jicama vine, its flowers blooming at regular two-meter intervals. She could detect the shapes of chairs and loungers buried beneath mounds of foliage. A few silken butterflies cooled themselves in the shade. But as for any sign of the Crown, there was none.

Magdalena passed through the crescent-shaped bungalow into the open air courtyard it surrounded. The courtyard itself was ringed with columns covered in the ubiquitous purple vine . . . but it was what stood in the middle of the columns that attracted Magdalena's interest. From afar it resembled a sarcophagus. On closer inspection, it turned out to be a dais—coated, of course, in a layer of grass.

Magdalena'a adrenaline surged. The blood began beating in her ears. A bolt of excitement swept through her. This was a shrine, built to honor the landscape's fallen master. Lying flat on the raised platform, covered (of course) by a blanket of grass, was the unmistakable shape of a human body. Judging by the contours of the turf, the body had its feet together and its hands across its chest. In eternal rigor mortis, it clutched a cockeyed cylinder: *A cowboy hat!*

Magdalena was so intent upon the grassy, regal tomb that she barely realized the air was filling with a new sound—the sound of a spacecraft. She looked through the foliage to the azure expanse of sky, but could see nothing. Still, there was only one possible culprit: her children. *Tenacious couple of munchkins, aren't you?* She was going to have to make this quick.

Magdalena stretched out a hand and touched the turf overgrowing the hat, carefully working her fingers into the soil. The gentle pressure was enough to punch through the hard crust. It was empty inside; the actual hat had disintegrated long ago.

Suddenly, a shadow fell on Magdalena. She almost cried out in surprise as a terrabot—almost identical to the ones that had been following her, except that it was about ten times larger—clawed its way to the top of the dais. Magdalena prepared to fight for her prize, if not for her life, when she realized that the monster was ignoring her entirely. It had more important fish to fry; specifically, restoring the torn soil that Magdalena was destroying.

Magdalena kept digging up, and the 'bot kept smoothing over. She worked briskly, trying to avoid the giant spider's spindly metal legs. Her hand darted in and out, snatching strips of grass and ripping them away. Eventually, she exposed a skeletal hand, its fingers covering something shiny. She raced the terrabot to the cowboy's corpse—touched something hard and cold, and yanked it free.

It was the Crown of Ixthathos, repulsive jewel and all.

Carefully brushing the dirt off her discovery, Magdalena tried to admire the ugly thing as best she could. The Crown itself was exquisite, a wreath of precious metals that sparkled brilliantly in the sun. The jewel, too, was astounding, but only because of how grotesque it was. In color and texture, it resembled nothing so much as rotting flesh. *It's one of the oldest known artifacts in the universe. No one said it had to be pretty*, thought Magdalena.

Cautiously, Magdalena set about extracting the jewel from the

Crown's metalwork. The archaeologist in her cringed as the treasure hunter in her hurried the task before any claim jumpers—Valentine *frère et soeur*, for instance—wandered by. The headband portion of the Crown was almost certainly Vedran in origin, Magdalena decided, and the jewel itself undoubtedly a piece of the Runes.

Magdalena was dismayed to find the disgusting thing even felt like rotting flesh, slick and pliable. The jewel eventually came free with a nauseating squish. She turned it over. On the back of it, just as she had hoped, was a set of indentations. She brushed her fingers over them lightly. Magdalena was convinced that these odd-shaped grooves would perfectly match a group of bumps along the underside of the Fist of Pac Tull.

Magdalena hurried as the whine of the *Maru*'s engines increased in pitch. The ship sounded closer, although there was still no visual sign of it. Rebecca and Rafael were probably trying to get a fix on her location. Magdalena expertly snapped the jewel back into the Crown, and curtsied good-bye to the cowboy.

She was crossing the courtyard, steps away from the bungalow, when she felt the first tremor. Another, longer temblor followed. The vines hanging from the bungalow's ceiling began to sway as the tremors increased in number and intensity.

Behind Magdalena, the dais splintered and broke apart. The outsized terrabot was thrown onto its back, its legs cycling helplessly in the air.

Okay. This doesn't look good. Magdalena wondered if maybe taking the Crown had set off a trigger. A sudden burst of blinding light from out on the horizon seemed to answer, "Ya think?" A searing flash opened a rip in the sky . . . and Magdalena didn't wait around to see more. She hit the bungalow at a gallop, her two terrabots following in pursuit.

As she crossed the field toward the *Hypatia*, another flash erupted from far out over the ocean. *And people wonder why I hate planets*, she grimaced. The ground continued to shudder violently. Large chunks of bungalow began to fall; the entire building was being shaken off its foundation. Terrabots swarmed frantically from hidden burrows, attempting to repair the damage to the foliage.

Magdalena ran full throttle, using her cane for increased leverage. She pole-vaulted aboard the *Hypatia*, jogged to the main cabin, tossed the Crown onto the dashboard, and slid into the pilot's chair. The ship's computer told her that a series of explosions had kicked off fusion reactions all across Bodega Blue. The good news was that . . . well, actually there was no good news. Blast waves from the bombs were fast approaching her current location, and in about a minute and a half she and the *Hypatia* would be toast. She engaged the engines and struggled for altitude.

According to sensor readings, someone had planted Maxim charges around the planet. Once detonated, the incendiaries literally ignited land, sea, and atmosphere. Bodega Blue was quickly turning into a fiery maelstrom that only a Pyrian would find resortlike.

Magdalena knew exactly who was responsible, of course. The cowboy. A player to the end, he was willing to melt his planet rather than relinquish it to any creditors: *Repossess this, asshole!*

As she approached the upper atmosphere, Magdalena could see the beach continent below, tinted blue from its acres of grass. It began to crackle and scorch as the blast waves bounded across the planetary surface. When Magdalena finally got high enough above the flaming surface that she considered breathing again, *Hypatia*'s sensors alerted her to a new danger: another ship. It was Rebecca and Rafael in the *Eureka Maru*, who had apparently figured it was time to leave when Bodega Blue began combusting.

They were only a few light-seconds away, and they had her dead in their sights. A light on the console began blinking. They were hailing her.

Magdalena hesitated, torn. Her hand hovered above the comm

button . . . but she couldn't bring herself to press it. Too many years had passed, too much had happened. . . . And as much as she wanted to talk to her children, there was something else demanding her immediate attention.

Because Magdalena realized with a start that she already possessed the very knowledge she had been searching for, knowledge she'd seen people die for—including her best friend. Magdalena knew where to find the next piece of the Vedran Runes.

EIGHT

The Nietzscheans call their system one of enlightened
self-interest. I'll believe that when I meet an enlightened
Nietzschean.

—PATRICIA "PAC" PETERSON,
"THE RIGHTS OF HUMANKIND," AFC 305

Rommie was bored sick of Lord Nyain Parchman's intercepted Dragan datalink transmission. She'd listened to it three thousand four
hundred fifty-three times, and it never got any more exciting. She
had dissected it completely, thoroughly analyzing every bit and byte
of information forward and backward, downward and upward, and a
few other-wards that defied categorization. Part of the difficulty was
the fact that the transmission *was* a datalink. Datalinks were low-
strength lasers that couriered secret information from missiles and
drones to ships, from ships to fleets, from fleets to High Command,
and so on. Theoretically, if you managed to hook up to an enemy's
datalink, you'd be holding the key to their every move, tic and hiccup.

The enormous suck of the universe alone helped keep datalinks safe: triangulating on a laser communication in that infinity of square nothingness was damn near impossible. Even if you got lucky and stumbled onto one, you'd lose it immediately, since the beams were constantly changing position. It was called "frequency hopping," and it had been around since before humanity set foot in space. And if you surmounted that hurdle, you still had to get around the encryption. Even in the High Guard, the datalink had been quadruple encrypted . . . and Nietzscheans are *careful.*

So the surest way of testing the authenticity of the Genite's transmission—by comparing it to an actual Dragan one—was impossible on the face of it, since there was no way of getting hold of a genuine Dragan military communication in the first place. Or, as Harper would say, about as easy as finding an honest Nightsider.

"What do you have for me?" asked Dylan, striding onto Command Deck, his thick-soled boots falling almost noiseless on the springy floor.

Well, hello to you too, thought Rommie, looking up. Only the don't-mess-with-me furrows on her captain's forehead prevented her from actually saying it. The avatar stepped aside as Dylan walked to the command post. "Which do you want first, the bad news or the good news?"

"Let me guess," said Dylan, who knew his ship all too well. "The bad news is that there is no good news."

"Almost, but not quite. The bad news is that I've been looking into the Genites' stealth technology, and I'm still stumped. So far, all I can figure is that they've perfected a sensor countermeasure that operates kind of like a false target generator."

"How 'kind of'?"

"Well, in the case of the false target generator, the evading ship would duplicate and then multiply the enemy's sensor signal and return it. But, apparently, rather than fooling an enemy ship's sensors

into seeing more targets than are actually there, the Genites are convincing the enemy ship's sensors that there are fewer targets out
there. To wit, none."

In other words, their ships could be within arm's length, right
under the *Andromeda Ascendant*'s sensor nose, and she'd never know
it. Dylan didn't like the sound of that. "Counteractive measures?" he
asked crisply.

Rommie's avatar shrugged, deferring to the Command Deck
viewscreen where her digital image blinked into existence. "I was
hoping you'd have a suggestion," said Andromeda's image. "In the
case of a false target, we'd pepper the decoys with active sensors—
eventually, we'll figure out what's a real target and what isn't. It's
time-consuming, but it works. But an invisible target somewhere in
open space—taking that approach is like looking for a nanobot in a
reactor pile. So . . . I'm working on options."

"Well, keep working on them," said Dylan. "And get our
esteemed chief engineer on the job. Two heads are better than one—
that is, if young Harper's even thinking with his upper-torso head at
the moment."

"You mean him and Arca? I think it's cute," cooed Rommie.

Actually, Dylan thought it was kind of cute, too. "And probably
healthy. I see the way he looks at you. I worry about him."

Digital Andromeda and avatar Rommie planted their hands on
their hips in simultaneous indignation. "Are you saying I don't merit
human attention?" they echoed.

"I'm not saying that at all, I'm just—" Dylan shook his head. He
wasn't going to get locked in to this particular death spiral. "Never
mind. Let's just try and stick to business, okay? I think you owe me
some good news."

Rommie cleared her throat. "Fine. It's about the datalink transmission. I was hoping I could compare the Genites' intercepted communiqué to a proven Dragan one, but that didn't pan out."

Dylan absentmindedly scratched his chin. "What about checking it against your own datalink? If the Genites generated the transmission themselves, they would have done it using their own equipment, which is probably based on High Guard technology."

"I thought the same thing," said Rommie, "but I couldn't find any similarities. Which seems to support the case that the transmission is authentic, although I can't be sure."

"This is the good news?" asked Dylan. "Why did you even call me in here?"

"And he still hasn't let me finish," said Rommie, as if there was someone else in Command invisible to mere mortals. "As I was going to say, I then switched to analyzing the pilots' voices, in order to verify that they were in fact Nietzschean. For comparison, I used a voice sample provided by Admiral Rasputin."

Rommie played the sample: Rasputin saying, "Move away, or I rip out your captain's throat."

"Interesting choice," said Dylan.

"Species which utilize verbal communication possess voice frequencies specific to that species, within parameters. Nietzscheans and humans are similar, but not identical. So I compared the frequencies of Rasputin's voice to the voices on the transmission. Perfect match."

"Score another point for the Knights of Genetic Purity."

"As a precaution, I also compared the pilots' voices to a human one, provided gratis by our favorite ladykiller, Seamus Harper. More specifically, I compared Harper's human-specific speech frequencies to the Dragan-specific ones. And here's the funny thing. The transmission contains *both* human and Nietzschean frequencies. Rasputin's voice unquestionably does not. Leading me to believe the voices on the transmission are human in origin, but have been altered to appear Nietzschean."

"Good work, although not technically good news. But at least it clears up a few things. In fact, I think it's time I introduced his lord-ship to the four-star accommodations of V Deck."

Dylan had taken but two steps before Rommie called after him. She listened internally for a moment, scanning some part of the "her" that is the ship itself, and threw a new image on the main screen. "Dylan? Wait. You should see this."

The comm screen showed the Observation Deck and, on it, Tyr and Lord Parchman taking swings at each other. Dylan sighed. Gen-ites and Nietzscheans on the same ship was inevitably the beginning of a bad day. What made him think Tyr Anasazi would step up to the plate as baby-sitter? Then he watched as Rasputin stepped between the pair, surprised by the fact that Rasputin appeared to be talking some sense into them. *Rasputin Genovese, the voice of reason? Tomorrow, they repeal the laws of gravity.*

"One more thing," said Rommie. "Harper needs to talk to you."

"Put him through."

The image of Obs Deck disappeared and was replaced by Harper, who was grinning just a bit more than Dylan was comfortable with. "Hey, Boss. Uh, thought you might want to know that Tyr and the Genite are on their way to hydroponics to bump knuckles. I've got the odds at six-two in Tyr's favor."

"Thank you, Mr. Harper. Way ahead of you." If stamping one's foot in exasperation was acceptable High Guard behavior, Dylan would have stamped his foot right through the Command Deck floor. How did he end up with a so-called crew that acted like a bunch of hormonal teenagers?

"Although, I tell you," continued Harper. "That Parchman guy? He may be bald as a Perseid's butt, but he's got a few moves on him. Not that I've actually seen a Perseid's butt, mind you."

"Enough!" said Dylan. "I'm on my way."

Arca wasn't as enthusiastic about the impending melee as Harper was. Tyr was a Nietzschean, after all, so she didn't totally trust him, and Parchman, while a potential ally, was . . . well, creepy. They could beat each other into identical pulps for all she cared. On the other hand, she was decidedly enthusiastic about Harper, and wasn't shy about letting him know it.

A few lingering looks and attentive smiles from Arca, and Harper was suddenly less enthusiastic about the fight himself. Not only did he quickly forget about the Tyr/Parchman matchup, but was so smitten with the HIA delegate he also forgot where they were going and led her on a random meander through the *Andromeda*'s corridors.

Harper tried to analyze the oversized impact this little gal was having on him. *First of all, she's hot,* he thought. She was also smart, funny, and a fellow mudfoot—more than that, a fellow survivor of the yoke of Nietzschean slavery. Someone who understands what that's like. *Oh, and did I mention she was hot?*

"Do you miss Earth?" asked Arca.

Harper thought about that one a minute before answering. "Yeah. But in the way you'd miss a gangrenous foot that got amputated. There isn't anything there for me anymore. Mostly, I miss the people I lost. I've got the *Andromeda* now, but I'll always think of Earth as my home."

"I've lost a lot too," said Arca. "Everyone has, I guess. I never even knew my parents."

Harper waited, but she didn't elaborate. He prompted her: "The Dragans?"

"One way or another," Arca said, shrugging. "The Dragans never did waste a lot of time and money on sanitation or medical facilities for the day labor. My mom died of tuberculosis when I was six. My dad . . . they rounded him up for work one day, he never came home—nobody knows what happened to him." She wasn't trying to elicit sympathy. It was just cold fact, similar to tales told by slaves all over the galaxy. She told it as mundanely as giving an old address, or a date of birth.

Harper felt a swell of tenderness in his breast. At least, he thought it was tenderness . . . and he thought it was his breast. Unlike most everyone else on the ship, Arca *got* it. You had to live through the horror to fully comprehend it.

"Yeah. Been there, done that . . . burned the vermin-infested T-shirt," sighed Harper.

Arca brightened. "But, hey—look at how far you've come. You're known throughout the universe. I feel like I should ask for your autograph."

Harper laughed. "Anytime. But don't blame me. Blame my good looks." He moved closer to Arca and all but held his breath as he snaked an arm around her waist. To his relief, she didn't slap him.

"Yeah," said Arca with an impish grin. "I can see how a lady might mistake you for being attractive."

There was an awkward pause; Harper wasn't sure how to respond to an open door. Not only had Arca not slapped him, but she also hadn't walked out snarling, or poured a drink on his head—which, historically, is how girls respond to Harper's advances. On one occasion, he'd had a gun pulled on him. More than one occasion. More than one gun.

He tried to phrase a suave response. All his head came up with was, "Me Harper. Me like you. Me happy." At least he had enough self-control to avoid blathering it aloud.

Don't screw this up, Seamus, he told himself. He took a deep breath and a leap of faith, and suggested, "Do you want to see my place?"

"Your place?" asked Arca, with a coy lift of an eyebrow.

"The machine shop. It's my own private corner of the *Andromeda*."

"Lead the way," said Arca, intertwining her hand with his.

As they walked, Harper felt like he was a normal person having a normal conversation about normal things, taking a normal stroll—a normal life the Magog and Dragans had made impossible. He led Arca into a passage that looked markedly different than the rest of the *Andromeda*. The artistic architecture and design flourishes were absent; this place was strictly nuts and bolts, straightforward and simple. By opening the machine-shop door, Harper felt as if he were opening his heart to Arca. This was where he spent most of his time, and the place had come to reflect who he was. Others saw the shop and saw stashes of junk, tools, half-dismantled 'droids, and leftover parts. He saw it as his own kind of art. His passion for his work rose to the surface, and he rattled on about inventions he'd built and projects he was working on.

Arca understood that this was Harper in his element. He might be a crew member on the *Andromeda*, but at heart he was still an Earther, scavenging what he could find, taking scraps and making them useful.

"Come here. I want to show you something special," said Harper. Arca leaned over his worktable as he displayed an elaborate device he was working on (something to do with teleportation, he claimed) and showed her a tiny scratch on the bottom. "I've never told this to anyone before," he said.

Arca looked at him inquisitively. "Told them about the scratch?"

"It's not a scratch—it's a 'z.' For Zelazny. I laser-etch a 'z' in everything I make—even Rommie's got my signature on her, and not even she knows it." Harper reached to his hip holster and pulled out his laser torch. He twirled the silver cylinder in his fingers. "I'm like Zorro, and this is my whip," he said, almost dropping it.

Arca was confused. "Zorro? Was that a friend of yours?"

Harper smiled. "Sort of."

Arca reached around her neck, and pulled off a necklace with a pendant of a simple circle of shiny metal. She handed it to him. "Here, do this one."

"What's this?" said Harper, taking the necklace. On one side of the circle was the name Arca Shel Roya, followed by the number 744568.

"My dog tag," said Arca.

Harper laid the tag on his worktable, spun his torch in the air, and turned it on. He aimed the narrow purple beam and made a few quick, precise movements across the tag. Then, blushing slightly, he held the necklace up to the light so Arca could see his handiwork. Clearly etched on the medallion was the inscription "Z + A."

Arca took the necklace and studied the inscription, her brow furrowing. "So you get top billing, huh?"

Harper got flustered. *Okay, now she's gonna slap me.* "I didn't mean anything by it. I mean, I meant, er . . ." She started laughing at him, and Harper realized she'd been messing with his head. To his surprise she moved in toward him, bringing her face so close to his he could feel her breath on his cheek. Harper dropped the necklace on the workbench and brought an equal and opposite reaction to her movement. Their lips met and they kissed. Arca's mouth was soft, and her skin felt warm enough to melt into his.

Suddenly Arca jerked her head away and buried it in Harper's shoulder. "Crap!" she whispered.

"What's wrong?" panicked Harper. "Is it my breath? Should I change my shirt? Anything!"

"Nothing like that," said Arca. "I'm supposed to check in with my counsel." She disentangled herself from Harper. "I have to go."

The blood was pounding in Harper's ears. *Stupid revolution*, he grumbled. *Can't I just score for once without interruptions?* Then another thought occurred to him. "I'll go with you. Hydroponics is on the way, I can stop and see how the brawl is going."

"All right," said Arca, already heading out of the machine shop.

Harper hurried after her. "You forgot your dog tag!" He turned around to go back and get it.

Arca grabbed him by the arm, pulled him close, and whispered, "I'll come back and get it . . . tonight."

Harper was outwardly calm, but inwardly his libido was high-fiving his id. He grinned and tried to keep his voice from cracking. "Anything you say."

Lord Parchman stood in the open area usually designated for Dylan's basketball games, at about the free throw lane. "Nietzscheans claim they tamper with their chromosomes to better the race. I say it's just a crutch, patching up mistakes to prop up weaklings. I doubt any mutation can really outmatch a true human."

Tyr knew the Genite was taunting him on purpose, but it still worked. There were a few things that would make the big Kodiak seethe. Disparaging the Kodiak Pride was one of them. If the Genite did that, then the Genite would die. Tyr shrugged his huge shoulders out of his chain-mail shirt, stretched his back and arms. He cracked his knuckles showily, then joined Parchman at the top of the key.

"Out of fairness," said Lord Parchman, "I should get one edged weapon. After all, you've got those foul toothpicks on your arms."

Tyr extended his bone blades to full fighting position. They looked as lethal as they, in fact, were. "You mean these little crutches?"

Rasputin, standing in the hydroponics entryway, enjoyed the show while keeping a watchful eye on the outer walkway, scanning for any meddlesome ship captains. "Are you here to fight, or to chat?" he goaded.

Tyr turned to glare at Rasputin . . . and Parchman saw this as an opening. He instantly charged at Tyr, trying to catch the Nietzschean with his shoulder. Tyr nimbly jumped aside and used Parchman's momentum against him. He grabbed Parchman's shirt and threw him into a shelf of Sintii cactus. Parchman toppled the shelf, loudly sending cacti and glass skittering across the floor. The Genite carefully climbed to his feet, pulling himself free from the debris, wiping granules of glass from his shoulders and arms. He inadvertently stepped on a few of the cacti, sending their pink innards squirting out onto his boots.

Now Tyr lunged, and took a few jabs at Parchman's face. Parchman deftly avoided them, backpedaling around hydroponics like a prizefighter. Tyr chased Parchman relentlessly, trying to keep him on his heels. When he saw his opening, he moved in quickly and threw a bear hug around the Genite, running him against a wall and pinning him there. Tyr's arms bulged as he slowly constricted them around Parchman's ribs.

At first it seemed as if the Genite were flailing his arms in desperation, but Tyr soon became aware of a sharp stinging in his back. He was being stabbed! Tyr tried ignoring the blows, but Parchman was mercilessly tearing into his flesh. Had the man smuggled a weapon past *Andromeda*'s scans? Parchman struck again and again, using all his strength. Tyr abruptly backed up, and threw Parchman to the ground. A burning pain lodged in the small of his back—he reached behind him, and found Parchman's weapon still dug into his skin. He pulled it free . . . withdrawing a Sintii cactus, covered in curling, jagged quills, slick with blood.

"Necessity is the mother of invention," the Genite said with a smile.

The fight continued. The two circled each other, both breathing heavily now, the adrenaline surging thick in their veins. As Parchman moved past the hydroponics entryway, his back to the open door, Rasputin quickly stepped in and, without warning, shoved the Genite toward Tyr.

Parchman cursed as he stumbled. Tyr grabbed his tunic and pulled him just upright enough to lay into his skull with meaty roundhouse punches. Parchman tried pulling away, but Tyr had a firm grip on his clothes and the force of his rough swings kept

Parchman off balance. Eventually the Genite went sprawling and Tyr stood over him, stomping him in the back with his boot for punctuation.

Parchman deftly flipped over and surprised Tyr with a kick in the stomach. The Genite rolled away and, using a wall for support, pushed himself upright. Thanks to Tyr, Parchman's pale skin was inflamed with scratch marks and reddening bruises.

Now it was Tyr's turn to be surprised by Rasputin. The admiral hadn't, apparently, been siding with his fellow Nietzschean at all, because he now did the same thing to Tyr as he had done to the Genite, shoving him unawares from behind. Tyr tumbled into Parchman, who hoisted Tyr by his armpits and then head-butted him on the side of the face. A splotch of blood—Tyr wasn't even sure at this point if it was his blood or the Genite's—was smeared across Parchman's forehead, glowing bright crimson on the man's pallid skin.

Tyr didn't hesitate to return the favor, and immediately head-butted Parchman back, hitting the Genite on the bridge of the nose. Parchman stifled a cry as the sharp blow sent him reeling. He let go of Tyr and stumbled backward, hands cupped to his nose, blood seeping through his fingers and dripping down his chin.

Rasputin's eyes lit up at the sight. His nose twitched—he loved the sharp, lusty smell of fresh blood. It smelled like . . . life. Excitedly Rasputin barked at Tyr, "Kill him! Kill him!" He was so exhilarated by the red liquid streaming down Parchman's face that he didn't register the sound of footsteps coming up behind him. Without warning, someone grabbed on to Rasputin's coat and spun him around.

It was Dylan. And the captain was aiming the plasma beam business end of an F-lance at Rasputin's chest. "Out of the way, Rasputin."

"Captain Hunt, don't be a wet blanket," said Rasputin, flashing his sharpened canines and spreading his broad arms across the entryway.

"Turn the other cheek, and let Tyr cure that Genite once and for all of his disgusting prejudices."

Dylan snapped his wrist and the force lance extended into quarterstaff mode; the admiral had to jerk his head back to avoid getting hit. Dylan placed one end of the lance firmly beneath the admiral's chin. "Are you hard of hearing? I asked you to move out of the way."

"So that would be a 'no.'" Rasputin frowned, slowly dropping his arms to his side. Dylan pushed past him to find Tyr in the process of turning Parchman into quivering hamburger. The big Kodiak followed the drunkenly staggering Genite around the room, launching punch after punch against his opponent's face and body. Each blow landed with a sickening thud, sending the Genite reeling.

Dylan swung his F-lance, deftly catching Tyr across the ankles and sweeping his feet out from under him. Tyr crashed onto his back, and Dylan firmly planted a boot on Tyr's heaving chest, the lance pointing in the Nietzschean's face.

"Three reasons I shouldn't throw you in the brig. Now!" shouted Dylan. Tyr's nostrils flared, his jaw was clenched tight enough to snap. He had a wild look in his eye that Dylan had never seen before. *So this is what it looks like when Tyr loses it.* Dylan was glad this sort of thing didn't happen often.

It took Tyr a few seconds to even realize who Dylan was. "Aren't you threatening the wrong person? That human is rabid," Tyr sputtered.

Rasputin watched the scene unfold with mounting disappointment. The fight was obviously as good as over, and while the Genite was bloodied, he definitely wasn't dead. *Time for Plan B*, sighed Rasputin. It was just that Plan B was so, well, coarse.

"I do apologize, Captain," said the admiral. "This really is my fault. I should have stopped them when I had the chance. But the Genite's loathsome sentiments about my people make me . . . well, unwilling *not* to want him dead."

Dylan guessed Rasputin had more to do with this than simply letting it go on too long—the entire fight had his manipulative fingerprints all over it. Dylan retracted his force lance and stepped back from Tyr. "I expected more of you," he said simply.

Tyr smiled inwardly at Dylan's unwavering—and unrealistic—optimism, then got to his feet and brushed himself off. He assessed his injures: other than the bruise on his cheek where Parchman had head-butted him and the cactus-shaped gash in his back, he was unharmed. He was aware of Rasputin's eyes chiseling away at him, but ignored the admiral. As his adrenaline-fueled anger began to dissipate, Tyr realized that Rasputin had finally gotten to him. *Idiot. You fell for it.* True, it was Parchman who had pressed Tyr's buttons . . . but only after Rasputin gave him the wiring diagram.

Dylan now went to examine the battered Lord Parchman, who was slumped against a wall with his head dangling in his chest. He appeared to be unconscious. Dylan carefully lifted up his head—he was breathing noisily, bubbles of blood popping around his nostrils as he exhaled. Dylan reached for Parchman's goggles to check the man's pupils when the Genite suddenly jerked his head back, whipping his arms around and muttering incoherently. In a panic, the injured man struggled to get to his feet.

"Andromeda," Dylan called out, "get Trance and Rev Bem to hydroponics. This man needs to get to Med Deck."

Dylan turned to find Rasputin standing behind him. "I'm feeling a little flushed from all the excitement. If you don't mind, I'd like to retire to my quarters now. Please call me when you're ready to resume negotiations. Unless, of course, you'll accede to my request and let me send a message to my flagship."

"Return to your quarters," said Dylan, and when Rasputin didn't move, he added, "I'm still considering your request." With a courtly bow and a flourish, Rasputin left. Dylan understood that the Nietzschean's bow was really just an elaborate way of giving him the finger.

Lord Nyain Parchman lay on an examination table, fading in and out of consciousness. It was a table Rev Bem was familiar with; it was where he'd recently been sitting, putting up with Trance's fussing over the nearly nonexistent bruise on the back of his head. Rev had already deposited the monumentally unnecessary bandage she'd applied in the trash.

Rev decided that the Genite was perfectly agreeable—when he was passed out. It was the moments of coherence that were problematic.

As was to be expected, Parchman wasn't overjoyed to find himself being ministered to by a Magog and a purple alien with platinum blond hair and a tail. When Parchman demanded to know what exactly Trance was, she answered with her stock "I'm Trance," accompanied by a quizzical smile that seemed to say, *Are you simple?* After four years of observing Trance, it was a response Rev knew by heart.

During one of the Genite's pleasant comatose moments, Rev Bem gently removed the man's goggles and set them aside, hoping to make him more comfortable—especially around his broken nose. Parchman's eyes were closed, underlined by a pair of very ugly bruises. Trance slid a nanobot cartridge into a healing needle. When the green light along the needle barrel announced that it was ready, she handed it to Rev.

One of Parchman's eyes briefly fluttered open, and a weak groan escaped his lips.

"I am about to inject calcium-producing nanobots into your sinus cavity, to knit the broken bone," said Rev. "Other nanobots will repair the other . . . the, uh . . ."

Rev Bem looked at Trance. "What did you say it was called, the material in the human nose?"

"Cartilage," piped Trance.

"Cartilage. We'll give you a second injection to repair your fractured rib. Hold still, this won't hurt . . . much." Rev delicately pressed the needle to the side of Parchman's nose. Parchman's eyes blinked open and he abruptly swatted the needle out of Rev's hand. He jumped up, panicked. "Get away from me, Magog. I'm not help-less!" Parchman felt at his face.

"My goggles! Where are my goggles?"

"Right there on the exam table," said Rev, cautiously backing away. "They must have been causing you incredible pain."

Parchman covered his eyes with one hand, snatched up his goggles with the other, and put them on. He pointed at Rev and Trance. "Don't touch me. I don't want either of you to touch me."

Trance slowly approached. "But, you're hurt. We only want to help you."

"I don't want your help, freaks." Parchman caught sight of the blood staining his hands. He touched his face, feeling the sticky patches of gore there. He snarled at Trance, "Give me something to wash this off with."

Trance padded to a small window that opened at her approach, reached in, and withdrew several medicated towels. She gave them without comment to Parchman, who began to scrub his hands and face, disregarding the pain as he pressed on the swollen tissue sur-rounding his nose. After that he scrutinized the surface of the exam table, carefully wiping away any traces of blood that he found.

Rev Bem offered to dispose of the bloody towels, but Parchman simply shook his head and slid off of the table. He limped toward the nearest disposal unit, even though it was obviously painful for him to move, and threw everything in the trash. Then he hobbled back to the table and lay down with a relieved grunt.

"Go. All I need is rest." He turned gingerly onto his side, giving Rev and Trance his back.

Rev sighed. "It pains me to admit it, but one simply cannot help a man who refuses to be helped."

"Then do you mind if I go to hydroponics?" asked Trance. "I think he may have squashed some of the poor cacti."

"Of course," said Rev. "I can handle this."

After Trance had gone, Rev picked up the healing needle and was about to remove the cartridge when he noticed a glistening droplet of blood on the tip. Rev glanced over his shoulder; Parchman was still turned away. Acting on a combination of curiosity and habit, the scientist quietly found a test slide and wiped the blood on it.

Before Rev could feed the slide into the computer, Dylan appeared on the comm screen, looking more harried than usual. "How's the patient?"

"His vital signs are stable," said Rev, pocketing the slide. "He has sustained a few injuries, though. They would be simple to fix, but he refuses any medical attention. I'm afraid my hands are tied."

"Well, if it's not life-threatening, his lordship is welcome to suffer as much as he wants. We've got another medical emergency. Admiral Rasputin's slave . . . uh, escort, is sick. Trance says she'll meet you in the visitors' quarters."

"Certainly, Dylan," said Rev. He looked over his shoulder at the curled shape of Parchman, who had apparently lost consciousness again. If the man was keeping a secret in his blood, whatever it was would have to wait.

As Arca crept through the corridor, she felt a sudden and intense pang of guilt for lying to Harper. *Stop it*, she admonished herself. *Guilt is a small price to pay. And what choice do you have?*

She passed by her delegation's makeshift headquarters on an unoccupied Crew Deck and she turned toward the Medical Deck. Or, at least, what she hoped was the Med Deck—the *Andromeda* was the largest structure she had ever seen, and every square meter of it was unfamiliar territory. Complicating things further was the array of androids and robots that ceaselessly patrolled the ship's corridors; the last thing she needed was for Andromeda to spot her and get suspicious. Here, however, Arca's experience fighting in the alleyways and crawlspaces of Xhosa served her well. *Andromeda Ascendant's* utility 'droids were nothing compared to regiments of marauding Dragans—ultrasonic-sensitive, scent-seeking, night-sighted Dragans.

Most useful of all proved to be a series of "M Deck" signs that helpfully pointed her in the right direction. Medical Deck itself was, like everything else on the *Andromeda*, overwhelming. Built to accommodate a multispecies crew of more than four thousand, it was enormous and stocked with every kind of medical instrument imaginable. Finding Parchman was easy, however, as most of the deck was shuttered in long-term standby mode; Arca just followed the lights and the regular beep of a vitals monitor. *And without even the benefit of ultrasonic hearing*, she smiled grimly to herself.

She was relieved to find Parchman alone. He was curled in a fetal position, apparently sleeping. Arca crept across the med suite and lightly tapped his shoulder. Parchman sprang up as if electrified. He clamped a hand around Arca's throat and growled, "I told you not to touch me!"

Realizing that it was a young woman flailing in his grip and not a Magog, Lord Parchman released Arca abruptly. He patted her shoulder apologetically, an attempt to soothe her. "Arca. I'm sorry. I mistook you for one of the hybrid abominations that crawl around this ship."

Well, just because she needed his help didn't mean she had to like him. "Don't worry. You scared me, too," said Arca with a disarming smile. She was surprised at how much better Parchman looked since she saw him being wheeled out of hydroponics. The violent bruises on his face and the swelling around his nose had already begun to subside.

"Are you alone?" asked Parchman, looking around.

"I am," said Arca. She stopped herself before continuing. This would be her last chance to change her mind. Her jaw tightened: *No turning back now.*

"Listen, Lord Nyain—and personally, I don't care whether you're a king or an indentured servant, and I don't care what you or the Knights of Genetic Purity believe in. All I care about are the people of Alpha Centauri. And they need your help."

"I'm glad somebody on this ship is finally making sense." Parchman smiled and swung his legs over the side of the exam table. "We've wasted enough time—grab your compatriots and let's get off this mausoleum. We can be on Natal and talking tactics within the hour."

"About Natal. There is one slight problem," said Arca. "See, my commander is practically a clone of Dylan and Harper. She means well—they all do—but that doesn't make her right. And the thing is . . . well, she won't agree with my decision. Not unless we can somehow convince her that it's our best option."

Parchman suddenly held up a finger and cocked his head to one side. "Someone's coming," he whispered. "Hide. Quickly."

Arca heard nothing, but his urgency moved her to scramble to the far corner of the suite. She crouched behind a supply cabinet that would give her cover—as long as nobody needed any supplies. Parchman quickly lay back down onto the exam table and feigned unconsciousness.

A few seconds later Rev Bem and Trance walked in with the human slave slumped over a medic 'droid in a fireman's carry. The 'droid hoisted the human onto the table next to Parchman. Rev Bem helped the human lie down, although he suspected the man could have managed well enough on his own. He complained of illness, but Rev couldn't find any support for his claim. Plenty of keloid-rippled scars—life as a Nietzschean slave was never kind—but no recent trauma.

"My preliminary readings show no signs of sickness or disease," said Rev. "Your bodily systems all seem to be operating effectively."

The slave avoided Rev's gaze and pointed vaguely to his stomach. "It hurts, right here. I'm nauseous, and I think I have a fever."

It was certainly possible that the man was in fact sick; Rev had never quite mastered the specifics of human physiology. What, in the name of the Divine, was the appendix supposed to do? And do they really need a pancreas, a spleen, *and* a gallbladder? But Rev also had a suspicion—one that aroused a keen sense of sympathy in him— that the human was just trying to escape the oversight of Admiral Rasputin for a while.

"Trance, could you hand me the flexi with his vitals?" called Rev as he examined the man's pupils for what must have been the third time. After neither symptoms nor Trance made an appearance, Rev Bem looked around the med suite. Nobody there with him except for the slave and Parchman. With a tingle of annoyance, Rev decided Trance must have gone back to hydroponics, taking the flexi with her. Only years of daily meditation gave him the patience to keep from being completely pissed off.

Rev apologized to the slave. "It appears that Trance has accidentally made off with your flexi." After getting meek assurance from the human that he would be okay on his own, Rev left the suite in search of his erstwhile Life Support Officer.

Parchman slowly swiveled his head around and peered at the slave. The slave was sitting on the exam table, hugging his knees. "Who are you?" Parchman demanded sharply. The slave simply looked at him expressionlessly. It was, he always found, best to avoid any conversation that could escalate into conflict. "Answer me! You're not a spy for the Nietzschean, are you?"

The slave turned away. "Not a spy," he muttered, hiding his face.

Arca slid cautiously out from behind the supply cabinet. The sight of the cowering slave moved her to an overwhelming sense of compassion . . . as well as a deepening fury. "You see what they do to us?" she hissed to the Genite.

Parchman was examining the slave as if he were a specimen pinned to a corkboard. "Nietzscheans are born evil. They're corrupted by their own genetic mistakes. You and I—we understand that the only way to stop evil is to annihilate it."

Parchman stood and leaned on the edge of his exam table, crossing his arms. "It has occurred to me that perhaps you, and not your commander, would be the best person to lead your people to victory."

"Pac will never stand down."

"Who said anything about standing down?" said the Genite, a slow smirk spreading across his pale features. Arca understood this, too: he could remove Pac Peterson for her, and she would align herself with him. It was exactly what she had been working toward, but hearing the words was no victory. She turned away from Parchman and put a reassuring hand on the slave's shoulder.

"Hey there," said Arca, gently pulling the man's hands away from his face. "What's your name?"

"Chutak," he whispered. It had been a long time since he'd spoken that word. It had been a long time since he'd fallen asleep with food in his stomach. A long time since he'd sat in the sunshine. A long time since he'd held his wife and his children in his arms. A long time . . .

Chutak held out his hands to Arca in supplication. In the left hand, the slave held a grenade. He closed his eyes, and tried to remember what his family looked like. Was it worth explaining? Was it worth apologizing? Chutak decided to try. "He said he'd kill them," mumbled the slave, and triggered the grenade.

Med Deck erupted into flames.

NINE

Listen very carefully to those who say very little.

—VICTORIA, ALPHA WIFE OF
BARBAROSSA ANASAZI

"Trance?"

The Reverend Behemiel Far Traveler shuffled down Med Deck's gleaming platinum corridors. He couldn't understand it; Trance had been just two steps behind him when they entered the medical suite. The disappearing act in itself wasn't a surprise—he was used to that kind of behavior from Trance Gemini. What bothered Rev was that the purple pixie hadn't just disappeared, but apparently vacated the physical plane entirely without leaving so much as a forwarding address. Surely she couldn't have made it to hydroponics in such a short time?

Rev boarded an inter-deck lift. Dylan didn't like the crew to use the lifts; real High Guard would use the ladders. But the Magog wasn't exactly regular army and, anyway, his toe claws got caught in the rungs. As the lift whooshed imperceptibly between decks, Rev contemplated the anomalous Life Support Officer. He was certainly fond of her, and he respected her mysterious nature. Of course, Rev Bem pretty much respected everyone's nature; that just came with being a Wayist. But, like the rest of *Andromeda*'s motley crew, he had long since realized there was more to Trance than she let on. How much more he couldn't say, and most of the time Rev didn't let that bother him. Trance's statistically improbable series of fortunately timed accidents always seemed to promote a certain balance and harmony on the ship.

Rev stepped off the lift and softly called Trance's name. As he entered hydroponics, it occurred to him that he might have been mistaken. Perhaps she hadn't come here after all; certainly, there wasn't a purple tail anywhere to be seen. Flattened Sintii cacti still dotted the floor, the gooey smears of their day-glo insides imparting a psychedelic effect to the room. The skeleton of the broken shelf still lay shattered on its side. A lone maintenance 'droid quietly regarded the mess, as if too overwhelmed by the destruction to act.

Rev sighed. *I could just do it myself—getting new readings on the human will only take a few moments.*

He decided to make one quick sweep, just to be certain Trance wasn't on the premises. He glanced into the atrium where their Vedran oak was proudly displayed—as tall as three decks, its top brushed against the crystalline skylight that provided the room's artificial sun. In the oak's shade was a small pen where Rev kept the cloned calves that constituted his dinners.

The sight of the pen always spoiled the beauty of the scene for Rev, and not simply because it reminded him of his dismal diet. Sure, eating the same cloned animal day in and day out didn't exactly put

Rev on the cutting edge of Epicurean adventure, nor did it fully meet the nutritional needs of a body that demanded sentient flesh (although, as Beka had once pointed out, "better a heifer than a Harper"). But what really bothered him was that the pen screamed an insistent reminder of his inherently bestial nature. Beka might accept it, and Harper might accept it, but Reverend Behemiel Far Traveler himself could never make peace with his inner cannibal. No matter how perfectly he walked the Wayist path, his DNA would always be that of a murderer named Red Plague.

Rev decided to take a quick peek at the rose garden and then be on his way; he'd neglected his patient long enough. As he approached the open doorway, he noted the residual singe marks from the meltdown of Tyr's force lance. If Rev remembered right, most of the water roses had melted down, as well. And there was Trance, kneeling at the corner of the low-slung hydroponics vat, tending to the one water rose that had survived the fiasco. Rev opened his mouth and was about to call her name . . . and then stopped. There was something about her attitude that made him slip behind one of the garden's accordionlike doors, and watch her through the cracks in its folds.

Trance, who claimed to be so tone-deaf she couldn't carry a tune in a bucket, was humming. Her pitch was perfect. She sang softly to herself, a haunting, lilting melody that Rev couldn't quite place. Now Trance carefully placed a hand in the vat, cupping it beneath the floating rose. She gently lifted the rose free of the water, holding it by the hollow sacks that constituted the root system and gave the flower buoyancy. Still humming, she took her other hand and grasped the flower by its slender stem, careful not to disturb the petals of globules. She delicately parted the web of balloonlike roots, reached in, and withdrew something nestled there.

Rev's pulse quickened. In Trance's hand was the most extraordinary object he had ever seen. It was an orb, smaller than her fist. The orb seemed to possess no color of its own, yet it radiated an ever-changing spectrum of light that shimmered across Trance's face. Rev became aware of the sound of his own rapidly thumping heart, drumming a rhythm to Trance's tune. He was quite unable to take his eyes off the orb. Everything seemed to focus on that one small object, as if the ship had contracted down to a single point, and this was it.

He didn't stay engrossed for long; a shipwide alarm began sounding throughout the *Andromeda*. Rev snapped his eyes shut against the lure of the orb, and stumbled out into the atrium. He pressed against a wall, trying to gather himself. Only the urgency of the alarm could overpower the attraction of the orb; obviously, there was a major emergency somewhere on the ship. Rev felt guilty for hiding in the shadows and spying on Trance, but he still couldn't bring himself to get her attention, lest he see the orb again. Instead, he gathered his robes and fled hydroponics.

Dylan was the first to arrive at the smoldering medical suite. Thankfully, the damage had been contained to the one room. But what damage there was, was extensive: the monitors had been blown out; the exam tables and medicine banks were blackened and shattered. *Andromeda*'s autonomous systems had already doused the room with fire-retardant foam, and her nanobots had started the job of resurfacing the scorched metal. But there was nothing she could do about the sweet, sick smell of death.

Dylan pulled his force lance as he stepped into the suite, his feet sticking slightly to the residue of the quickly evaporating foam. The first thing he saw was Lord Parchman, pushing himself out from under the bulk of an upended exam table. Gingerly, the man stood and patted himself down, checking for damage. No gross injuries, apparently.

An Andromeda hologram appeared beside Dylan. "Plasma

grenade, medium yield. I'm detecting traces of tissue and dried blood. My readings indicate there were three people here when the bomb went off."

Dylan looked around the suite. No sign of anyone but Parchman. Dylan was fully aware that a plasma grenade would completely vaporize any living entity within range; what made his stomach churn was speculating on the identity of who that entity might be. *The human, and who else? Surely not Rev. . . .* Trance was also a possibility, although Dylan had personally seen her die at least once, and it didn't seem to do her any lasting harm. Still, he doubted even she was resilient enough to withstand the brunt of a plasma grenade, and the very thought made his jaw clench.

Dylan aimed his F-lance at the bridge of the Genite's aristocratic nose. "Why is it that wherever you go, death is always right behind?"

Parchman's tunic was torn and dirty; smudges of soot striped his face. He spoke in a dazed, halting rhythm. "I jumped . . . behind the exam table . . . there was barely any time."

Unfortunately for Nyain Parchman, Dylan's legendary patience was in short supply; right now, Dylan wanted nothing more than to wrap the Genite in a bow and hand him to Rasputin as an early Empress Day present. Dylan poked the force lance in Parchman's chest. "I want answers, *now!*"

"It was the slave," coughed Parchman. "He was carrying a grenade."

Dylan blanched. If the slave had a grenade, there was only one person who could have given it to him. "Rasputin Genovese," he whispered. It came out like a curse.

Tyr strode into the medical suite chest first, like an icebreaker slicing into a glacier. He looked around at the damage. He smelled the fire-extinguishing chemicals. Smelled the blood. Smelled the fear. Then he saw the Genite, and immediately regretted not killing him earlier.

Tyr didn't need *Andromeda*'s sensor readings to know that Parch-man wouldn't have been on Med Deck alone. He looked at Dylan, who saw a surprising depth of concern in the Nietzschean's eyes, and then spoke two words. "The priest?"

Dylan clenched his jaw and didn't answer. He spoke impatiently to the hologram: "Can you identify the casualties?"

"Only by elimination," said Andromeda, furrowing her ethereal holographic brow. "I've accounted for Rev and Trance."

Tyr's face brightened with relief, which he immediately tried to cover—but not soon enough to hide it from Dylan. Dylan, for his part, was as confused as he was relieved. "Who else could have been on Med Deck?"

That's what Andromeda wanted to know. Well, she did know, but it didn't make a whole lot of sense. The hologram shook her head. "The only people unaccounted for are the slave, and Arca."

For the first time since he was pulled back from the event horizon and found himself in this dystopian future, Dylan truly felt every minute of three hundred and five years old. His first thought: *Poor Harper.* He'd seen the way the kid looked at the feisty freedom fighter. He remembered how he felt, when he first met his fiancée Sarah. And he remembered how he felt when he realized she was gone forever. He had no idea what he was going to say to his scrappy engineer to help him through this.

And then Dylan had another thought: *Why was Arca meeting secretly with the Genite in his hospital room?*

As if anticipating these questions, Parchman began speaking. "The girl came to talk. She wanted my help." Parchman seemed to be recalling it as if from a dream. "Then the Magog arrived with the slave. He said he was sick. The slave, not the Magog. Then the Magog left." Parchman pointed to a half-melted exam table. "The girl grabbed for the grenade, tried to throw it."

Parchman turned to Dylan. "That grenade was intended for me."

Tyr raised the corner of his full lips into a sneer and noted, "It was intended for you, but others died. Either you're very lucky, or you're a coward."

"Tyr, this isn't the time," snapped Dylan. He glowered at Tyr, and Tyr glowered right back. Dylan was going to have to keep Tyr on a very short leash right now—whether the Nietzschean liked it or not. Tyr cut their staring contest short, however, abruptly diverting his eyes to a fallen display monitor, which had been wrenched from the wall by the blast and currently lay at an angle on the floor. He motioned for silence. Tyr's acute senses were picking up movement.

"I think there may be another survivor," said Tyr. Silently, he picked his way through the smoking debris toward the monitor. He placed his hands beneath an edge and lifted, stifling a grunt as he slipped the monitor aside. There was someone underneath it: the slave, Chutak. Unconscious, cut and bruised . . . but alive. Tyr bent and checked the man's pulse.

"Andromeda," shouted Dylan, "where's Rev and Trance?"

"I'm right here," said Rev, hurrying into the room. "I came as soon as I heard." Rev caught sight of the slave. "Is he—?"

"He's alive, but just barely," said Tyr.

Dylan led Rev toward the slave. "I'm more relieved to see you than you'll ever know," he whispered.

"I went to get Trance . . ." said Rev, letting the sentence trail off. Once more, Trance's small action had created enormous conse-quences. "She's in hydroponics. She should be here shortly."

But Trance was not the next arrival. The next arrival paused in the doorway, and all conversation immediately stopped. All eyes turned to the newcomer. Seamus Zelazny Harper looked at the faces of the people in the room. He read them like there was an LED crawl across their foreheads. A haze clouded his eyes and he balled his hands into fists.

"Where is she? What happened? Arca? Arca!"

Frantically, Harper pushed aside the broken medical equipment. Cabinets toppled. Exam tables caromed. Harper massed about fifty-two kilos, and the top of his head cleared maybe 165 centimeters, but he easily hoisted a diagnostic computer and sent it flying. Tyr looked at Dylan with a silent offer to stop the destruction, but Dylan just shook his head. *Let him do what he has to do.*

Two computers, three tables, and an instrument tray later, Harper finally wore himself out. The room started to spin . . . he had to put out a hand to lean on Tyr's shoulder. And while it would have been entirely un-Nietzschean of Tyr to actually comfort Harper, he didn't shake Harper's arm off, either. It was more than he would have done for anyone else in the galaxy.

"Harper, I'm sorry. We got here too late. There was nothing we could do." Dylan wasn't afraid to offer comfort. What bothered him was that he didn't have anything else to offer. The worst part wasn't telling Harper that Arca was dead. The worst part was telling him that there was no corpse to identify, no body to bury in a hero's grave. Not one piece of Arca left for him even to cry over.

Harper had mourned a lot of dead people in his time. His mother. His father. His cousin. But today, he had nothing to mourn but a fine red mist. He felt like mercury dropped on the floor from a great height, shattered into a thousand skittering fragments. He slumped to the floor.

"You know who did this," Parchman hissed to Harper. Harper looked up at him, but made no reply. His face was blank, comatose.

Gently, Dylan picked Harper up by his armpits and started him toward the door. "Leave the man be," said Dylan, not bothering to hide his disgust for the Genite. "This is no time to play politics."

"This is no time *not* to play politics," insisted Parchman. "Every human in Alpha Centauri could die while you're kowtowing to the Nietzscheans."

Dylan handed Harper off to Tyr and took a deliberate step

toward Parchman. He reached over deliberately, and grabbed the Genite by the now-frayed collar of his tunic. "Not another word," he said quietly. "I don't want to hear another word out of you for as long as you're on my ship." Parchman flinched and Dylan noticed the reddening burn marks along the left side of his body. It didn't make him loosen his grip.

Dylan leaned in closer. "I know you faked the datalink. That makes you a murderer, the same as Rasputin. So you can step off that high moral ground anytime."

Parchman laughed hoarsely. "Fine. But remember, I'm the one with three battleships outside. At least, three ships that *you* know of. I'd take good care of me, if I were you." His laughter gave way to a racking cough.

Rev approached with a med 'droid. "Captain, Lord Parchman's burns require immediate attention."

Dylan's face soured. "Let him hurt. This is his own doing."

"You don't mean that," said Rev Bem mildly. "At least let me be sure his life isn't in danger."

Dylan let go of Parchman. "Go. But if that bullet head of yours so much as gleams in the wrong direction, I'm all over you."

Parchman defiantly pursed his lips, but said nothing. Dylan watched him limp painfully away. The *Andromeda* hologram sprang to life. "Orders, Captain?"

"I want you on full alert mode. Neither Rasputin nor Parchman is to make a move without my permission. I want all internal defenses ready to roll at my command—anyone else around here pisses me off, be ready to hit them and hit them hard."

With a nod, the hologram blinked out of existence and began the task of marshaling her Intruder Control systems and surveillance 'droids. Dylan walked over to Harper and put both his hands on the engineer's shoulders. Harper barely noticed his touch.

"I know how hard this is for you, Harper," said Dylan. "I do."

Harper still said nothing. He looked like a marionette whose strings had been cut. Dylan had seen it before: trauma. The boy was in shock.

"What do you want me to do with him?" asked Tyr. His patience for this kind of thing had its limits.

Dylan looked at Harper, and his heart hurt. But he knew there was nothing he could do for him, not yet. These things take time.

"Get him to his quarters, leave him some hot food and a stiff drink. Then report back to Command. I want you in Lancer Armor and fully armed. We're going to pay a visit to Rasputin."

Tyr nodded and the corners of his mouth twitched in the faintest impression of a smile.

Rev's first order of business was to get Chutak into immediate treatment. He worked efficiently and quickly, the healing needles clattering like chef's knives. He could feel Parchman's eyes on his back.

Rev was in a somber mood; Arca's death was senseless and unnecessary, and it did not bode well for Dylan's fragile negotiations. While Rev never questioned the Divine's motives—why some died when others lived was one of those eternal mysteries that would never be resolved—that didn't necessarily mean he always agreed with them.

"You were the lucky one," said Parchman. "If you had lingered one minute longer, you'd have been exterminated."

Parchman didn't need to remind him. It was something Rev was already giving considerable thought to. He was going to have to speak with Trance. *Did she disappear on purpose, knowing I'd look for her?*

"You really should let me check the severity of those burns," said Rev.

Parchman groaned as he lay down on an exam table. "You touch me and you die. All I need is sleep."

"Dylan won't be pleased."

"Tell Dylan he can go to hell."

"As you wish," said Rev. The truth was, Rev wasn't nearly as concerned with Parchman's health as he pretended to be. In actuality, Rev had thought he might talk some sense into the man. Rev surreptitiously reached into a pouch under his robes, and removed the test slide that carried Parchman's drop of blood.

The Magog made a show of rearranging healing needles and activating the dormant medical machinery that lined the wall beneath the status monitors. Once the medical computer was on-line, he opened a tray, inserted the slide, and closed it. The computer began to analyze the blood: blood type, blood gases, white cell count . . . As the analysis got down to genetic information, Rev smiled. He had guessed right.

Parchman lay on his back, awkwardly trying to keep his weight off of his burns. "Why are you still here?" he spat. "I told you I don't need your help."

Rev shut off the computer and stood at the human supremacist's side. "Perhaps I can offer more than just physical help."

"You can help me by leaving."

"I was referring to spiritual aid," said Rev. Parchman sniggered. Rev ignored it, continuing, "The Magog have contributed little to the universe besides pain and death. As a monk, I understand what it's like to renounce one's kind."

That got Parchman's attention. He sat up, grimacing as he did so, and stared at Rev.

Rev absently fingered the Wayist medallion he wore around his neck. The symbol was a triangle enclosed in a circle, bisected by an irregular line. It represented the Anointed's vision of the Way, the journey to enlightenment. From one perspective, it's a road disappearing into the infinite horizon. From another, it's a path to the top of a mountain. Rev Bem believed that both were true, and that the Anointed was saying all roads, finally, lead to the same destination.

"I turned away from the Magog, but I never turned *against* the Magog. Because the very fact of my existence proves that we are not all evil."

Parchman spoke coolly. "You know, this really is your lucky day. If I weren't injured, I'd have killed you by now. Know this, Magog. I'm not some uneducated bigot blaming the universe's troubles on Nietzscheans because I don't understand them. I know *exactly* what treachery lies in the hearts of those mutants."

"Biology is not destiny, Nyain. Our actions determine our fate. Sow hatred, and it is hatred you will reap."

Parchman brushed Rev Bem away as if he were an annoying bug. "I didn't come here for sermons. I ask you again—leave me. Please."

Well, thought Rev, *the Divine knows I tried. I only hope his secrets don't kill him . . . or anyone else.*

The door to Rasputin's room was wide open. Dylan glanced in, and was startled to realize this was the same room once occupied by another Nietzschean: Gaheris Rhade. Dylan cast a questioning glance at Rommie; was she trying to tell him something by putting their guest in the quarters of the man who had been both Dylan's best friend and his most lethal enemy? It was, after all, Gaheris Rhade, his handpicked first officer, who had finally betrayed Dylan in the name of the Nietzschean uprising.

But if Rommie was making a statement with her room assignments, she wasn't saying.

Dylan entered to find Rasputin sitting at the multileveled Go board, studying the pieces. He was playing one of his guards, and judging by the sour expression on the soldier's face, Rasputin was winning.

"That was an all-hands Code Black," said Rasputin, swiveling in his chair as he heard Dylan's soft step on the plush carpet. "I've been dying to know what the excitement was all about."

Tyr and Rommie followed behind Dylan and took up positions on either side of the door.

"Nice try. But I know you tried to kill Parchman."

"Tried?" Rasputin arranged his face into a fairly convincing puzzled smile.

"Nyain Parchman is still alive. And so is your slave, but just barely."

Rasputin's face slowly turned grim. His guard remained focused on the game, ignoring Dylan.

"But," continued Dylan, "you did manage to murder a rather nice young woman, if it matters. Arca is dead."

It was impossible to read Rasputin's expression. He steepled his fingers, deep in thought. Dylan couldn't tell whether Rasputin was contemplating what he'd just heard, or his next Go move.

"That is unfortunate," said Rasputin. "But . . . may I ask what she was doing with the Genite?"

"No, you may not," said Dylan. "It's none of your business."

"I wouldn't say that. Especially if the meeting involved a Genite attack on my system."

" 'Your system.' Interesting choice of words."

"Captain, you know perfectly well that one man's slave world is another man's colonial outpost. And 'tribute' is just an impolite way of saying 'taxes.' Who are you to judge the Drago-Kazov Empire?"

Rasputin stood up and frowned at Tyr, fully kitted in obsidian breastplate and carrying a Gauss rifle larger than an adult Mugani. "Playing soldier, are we?"

"Just taking out the garbage," Tyr replied laconically.

Amusement flickered momentarily across Rasputin's face, and then he spun around on his heels, addressing Dylan. "I'd like to speak with you alone, for a moment."

Dylan nodded at Tyr and Rommie. "Wait for me outside." Rasputin signaled, and his own soldiers followed them out.

Rasputin sat at the Go table, and nodded for Dylan to take the opposite chair. Rasputin was sitting, Dylan noted wryly, in the same spot where Rhade used to sit. "My guards make excellent warriors," said Rasputin, "but their Go skills are appalling. Do you play?"

Dylan hesitated before answering. "Not as much as I used to."

"We'll have to try a game sometime."

Dylan glared at Rasputin. *Something tells me that, for you, this is already a game.* "Maybe later—after I decide whether or not to put you and your buddy Parchman in chains."

"I would prefer you not call him my . . . buddy. Although I do understand why you're angry. I can't imagine a worse diplomatic faux pas than killing the other party's diplomat, can you? But whatever you think, I'm terribly sorry Arca died. That was never my intent."

"That still doesn't get you off the hook."

Rasputin's eyes closed to slivers, and his voice took on a menacing tone. "The hook? There is no *hook*, Captain. You're not the law in this system. I am. You have a bad habit of forgetting that your Commonwealth no longer exists."

The admiral suddenly leaned back and smiled. "But I wouldn't worry about that now. I'm more concerned with the fact that the HIA will be calling for my blood. Even if you tell them Arca's death was accidental, they wouldn't believe it."

It was true. As much as Dylan hated to admit it, there was little he could do to hold Rasputin accountable for Arca's death. There was no court to try him, no jail to hold him—and anything Dylan did personally to exact justice would certainly bring down the wrath of the admiral's flagship on the *Andromeda*. No, his best bet was to use the incident as a lever . . . or a club.

"There is one way you can placate the HIA," said Dylan. "And placate me at the same time." Rasputin looked at him with feigned disinterest. "Free Alpha Centauri."

Rasputin broke into laughter. "Please. If I walked away from

Alpha Centauri now, I would be dead at the hands of my own Pride by dinnertime."

"You're not thinking of the big picture," said Dylan. "You study history, Admiral. Look at the Vedrans, the most influential species in the universe. They were a warrior race—not unlike the Drago-Kazov, really. But when they made a decision to become statesmen instead of soldiers, it ushered in the greatest civilization ever known. Because in the final analysis, peace is profitable. It's practical. It's productive. It costs less than war.

"Frankly, I'm surprised that the Nietzscheans aren't the biggest boosters of the New Commonwealth out there."

Rasputin intently examined the Go board, placing one of the small smooth pieces in his palm and closing his fist over it. "You're good, Captain. Cost efficiency is an argument every Nietzschean understands. But don't deceive yourself that your dream of a restored Commonwealth is practical. It is not. It's a fantasy. And fantasy doesn't do me any good—not right here, not right now.

"You are a man out of your time, and you're too blind to realize that's a liability. You're so used to seeing things as they were, you don't see them as they are."

He returned the Go piece to the board. As Dylan expected, he returned the pebble to a different grid than where he had found it. The admiral was cheating.

"If freeing slaves equaled productivity, I'd free them all tomorrow. But home rule for kludges will not recoup the Drago-Kazov investment on Natal. Did it ever occur to you that these negotiations might simply be a stalling tactic?"

That made no sense to Dylan. "Why would the HIA want to stall their own revolution?"

"Not them. Me. Try this scenario: I talk to the HIA, the rebellion is put on hold, and I stop losing money. I wait for the fleet to finish fighting the Maroon Pride, and as soon as the fleet comes to Alpha

Centauri I put an end to the HIA once and for all. The slaves go back to work, productivity is restored . . . Rasputin emerges victorious yet again."

Dylan couldn't believe his ears. Was Rasputin toying with him? Surely a Nietzschean wouldn't reveal his game plan so openly. "No, Rasputin. I can't believe you would have gone to all this trouble unless you thought freedom for the humans was an option."

Rasputin chuckled approvingly. He prepared to answer Dylan with an appropriately confounding assertion when an Andromeda hologram appeared with an urgent message from Parchman. And much as Rasputin would have given his backbone blade to overhear the message, there was no way he could hack into the subvocal communication system between the captain and his ship. Rasputin had no choice but to wait impatiently, contemplating the Go board, as Dylan stood and walked to the other side of the room, listening to the Genite's vital communiqué. *Probably either an attack or a retreat*, thought Rasputin. *Wasn't that the nature of all conversations?*

Rasputin watched Dylan as he listened intently to Andromeda's transmission. He admired the fact that Dylan was a man of honor, truthfully, but that made him predictable, and predictability was a weakness. Rasputin had just revealed his true motives and the captain, true to form, didn't believe him.

Certainly Rasputin did think freedom for the humans was an option. If all else failed, he was perfectly willing to agree to the HIA's demands—they could even have a ceremony, sign a truce of some kind, have a parade. And Rasputin would honor that agreement for precisely as long as it took for his fleet to arrive.

Who would stop him from reneging? Dylan and his rattletrap Commonwealth? Not likely. *I know the extent of his battle group*, Rasputin gloated. *I'm sitting on her.*

The admiral smiled as Dylan ended his subvocal conversation. "Sorry about that," said Dylan.

"Apology accepted. You know, Captain," said Rasputin. "It's too bad you didn't let me blow the Genite out of the sky when I had the chance. You could have saved us all a lot of trouble if you allowed me to dispatch him from the beginning."

"You won't have to worry about Lord Parchman anymore."

"What do you mean?"

"He's leaving." Dylan took his seat at the Go board. "That was the urgent message. He's taking his ships and leaving the system."

"He said that? And you believed him?"

"He was quite convincing."

Rasputin watched Dylan for a moment; the man's face was an impassive mask. Surely Dylan knew that Parchman had lied from the beginning, that he was guilty of destroying the Nietzschean fighters without provocation. Yet here he was, allowing the Genite to just pick up and leave. For a High Guard officer, a supposed man of honor, this was exceedingly unusual.

Unless . . . unless he believed me after all. Rasputin suddenly wondered if Dylan would release the Genite just to spite him. He had difficulty accepting that. Dylan was, after all, predictable.

Wasn't he?

TEN

We must always praise virtue in others. It gives us great
advantage over them.

                    —FRIEDRICH NIETZSCHE, CY 6811

Beka Valentine crossed her fingers as the onboard computers gathered and regurgitated sensor information. As usual, crossed fingers
failed to deliver; there was no sign of either Magdalena or her ship.

The *Eureka Maru* skimmed across a quiet piece of real estate
called the Bodega system. They'd just been spit out of the nearest
Slip point, and Beka made some quick calculations. She figured
Magdalena's speed to be about thirty PSL—which meant that given
her lead she couldn't have made it to the next closest Slip point,
which was well on the far side of the system.

"So, where is she?" asked Rafe, seemingly picking up on Beka's
thoughts. It was the first thing either of them had said since they left

the Gallipolans and the pirate's Salvager. Beka was still reeling after realizing she actually gave a damn for her brother. And Rafe—who had almost convinced himself that he was responsible for the Salvager's supernatural performance—was reeling because Beka was reeling.

"Well, she either found some way to cheat the speed of light, which at this point I wouldn't put past her, or . . ." Beka pointed to the cluster of the Bodega system's six planets. "Or she's hiding."

Beka closed her eyes and scrolled what she had seen of the *Ot* past her retinas. She'd had so little time with the document, she couldn't recall much of it. The text had mentioned a false star, she remembered that clearly, but as Beka scanned Bodega's planets she couldn't find any promising candidates. Her false star seemed more like a false lead at this moment.

"What about you? Any bright ideas?" Beka asked, even though she was well aware of their options. They could either pull up a chair and wait, hoping Magdalena would show her face, or they could try the planets. Painstakingly. One by one. And it was possible their mother wasn't in Bodega in the first place.

"I say we check out a few of these rocks," said Rafe. "We found her once, we can find her again." Rafe wasn't as convinced as he tried to sound. At this point, he was ready to believe Magdalena could disappear at will. She made them look like amateurs when they had the element of surprise; now that she knew they were on her trail, he calibrated the odds of finding her as somewhere between minuscule and why-even-bother.

Beka agreed that if they were going to check out any planets, they should start with whichever one was the least annoying and, well, planetlike. The choice was easy. If you have to go to mudfoot territory, Bodega Blue was about as good as it was going to get. Beka fired a drone to keep watch (in case they missed anything while they were landlocked), then initiated the *Maru*'s atmospheric entry sequence.

She knew that finding Magdalena on a planet, especially if she didn't want to be found, was most likely an exercise in futility. *I'd have an easier time finding Tarn-Vedra.*

"I'm giving this half an hour, tops," said Beka. "Then we're on to the next ball of dirt."

Twenty-nine minutes and fifty-nine seconds later, as Rafe was dozing in the copilot's chair and Beka glumly prepared coordinates to the next closest planet, the first of the Maxim charges on Bodega Blue detonated. The explosion jolted Rafe upright. "What the hell was that?"

Beka grinned; her black mood had just done a vigorous one-eighty. If she'd ever seen the calling card of a Valentine, a few Maxim charges evaporating half a planet was certainly one of them. Good thing the resort didn't have any paying guests on the premises.

"If I was a betting woman—and I am—I'd bet that was Mom," said Beka. "And my guess is she'll be making a hasty getaway."

It didn't take long before Magdalena's ship, punched at full acceleration, blasted by, riding the edge of a deadly shock wave. *Gotcha*, thought Beka. She accelerated the *Maru* and trailed Magdalena to Bodega Blue's upper atmosphere, squeaking to within a few light-seconds of the elusive prey.

Beka looked at Rafe. "Get her on the comm. Talk to her."

Rafe had always considered himself a capable orator (a nice way of saying bullshit artist), especially when it counted most. But not even a lifetime of smooth talking had prepared him for this. Rafe was at a loss for words. "Me? Talk to her? But . . . what do I say?"

Beka didn't know how to answer that. What do you say to a mother that, until a few days ago, you didn't even know was alive? A mother who did a damn good job of not knowing whether you were alive, either.

"For starters," said Beka, "try, 'Hey, Mom, slow down.'"

Beka tapped a few buttons, activating the hailing unit. She kept the *Maru* right behind Magdalena's ship, and was soon close enough to get a visual on it. It was a beat-up research vessel, and from the looks of it, it was held together with string and chewing gum. But Beka knew looks could be deceiving; the *Maru* was proof of that.

"Will you get on the comm unit already?" Beka was getting impatient.

"What do you think I'm doing over here? Writing her a letter? The channel's open, but I can't talk if she doesn't respond."

Rafe was right. All they could do was keep hailing and wait. And wait.

It quickly became obvious that Magdalena didn't want to chat. Beka found herself in a strange position—now that they had caught up to Magdalena, what exactly would they do about it? Blow her out of the sky? That seemed somehow self-defeating. But Beka couldn't just let Magdalena thumb her nose at them, either. She'd done that for a lifetime too long.

Well, she's gotta land that bird sometime, and I'll be right there when she does. Beka continued the pursuit. Magdalena wasn't even trying to shake her.

"You think she found anything back there?" said Rafe.

"Of course she found something. Planets don't get cremated for no reason." And Beka had a good idea what Magdalena found: the Crown of Ixthathos, a score worth melting half a world for.

Beka initiated the Slipstream drive. "Get ready. I think she's gonna jump."

Moments later they were thrust into the spaghetti junction of the Slipstream, bouncing from one string to another. The ride was a lot smoother than their last jump. Beka got to see Magdalena's 'streaming skills up close and personal, and was pleasantly surprised. Her mother was a deft pilot, effortlessly jumping from one connection to the next. It was the moment they were spewed back into normal space that made Beka almost choke. *Milky Way galaxy. Triadic system. No, it can't be. . . .*

The nav computer had a lock on their location: they were at Alpha Centauri, just a few light-minutes away from the *Andromeda Ascendant* herself.

"Hey, I recognize this place," said Rafe. "What are the chances we'd end up back here?"

Rommie could have rattled off a statistical solution, but all Beka knew for sure was that it was a bit too coincidental for comfort. Could their return to Alpha Centauri really be just a random occurrence? You could travel the Slipstream a lifetime and never see the same place twice.

However, Beka's concerns were soon forgotten; the *Maru* was receiving a message. It looked like Magdalena was finally ready to talk.

About time! Beka looked at Rafe. "You ready?"

He nodded. Beka took a breath—she was surprisingly nervous.

Magdalena appeared on the comm screen. A sly smile graced her lips as she pushed an errant lock of hair out of her eyes. She looked—well, almost as young as Beka, frankly. It was a big difference from the security scan image. In fact, her appearance was *too* good; Beka immediately suspected that an "image enhancer" program was glamorizing Magdalena's transmission—a virtual facelift, as it were.

"Well, I'll be. Look at the two of you! You're all grown up . . . and gorgeous," exclaimed Magdalena. (*Not too shabby yourself*, thought Beka.) "Hey, I apologize for being so inaccessible. It's just that I . . . had a few errands to run."

Rafe sat silent with his mouth hanging open. Beka leaned over and backhanded it shut for him. "Ow. Uh, hi, Mom. Er, Magdalena. Uh—"

"What I think my brother is trying to say," Beka cut in, "is that you're one hard lady to get ahold of. But we're glad to finally meet you."

Magdalena's smile became more tentative, less studied. It occurred to Beka that their mother was as nervous speaking to them as they were to her.

"This is awkward, isn't it?" said Magdalena, voicing Beka's thoughts. "I've never been good at hellos . . . or good-byes, for that matter. Is there anyplace we can talk? Do this the right way?"

"The *Andromeda Ascendant* is nearby," said Beka. "We can go there."

The vulnerability bled from Magdalena's expression. She showed her teeth in a camera-ready smile and nodded. "The *Andromeda*. I've heard about her. Sounds perfect; I'll follow you there."

After Magdalena signed off, Beka looked at Rafe and mouthed, "Wow."

Rafe was grinning. "So that's Magdalena Valentine."

Beka set a course and nudged the *Maru* toward *Andromeda*, keeping a close eye on Magdalena to make sure she did indeed follow them. In the process, Beka nearly ran right through a two-kilometer-wide, octagonal mylar mirror, all but invisible from the wrong angle. In fact, there were three of the huge constructs fanning out from the ship. She gave them plenty of berth. *What harebrained scheme of Dylan's are those things a part of?*

Beka activated the comm. "Andromeda, it's Beka. So, did you miss me or what?"

He's drunk, thought Tyr. Harper was splayed across the mattress in his quarters, head cocked at an ungainly angle. Like Beka, Tyr never became intoxicated, although for different reasons. For Tyr, intoxication was an indulgence. It dulled the senses. It was antisurvival.

Harper spoke without moving. "Get bent, Tyr. I want to be alone."

So he wasn't drunk. *Good*, thought Tyr. He came closer, and casually kicked Harper in the ribs. Harper yelped and jumped to a sitting position. *Better*, thought Tyr.

Tyr squatted on his haunches next to the bed and spoke softly. "What do you know about the Maroon Pride?" he asked.

It was perhaps the most unexpected question Harper had been asked since Dylan said, "Would you like a berth on the *Andromeda Ascendant?*"

Harper answered: "What do you want to know? Maroons. Fierce, ruthless, hated, and feared—the usual. After the Dragans and the Jaguar-Sabra Alliance, they're probably the most powerful Nietzschean Pride out there."

"How many slave worlds do they have?"

"This is a trick question, isn't it? If you already know the answer, Tyr, why are you asking me? None. The Maroons aren't slavers. Never have been. What's this all about?"

That's when Tyr told Harper a story. It was a story about Old Earth, a topic they both knew well. Except Harper didn't know the story of the Maroons.

He did know about Christopher Columbus, of course, the woohoo-the-world-is-round guy. Columbus landed on the Caribbean island of Jamaica in Earth Year 1494. Like all the explorers' "discoveries" in the New World, the place was already inhabited—in this case, by a hundred thousand peaceful Taino Indians. The Spanish immigrants murdered thousands of the natives outright, and thousands more died of smallpox and other imported diseases. Survivors were impressed into brutal slavery.

The Taino did not want to be slaves. Rather than cut the Spaniards' sugarcane and mine the Spaniards' ore, they opted to commit mass suicide. By the time the English arm-wrestled the Spanish for control of Jamaica a century or so later, the Taino had all but disappeared from the Caribbean.

The English, then, had to import their own slaves to brutalize in the cane fields and the mines. They brought black-skinned people from Africa, and these people did not want to be slaves, either. But rather than killing themselves, they killed the English. Twenty thousand rebels hid in the mountains, sending raiding parties to raze plantations and ambush planters. The Spanish called these guerrilla fighters *"cimarrones."* "Wild ones."

The British shortened it to "Maroons."

The Maroon Wars lasted for more than eighty years. At the end of them, the island of Jamaica abolished slavery.

Harper listened to the story. It was a good story. But it had nothing to do with him. "Tyr, I like history as much as the next guy. But why this, and why now?"

"Because while you're sitting here contemplating suicide, I want you to think about the Taino. I want you to think about why there is no 'Taino Pride,' and not a soul alive with Taino blood flowing in his veins. Then I want you to think about the Maroon Pride, and why they don't have slave planets.

"And I want you to remember this: I, too, was a slave."

Harper was speechless. His mouth worked slightly, but no sound came out. *He's good*, thought Harper. *No one else got it.* Tyr had picked up on the one thought that had consumed Harper since Arca's death, the thought he didn't want to admit to anyone—not even to himself. Harper wanted to kill himself. He wanted to commit suicide. It just hurt too damn much and he didn't want to be around to feel it anymore. He just wanted to die, like Arca.

And here comes Tyr with a different idea.

"I think I get it. You want me to go back to Natal, take Arca's place. You want the HIA to bite at the Dragans' ankles just enough to give the Maroons a clean shot at them, even if it means siding with the Genites. Because you like the Maroon Pride better than the Drago-Kazov. You're playing politics with my personal life."

"The personal is always political. You know that."

"So I shouldn't kill myself . . . for *you*."

"If you want to put it that way. Or you can put it this way: Rasputin Genovese murdered Arca. For that, he should pay."

Tyr got up and left Harper to make his decision. He hoped the boy wouldn't take his own life: it was unnecessary, it was wasteful, and it was un-Nietzschean. Also, he felt a kinship of sorts with the cocky engineer.

Because what Tyr Anasazi didn't tell Harper was that he knew damn well Rasputin Genovese had betrayed the Kodiak, had murdered his parents and destroyed his Pride. And for that, he *would* pay.

Beka eased the *Eureka Maru* into the *Andromeda*'s Hangar Deck. *Home, sweet home.* She was a little nervous; she hadn't left on the best of circumstances, and didn't know how well she'd be received. *Well, if Dylan can't take a joke, then too bad for Dylan.*

Sure enough, the *Hypatia* was right behind them. No last-minute getaways, no marauding pirates. For once, something was going right. Beka set the *Maru* down softly; the ship came to rest with a relieved groan. Rafe pried himself out of the copilot's seat and stretched his back. Beka could see the lean muscle unknot, could hear his compressed joints pop.

"Booster Rocket, you really have to do something about that chair. It's too short for my back, and too wide for my ass."

"Shut up and get off my ship," Beka said with a grimace.

"Oooh, I'm telling Mom you yelled at me. You're going to get in trouble!"

Beka retrieved the hangar access key from the computer and slipped it into her pocket; depending on how mad Dylan was, she could try to trade it for some forgiveness. Then Beka slipped her Gauss pistol into its holster and led the way to the *Maru*'s main airlock, tapping in the code to open the doors. She sauntered out into the hangar bay, bracing herself for an earful from Dylan or a lecture from Rev. Beka was surprised to find only Tyr Anasazi on deck.

"Rafe, you remember Tyr, don't you?"

"How could I forget?" said Rafe.

Tyr looked down his nose at Rafe and asked archly, "Still spying for the Free Trade Alliance?"

"Tyr, behave," said Beka. There was an unusually querulous quality to Tyr's question. Surely he wasn't jealous of her brother? No, she decided. More likely it was just a Nietzschean male reflex: the everything-here-is-mine scent spray.

Rafe took the jab good-naturedly. "Self-employed, thanks. Those big bureaucracies aren't my style. I like to keep my own hours, you know?"

"Yeah, Rafe figures why cheat for someone else when he could be cheating for himself," added Beka.

Rafe feigned a pout. "That hurts."

Tyr studiously ignored Rafe and turned to Beka. "How was the family reunion?"

"You're looking at it. This is actually going to be the first time we'll see our mother face-to-face."

Tyr skeptically eyed the *Hypatia*. "Am I to assume that's her ship?"

"The one and only," said Beka. *And apparently, she's not in any rush to get out of it.* The *Hypatia* was locked up like the vaults of Orgishnu, with no sign of pilot or passenger. Beka considered the possibility that her mother had somehow ditched the ship before landing. *Impossible. I would have seen it.*

"So," said Beka, stalling for time. "How's the boss?"

"Why don't you ask him yourself?" boomed Dylan from across the hangar bay, stepping in from the far access corridor. Rommie and

Rev Bem followed. "Although I wish you'd thought of me as your boss when you up and left."

Note to self, thought Beka. *Voices in the hangar bay tend to carry.* "It was just a figure of speech."

"Next time you run out for groceries, tack a note to the refrigerator or something, okay?" As Dylan got closer, Beka was struck by how weary he looked. Now that she thought about it, the whole group seemed a little the worse for wear.

Dylan turned to Rafe. "Any more crew you need to kidnap today?"

Rafe grinned sheepishly. "No, one was enough."

Rev Bem politely coughed. "I, for one, am glad to have you both back safely." Rev had been feeling fairly buoyant, actually. In many ways, things were going quite well. The Genite had responded to his . . . encouragement. They had come to an understanding that was satisfactory to both, and based on what he'd heard, Parchman had been true to his word.

But seeing Beka, Rev was reminded of the way Trance had enabled her departure in the first place by providing her with a key. Trance Gemini was purposely intervening in events; Rev Bem was convinced of it. But he didn't know why, and it worried him.

"Thanks, Rev," said Beka, once again grateful for the Wayist's gift for saying the right thing at the right time. "As you can see, we're still waiting for the guest of honor."

"I imagine your mother was pleased to see the two of you," said Rommie.

"I don't know about 'pleased.' 'Energized' might be a better word," said Beka, somewhat obscurely. "She can be . . . a little hard to follow sometimes, and we had some trouble . . . connecting. But, all in all, Rafe and I are pretty happy with the whole thing." *Ugh, did I just sound like an idiot or what? Why does my family have to be so bending insane?*

"What about you guys?" asked Beka. "Anything interesting happen while I was gone?"

She was greeted with deadpan silence. Beka could have sworn she heard a Silonian cricket chirping in a corner of the hangar. Dylan decided against even attempting a two-minute recap. Instead, he pointed at the *Hypatia*. "Is that her?"

Beka felt a little levity was in order; everyone was just being so damn serious. She held out her hands to the ship like a hostess presenting prizes at a raffle. "Observe. This is a spacecraft. And, contrary to popular opinion, I did not technically spring from one. No, I'm afraid my mother is what's *inside*."

Dylan didn't even crack a smile. *Tough room*, thought Beka.

Finally, the *Hypatia*'s airlock slid dramatically and noisily open. Magdalena Valentine nimbly jumped out, jovially swiveling her walking stick like a bandleader's baton. She didn't mind making everyone wait. Hey, she deserved a few minutes to make herself presentable, didn't she? Especially after being chased halfway across the cosmos.

Of course, she also needed to spend some quality time with the Crown of Ixthathos. After landing, her first order of business had been to carefully lay out each of her four pieces of the Vedran Runes. They were by now separated from their ornamentation; those bits of jewelry were collecting dust in *Hypatia*'s cargo hold. As she predicted, the Crown's stone fit perfectly onto the Fist of Pac Tull. The moment the pieces meshed, the hairs on Magdalena's body stood on end. There was an undeniable sense of growing power about the half-formed object in her hands, a field of emanating waves that played invisibly against the skin. She could *feel* that the artifact was near completion.

She carefully dropped the pieces into a specially made pouch—nanobots inhabited its fabric and secured the contents in a froth of preservative silicone. The pouch had a long strap, allowing her to wear it around her neck. She then hid it beneath several untidy layers of necklaces and jangling trinkets.

Then it was, as claimed, off to the mirror for some primping . . . and a peek at *Hypatia*'s external surveillance monitors. Magdalena had learned long ago that people said the most interesting things when they thought you weren't listening. Anyway, knowing when others were talking about you was essential for timing a proper entrance.

All eyes turned to the lean, muscular woman striding off the *Hypatia*. As Magdalena walked—whisked, was more like it—toward Beka, Beka noted that her appearance had changed from the glamorous image projected earlier over the comm. Now presenting a more accurate, yet still youthfully indeterminate visage, Magdalena sported a different hairstyle (down as opposed to up), hair color (pink as opposed to blond), and eye color (gray as opposed to green). She wore a simple, formfitting jumpsuit that took on the hue of the surrounding environment. Wherever Magdalena went, she blended in . . . quite literally. It was quite flattering, yet Beka had a feeling it was done less for looks than to keep her identity hidden.

Magdalena went up to Rafe, tucked her cane under one arm, and wordlessly took his head in her hands. Actually seeing him, touching him, she wondered for a moment—only a moment—how she could ever have left such a beautiful boy behind. Her bravado began to wobble, but she quickly reminded herself: Rafael wasn't a child anymore.

Sobering, she approached Beka and pushed the hair back from her daughter's face, pressed her palms gently against her cheeks. In Beka's eyes she could still see the clear gaze of the baby girl she had left so long ago. Again, a pang of doubt—could she have ever made a real mother to her kids? A good mother? Magdalena was painfully aware that the time for such questions had long since passed. She'd made her decisions, and there was no way to change that.

"It's been a long time," she said. "Too long."

Beka inhaled her mother's scent. She couldn't believe how soft her hands were. It was a sweet thrill—and now that she felt it, she didn't know how she ever got along without it.

Overwhelmed, Beka said the first thing to pop into her head. "So, what have you been up to?"

Magdalena laughed, a sound like silver chimes. "Got a year? It's a long story."

Rafe's eyes were drawn to Magdalena's walking stick, specifically the handle, an intricate metal gargoyle that had "valuable" written all over it. In spite of himself, he was calculating what it would go for on the open market.

Beka was suddenly aware that there were people in the room other than the three of them. Self-conscious, she drew away. "You have to meet the rest of the crew."

Beka pulled Magdalena toward Tyr for the first introduction . . . not that she needed much encouragement. She had noticed the big Nietzschean when spying on the Hangar Deck. How could she not? That velvety brown skin, those bulging triceps, the tightly coiled dreadlocks that fell down his chiseled back . . . *By the Vedran Empress, the man's buttocks striate.*

Tyr, for his part, fairly melted when Magdalena approached him at full wattage. He not only let her playfully squeeze one of his biceps, but even coaxed her into flexing one of her own. Beka didn't know which bothered her more, that Tyr was stroking her mother's arm—or that her mother had better muscle definition than she did.

Tyr caught a raised eyebrow from Dylan and quickly stepped back. He wouldn't want anyone to think he was actually enjoying himself.

Magdalena now turned her attention to Rev Bem. She was in awe. "I've never met a Magog before."

"That's because they usually eat you right before shaking hands," said Rafe.

"Shush," scolded Magdalena. "Be nice."

Rafe blushed. *Is this what it's like having a mother?*

Rev stood politely as Magdalena inspected his cheek horns and patchy fur. "By the Divine, you are fantastic," she said. Rev went nuclear with embarrassment; it took all his restraint not to mutter something on the order of "Aw, shucks."

"Let me show you something," said Magdalena, reaching into the noisy tangle of necklaces, charms, and juju bags that hung around her neck. Her hand emerged from the mess, surprisingly, with a Wayist medallion. Now it was Rev's turn to be in awe.

"You're a follower of the Way?" he asked.

With a playful wink, Magdalena whispered, "When it suits me."

Beka next introduced Magdalena to Rommie. "This is the *Andromeda Ascendant*'s public interface avatar. 'Rommie,' to her friends."

"She's a ship?"

"Yes, but I watch my weight." Rommie smiled absently at Magdalena; she was preoccupied with other matters. She was getting an odd kind of sensory buzz, picking up readings on something almost too infinitesimal to notice, but too distinct to ignore. It was an energetic phenomenon that defied categorization, and Rommie didn't like to be defied.

Magdalena looked Rommie up and down. "Is that how you get a body like that? Because I want one."

"You'd have to talk to Harper about that," answered Rommie distractedly. She was trying to pin down exactly when she became aware of the odd sensor readings.

"Speaking of which, where is the twerp?" asked Beka.

There was an unusually long silence before Dylan spoke up. "Harper . . . stepped out."

"You must be Captain Hunt," said Magdalena. Her first impression of Dylan was that he was about the handsomest man she had ever seen. Her second was that he was a hopeless prude. The old-fashioned High Guard uniform and his determined expression didn't help. She extended her hand for a firm, soldierly shake.

Dylan shook Magdalena's hand. He was struck by how much she looked like Beka, and how little like Rafe. He also couldn't deny that Magdalena had an energy about her that was palpable.

"Why the long face?" asked Magdalena.

"It's been a long day," said Dylan. "But I won't bore you with the details."

Thank goodness for that, thought Magdalena.

"Tell me," he continued, "what brings you to Alpha Centauri?"

"My children, of course. I thought it was high time I paid them a visit."

Beka shot a glance at Rafe. Who paid whom a visit? Wasn't someone riding someone's tail at the time? Which reminded her . . . "Hey, where's Trance?"

A flash of purple bounded into the cavernous room, waving as it sped past and skittering to a stop in front of Magdalena. Trance threw her arms around Magdalena's middle and hugged her excitedly.

"I'm so happy for the three of you!"

"Uh, thanks?" said Magdalena, a little discombobulated to find this enthusiastic, if unidentifiable, being clutching her around the midriff.

"And last but not least," drolly announced Beka, "I'd like you to meet Trance Gemini."

Magdalena looked at Trance with curiosity. In all her travels, she'd never seen anything quite like her. Although she had heard stories. . . . "What exactly are you?"

Beka cut her off. "Trust me, don't even bother asking."

Trance squeezed Beka's arm. "See? Isn't it nice, being back with her?"

Beka felt awkward, especially with her mother standing right there and everyone watching. "Yes, it is," she said diplomatically.

"I'd love to see the rest of the ship," said Magdalena, sensing her daughter's discomfort. "I do admire anything older than me that looks this good."

"Please, make yourself at home," said Dylan. "I wish I could be a better host, but I'm afraid I've landed myself in the middle of a war. You'll have to excuse me."

Beka turned to question Dylan, but he was already heading out. "Rev, you're with me," he called over his shoulder.

Trance clapped her hands. "I can show you around. Beka? Are you coming?"

"Thanks, I've already taken the tour."

While Trance attempted to recruit Rommie and Rafe, Beka took the opportunity to sidle up to Tyr. "Want to tell me what's going on?"

"Do you want the short version or the long version?"

"How about something in between."

Tyr explained the basics: Dylan invites Admiral Rasputin Genovese on board in hopes of negotiating a settlement between the Drago-Kazov Pride and the insurgent HIA. As soon as he arrives, the Dragans are blindsided by Genites. In response, Rasputin ambushes the Genite commander, accidentally killing the HIA representative . . . who also happened to be Harper's girlfriend. Now the Genite has left the ship, presumably gearing up for a wholesale conflagration. Oh, and Harper's gone missing.

Beka groaned inwardly. It was too much information to absorb all at once. Worse, it was probably all her fault. She deflected with a joke: "I leave you guys alone for a couple days, and this is what happens?"

When Dylan had said he'd had a long day, he hadn't been kidding.

Beka looked at her mother, currently in the capable hands of Trance. The Valentines definitely needed to have a sit-down, but it would have to wait. *I've had to wait a whole lifetime, what's a few extra minutes?* "Rommie, find Dylan and tell him to stay put. We need to have a talk."

Rommie nodded and waited for Beka to catch up to her; she was already pointed for Dylan's twenty. Something strange was happening, and while she didn't know what it was yet, she did know when it started: as soon as Magdalena Valentine had jumped into Alpha Centauri.

ELEVEN

Human beings, while for the most part intelligent, labor under two strangely irrational beliefs. One is that if they do everything right, they will live forever. The other is that their mothers love them.

—AKFAK YUXHEL, *SENTIENT SPECIES OF THE MILKY WAY GALAXY,* CY 8742

Any suspicions Rasputin had when he learned of Parchman's sudden departure quickly turned into full-fledged conspiracy theories the moment he realized Seamus Harper was gone too. Disembarked without permission, his intelligence told him, taking the remaining Human Interplanetary Alliance delegates with him.

Rasputin's already foul mood darkened another notch. Forget simply losing the slave worlds; if the Knights of Genetic Purity combined forces with (and provided advanced weaponry to) the rebels, there was the potential for losing the entire Drago-Kazov regiment stationed at Alpha Centauri. And if that stunted "hero of Bunker

Hill" became the HIA standard-bearer—well, Rasputin didn't like the way the pieces were playing out on this board, not one bit.

And here stood Captain Dylan Hunt, blithely confirming the information, as unconcerned about Harper's desertion as if his crew regularly wandered off to all corners of the universe at whim. Rasputin brought his fist down in the middle of the Go board, sending pebbles spraying across the floor and Dylan.

"This is pathetic," said Rasputin. "You have zero control over this cast of misfits you call a crew." Rasputin knew there was still a chance the High Guard fossil was motivating all these events . . . but his instincts told him he wasn't. Hunt had that touchy-feely spinelessness so common to peacemongers. He couldn't imagine the man doing anything that might jeopardize his image as a moral leader.

"You call this statesmanship? You've allowed this Genite, the murderer of my pilots, to skip off into the waiting arms of the insurgents."

Rasputin's mind quickly weighed options. Truth be told, he quite enjoyed it when his carefully laid plans fell apart; there were few things more intellectually stimulating than relying on sheer wit and improvisation. He looked at Dylan. *Time*, thought Rasputin, *for a little social engineering*.

"This is your fault, you know." Rasputin frowned. "You brought the HIA and the Genites together in the first place. For all your fine intentions, you've managed to turn a simple negotiation into a full-fledged war."

Dylan was tempted to mention that Rasputin had already admitted to negotiating in bad faith from the get-go, but he didn't see what that would gain him. The fact that Rasputin had announced it in the first place was, to Dylan, a clear sign of the Nietzschean's rabid arrogance. As Dylan saw it, Rasputin's biggest weakness was that he was too enamored with the genius of his own machinations to keep them secret for long. And Rasputin's failing was Dylan's edge. He waited for the Nietzschean to continue.

"That girl never would have died if it wasn't for you," said Rasputin. "All because you made the insane mistake of actually trusting the Genite. Her blood is on your hands as much as it's on mine. And you'll have the blood of my soldiers on your hands as well."

Dylan looked mildly at Rasputin. "Why should I care about your soldiers, Admiral?"

"Because you just introduced a genocidal maniac to a willing army numbering in the hundreds of thousands." Rasputin's nictitating membrane flickered. "Do you really want to go down in history as the man responsible for the next Holocaust?"

This is the stuff that nightmares are made of: the Magog descended on Brandenburg Tor in CY 9766, and they scoured it clean of all sentient life. The Magog aren't neat eaters. The inhabitants died limb by torn limb, intestine by eviscerated intestine . . . three billion times over. If Dylan Hunt had been prone to insomnia, Brandenburg Tor would be the image that haunted his sleep. So you can't blame the man if, when he first met Rev Bem, he'd had his doubts. *Am I friend? Am I foe? Am I food?* Dylan soon discovered that Rev Bem was a being he could trust implicitly, which is something he couldn't always say for the rest of Beka's crew—Beka included.

Suffice to say that if Rev had lost his life to Rasputin's proxy grenade attack, the Nietzschean admiral would no longer be in possession of a pulse. Reverend Behemiel Far Traveler was smart, he was loyal, he was (when it was needed) fierce. Dylan was damn glad he was on his side, and not wreaking havoc as an armor-clad Magog chieftain. Of course, that was about as likely as his joining the Genites. . . .

Dylan thought about all this as he walked silently alongside Rev Bem toward the Observation Deck. Rev Bem waited patiently for him to speak. Finally, Dylan smiled. "You may be wondering why I called you all here today," he joked. Rev grinned back at him, then quickly stopped when he saw the effect his display of flesh-rending teeth was having on Dylan.

Oh, dear, guessed Rev. *He's thinking about Brandenburg Tor again.*

Dylan snapped out of it. "I was surprised that Lord Parchman was so quick to pick up his ball and go home."

Rev looked at Dylan quizzically. "He had a ball?"

"Never mind. You were the last person to talk to him, weren't you?"

Rev played innocent. "Was I?"

This was no time for humility; Dylan decided to cut to the chase. "He's a Nietzschean, isn't he?" It wasn't really a question. It was a statement. "That's what you two talked about."

Dylan half expected Rev to deny it, to pretend that he had forgotten who it was they were even discussing. But Rev simply lowered his eyes. He should have realized Dylan would guess. "I hoped I might be able to help him."

Dylan wasn't surprised; if anything, he was proud of his ad hoc spiritual advisor, both for intuiting the man's secret . . . and for keeping it. His own suspicions had been building since Parchman's fight with Tyr. The Genite fought too well, and healed too quickly, to be only human. While Parchman was unconscious, Dylan peered under his goggles. Parchman instantly jerked awake, and Dylan caught the rapid flash of a third eyelid. He must have had his bone blades surgically removed. It's been done, but usually only in cases of deep-cover espionage—and Dylan would have bet *Andromeda*'s starboard milk cupboard that this was no mole. This was a man who hated Nietzscheans with every fiber of his being.

"Mind if I ask how you knew?" said Dylan.

Rev matter-of-factly described how his professional curiosity (as he called it) had been aroused when Parchman refused treatment, and didn't want anyone handling his blood. From there, a simple—albeit surreptitious—check of his DNA had revealed everything.

Dylan marveled at Rev Bem. So unassuming, yet so incredibly effective. He'd managed the one trick that Dylan couldn't pull off.

"I didn't want to have to use the information against him," said Rev. "But he was being difficult. Ultimately, I felt it was more important that he disappear from the picture. I can't guarantee what he will do next—but at least he will be doing it from a distance."

Dylan hadn't been able to muster the sympathy for the human supremacist that Rev Bem had. Whenever he tried to look at things from Parchman's point of view, all he could see was bigotry and narrow-mindedness. Even when the self-styled Knight of Genetic Purity was complimenting Dylan, he had to spoil it with some poorly timed blather about pure humans. He didn't approve of Dylan's racial leniency, he said, but he was gratified to at least be dealing with a "natural man." Then he threw in some rhetoric about sanitizing the cosmos.

So when Dylan bid the Genite farewell, he made a point of adding, as a parting gesture: "For the record, my mother was a Heavy Worlder, genetically engineered for high-gravity environments. In case you can't do the math—that makes me half a mutant." Dylan enjoyed the expression on the Genite's face just as he clicked off the screen.

Dylan clapped Rev on the shoulder. "Remind me not to try to keep any secrets from you."

"Your secrets are safe with me, Dylan. Always," said Rev seriously.

Dylan knew that. But it still felt good to hear it. "How's Rasputin's slave doing? Chutak."

"Peacefully sedated," said Rev. "It will take a few days for the nanobots to repair all of the injuries, but he should be fine." Then, as if reading Dylan's mind, Rev added, "There was nothing you could have done to prevent this, my friend. Dwelling on ways you might have been able to save Arca serves no one. We simply can't foresee everything. Sometimes, all we can do is accept the Divine's plan."

"I just hope the Divine knows what it's doing," said Dylan grimly. Well, if there was nothing he could do anymore to help Arca, perhaps he could atone somewhat by cushioning Chutak from Rasputin's retribution. Failure wasn't exactly an approved option for Nietzschean suicide bombers.

"If the admiral asks, tell him Chutak's injuries are too severe and we're not releasing him until he's better. Maybe Rasputin will forget all about him. He's just a slave, right?"

Dylan and Rev turned to the sound of a tentative banging at the entryway. "Knock, knock," said Beka. She stood at the door to Obs, hands clasped behind her back. "Is this a private party?"

"Not at all," said Rev.

Beka walked in, nervously chewing on a nail. She addressed the captain, but kept glancing at Rev Bem for moral support. "So, look. Tyr filled me in on what all I missed. I wanted to make sure you weren't freaking out or anything."

Dylan appreciated her concern, although at this point, all the concern in the world wasn't going to help his position. "I've gone beyond the pale of merely freaking out. They don't have a name yet for where I'm at."

"That bad, huh?"

"A war between the Drago-Kazov and the Human Interplanetary Alliance is inevitable, I think. And I think that's my fault. I should never have let Nyain Parchman on the ship with Rasputin here. Hell, I shouldn't have let Rasputin on the ship in the first place, and I damn sure shouldn't have let either of them out of my sight once they were here. It's one very large, very hot coal—and I'm raking myself all over it."

Beka, never very good at finding the rights words, tried to find the right words. "My dad used to say: 'Run first, talk second, fight last.'

But then, Ignatius was kind of a coward. You always talk first, and I like that about you. But when the talking's all over . . . sometimes, peace isn't the answer.

"Anyway, for what it's worth, I'm . . . uh, you know . . ." Her mouth was working, but the words weren't coming out. Pronouncing the phrase "I'm sorry" was giving her as much trouble as the name of the Vedran city Shthoxxos Arghtoxyth.

Dylan smiled. As apologies went, this was actually one of Beka's more successful. "I'm sorry, too, Beka. I forget you're not a real officer. But if you're going to be a part of this crew, you have to follow the rules. You're acting X.O. on this ship, and I rely on you."

Uh-oh. Here it comes, Beka groaned.

"As well as trust you, and depend on you." Dylan looked at both Beka and Rev warmly. "Believe it or not, the two of you are my primary voices of reason. I need you both."

Beka didn't know whether to take Dylan's compliment, or punch him. Even if he was letting her off the hook a lot more lightly than she expected. "Thanks?" she offered tentatively.

Beka looked so uncomfortable standing there, waiting for a chastisement that never came—quite unsure how to respond to unconditional support—that Rev felt the need to rescue her. "Tell us, Beka," he said, "what's it like to reconnect with your mother after all these years?"

Beka shot him a look of gratitude. "Well, she's definitely a Valentine. She's as smart as I am, and as weaselly as Rafe." And, Beka thought, just as full of bluster and energy as Ignatius ever was. What a clash of the titans that must have been! That they were together at all must have had something to do with mutually assured destruction.

"You know what she did when we first showed up? She ran for the hills. No 'Hey, kids, how ya doing,' just a face full of thruster exhaust. We've been chasing her ever since. But . . ." Beka finished the thought in her head. *But everything about Magdalena is wrapped up with the Vedran Runes. Same with Rafe. Hell—me, too, for that matter.* She shrugged. "You know. It's all weird and messy and emotional."

"I take it you haven't asked her why she left you and your brother," said Dylan.

"There's a lot we haven't talked about yet. What am I saying? We haven't talked about squat!" Beka shook her fists in frustration. "Look at her. She's impossible." Beka always thought mothers would have the decency not to look better than their daughters. And they shouldn't make goo-goo eyes at the captain, and certainly not lollop all over big brawny Nietzscheans named Tyr. . . .

Dylan chuckled. "Well, it sounds like one big happy family. An eccentric mom and a fly-by-night brother."

Beka bristled. For some reason, she didn't like Dylan talking about her brother that way, never mind that she had just described him as "weaselly" moments before. "There's more to Rafe than you know," said Beka. "He's . . . brave. And he's a really good pilot." Plus, she realized, he was the only other person who shared her curse: the awesome burden of being born a Valentine.

"I'm sorry, but did I just hear Beka Valentine defend her brother?" An Andromeda hologram winked into existence.

"You were listening in on our conversation?" asked Dylan.

The hologram rolled her virtual eyes. "I wasn't eavesdropping. You ordered me to start keeping close tabs on everyone on the ship; I don't recall that you three were exempt."

Dylan was used to Andromeda's machine logic, so he didn't take it personally. But as a High Guard lieutenant herself, Rommie should probably learn to couch her criticisms of superior officers a little more tactfully. Dylan said mildly, "With both Lord Parchman and the HIA delegation gone, I think it's safe to confine your scrutiny to Rasputin and his men." *And the Valentines*, he added subvocally . Just in case.

Rommie made the appropriate adjustments, noting that the admiral was currently admiring his reflection in the glazed surface of a Than vase.

"And to what do we owe the honor?" said Dylan.

"I thought you should know. My sensor array has been picking up a series of aberrations," said Andromeda. All eyes turned to the hologram. This was not good news.

Dylan asked, "What are you seeing?"

The hologram enumerated her observations, and Dylan's face darkened at each entry to the list. Increased flare activity on Alpha Centauri's three suns. Changes in the magnetic field around Natal. Gravity fluctuations surrounding a locus between the ship and the planet. Andromeda voiced Dylan's concern: "It has all the characteristics of a singularity."

As a scientist, Rev Bem was incredulous. "A black hole? In the middle of a star system? How is that possible?"

"Technically, it isn't," said Andromeda. "And there's a chance that these anomalies are just that—anomalies. But I've pinpointed the exact time the first signs of the phenomenon began, and they started the moment the *Maru* and the *Hypatia* entered Centauri space."

Dylan, Rev, and Andromeda all looked at Beka. "Don't look at me!" cried Beka.

"Call Harper in for a tech consult. And keep me posted," instructed Dylan.

Andromeda stood there and said nothing. Dylan couldn't tell if she was making a sensor sweep of the decks, or if she was merely pausing for dramatic effect. Finally, she answered: "Harper still hasn't reported back."

Dylan clenched his jaw. First Beka, then Harper . . . and now it looked like he was losing control over gravity. What next? "And the rest of the Valentines? Any particular mischief I should know about?"

Andromeda checked internally. "Magdalena and Rafe are with Tyr and Trance. They're enjoying the sights and sounds of the officers' mess." Andromeda wasn't being facetious; she truly believed the sights and sounds of the officers' mess were worth exploring. Dylan didn't have the energy right now to contradict her.

"Keep me posted. Reports every half hour on the half hour."

With a nod, the hologram winked out.

"It could be nothing," Beka said optimistically.

Dylan looked from her to Rev. "I hope it is nothing. With what we've been through already, we deserve a false alarm."

Rev didn't think Dylan was going to get his wish. Neither, for that matter, did Dylan. "Any more bad news before I go beard the Dragon in his den?"

Hesitantly, Rev raised a paw. "There is one thing, since you're both here."

"Magdalena's counterfeit Wayist medallion?" offered Beka lightly.

"No, although that is charming. Actually, I've been concerned about Trance."

Dylan wasn't expecting that. "Concerned, why?"

"I don't know exactly. But it was because of her that you were able to leave the *Andromeda*, Beka. And she was the reason I wasn't with Lord Parchman when the grenade exploded. It seems as if her little, ah, intercessions are getting more frequent, and I can't shake the feeling that these events are leading up to something."

Rev didn't dare mention his biggest cause for suspicion—seeing Trance with the mysterious object in hydroponics. But he wanted to gather more information before he brought it to anyone else's attention.

Dylan, like everyone on the *Andromeda*, was aware of Trance's cryptic nature. He had only to think back to her "goof up" that brought them to Hephaistos in time to change the course of history . . . or her "lucky guess" that found him on the prison planet Helios Nine . . . or her uncanny sense of direction in the labyrinths of Mobius. But, like the rest of the crew, he had come to accept it as a part of who Trance was. Beka always said that some people have perfect pitch, and some people have perfect luck. Trance was Beka's good luck charm. Always had been.

But Dylan also knew that if something was bothering Rev, it should bother him, too. Could this have anything to do with *Andromeda*'s bizarre sensor readings? Dylan had a bad feeling he was going to find out the hard way.

TWELVE

Anyone who says "living well is the best revenge" has just never had a really good revenge.

—TESTIMONY OF BREXOS GERENTEX, AFC 302

Dylan heard Rasputin long before he saw him; the Nietzschean was preceded by a colorful parade of threats and profanities. The admiral and his two guards stormed onto Command Deck, a flurry of baleful glares and clanking boot buckles. Dylan and Rommie looked up from the communications consoles as they stomped in.

"Captain Hunt, my second in command informs me that a battle group assembled in the shadow of Natal's moon is vectoring for my flagship!"

"Yes, we just began picking up the transmissions," said Dylan. "These are the first real-time images." Indeed, popping up on the Command main viewscreen at that moment were visuals of the fleet en route to the Drago-Kazov battle cruiser, an advancing shield of sails some few hundred kilometers long in all directions.

Rasputin fumed. *And Nietzsche only knows how many Genite stealth fighters there are, invisible to* Andromeda*'s sensors.*

"On Drago's bones, I swear this is your fault," shouted Rasputin, closing in on Dylan. His guards circled around and took up positions on either side of the captain. Rommie tensed, ready to concentrate the entire ship's artificial gravity field underneath Rasputin's feet, and raised an eyebrow.

"Shall I squash him?" she asked subvocally. Dylan declined her offer with an almost imperceptible shake of his head. Things were actually playing out just fine.

Rasputin looked around Command. "Isn't this where we were standing yesterday? And wasn't I about to tear your head off its stem?" He turned his feline pupils on Dylan. "You *owe* me. And you can start by protecting my flagship from those genocidal Knights of Revisionist History."

Dylan looked pensive for a few seconds, then suggested, "I suppose I should bring the *Andromeda Ascendant* in to cover your flank. . . ."

Rasputin smiled. He knew the captain's Boy Scout tendencies would work in his favor. Morality was a crippling human weakness.

"Assuming you were a member of the New Systems Commonwealth, of course," Dylan continued.

Rasputin burst out laughing. "Are you kidding?"

"Do I look like I'm kidding?" asked Dylan. In truth, he did not. The indecisiveness Rasputin had sensed was entirely gone. Instead, Dylan stood ramrod-straight and stared the Nietzschean down. "Which means, of course, granting independence to Alpha Centauri. Slave worlds are forbidden by Commonwealth Charter, no matter how you label them."

Rasputin was speechless. He finally sputtered, "And what in the name of the Great Progenitor would make me do such a fool thing?"

"Well, the way I see it, you don't have much choice—unless you can outgun the Genites, which I don't think you can. You lose a fire-fight, and there go both your system and your troops. This way, at least a big chunk of the Dragan Navy doesn't get vaporized."

Rasputin tested the points of his incisors with the tip of his tongue, studying the board. Wait. This could work. He could sign Dylan's treaty. And since this pipe dream of a new Commonwealth was no stronger than the flexi its charter was printed on, Rasputin didn't see how anyone could hold him to it. As Rasputin now viewed it, the game would play out like this: with *Andromeda*'s help, the Genites would be destroyed, Rasputin would make a big show of withdrawing from the system, and then, when his fleet returned, he'd come back to Alpha Centauri and reclaim it. This Glorious Heritage antique was a formidable asset, but hardly a match for the Drago-Kazov armada.

Rasputin hemmed and hawed for a moment, then relented. "You drive a hard bargain, Captain, but I don't have any choice. Help me rebuff the Genite attack, and I will sign your charter."

"And cede control of Alpha Centauri."

"Yes, yes, cede control of Alpha Centauri. And you can be sure I'm going to hold you to your side of the agreement." *Although I won't hold to mine.*

A flexi appeared in Dylan's hands as if out of thin air. He gave the sheet to Rasputin, who activated the screen and skimmed the data. It bore the seal of the Systems Commonwealth, and announced that on behalf of Charter Member the Drago-Kazov Pride, Admiral Rasputin Genovese hereby and in good faith cedes the system of Alpha Centauri, blah, blah, blah. Dylan handed him an authentica-tor pen that included a DNA stamp so the signature could be verified. Rasputin scrolled through the contents, then signed on the flashing line.

Rasputin handed back the flexi and pointed to the viewscreen. "Now, if you don't mind, please make yourself useful."

The corners of Dylan's lips turned up briefly. "My pleasure. Rommie, did you find Master Harper?"

"As a matter of fact, I did, Captain."

"Put him through, will you?"

Those old solar sails were only equipped with voice communication, but there was no mistaking Harper's snide tone. "Hero of Humanity Seamus Z. Harper, reporting for duty," the speaker squawked. "Yo, Dylan, is that a force lance in your pocket, or are you just happy to see me?"

Command Deck was silent. Rommie's eyes rolled; Rasputin's bulged. No one laughed. "Uh, anyone there? This is the *Andromeda*, isn't it?"

"I'm afraid so," responded *Andromeda*'s AI image.

"Report, Mr. Harper," said Dylan.

"Well, we got all our sailboats in a row, and the HIA is launching a systemwide attack. Everyone and their mom's grabbing an oar. Or a gun. Between you and me, Boss, that Dragan flagship is going *down*."

Dylan wished he could record the look on Rasputin's face, it was that good. Rasputin gasped, "You knew about this all along."

"Whoa, bozo on deck," said Harper. "I didn't hear him standing there."

Rasputin leaned in close to Dylan. "I don't know what game you're playing, but we have a deal." Rasputin knew Dylan *had* to live up to his end of the bargain. He was a man of his word.

"That's right," said Dylan. "I'm sworn to protect you from a Genite attack." He kept his eyes trained on Rasputin. "Harper, any Genites out there?"

"Genites? Nope. Haven't seen a one of them. Nobody here but us kludges."

Rasputin looked at Dylan, puzzled. "I don't understand."

"If you wanted my help fighting the HIA, you should have asked for it. Although I'm not sure I would have agreed. I have this thing about underdogs; must be the Boy Scout in me."

Rasputin was stunned. Dylan had planned this! The mealy-mouthed High Guard had been ahead of him at every step. Rasputin's face glowed lobster red. "You don't really think you can make me adhere to that document, do you?" he seethed, barely able to control his voice.

Dylan controlled his own voice just fine. "As I see it, you have two choices. One, you make good on this agreement. Take your lumps. Tell everyone you got beat—tell them you were outnumbered, tell them Alpha Centauri is no longer economically viable as a slave colony. Tell them whatever you want. In the end, maybe you get demoted.

"Alternative two, I send a copy of this signed, DNA-stamped agreement to the Drago-Kazov leadership council. Giving away the system *and* losing your flagship . . . that's going to look real bad on your résumé. Won't do much for your life span, either, if I know the Dragans."

Rasputin wished he had torn out Dylan's throat when he had the chance. Dylan was, in essence, blackmailing him to be honorable. The gall! But still—the wheels in Rasputin's brain were already turning. There had to be a way to save both his rank and his reputation.

"If I ever see you again, I'll kill you," he said flatly. Dylan believed it to be the most sincere sentence he had heard Rasputin Genovese utter to date. Then the admiral turned on his heels and, in a flap of coattails, marched out of Command, his guards in tow. *Our forces were absolutely outnumbered and woefully undersupplied,* he rehearsed, already preparing the testimony he'd give to the Dragan High Command. It occurred to him that the Genites might prove useful after all. Even if they didn't take part in the attack, he could claim they did. For that to work, of course, he'd have to destroy some of his own installations. *Call it collateral damage*, he rationalized. *And it will support the claim of being undermanned. . . .*

Rasputin walked faster. He had a lot of work to do.

Beka caught up with the sightseeing caravan in hydroponics. The party consisted of tour guide Trance and her captive tourists, Rafe and Magdalena. Bringing up the rear was Tyr Anasazi, either unwilling or unable to escape Magdalena's attentions. Trance busily pointed at and explained the workings of everything in sight . . . very quickly, lest anyone get a word in edgewise. A word like, "I have to go to the head," for instance.

Trance ushered Magdalena and Rafe into the rose garden. Tyr managed to sneak away for a brief reprieve and remained outside, holding up the wall outside of the garden entryway. He idly flexed a tricep and, admiring it, had to agree with Magdalena: they were impressive.

"Enjoying yourself?" asked Beka, hoping to startle Tyr but knowing his acute Nietzschean hearing would have already sensed her step on the hydroponics floor. The shelf of Sintii cactus had since been restored, although not the cacti themselves. Not that Beka would have cared either way. She rarely visited hydroponics; plants and trees fell into the general mudfoot category of things-that-don't-go-fast-and-aren't-worth-much.

"Not really," said Tyr, yawning. Beka could tell he was lying. She decided that Tyr had spent quite enough time with Magdalena.

Beka passed through the arched entrance of the rose garden. The sightseers were at the far end of the room. Rafe sat on the edge of the hydroponics vat that had previously hosted the water rose bed, while Magdalena reclined attractively on an adjacent bench. Trance animatedly regaled them with the tale of the exploding F-lance, complete with mimed reenactment.

"And then Tyr had me stuffed under one of his arms when the F-lance started making this really weird sizzling sound, and it totally hurt my ears, and Tyr was totally hurting my neck. . . ." Trance put herself in a headlock and stuck out her tongue in mock pain. She was so engrossed in her story that she didn't hear Beka coming up behind her.

"And then Tyr pulled me onto the ground and there was this flash!" said Trance, pausing when Beka placed a hand on her shoulder.

"I can take it from here," said Beka.

"Oh, hi, Beka," said Trance. She looked puzzled. "But you weren't there. How do you know what happened?"

"What I mean," said Beka, "is that Magdalena, Rafe, and I need to talk."

Trance nodded. "Sure. I don't mind if you talk."

"Alone," underscored Beka.

Trance's face lit up. Happy families made her feel squishy all over. She squeezed Beka's hand and whispered, "I understand." Trance looked at Magdalena and Rafe and gave them a knowing wink. "Let me know as soon as you're done," said Trance, who began backing out of the garden. "We still have to see the plumbing on Decks One through Eight!"

"Wouldn't want to miss that," said Rafe. Then he carefully added, "I'm kidding." The purple girl seemed to take things so very literally.

Trance gathered up her tail and was gone. Beka turned to Magdalena apologetically. "Trance can be a bit overenthusiastic at times."

Magdalena smiled. "So I noticed. She's something, though. I've never seen anything like her, although I think I read about a similar species in one of the older mythologies."

"And of all the pilots in the universe, she meets up with good ol' Beka," said Rafe. "Plus, look where they end up." Rafe waved at the rose garden. "A classy ship, lots of travel, important jobs. A bit too regimented and by-the-book for my tastes, but still . . ."

"Yes, you've done very well, Rebecca," said Magdalena. She was glad to see that at least one of her children had managed to put the Valentine wanderer spirit in check. She admired Beka: her daughter possessed both a sense of adventure and a sense of responsibility. At least, that's how it seemed to her. She, of course, hadn't been there when Beka and Rafe made their unexcused exit from the *Andromeda*.

For a moment, Beka glowed in this unfamiliar praise from her mother. Then, abruptly, it put her on the defensive. People just didn't talk that nicely, especially people related to her, and she was getting really tired of trying to guess whether anything her kinfolk said was sincere or not. Beka braced herself. She came here for the Big Talk, and they were going to have it whether Magdalena liked it or not.

Rafe, Beka noted, was paying rapt attention to the lone water rose floating in the vat, removing himself from the conversation. *I always have to do the hard stuff myself*, groaned Beka. She sat down next to Magdalena and took her mother's hand. Didn't say anything for a long breath and then, finally, started with, "Look, there's something we need to get out of the way.

"Yes, I want to know why you up and left us and yes, I want to yell and hug you and make you tell me a hundred stories about my father. But not now. Now, we need to talk about the En . . . about the Vedran Runes."

Beka wasn't sure why she couldn't just say "the Engine of Creation." Did she really distrust this mother of hers that much? *Yeah, I guess I do*, she sighed.

Beka waited for a response, got none but the watery burbling of the hydroponic's vat. Magdalena looked down, idly running her fingers along the head of her cane. She knew this had to come up sooner or later; she was just hoping for later. Magdalena nodded slowly. "I'm glad we're having this conversation, finally."

Beka waited, but Magdalena apparently wasn't going to continue. "Mom," she tried again, and stopped. The word "mom" still felt too strange. "Magdalena, we know you've got at least three of the pieces. I read the *Avrexat Vingareth Ot*, and we think you might have gotten one more. The only reason I bring this up is . . ." Beka suddenly felt silly. Technically, what business of hers was it whether Magdalena possessed pieces of the Runes or not?

Magdalena turned her thickly lashed eyes on Beka. She knew why the girl had brought it up, even if Beka didn't. Magdalena knew better than anyone that the Runes weren't something you could ignore. They got under your skin and colored your every action.

"The reason is, you have no choice," said Magdalena. She looked at this strong, intelligent woman: her daughter. She was overwhelmed with affection—for about a nanosecond. Then she was overtaken by a stronger, more selfish impulse. She wanted the Vedran artifact for herself. After all, she'd devoted her life to getting it. Her every fiber was lit up with a base desire to assemble all the pieces.

And she had a strong feeling that Beka and Rafe could help her do that.

"The Runes have affected your life more than you know. You could say I left your father for them. They're the reason I've spent most of my life floating from one galaxy to the next, getting myself into and out of danger so often that I can hardly tell which is which anymore. It's the reason everyone I've ever trusted or called a friend is either dead or left behind.

"I'm not complaining. I made my bed, and I willingly lie in it." *I just never knew it would be a bed of nails*, thought Magdalena.

"It's almost over, I think. I'm close. Don't ask me how I know, because I can't explain it. But the pieces seem to be gaining momentum somehow. And I think . . . that a piece of the Vedran Runes is on this ship."

Beka clenched. *How did she know?* There was a piece of the Runes on the *Andromeda.* Her piece. But there was no way Magdalena could have known that. *Unless . . .* She looked at Rafe, who was still pretending to be engrossed in the water rose. Did he know? Could he have told her?

Rafe stared at the translucent flower. He didn't want to say anything until he could calculate how things were going to play out. Magdalena had it wrong, there was more than one piece of the Runes on the *Andromeda.* There were two: Beka's, and his. And he wasn't about to show his hand until Beka showed hers, no matter how much he was coming to like his little sister.

Rafe caressed one of the buds on the flower but squeezed too hard and popped it, getting slimy goo on his fingers. Suppressing his first instinct to wipe the stuff off on his shirt, he dipped his fingers in the water instead. As he wiggled his fingers clean, the gelatinous insides of the petal formed a soapy slick on the pond's surface, a miniature shimmering rainbow. Rafe looked at the colors prism in the light, and then he noticed something odd on the bottom of the vat, reflecting back the dancing hues. He put his hand in the water and ran it along the bottom of the vat. When he waved it beneath the approximate underside of the rose, the light rippled across the back of his hand.

At that point, things got a bit weird.

His curiosity piqued, Rafe grasped the flower's fragile stem and lifted the rose from the pool. Beka's and Magdalena's attention turned to the odd sight of Rafe peering into the flower's bundle of saclike roots. He reached into the dripping root ball and gently inserted his hand. Something fell out and landed with a crack on the edge of the vat. The noise sent goose bumps racing across his skin. The object bounced onto the floor and rolled straight toward Magdalena, coming to rest against her foot. It was a globe, small enough to fit easily in the palm of a hand. It gave off a kaleidoscopic light, and in fact seemed carved out of the very light itself.

Magdalena knew instantly what it was, just as she had known to find it on the *Andromeda*. So did Beka and Rafe. Anyone who searched for the Vedran Runes had heard of the Triangulum Eye. It was the mythical centerpiece of the mythical artifact, and it was sitting right in front of them.

Magdalena's foot, where the orb was touching, began to feel warm. She watched the halo of light play along the legs of her dress. Her throat felt dry, she fidgeted with her cane—it all felt disconnected, as if she were watching herself from a great distance. From underneath the collection baubles Magdalena wore around her neck, she removed a large black pouch. She opened it, breaking the protective seal, and began to place its contents on the bench.

Beka's breath caught in her throat. The objects were unlike anything she had ever seen. Intricate, unworldly . . . lit from within not so much with luminescence but with sheer *power*. There was no doubt about it: these were all fragments of the Vedran Runes. As Magdalena removed each item, she connected it to the one before it. Beka counted: four pieces. Four pieces of the Engine of Creation. But four out of . . . how many?

The partially completed Runes resembled a hollow nest, the pieces curving around an open concave space. Magdalena bent over and picked up the Eye. The blood roared in her ears. Or was that sound coming from the orb? She couldn't tell. She gently slid the orb into the cavity. As the Eye clicked home, the artifact sent out an invisible shock wave, a shudder they all felt.

A sudden realization struck Magdalena with such force that she reeled with the sheer obviousness of it all. The abrupt and timely reappearance of her children was no coincidence. She was no longer pursuing the Vedran Runes; the Runes were pursuing her.

Magdalena held out her hand to Rafe. "No games, Raphael," she said. "Give it here."

Rafe could sense the power rolling off of the artifact. His brain was like a small raft, tossed and twirled with each successive swell. If he had any self will at this point, it was relegated to some small and insignificant corner of his mind. With one hand still holding the soggy water rose, he obediently placed the other into the collar of his shirt and from a hand-stitched pocket withdrew a wide black bracelet. It felt uncomfortably alive in his hands. He handed it to Magdalena.

From the moment the Eye fell into place to the instant Rafe handed Magdalena the black circlet, only about thirty seconds could have elapsed. To Beka it seemed to take hours, maybe days. Everything was going in slow motion. It was as if Beka's whole being was focused on the construct in Magdalena's lap. No room to wonder when and how Rafe had gotten hold of the Wixan Ring, or even why he hadn't said anything about it. Or, for that matter, what the Triangulum Eye was doing in the hydroponics rose garden in the first place.

Magdalena dropped Rafe's piece over the orb and the ring fell snugly into place, completely covering the globe. There was another shock wave, this one more powerful than the first. Beka felt her body bend slightly as it passed through her, like the cone of an old-fashioned audio speaker. She thought perhaps she was making a sound. *Ka-shummm.* . . .

Beka became aware that Magdalena was looking at her. She couldn't recall if this had been going on for a few seconds, or for a millennium. Furthermore, she didn't know how long it took exactly for her to respond. It was an answer to a question Magdalena didn't have to voice; Beka knew what was coming. "Now yours," is what Magdalena would have said.

Beka's response to the question was this: she drew her sidearm.

Rafe steeled himself, but Magdalena just sat there and waited. Instead of shooting, Beka deftly twisted the grip of the Gauss pistol and a cube unlatched itself from the stock. It was called the Song of Silence, and it was her piece of the Engine of Creation, a prize she had tracked across half the universe. She handed it to Magdalena.

The cube pulsated in Magdalena's hand. She pushed it into the underside of the nest. Synapses fired behind her eyes and her breath went shallow as she experienced a sudden sensation of acceleration. The Song settled into its slot, and Magdalena examined the finished product. *No, not finished.* There was still one missing piece. The last piece, the vital piece. And it was nearby, she was sure of it. She tried to concentrate, but there was a sandstorm of white noise in her brain. She wanted to say something to Beka, to explain what she was doing, and why she was doing it. She had only just opened her mouth when the noise in her brain crested and her body went into convulsions.

THIRTEEN

Pray with two hands, but dig with six.

—THAN-THRE-KULL PROVERB

Harper didn't like the Human Interplanetary Alliance's solar sails when he first saw them. Gigantic octagons made of aluminized Mylar film that encircled a rickety cylinder with a bubble of a cockpit at one end—they looked flimsy, unspaceworthy, like an interstellar hang glider with elephantiasis. His opinion hadn't changed since. The only difference was that now he was piloting one.

In principle, of course, the engineer was all for solar sails. They're a virtually fuel-less method of scooting around space, great for leisurely cargo hauls across a star system. The key word here is "leisurely." Starsails accumulate momentum at eleven-point-three kilometers an hour. While their top speed can reach into thousands, even hundreds of thousands of kilometers per, it takes, oh, about half a decade to get from zero to sixty. It was the kind of technology even a neo-Luddite Restorian could be proud of.

However, a raid on a Nietzschean flagship is far from leisurely. It's a dangerous task in a Slipfighter, let alone in one of the far less maneuverable solar sails. To try to make up for the sails' lack of get-up-and-go, the insurgents had incorporated a dubious-looking rocket engine into the design. *Great. Not only am I steering a hang glider the size of a football field, but I'm doing it with my ass parked on a metric ton of napalm.* And Harper didn't even have the worst of it. Every other star sailor in the fleet was chest-deep in a pile of jury-rigged plasma bombs, waiting to crack the seal on their cockpit and then launch them at the Nietzschean battle cruiser. Talk about your desperate measures. One stray spark and it's tuck your head between your knees, kiss the universe good-bye.

But if the HIA wanted an air force, the sails were going to have to do. When the Dragan slavelords first moved into Alpha Centauri, they stole—"repurposed," they called it—every spaceworthy vessel in the system. Except, that is, for solar sails, which they deemed too primitive to even bother destroying. They were cheap, they were plentiful . . . and as far as Harper was concerned, they were two degrees shy of useless. Eager as he was to drop-kick some Dragans, Harper would have much preferred to do it in something with an antiproton drive, or at least an ignition relay.

Such were the thoughts of Seamus Zelazny Harper as he got on the primitive two-way, a souped-up long-range walkie-talkie, and hailed HIA leader Pac Peterson. "My work here is done. The boss is calling me back home."

After a moment's time lag (*What do they make these with, waxed string?*), the box chirped in response.

"Thank you, Harper," came a tinny version of Pac's otherwise velvety tones. "But are you sure I can't convince you to join us? We could use another hero."

Much as Harper loved being called a hero, and much as he wanted to avenge Arca by carving up her weight in genetically engineered flesh, he knew he couldn't stay. After all, an order was an order—although that didn't stop a very loud (and very obnoxious) slice of his personality from arguing otherwise. *C'mon, Seamus, just stick around for the first volley.*

Harper scolded himself for even considering it. They needed him back on the ship. Anyway, Dylan had a better idea.

"It's tempting, you know it is," said Harper. "But I think I can do more for humanity in the long run on the *Andromeda.* Anyway, you guys are already halfway to booting the Dragans' booty out of Alpha Centauri altogether."

"From your lips to God's ears," said Pac. Then, with an audible smile, she added, "If you ever change your mind, you know where to find us."

Harper looked one last time at the formation of sails behind him. It was impressive . . . and useful. What the Dragans didn't know was that dogging it behind this reflective barrier were a couple more waves of sails, as well as the heavy hitters of the HIA fleet: armed courier ships, scavenged Slipcraft, and one worse-for-wear (but still dangerous) Juno fighter.

"Now be a good Harper and turn this piece of tinfoil toward the *Andromeda,*" he mumbled. *First thing, check the ship's excuse for a radar display and find out where the hell we are.* Harper glanced at a display screen, the only piece of decent equipment on the whole sail (for obvious reasons), one that closely monitored the nearby suns and their location in relation to the sail. *So far, so good,* thought Harper. Then he confronted the sail's steering mechanism. It was, believe it or not, a row of levers. Each lever controlled a gas-filled tube that when inflated or deflated altered the shape and angle of the sail.

Harper stared at the levers, and stared some more. He knew what he had to do, but he wasn't doing it. *I know what you're thinking, Seamus. Just walk away and fly this stupid thing home.* Nothing happened. *I repeat . . .* No use. His hands were acting in open defiance of his brain.

Screw it, thought Harper. *Just one run.* He'd never been very good at taking orders and figured there was no need to start now. Besides, the battle group was about to begin its attack—one little pass, and then he'd head home. He had to get at least one punch in. Okay, two. One for himself, and one for Arca.

Harper got back on the walkie-talkie. "Pac. Harper here. You know, the more I think about it, the more I realize I can't pass this opportunity up. Count me in for the first run."

The reply came a few seconds later, the two-way carrying the delayed notes of Pac's laughter. "I knew you wouldn't abandon us. Fall back and slot into the left flank."

Harper adjusted the trim of his sail and carefully applied some short bursts of thrust, careful not to apply too much force lest he damage the sail. Whether he could do something as graceful as slotting into a given location was doubtful. He figured he'd just float over in the general direction of the left flank and pray he didn't hit anyone.

The battle fleet was soon within range of the Drago-Kazov flagship. The Nietzschean cruiser welcomed them by firing off a volley from its AP guns. A number of sails engaged their rockets, breaking ahead of the main group. These were in fact decoys, remotely piloted by the HIA. Once the sails were shredded by the inevitable Dragan projectiles, their engines fired full blast and they kamikazed straight at the flagship. Pinpoint accuracy was impossible, but the

results were impressive anyway. The Dragan ship rocked with billowing explosions as the unmanned sails rammed it one after the
other.

The flagship responded by unleashing a squadron of fighters. It
was a big group, and Harper watched their approach with some trepidation; they'd be able to mow through the rows of sails without
flinching. But then, to Harper's amazement, the Dragan fighters split
up. Most of them headed off in the direction of Natal or Sisulu; only
a handful remained to deal with the sails. Apparently, the Drago-
Kazov leadership didn't think the HIA space force was much of a
challenge. Harper grinned. The humans had more tricks up their
sleeves than the Dragans knew. As the remaining dozen or so Dragan
fighters got closer to the battle group, the HIA formation split down
the middle. The slavers should arrive just in time to find the HIA's
space fighters emerging from behind the wall of sails, ready for a
serious brawl.

The HIA battle group was now close enough to fire. Harper
briskly checked the connections on his E-suit (and wished he'd
thought to do this ahead of time, as the antique looked like it could
spring a leak in a million places). He picked up the simple grenade
launcher Pac had provided for him. It was little more than a glorified
slingshot outfitted with a rudimentary target detector. He loaded it
with a handful of plasma grenades, then made sure he was securely
strapped in. *David, meet Goliath. Goliath, meet your Maker.*

Harper took a deep breath and released the latches on the cockpit,
a vestigial feature left over from the days when the sails were sometimes trimmed by hand. Most of the decoys had already been
destroyed. All around him, sail pilots were unloading their cargo of
grenades. Harper got the flagship in the shoulder launcher's sights,
and began plugging away.

Either it was Harper's imagination, or the Nietzscheans weren't
putting up a very enthusiastic fight. He'd thought this assault was

going to be a lot harder. He was already launching the last of his plasma grenades, and he hadn't even been fired on yet. Harper didn't know which of the small explosions peppering the flagships were his, but that didn't matter; it was a gratifying sight all the same.

Just as he was beginning to rest on his laurels, a well-aimed shot from one of the Dragans' point defense lasers struck a bull's eye, vaporizing the sail to Harper's immediate left. The cockpit exploded, erupting into a white fireball that engulfed the entire sail. The huge mirror blazed for one very intense, very brief moment, then disintegrated into nothing.

Harper winced, and was glad he couldn't put a face to the rebel pilot who had just been reduced to space dust. His reservations about the solar sail made a speedy encore. *Brave is one thing, but this is suicidal.* The sail's size and awful maneuverability made its pilot a sitting duck. Whoever came up with the plan of using them to attack a Dragan flagship had a screw loose. *Make that a hundred screws.*

The worst part was that a sailor had no second chances. If the engine got hit, it was game over, no question. If the sail got hit, there were two choices: make a futile attempt to steer to safety (although Harper knew the sails weren't carrying enough fuel to make it back to Natal), or head straight for the fighter on a kamikaze run. In other words—game over, take two. Harper decided that since he was out of ammo anyway, now would be a good time to make good on his promise and head back for the *Andromeda*. He fired off his last grenade, closed the cockpit, then got on the two-way and said goodbye to Pac one last time. He fired the sail's rocket and pulled away from the HIA formation.

What Harper didn't know was that Rasputin had other plans for him. The admiral, off of the *Andromeda* and en route to his flagship, gave a burst of orders to his bewildered second in command. For reasons the captain couldn't comprehend, Rasputin intended to send lone units of Dragan soldiers against entire battalions of HIA, and spread their fighter ships so thin that they were nearly ineffectual. All the while, the admiral was loudly blaming the Genites for the human attacks, even though there were no Genites visible.

Rasputin did manage to give one very specific instruction that made perfect sense. It was a mission to be carried out by a fighter pilot who was to succeed at all costs—if she didn't, the pilot shouldn't bother returning to base. The order was simple: kill Harper.

Rasputin knew he couldn't touch Dylan, but he could touch Dylan's pet engineer. And if he couldn't best the High Guard, he would at least hurt him. The Dragan pilot was told to blow every solar sail out of the sky until he blew up the one carrying Seamus Harper. She was also told to be especially watchful for any ships breaking away from the battle group and heading toward the *Andromeda*, as there was a ninety-nine percent chance that this craft would be carrying you-know-who.

It was with growing dismay that Harper watched a fast-moving blip on his radar veer off from the phalanx of Dragan fighters and head straight for him. He ran through a mental list of available defensive weapons: zip, zero, and zilch. Supposedly the sails were equipped with electronic countermeasures, but that didn't give Harper any confidence. If the ECM was as antiquated as the rest of the sail's technology, it would be useless against anything built within the last 350 years . . . give or take a century.

The one thing Harper had going for him was the sail itself. Being a mirror, it reflected surrounding space, and therefore blended in almost perfectly—unless it did something too obvious, like reflecting a sun. In an ideal world, the Dragan sensors would consist of the pilot's eye stuck to a telescope, scanning the stars for enemy ships. But even the harsher truth wasn't all that bad: the fighter's sensors would be checking for engine signatures, as sensors are wont to do. Harper's rocket spurts would be a dead giveaway, but if he cut the engine he'd be much harder to see.

Harper still didn't like his chances, and getting his butt blown off was not on top of today's To Do list. He shut the engine down and tried hailing a new frequency on his radio. "Hey, Rommie, think you can send out that Slipfighter now? I've got some company. . . ."

He waited for a response, but got only audio feedback. He tried again, and got the same result. *Okay, that was strange.* His radar was acting oddly too, showing large swaths of signal interference. To make matters worse, the ship was inexplicably losing speed and deviating off course. He worked the steering levers but they weren't responding correctly. Harper looked out at the sail. What he saw didn't inspire confidence: the sail was crumpling like a piece of used tinfoil.

Harper cast a wary eye at the temperamental radar. Its display was breaking up and the data erratic, but he could still determine the Dragan's location. The fighter was making systematic sweeps through nearby space, crisscrossing back and forth trying to find its lost prey. Harper knew that as slow as he was moving and as fast as the fighter was going, it was only a matter of time before the Nietzschean ran right through him.

Then something else grabbed Harper's attention. The good monitor, the one with the suns on display, was flashing several warning messages simultaneously. Each of the sector's proximate suns was showing an uncommon amount of sunspot activity. A mammoth sunspot, easily two hundred thousand kilometers in diameter, crossed the face of the sun closest to Harper, enormous solar prominences curling visibly along its surface.

Now it all made sense. No wonder he couldn't use the radio. Charged particles cannoning from the sunspots were causing magnetic havoc, disrupting his low-tech broadcasts. That was also what was deforming his sails. He was caught in a magnetic storm.

Okay, Seamus, don't go wetting your pants. He took stock of the situation. With his sails all but dead to him, his little ship was veering uncontrollably. He ran a few projections and was chagrined to see that his course was curving not toward the *Andromeda*, but rather toward the nearest sun. *Of course. Wouldn't want to make it easy for me or anything, would you?* he railed at no deity in particular.

Harper considered flooring the rocket and making a run for the *Andromeda*, but he knew he'd never beat the Dragan fighter in a race, especially if he couldn't steer properly. There had to be another way.

Think, Seamus. You know how to think, don't you? Just put your lobes together and . . . The answer came fully formed. If he went into a spin, centripetal force would spread and flatten the sails. Then he could steer himself home. Only one problem: he'd have to fire the rocket to initiate the maneuver, meaning the fighter would see him. *So, how do I lose the* uber?

Well, he had one idea. Unfortunately, it was being suggested by the same part of his brain that had convinced him to take part in the HIA assault. And look where that had gotten him. Harper waited for the more responsible side of his intellect to kick in with a better suggestion. But that was a waste of time; as Harper well knew, he had no responsible side.

Harper checked on the fighter one more time; its last pass was uncomfortably close. *Well,* he thought, *a crazy plan is better than no plan at all.* He fired up the rocket and kicked the sail into a spiral. The cockpit, thankfully, was rigged so that it stayed stationary while the engine spun behind it. The last thing he needed right now was a dose of motion sickness.

With a taut snap, the sail bounced open. *Excellent! Time for Phase Two,* thought Harper. He paused a second, hoping he was doing the right thing. Or, if not the right thing, then at least the *only* thing. He switched a couple of the levers, and aimed straight for the sun.

Sure enough, the fighter did a sudden about-face, reversed its trajectory, and headed straight for Harper. And, as Harper had so carefully calculated, it did it just as it rounded the far end of its elliptical pass and was the maximum number of light-minutes away.

Harper watched the solar readout. On the monitor cascaded the looping lines of the star's magnetic field, several of which arced from the largest sunspot like bows on a package. A stampede of charged particles spewed along these lines. Harper headed for the nearest loop. He knew that the high particle fluxes would make for a bumpy ride; he just hoped that it would be bumpy enough.

Harper had the rocket going full blast, and it didn't take long to reach a field line. He raised a hand to wipe the sweat off his brow, and his bulky glove whapped the bubble of his E-suit mask. *Stupid Buck Rogers space helmet!*

Harper shut off his engines and let inertia spiral him along the path of the field line toward the sun. As he entered the stream of charged particles, the turbulence quickly escalated. Harper's head slammed against the roof of the cockpit, and he tasted blood as he bit his tongue. It was like being kicked back and forth by a soccer team of rhinoceroses.

But the little ship's simple construction was Harper's saving grace. The gas-filled tubes that supported the sail gave it a flexibility that allowed it to absorb the sharper jolts. It was the fighter, Harper knew, that would be having a rough time—under these conditions, an expensive tungsten alloy frame and sensitive flight controls were a handicap. On the sail, only a handful of things could break, but the complex fighter boasted thousands of parts and systems that could fail.

There was nothing Harper could do except let himself be knocked around like a rag doll. With his radar useless in the magnetic barrage, he had no idea what was happening to the Dragan fighter. He waited as long as he could, until he thought he would be torn quite literally limb from limb, then he reached for the levers and steered himself away from the sun. As soon as the ride started to smooth out, his monitors come back on-line. The radar was fuzzy, but it picked up the fighter's signal.

"Yes!" shouted Harper. The fighter was still caught in the magnetic field, either unaware that Harper had already made an exit, or unable to do anything about it. Given the speed the fighter was traveling, Harper assumed it was the latter—nobody in their right mind would be racing at that speed into a sun unless they actually wanted to get burned to a crisp. By the looks of it, the fighter's ion drive had been knocked out of commission.

He could rest easy now; the Dragan wouldn't be giving him any more trouble. Harper gunned the engine, deciding he was going to use up every last drop of fuel to get him as close to the *Andromeda* as quickly as possible.

Harper was still congratulating himself when his going away gift from the Dragan fighter pilot arrived: an offensive missile vaporized the top half of his sail with a screaming blast. The little ship flailed out of control. Harper tried deforming the lower half of the sail, to make its shape as symmetrical as possible. It helped, but not much.

Harper cut the engine; an extended blast of the rocket would send him wildly out of control. He hated to give up on the sail, though— the ship could be piloted without it, but it would be difficult to steer. And steering would come in handy since he was aiming for a very specific target: the *Andromeda Ascendant*. Harper knew he had no choice. The tattered sail was likely to destabilize the ship, doing him more harm than good.

Harper pulled down on a steering lever and the sails (what was left of them) began to retract. He picked out a blip on the radar that he hoped was the *Andromeda* and gradually began pushing the rocket faster, all the while keeping its trajectory in check. He was still several light-minutes away and the rocket, even at full blast, would never break any speed records. Making things worse was the fact that

Harper couldn't let up his concentration for a second, having to keep a close watch at all times on his fuel level and bearing.

He repeatedly tried rousing Rommie on the walkie-talkie. The farther he got from the sun, the easier it was to find patches unaffected by magnetic interference. Finally, about two light-seconds from the *Andromeda*, the radio warbled at him. "Harper, can you hear me? Come in."

Harper cut to the chase. "Rommie, I'm running on fumes and this thing steers like a zeppelin. You're going to have to catch me."

"Say again?"

"I'm adrift in a fuel-less, sail-less dinghy. I'm heading in your general vicinity, but that's about all I can guarantee. The rest is up to you."

Harper tried carefully engaging some reverse thrust, but he had no more thrust. The fuel supply was dried up. He picked up the walkie-talkie again; at least Rommie could get a lock on his position from the signal, and if this was going to work, she was going to have to know his exact location.

"More bad news," Harper yelled into the staticky two-way. "No brakes!"

"I've got a bead on you," squawked Rommie's voice on the speaker. "Don't do anything stupid, like change your trajectory. I'll do the maneuvering from my end so that you'll make it to the aft hangar." Harper was about to make a salacious comeback when he was brought back to the genuine peril of the situation by her next comment: "Prepping for emergency landing. Medical team on alert."

There was nothing more he could do; Harper sat back and waited. He would have preferred it if Beka were behind the *Andromeda*'s controls—she could thread a needle in space. But for this kind of micro-precision, Andromeda was a good second choice.

The *Andromeda Ascendant* herself quickly came into sight, a sleek integration of gentle curves and fierce armament. Harper resisted the temptation to fiddle with the sail's angle of approach. A hundred meters in the wrong direction and he'd be bug smear on *Andromeda*'s windshield.

Now the heavy cruiser filled Harper's entire field of vision. He could see the open hangar, a small blinking rectangle awash in red emergency light. Inside there would be a cage of safety netting ready to catch the solar sail and slow its momentum. Harper hoped he wasn't going too fast—the fullerene mesh was unlikely to break, but it might slice and dice him for sashimi if he hit it wrong.

The hangar was now only a thousand meters away. Harper stuck his hands under his armpits and pushed his feet against the controls, lodging himself against his seat. His stomach lurched—the rocket had picked up a slight end-over-end tumble along the way. Not a good sign. Harper closed his eyes and prayed.

Hey, God. I'm a friend of Rev Bem's. . . .

FOURTEEN

What is the price of experience? Do men buy it for a song?
Or wisdom for a dance in the street?
No, it is bought with the price
Of all that man hath, his house, his wife, his children.
Wisdom is sold in the desolate market where none come to
buy,
And in the wither'd field where the farmer plows in vain for
bread

—"POET SAVANTS OF PRIMITIVE PLANETS,"
BY TEARDROPS IN EMBERS, CY 7121

"Nicely done, Captain," allowed Tyr. The honorific may have been tinged with sarcasm, but the praise was genuine. Effusive praise it was, coming from Tyr, but well deserved. After all, in the brief span of time that the big Nietzschean had been following Magdalena and Rafe around the ship, Dylan Hunt had managed to initiate an offensive by the Human Alliance effective enough to gain control of Alpha Centauri.

"You knew, of course, that Rasputin would never honor the peace."

"Naturally. He's a Nietzschean," Dylan said with a twinkle, enjoying the way Tyr's skin twitched as he withheld his response. When

Tyr's skin twitched, it meant someone was getting under it. And getting under Tyr's skin was fast becoming Dylan's guilty pleasure.

"Not a very good Nietzschean," said Tyr dryly. What he didn't add was: the idiot left a blood enemy behind, alive. Worse, he left a blood enemy alive whom he didn't even *know* was an enemy. And if you can't be bothered to take the time to find out who your enemies are, you can hardly complain when they stab you in the back.

Rev Bem, arriving on Command after checking on Chutak's condition, felt as if he could finally exhale. Rasputin had left in such a huff that he forgot to collect his slave, and while Rev would have preferred to see a negotiated settlement between the Drago-Kazov and the Human Interplanetary Alliance, he was at least satisfied that, given the circumstances, Dylan's ploy resulted in the best possible outcome.

"Having won the war, let us make sure that the HIA also wins the peace," said the monk. To Tyr he added, "Was it not your own Great Philosopher, Nietzsche, who said, 'He who fights with monsters must take care lest he become a monster'?"

Trance's voice piped up from behind the pilot's chair, where Rev hadn't seen her. "I don't think the humans will become monsters. Do you?" she asked, sounding terribly concerned. Rev was quick to assure her that he expected no such metamorphosis. The purple pixie seemed relieved.

"Don't break out the champagne just yet," said Dylan, turning serious. "The HIA seems to have the upper hand but the Dragans are still dangerous, as I'm sure Harper can attest. I also don't like the look of that freak mag storm. I hope we haven't traded Rasputin Genovese for something even more dangerous."

"Still no idea what's causing these anomalies?" asked Rev. His eyes wandered toward Trance. Maybe he was reading too much into things, but she seemed exceedingly pensive.

Rommie worked the tiny hydraulics in her jaw to make an answer when Harper traipsed onto Command Deck, still clothed in the bulky HIA E-suit. He held his arms out wide, giving everyone the chance to hail the conquering hero.

"Hail the conquering hero!" he cried helpfully. It didn't help. He soldiered on. "It was close, people . . ." Harper took a good look at the occupants of Command: an android, a Nietzschean, a Magog, a whatever-the-hell-Trance-was, and added, "or not people. Let me tell ya, being target practice for a Dragan fighter is not a pastime for amateurs." He ran his fingers through his hair. "Good thing I'm sooo cool under pressure."

Dylan smiled as Harper basked in the glow of positive attention. For once, the kid's cocky presence was welcome. "You had me worried there for a minute. Glad you made it home in one piece, Mr. Harper."

"Not nearly as glad as I am. So, what's going on out there? Don't get me wrong, I'm all for giganto magnetic effects that take out bad guys, but it isn't exactly kosher according to Hoyle."

"I know. That's what you and Rommie need to figure out," said Dylan.

Rommie accessed the preliminary data scans from her CPU. "The storm was a result of increased flare activity on the sun closest to us. This activity has been building consistently—and there were two more significant jumps in intensity five-point-three and three-point-two minutes ago." Rommie quickly filled Harper in on the formation of the nascent black hole. Not surprisingly, all these phenomena seemed to be growing at exactly the same rate.

But the strange part, she said, was that according to her readings, there was a measurable increase in the attractor forces on board: electromagnetic force, gravitational force, strong and weak nuclear forces . . . all were fluctuating wildly. Andromeda, with a brain the size of the proverbial planet (not all in one place, of course, for security's sake), was unable to explain the shifts in the normal physical spectrum happening around her.

"It's most obvious, quite illogically, between objects of negligible mass, like sentients," noted *Andromeda*'s AI image.

"Who you calling negligible?" objected Harper. "Even yours truly exerts measurable gravitational pull. Not nearly enough to get me a moon, admittedly, but it does exist."

Suddenly the lights on the Command Deck sputtered. A shiver zipped up Dylan's spine. Harper got an odd look on his face; he felt it, too.

"What was that?" said Tyr.

"I don't know, but I think a ghost just copped a feel," said Harper.

"Dylan, I'm getting new readings," said Rommie, sounding as worried as an android can sound. "You need to see this."

A cutaway diagram of the *Andromeda Ascendant* appeared on the main Command screen, showing the frequency-filtered results of a shipwide scan. An irregular pattern, some kind of fractal, was replicating itself, expanding and then coalescing into a stringy, cloudy mass trailing tentacles throughout the ship. Bands of energy undulated on its surface, then circulated back within themselves like a whirlpool. At its tallest points it extended right out into space, apparently unconstrained by the physical form of the ship itself.

Trance moved again. Rev Bem had been watching her for a while, shifting irregularly around Command—crossing from one side to the other, waiting, then crossing back. She'd concentrate on the air in front of her, then sidestep or climb a ramp to an upper tier, sometimes walking slowly, sometimes jogging. She was doing this as quietly and discreetly as possible, and no one but Rev seemed to notice. But as the display on the viewscreen took shape, he realized that Trance moved whenever a tendril of force passed through the blueprint of Command Deck. It was as if she could *see* these waves of energy.

Trance, in fact, was seeing them. She was also trying to avoid them. She knew that she'd soon be within reach of the Engine's power, but she wanted to play keep away with it for as long as possible. Trance hoped, as always, to skew the odds in her favor.

You could say that what Trance saw was probabilities. For her, the fractals represented ripples of possibility, compressed and powerful—pillars of terrible choices, fifty-fifty, one way or the other. In any square meter of space, an infinite number of unique potentialities existed—any square meter, that is, except for the square meter in which the Vedran Runes resided. The Runes eradicates all probabilities, save two. All or nothing. Light or dark. Chaos or entropy. Die or survive.

One or zero. A binary future. Trance looked at the shifting diagram on the viewscreen and she knew that what she was looking at was the silhouette of the Engine of Creation itself. She tried to see to her next move, but Rommie interrupted.

"There's been an additional burst, Dylan, the strongest one yet. It's getting worse." The avatar paused and read data internally. Then she reported, "I believe this singularity could be the anchor for a forming quasar."

Rev Bem glanced at Dylan. They both knew exactly what this meant. If a new galaxy was forming around it, the baby black hole would have to be pulling more matter and energy into itself than it could absorb. And the only way this could happen was if Alpha Centauri's suns went nova. All three of them, all at the same time.

Uneasy, Dylan pointed to the wireframe graphic of the *Andromeda Ascendant* on-screen, and followed the bands of energy to their point of origin. "Where is that?"

"Hydroponics," said Rommie. "Beka, Rafe, and Magdalena are there."

Why am I not surprised? Dylan clenched his jaw. Leave it to Beka to tramp in with catastrophe stuck to her shoe like a piece of toilet paper. Only now she'd got not just the *Andromeda* in trouble, but potentially all of Alpha Centauri. He swore that if she turned out to be a willing party in this, there was going to be hell to pay.

"Get them," said Dylan.

Rommie nodded and sent her holographic self to collect the trio. She looked up at Dylan, shook her head. "They're not responding to my hologram."

Dylan checked the charge on his force lance and signaled Tyr with it. "Let's move. Fast. Rommie, you come too."

"What about me, Boss?" asked Harper. He wanted to see what kind of trouble Beka had gotten herself into this time. As always, with Harper curiosity overpowered caution.

"Stay here," said Dylan. "I need you to figure out what's going on with these attractor forces, and find a way to counteract them. Rev Bem can help you."

Dylan hastily headed out of Command Deck, Rommie and Tyr falling in quickly behind. "Wait for me," shouted Trance, bounding past Rev, hurrying to catch up. Dylan didn't hear her; he was busy mentally preparing a riot act to read to Beka while tearing her a new one.

Harper smiled at Rev Bem. "Looks like Boss Lady's up to her old tricks."

But it was Trance's tricks that concerned Rev. His intuition told him she was somehow orchestrating these events. The Magog started up the walkway to the Command Deck entrance; wherever Trance was going is where he wanted to be.

Hydroponics seemed somehow changed to Dylan. It was subtle: the light in the room appeared brighter and harsher than usual, painting the plants and burnished copper walls with a brutal glare. Dylan's pupils contracted so quickly it was almost painful. It was worse for Tyr; his heightened senses were acerbated by the garishly charged atmosphere. A low-frequency buzz throbbed in his ears and the air felt heavy, as if he were pushing into soup.

Dylan stepped into the rose garden and found Beka, Rafe, and Magdalena silently standing in a circle, staring intently at an object in Magdalena's lap. They appeared neither to have seen nor heard his entrance. Dylan felt a slight nudge as Trance quietly squeezed past him.

Rev Bem, meanwhile, stood hesitantly in the entryway. He felt a sense of dread about entering the suddenly lurid garden. It was the same strangeness he'd experienced when he first saw Trance with the orb. He gripped his Wayist medallion, finding some reassurance in its cool strength. Then he steeled himself and walked in.

"Beka! What are you doing?" asked Dylan sharply.

At the sound of her name, Beka looked up. She blinked and peered at Dylan. No, not *at* him. *Through* him. With effort, she lifted an arm and listlessly pointed at the object in Magdalena's hand.

"The big score, Dylan. The Engine of Creation."

Weirdness, incoming, thought Dylan. He knew all about the Engine of Creation, of course. What he knew was that it was a myth, a legend of long-lost Tarn-Vedra. A fairy machine from the land before time, a destroyer of planets and maker of stars. No such thing actually existed, of course; it was only poetry and fable. A Vedran nursery rhyme about the Engine tickled at his memory: *Into the black hole and out the other side, starburst and moonshine are my guides . . .* something like that. It scans better in Common.

But Engine or no Engine, something around here was causing all hell to break loose, and Dylan had to address it. He looked at the object in Magdalena's hands. Definitely not your run-of-the-mill dusty artifact. There was something about it . . . it didn't just look otherworldly, it looked other-dimensional. He could have stared at the machine for hours, it was that fascinating.

"That object is what's causing the trouble," subvocalized Rommie.

She noted Dylan's unusually sluggish response to the information. In fact, every organic sentient in the rose garden was behaving oddly. Rommie could detect no alteration in her own operations, thankfully, nor the *Andromeda*'s in general. She tapped her captain on the shoulder. "Dylan!"

Dylan blinked at Rommie. Funny. His mind must have wandered. He cleared his throat. "Big score or not, Beka, this Engine, or whatever you want to call it, seems to be causing magnetic fluctuations in this sector. If we don't do something about it, it could seriously affect Alpha Centauri."

Trance spoke softly from behind him. "More than seriously. And more than Alpha Centauri." Dylan wasn't sure if he was imagining her voice or not. The words fluttered around his head and then broke apart into meaningless strings of sound. Even Rev Bem, who was concentrating, couldn't make out what Trance was saying.

"One more piece," said Beka haltingly. "All we need is one more piece."

She thought she heard Trance say, "It's already in your hands." But she wasn't positive. She might have dreamed it.

Magdalena felt as if every joint in her body was fused shut. Movement was excruciating. She thought she might have blacked out a few times. It was from being so close to the Engine's power, she was sure of it. She forced herself to think. The Runes were still incomplete. *Where is the other piece?* Beka's should have been the last. Then words came swirling, bubbling up into her brain: *It's already in your hands.*

"It's already in your hands." Somebody was saying it aloud. Magdalena looked up; it was Beka. She was pointing to Magdalena's walking stick. The handle, once a graceful silver gargoyle, had changed. Red light seeped through its folds and crevices; along its top glowed a familiar trisected pattern. The cane was a gift from Ignatius, and she always thought her attachment to it was sentimental, a reminder of a life that could have been. Now, she wasn't so sure.

Magdalena had carried a piece of the Engine of Creation with her the whole time, and never knew.

Tyr leaned toward Dylan, his speech halting and precise. "A weapon. Control it, and there would be no stopping us."

"Us?" Did Tyr really say "us"? Dylan thought surely he meant to say that "there would be no stopping *me.*" Didn't he?

"It's not a weapon," came Trance's voice, fading in and out. "It's a do over."

"Do what over?" asked Dylan. Or maybe he just thought the question. Either way, he got no answer.

Magdalena placed the partially constructed Engine of Creation on the floor at her feet. Then she turned her walking stick upside down and lowered the head into the cavity formed by Rafe's ring. The cane perfectly fit into the Engine. The universe took a sharp left and, suddenly, the crew weren't themselves anymore.

Rev stared into a fractal vortex that unspooled from the Engine of Creation. It roped its way straight toward him, reached out, and with a hungry snap, enclosed him. It formed a long echoing hallway, a black endless void. All was darkness, all was oneness. It was strangely comforting. He was drawn inexorably toward the Engine. It spoke to him in a language that he understood at a molecular level; it conversed with the deep and buried parts of his mind, the places where there was and always would be a Child of the Abyss: a Magog.

Now somebody was blocking Rev's path. Why? Who? He couldn't tell. There was only the Engine; everything else was reduced to vague shapes, to restless shadows, to muffled sounds. Something touched his chest, holding him back. An arm.

The Engine's call was more insistent. Rev grimaced, pulling back his lips to unsheathe needlelike teeth. He turned his head in the direction of his assailant and spat. Paralytic poison sprayed from sharp, hollow incisors. The arm disappeared. Rev dutifully continued until the Engine was at his feet. He was completely unaware of Magdalena, sitting just on the other side of it, or Beka and Rafe, also nearby.

Rev Bem knelt and placed his hands on the Engine's sides. Or maybe the Engine pulled his hands, as it was pulling at every cell in his body. A silence enveloped him, a sense of belonging. He felt almost . . . whole. He was one with his people. He was one with All That Is. But to fully connect, he had to become one with the Engine of Creation. He had to let it finish its work.

Is this what God wants for me? he asked himself. And then, *Is this God?*

There was one small doubt, one small voice inside him. He tried to ignore it, but it was persistent. The voice was the Way.

The siren song of the Engine was deafening, unyielding. *Come to me! Be with me! Complete me!* Rev choked on bile as it rose up in his throat. He wrenched his hands free of the Engine, his fingertips sizzling. He placed his hands on his temples, sticking the points of his claws into his own flesh. He jerked his hands downward, tearing open the sides of his face. The sensation sliced through the haze of his thoughts. The thunderous drone of the Engine was blotted out by the searing pain. He pulled his claws still farther, deeper, stumbling backward from the Engine, getting as far away as he could until his legs gave out from beneath him.

His legs buckled. His face bled. But Rev Bem was triumphant: his mind was his own again.

There was no more time for planning, no more time for scheming. No more diplomacy, no more waiting. Here was the key. He could feel the Engine's power. It was tactile, it crackled against his skin.

With the Engine of Creation at their command, the Kodiak would be reborn as the single most powerful Pride in the Known Worlds. Reunited, they would be more than powerful; they would be Gods. He, Tyr Anasazi out of Victoria by Barbarossa, would rule the future.

But Tyr knew he'd have to move fast. He'd have to steal the Engine and get it off the *Andromeda*. There'd be the crew to contend with, of course, and they wouldn't go down easy. But he couldn't let them get in the way of his plans.

He took a step toward the Engine, but felt something around his legs. It tickled. Something swept around his feet, grabbing his ankles. He tripped, fell . . . quickly righted himself. He reached down and took hold of the squirming cord that was still wrapped around his right ankle. He was positive that Dylan had somehow lassoed him. *You've tripped me up too many times already*, thought Tyr, as he yanked on the cord. He was surprised to find the cord was a tail, and it was attached to Trance.

She snapped her tail free of his grasp and bounced nervously from foot to foot, watching Tyr warily. "Don't do this," she warned.

"I'll kill you," said Tyr, simply. As of this moment, the *Andromeda Ascendant* and all aboard her were a footnote. The *Andromeda* would never bring him what the Engine could.

Trance didn't move. Tyr launched a punch in her direction, but she ducked and scrambled behind him. As soon as Trance was out of his sight, Tyr immediately forgot about her. The Engine demanded all of his attention. Tyr took another step, but now something landed on his back. Purple arms wrapped around his neck. He knelt, dropped his shoulder, and flipped Trance off of him, slamming her on the ground. Tyr put one arm beneath her back and another beneath her knees.

It was a reflex; years of training and exercise had hammered the art of combat into his muscle memory. Even the look in Trance's eyes, a mixture of fear and surprise, didn't stop him. It was a look he'd never seen on her face before, but he didn't care at this point. He pulled back and unceremoniously threw Trance in the direction of the hydroponics vat. She flew nine meters through the air to land in the tank, sending nutrient-rich fluid cascading over its edge and frothy waves ricocheting across its surface. Tyr didn't bother waiting to see where she had landed or how she had fared. He was much more concerned with Rev Bem, who was already nearing the Engine. Rev was sorely mistaken if he thought he was going to use the Engine for himself.

Growling, Tyr muscled Rev Bem out of the way. He reached across the monk's hairy chest, preparing to throw him to the ground. Rev just looked at him. The Magog's eyes were bloodshot, his mouth unzipped into a carnivorous leer. The rank stench of his breath reached Tyr's nostrils. Tyr reacted, tried to cover his face . . . but it was too late. Rev hissed and sprayed him with a foul, oily liquid that got in his eyes and ran down his torso. It burned at the touch; Tyr's very pores were being cauterized, seared closed. His limbs were so heavy it seemed his chain mail had grown into a suit of lead.

Tyr stumbled and fell to the floor, rigid.

The Vedran Runes were complete. The Engine of Creation's power would build inexorably until it achieved critical mass. Trance could see that everyone in hydroponics was in thrall to it. It was powerful, it was lethal . . . and it was getting stronger by the second.

The object at Magdalena's feet was merely the physical manifestation of the Engine, of course. Three dimensions—four, tops. When Trance looked at it, she saw something else entirely. In her multidimensional field of perception, the finished object was a pumping organ, a kind of cosmic heart. Except where another heart sustained life, this one would obliterate it.

The Engine affected Trance just as strongly as it did the others, but very differently. Where it drew them, it quite literally repulsed her. The nearer she got, the harder it seemed to push her away. She would have been just fine with the Engine staying broken into pieces, but that was a naïve hope. The Engine would have been restored eventually, no matter what. At least this way it was happening in her presence, where she could hope to affect the outcome.

Trance looked at Beka, Rafe, and Magdalena with a twinge of remorse. *It would be one of them, certainly.* Which one, she couldn't tell yet; the Engine was blurring her vision. Normally, probabilities would branch out in front of her like the glowing ropes of the Slip-stream; she could choose a likelihood the way Beka could choose a destination. But the power of the Engine was overriding her.

She worried about Rev Bem. The Engine resonated especially strongly with him. More important, though, Tyr must not get his hands on it. That would be a catastrophe. She carefully watched the two of them. Tyr moved first. Trance pushed against the force of the Engine and ran up behind him, wrapped her tail around one of the Nietzschean's ankles. She pulled his foot out from under him and brought him to his knees. He reacted faster than she expected, though, and grabbed her before she could get away. Out of the corner of her eye, she could see Rev walking toward them. She desperately yanked her tail out of Tyr's hand and ducked his inevitable punch.

She was going to have to put Tyr out of commission and do it fast, before Rev got too close. Tyr turned away, and she abruptly jumped on his back. Just as quickly, the room spun as Tyr flipped her over his shoulder. She landed with a jarring thud. Trance was stunned, both from the blow and by the fact that the move had caught her off guard. *I didn't see that coming. How could I not see that coming?* It had been a long time since she'd been shocked by anything. With so much at stake, this was definitely not the time for surprises.

She tried to cry out, but Tyr was on top of her, roughly lifting her into the air. He tossed her and she went flailing across the room, landing in the cold fluid of the hydroponics vat. She came to a stop against the far corner of the tank and sank beneath the surface, darkness enclosing her.

As the final piece of the Engine fell into place, Dylan felt something within him fall loose. He dropped to his knees. Here in front of him was the Engine of Creation itself, a fictional object whose existence Dylan could no longer doubt. It was magnificent—and all he could feel was despair. He knew that this much power was dangerous, that none of them should control it. He had to do something. He had to stop them.

But his mind chattered back at him. Why was it always up to him to save the others? Why, for once, couldn't they save themselves? He always did everything right, and it was never good enough. In the end, even his successes didn't accomplish anything lasting. And they never came when he needed them the most.

Memories of Hephaestos washed over him like a black tide. He was there, right there at the cusp of the Nietzschean uprising. He could have stopped it, but he didn't. He should have been smarter, seen the signs. He should have known that Gaheris Rhade would betray him. He should have used his Nova bombs against the attacking Nietzschean fleet, even if Hephaestos was an inhabited system. But he had been weak. He was weak then, just as he was now.

Why couldn't I have just died? Dylan whined silently. Rhade should have killed him right there on Command. He should have died alongside Refractions of Dawn, his pilot—along with the rest of his crew, along with the Commonwealth. Instead, here he was, an unwilling survivor, three hundred years later, trying to resurrect a world he once knew. Gluing the pieces of a shattered Commonwealth back together, one by one—it was pathetic. It was futile. He was going to fail now, just as he had failed before. Why did he even bother? One man was useless against the universe.

Dylan's hands fell impotently to his side. He heard someone call his name. "Go away," he grumbled. "Leave me alone." Someone lifted him to his feet, but he didn't have the strength to stand. He felt himself being carried away. "Leave me," he muttered. "Let me die."

Magdalena ignored the nausea. She ignored the throbbing headache; she ignored the pins and needles. *Focus!* Now was not the time to lose it, not when they were at the brink of succeeding.

What she needed to do was take the Engine and leave. Of course they all wanted to take the Engine from her, even Rebecca and Rafael. That, she could handle later. Right now, she needed Rebecca to get her off the *Andromeda*.

Magdalena looked at her daughter. She cleared her throat twice and said softly, with effort, "We did it." Beka and Rafe raised their heads, stared at her groggily. Magdalena managed a crooked smile. "What do you say we hit the road? Just the three of us."

No response. She tried again. "We can be a family." She picked up the Engine by the base. "And we'll have this."

Magdalena's voice brought Beka and Rafe momentarily to their senses. Beka looked around the rose garden. She saw:

Tyr lying motionless on the floor.

Rev Bem hunched at the far wall, cradling his face, black blood staining his fingers.

Trance floating facedown in the hydroponics vat.

And Dylan . . . Dylan was nowhere to be seen.

Beka had no emotional response to any of this.

"What do you say, kids?" asked Magdalena, getting painfully to her feet. Moving helped; she was starting to feel herself again.

Beka looked at Rafe. He smiled back at her. She knew what he was thinking: they'd done it. They had the Engine of Creation. And they had each other.

Beka turned to her mother and her brother. "The *Maru*," she said thickly, patting her pocket. "I have a key. We can take the *Eureka Maru*."

FIFTEEN

A moment of indiscretion can destroy a reputation. A
lifetime of indiscretion, on the other hand, can make one.

—SAM PROFITT, AFC 313

Rommie wasn't quite sure what she was looking at. The moment
Magdalena placed the glowing handle of her walking stick into the
construct of *objets trouvé* at her feet, everyone in the room underwent
an immediate and profound change. At first Rommie thought that
being a machine, she would be the only exception. Then she noticed
that Trance, too, appeared to be acting normally. She certainly wasn't
slack-jawed and drooling like Tyr was.

It was Dylan's response that concerned Rommie the most. He
sank to the ground, inert. At first she was worried that he had been
badly hurt or, worse, dead. But an emergency med scan showed
nothing wrong with him physically: no stroke, no heart attack as she

constantly feared. Rommie never told Dylan this, but she spent a good percentage of her energy worrying about his health, and another percentage monitoring it. The tendency of organics to drop dead terrified her.

But even that was nothing compared to the terror she felt as she watched the basic building blocks of reality shift. Subatomic attractor forces had, for no good reason, quadrupled in intensity. Using a full-spectrum visual feed, Rommie could actually see the connections webbing from the crew to every other object in the garden and, most prominently, to the core of the Engine of Creation itself. These last were thick trunks of energy, with pulses of light playing along their taffylike strings.

"Harper? Are you there? Can you see this?" Rommie trusted that back in Command, deep in the belly of the ship, Harper would be less affected. The energy seemed to diminish proportionally to its distance from the Engine.

"I see it," came Harper's voice over the comm. "It looks like quantum strings, like what you see when you're piloting in the 'stream."

Of course. Being an organic, Harper experienced the Slipstream quite differently than Andromeda herself did.

"You know, Rom Doll, if we live through this, we could end up with some exciting insights on Unified Field Theory."

"That's nice, Harper, but do you have any exciting insights on saving Dylan's life right now?"

Rommie leaned over her captain and called his name one more time. "Dylan?" He still wasn't responding. His head hung to his chest, his hair fell into his eyes. Rommie placed a gentle hand on his neck . . . and discharged a low-wattage electrical current into it. Nothing. He didn't appear to feel a thing.

She looked at the others. Beka, Rafe, Rev Bem—no help there. They were all tottering on their feet as if they'd just chugged a case of Harper's contraband Neubayern Weisbrau. As with Dylan, she couldn't find a physical reason for their fugue, although she did detect some signs of physical deterioration in Magdalena. Beka's mother was finally starting to look like she could be Beka's mother. Apparently the Engine did take a physical toll. Or perhaps Magdalena was being affected because she had been with the Engine the longest.

On second glance, Rommie decided that Trance wasn't as immune to the effects as she had thought. The pulsing bands didn't connect her to the Engine like the others; rather, they accumulated *between* her and the Engine. To Rommie's visual sensors, it looked as if Trance were pushing against an invisible wall. Like an Old Earth art form Harper always made fun of. *Mime*, that was it. Trance looked like someone struggling against an imaginary wind.

Rommie thought about Trance and the Engine of Creation. The creature seemed to have special knowledge of the Vedran machine. At one point, Rommie thought Trance had been instructing Beka and Magdalena how to complete it. But everything was so confused then . . . she'd have to consult her datafiles to be sure of what actually happened. And that would have to wait.

First, Rommie had to get everyone out of harm's way. Deciding whom to save first took fractions of a nanosecond—really, it wasn't a decision at all, as there was no active consideration on her part. She just grabbed her captain.

Rommie attempted to pull Dylan to his feet, but he kept shrugging her off. *No more Mister Nice Robot*, she frowned, then lifted him up by the scruff of his collar, threw him over her shoulder, and carried him out of the rose garden. At heart Rommie was a Type II utility 'droid capable of bench-pressing two hundred kilos, and she had no trouble hauling Dylan across the large atrium in a vector 180 degrees from the Engine. She finally stopped at the far side of the garden, by the mighty Vedran oak. She gently leaned the semiconscious Dylan against the tree's trunk, nestling him between two knobby roots that descended into a patch of aerated sand.

It took only a few meters' distance before the connection between Dylan and the machine loosened and he began to revive. The intense psychological influence of the machine seemed limited to about fifty meters, thank the Empress.

Not so with the collateral effects. The EM flux was playing havoc with Alpha Centauri's unstable suns and the newfound black hole, and it was going to get worse before it got better. *If it got better.* Andromeda put herself into Code Black mode; they were now in grave and immediate danger.

"Dylan, we need you."

Rommie lifted Dylan's head up and stared into his eyes, marveling (not for the first time) that genetic random chance could yield a face so esthetically pleasing. That sentiment alerted her inner cop. *Stop that*, she scolded herself. Such thoughts were inappropriate at the best of times, and this was definitely not the best of times.

Rommie ventured an optimistic smile as Dylan slowly began to acknowledge her presence. *At least he's not asking to be left alone to die anymore*, she thought. That had been particularly worrisome. She'd always known Dylan bore a burden of guilt so huge few could carry it. He sublimated the pain, poured it into his dream of the Commonwealth. And he had amazing resolve; even in the face of incredibly long odds, he doggedly retained his belief in himself and his mission. To see him this demoralized, so ready to give up, made Rommie ache to her core.

Dylan became aware of Rommie's hand against his cheek. It felt so . . . real. How did Harper do that? How did he get her skin so warm and pliable? It was easy sometimes to forget she was an artificial intelligence—especially right then, when she was being so tender. Were her eyes always this dark and lustrous? How could he have not noticed before? Lying together here under the oak, dappled in shade, it was all so . . . romantic. Dylan basked in the feeling, soaked up the sensuous warmth of Rommie's synthetic flesh. He smiled up at her.

"How are you feeling?" asked Rommie.

"Better than I was," said Dylan. "I don't know what happened in there. I just . . . I just gave up." It was like he just clawed his way out of a toxic mire of guilt and self-doubt. The doubts were still there, of course; but then again, they always were. They had just reverted to the familiar job of gnawing on his soul, as opposed to shredding it entirely.

"It's not your fault," said Rommie. "When she attached that last piece, Magdalena increased the Engine's sphere of influence almost fourfold. Everyone in the rose garden is under a tremendous strain. That's why I pulled you out here. The farther away you are, the less of an effect it has."

Dylan placed his hand over hers. It covered it completely, cupped it as if she were carved of finest porcelain, and protected it like . . . he quickly withdrew his hand. The moment was getting a bit too intimate. Was it him? Or was it the residual effect of the Engine?

"I think I can manage from here," he said, slowly getting to his feet.

Dylan rested against the oak, massaging his temples. His memory of events was a bit confusing. He remembered coming to hydroponics—after that, things got vague. The one fact he could recall clearly was one he couldn't quite believe: that Beka and her family had actually found the Engine of Creation. From the looks of things, it would have been better left unfound.

"So, where do we stand?" he asked Rommie, his voice sounding stronger and more confident with every syllable.

"Right in the middle of a self-destructing system," said Rommie.

"The singularity is growing exponentially, and the suns are flaring uncontrollably. They could go nova in a matter of hours."

Dylan groaned. "Oh, good. Glad it's nothing major."

"It sort of is," added Rommie reluctantly. "What's happening now is just a warm-up. The Engine's power is still building. What happens when it's fully operational?"

If the device could destroy a system just by being assembled, Dylan was willing to bet that its continued activation wasn't going to fill the universe with flowers, rainbows, and puppies.

"Do we even know what it's supposed to do?" asked Dylan, not really wanting to know.

"Harper's working on some theories," said Rommie. "And I think Trance might know a thing or two." That got Dylan's attention. He didn't even remember seeing Trance in the rose garden. *Why is she always in the middle of everything inexplicable?* thought Dylan. *And why is Rev Bem the only one who notices?*

"What did she say?" asked Dylan.

"She seemed to recognize it. She called it a 'do over.'"

A "do over." It sounded like something from a child's playground game. Dylan was about to ask Rommie another question when he realized she had twisted her head to one side as if listening to a faint noise. Dylan recognized this look; it meant she was carrying on a simultaneous conversation with someone else on the ship. She turned her head to look at him.

"I'm talking to Harper right now," said Rommie. "He's got some ideas he wants to run by you." As the comm screen was off-limits, back in the direction of the rose garden, Rommie routed Harper's voice through her own speech system.

Dylan was almost thankful. Nothing was quite so unattractive and off-putting as hearing Harper's voice come out of Rommie's mouth. It pretty much obliterated all of her fetching qualities.

"Hey, Boss," said Rommie—or, rather, said Harper's sarcastic voice emanating from Rommie's lips. "You should see what's happening down there. That's some freaky stuff."

Not as freaky as what I am seeing right now, thought Dylan. "What have you got for me, Harper?"

"Well, if that is the Engine of Creation, this is like the hugest find in the history of the universe. There's been rumors of it being buried on every planet from Shintaida to Gehenna. The thing's supposed to predate the Vedrans, and we can't even find the Vedrans, much less their grandparents.

"Judging by what this hunk of hardware is doing to our corner of space at the moment, all I can say is someone truly major must have built it. All the chinheads on Ugroth couldn't come up with something this powerful."

"Enough setup," said Dylan. "Get to the punch line. What does it do?"

Rommie grimaced. Dylan didn't know if she was doing it on purpose or not, but she had begun to assume the engineer's irritating mannerisms as well.

"Okay, okay," said Rommie/Harper. "Here's what I'm thinking. Start with string theory, which explains how everything in the universe is connected to everything else in the universe through eleven dimensions—give or take a dimension. The most obvious example of this is Slipstream, where some of the strongest of these connections between planets, stars, and stuff are actually visible.

"The Engine is increasing the attraction in these attractors. Things with names like 'strong force' and 'weak force,' which they got the same way rashes get names like 'red bumps' and 'pink bumps'—because no one knows what the hell they really are. And if we're seeing this kind of chaos with the thing just sitting there humming . . . well, my guess is that left to its own devices the Engine is going to overload the quantum connections in the fabric of space and time. If they collapse, then blammo—eleven dimensions go adios."

Dylan knew the answer couldn't be good, but he asked anyway. "What exactly do you mean by 'go adios'?"

"The known universe, all twenty-eight billion light-years of it, is reduced to the size of a proton. It would be like it was before the Big Bang."

And that was the "do over," Dylan realized. Everything collapses back into the primeval black hole, waiting to explode out all over again. This damn machine was a reset button for the universe.

Who could have built such a device in the first place? Dylan wondered. Then another thought struck him: *When did they build it? And . . . has it been used before?*

Much as he would have loved to debate these cosmic imponderables, Dylan realized he first needed an immediate plan of action. "How can we neutralize it?" he asked.

Harper/Rommie chewed on a nail. "Well, reversing a black hole and a trio of supernovas isn't exactly something they teach you at All Systems University. Honestly, I don't know if there's anything we can do, besides taking our fight to the source. The Engine didn't hurt anyone when it was a bunch of little pieces right? So, maybe we break it up again. I don't know how to do it, yet, but I have a hunch that without the Engine feeding it, this here apocalypse won't be able to maintain."

"Sounds reasonable. Keep working on it," said Dylan, his mind racing. He had to take charge of this situation and fast. "Any way you can damp down the thing's effects now would be appreciated. In the meantime, I'll try and get some answers from Trance."

"I'll do what I can," said Harper/Rommie. The Harper smirk melted from Rommie's face and her normal voice returned. "So, how did you like my Harper impression?"

"It was very . . ." He was about to say "creepy," but he didn't want to offend her. "Ah, accurate," is all he said.

Rommie suddenly got that faraway look again.

"Harper?" asked Dylan.

"No," said Rommie. "The Engine. It's moving." Without warning, she ran at Dylan and scooped him up in one smooth move, bending slightly to catch him at the waist and carrying him to the far side of the atrium. There, she pinned him to the wall and wrapped her arms around him protectively.

"Is this really necessary?" asked Dylan. Rommie just leaned in farther. Dylan could hear the faint echo of footsteps from the other side of the atrium, but he couldn't see anything; the big oak was in his way. He was about to protest again when he felt a familiar heaviness pressing in on him. The air became stifling, and he was overwhelmed by a burst of black, bilious self-loathing. It threatened to engulf him, to submerge him in an avalanche of remorse and guilt.

Just as quickly, the sensation began to recede.

"They've taken it. Beka, Rafe, and Magdalena have taken the Engine," said Rommie. "They crossed right in front of us. They're heading for Hangar Deck Twelve. I sent a hologram, but they just walked through her." Rommie shivered, as if the effect were physical.

The Engine was no longer close enough to affect Dylan, and he began feeling normal again. He also felt a little ridiculous; Rommie still had him fastened to the wall.

"Uh, Rommie? I think you can let go of me now."

Rommie put Dylan on his feet. He took a second to regain his composure and straighten his uniform. He was starting to get angry. He'd had it about up to here with reckless, thoughtless, self-centered Valentines. There was no way he was going to let them off the *Andromeda* with the Engine.

"Are your systems immune to the Engine?" asked Dylan.

Rommie nodded. "Apparently."

"Then it's up to you to stop them."

"I have been trying, you know," said Rommie, with a snarkiness level of about a seven. She had naturally armed the self-defense system immediately, and dispatched Intruder Control nanobots. "Unfortunately, as far as my operations are concerned, the Valentines are friendlies."

Dylan mentally shuffled through the usual options. Forget Gauss guns and other conventional lead-spitters; they were unreliable, and anyway, Beka was littered with electronic countermeasures, courtesy of his own armory. A targeted high-gravity field was a bad idea in an area of space where a black hole was already in progress. With no I.C. nanobots, that left the ship with Rommie's human avatar and her various 'droids. What he needed was something with surefire stopping power. . . .

"Tweedledum and Tweedledee," said Dylan. It wasn't as much a nonsequitur as it sounded. Tweedledum and Tweedledee were the enlisted men's nicknames for *Andromeda*'s Planetfall Defense Robots. "The twins" were only brought in for special occasions, like fullscale warfare; they weren't exactly synonymous with finesse. But Dylan couldn't leave Alpha Centauri to its own devices, either, and he didn't have much choice.

The only problem with the warbots was that as their name suggested, they were meant to be deployed on actual planets. On a planet there was plenty of room to run roughshod, and lots of interesting things to knock over and blow up. The *Andromeda Ascendant* may be 1,300 meters long and 325 meters high, but its corridors were still a tight fit for one of those juggernauts.

"Can they pull it off?" asked Dylan.

"Well, Tweedledee is in about five thousand pieces right now— one of Harper's long-term upgrade projects. As for Tweedledum . . ." Rommie did a quick calculation. "It'll be a close shave, but if he sticks to the main halls and if I keep him low to the ground, he should make it."

He'd better make it, thought Dylan. "Good. Get him on-line and cut the Valentines off. I want you to go, too. You're the only one who can get close enough to talk any sense into them."

And she was the only one he could trust absolutely. Especially now.

"What do you want me to do when I find them?"

"Just stop them," said Dylan. "If they try to activate the Engine . . ." Dylan let the thought trail off. Rommie knew what had to be done, what Dylan couldn't voice. And she was capable of doing it. She wasn't some dustbuster house robot, programmed never to harm an organic. She was a warship. If she had to sacrifice the few to save the many, she would. Even if it meant sacrificing Beka Valentine.

"Good luck," said Dylan. Without thinking, he put out an arm. He wasn't sure what he'd intended to do with this gesture, but apparently he'd meant to give her a hug. He stopped short and lamely patted Rommie on the shoulder.

"Is it okay to check on the others?" he asked.

"Yes, the Engine's at a safe distance," said Rommie, somehow flattered by Dylan's awkward caress. She turned and began jogging away. She was going to have to be quick. Luckily, nobody knew the *Andromeda Ascendant* better than, well, the Andromeda Ascendant. If she hurried, she could take a shortcut through the Gamma Deck repair conduit and head off the Valentines outside the hangar entrance. The warbot was already on its way.

Dylan watched her go, then walked around the girth of the tree and crossed the atrium floor. As he approached the garden, he felt a twinge—a sense memory, a rush of despair . . . even the reminder of the Engine's power made him nervous.

The sight of Rev Bem jolted Dylan out of gloom and into action. Rev was crawling painfully across the floor, leaving a smeared trail of blood. Dylan sprinted into the room, and what he saw was even more shocking. Not only was Rev Bem obviously injured, but so was Tyr. The Weapons Officer was lying on the ground, his body contorted and stiff.

Dylan ran to the monk's side, kneeling in one of the puddles that dotted the floor. Rev lifted his head at Dylan's touch, and Dylan saw the two terrible gashes on either side of Rev Bem's face. He didn't know what to think. Was this caused by the Engine—or was it caused by one of the Valentines?

"Rev. What happened to you?" asked Dylan.

Rev responded groggily. "I'll be fine. I . . . I only scratched myself." Dylan could see thick gouts of blood sticking to the claws on the Magog's gnarled hands. "Forget about me. I'm more worried about Tyr."

Dylan decided not to push him. He put an arm around Rev's shoulder and helped him to his feet. They walked together over to the fallen Tyr. Dylan felt for the Nietzschean's pulse. He gave a sigh of relief; there was a steady beat at Tyr's jugular. Tyr was also breathing—always a good sign. But his eyes were frozen in a dead stare and he wasn't responding to Dylan's voice.

Dylan shook his head. "He looks brain-dead."

Rev Bem turned his face away, ashamed. "No, Tyr's quite lucid, more's the pity. I'm afraid I did this. I can taste it, you know. My paralytic venom, it leaves an aftertaste." Rev looked at Dylan with an anguished expression. "I poisoned him."

Dylan looked around in disbelief. *What in the name of the Vedran Empress happened in here?*

Rev Bem shook his head. "At first I thought I was imagining it, or dreaming it, but it must have really happened. It was the Engine of Creation—it was overpowering. I was trying to get to it. I *had* to get to it. It was calling me. Consuming me.

"I finally tore my own skin. The pain was the only thing that broke its spell."

Dylan could see Rev's shame, and he empathized. "I know what you went through. It happened to me, too. I suspect it happened to all of us."

The Engine of Creation threw Dylan into a pit of despair. It made Rev Bem turn violently against a crewmate. Who knew what it had done to Tyr, or Trance for that matter. *Trance!* Dylan looked around the room. "Where's Trance?"

Rev had completely forgotten about her. "That's a good question."

Trance wasn't in the garden, and she hadn't left with Beka and the others. Dylan was reminded that Trance had aided Beka's escape in the first place, and wondered if the two of them were working together the whole time. Maybe Beka really was to blame for what was happening. Or maybe she had been manipulated. Could Trance pull off something like that? Would she want to?

"Andromeda," called Dylan. "Any sign of Trance?"

"No, but that's not unusual," answered the ship. "Trance is harder to keep track of than most. She never scans as alive in the first place."

"Keep looking," sighed Dylan. "Let me know when you reach the hangar bay. And send over a med 'droid."

At first Dylan had only been hoping Trance could shed some light on the situation. Now, he also wanted to keep a close eye on her in case she had any other surprises in store.

Rev Bem, meanwhile, was trying to maneuver Tyr into a more comfortable position. Bad as he felt for spraying a sentient being, a child of the Divine—and a colleague, to boot—he also knew that with Tyr's efficient immune system, some simple medical attention would nullify the paralysis within hours.

Rev leaned over and looked at Tyr's frozen face. "Tyr, I meant you no harm. Please forgive me." The Nietzschean was unable to return his normal look of disdain, so Rev took it as acceptance of his apology. Then he and the 'droids shifted the patient toward Med Deck.

"Vector *away* from Hangar Deck Twelve," instructed Dylan. "I'll be on Command, trying to figure out what to do about this Engine. Beka, Rafe, and Magdalena obviously have their own plans for it, but I doubt they realize exactly what that thing is capable of."

Rev shuddered; Dylan had no idea how close he had come to activating the Engine, and Rev hoped he never would know. He found some consolation knowing that he had at least managed to resist the Engine's awful lure.

"Beka can be hotheaded," said Rev. "But her heart is in the right place."

"Normally, yes. Under the influence of the Engine, who knows what she might or might not do," said Dylan.

Dylan wondered what Tyr's trauma had been, what demons had clutched at his soul. He doubted that he'd ever get a full account of what transpired in the rose garden. He knew he didn't want to talk about his own experience, and he imagined that everyone else felt the same. In the end, maybe it was best not to know. As the 'droid wheeled Tyr away on a gurney, Dylan leaned over him. "He can still hear and see, right?" Dylan winked at Rev. Then, to Tyr, he said seriously, "You know, this might be a good time for us to have that discussion about crew loyalty and shipboard discipline."

Poor paralyzed Tyr simply stared. Dylan laughed. It was the first laugh he'd had since Magdalena jammed the head of her cane into the Vedran Runes. Maybe by the time he made it to Command Deck, Harper would have some good news for him. He slapped Rev on the shoulder and made his way out through the doors of the rose garden.

Rev Bem shuffled alongside as the 'droid slowly pulled 140 kilos of Nietzschean dead weight. Tyr Anasazi watched the passing ceiling tiles. Each second away from the Engine filled him with growing relief. To have been under the machine's influence, but to be immobilized and unable to act, had been maddening. Literally. Tyr's mind had been like a rabid, scrambling animal, driven quite insane.

With the Engine receding to the distance, Tyr's rational intellect was back up and running. Its first conclusion: failing to possess the Engine was a significant loss. With it, long-range goals for himself, his son, and his Pride would surely have been realized. Had the Engine exerted no influence over him at all, Tyr supposed, he would still have wanted to steal it. The only difference was (though he would never openly admit this) that his affection for the rest of the crew would have made him feel some remorse as he made off with their prize.

The horror he had just experienced cured him of any such desire. He never wanted to get close to that cursed thing again. As far as he was concerned, Beka was welcome to it.

As Rev Bem and Tyr exited hydroponics, the room automatically kicked into power conservation mode. All nonessential systems turned themselves off. Since there were no longer any actual roses in the rose garden, the UV lamps dimmed. The filtration system sighed to a stop. The heaters slowly grew cold.

The room went dark and silent. But what nobody realized, not even Andromeda herself, was that the room was not empty. Trance was still in the garden. She was lying motionless at the bottom of the hydroponics vat.

SIXTEEN

The disciples said to him, "Tell us what our end will be." Jesus said, "If you haven't found the beginning, why ask about the end? For where the beginning is, the end is also."

—THE GOSPEL OF ST. THOMAS,
EARTH (PREHISTORIC)

Beka steered through the *Andromeda*'s corridors on autopilot, her body hunched forward, her arms swinging heavily at her sides, her face devoid of visible emotion. Everything was bottled up inside. *We did it, we did it, we put it together,* her mind echoed, keeping time with her footsteps. *We did it, we did it, we put it together.* The words became a hypnotic doggerel, a chugging locomotive powering her progress. *We did it, we did it—*

Her thoughts coalesced. *I put us together, and we put the Engine of Creation together, and now nothing can break us apart. Nothing can break us apart. Nothing can break us apart. . . .*

Rafe and Magdalena followed in Beka's wake. Magdalena had the

base of the Engine cradled in her arms, the long staff of the cane jut-
ting out into the air. For once she could actually have used that cane;
she was barely keeping up with Beka and Rafe, hobbling along as if
her feet were chained.

Beka didn't notice that her mother was in pain, or if she did
notice, she didn't care. What mattered was that she was *there*, finally.
With Beka. With her children. That's what was important. Magdalena wasn't concerned about her own condition, either. It didn't
feel to her as if she was having trouble walking. It didn't feel like she
was walking at all. It was more like she was being pushed, like the
Engine was taking her where she needed to go. Magdalena also failed
to notice the intense chill that radiated from the Engine into her
arm, and the subtle crackle of distorted space surrounding it.

One thing she did notice, however, was the impromptu appearance of her old friend Estrella Alejandro. Magdalena first became
aware of her presence soon after leaving hydroponics. What started
as an annoying flicker of color in the far corner of her peripheral
vision manifested itself into the proud step of her onetime mentor,
now effortlessly keeping pace alongside her.

Estrella looked exactly as Magdalena last saw her, as if she'd been
plucked straight from her memory: long black hair, piercing eyes, a
smile that was more a dare than a sign of amusement.

"What are you doing here? I . . . I killed you," said Magdalena.

"Why, yes, I believe you did," said Estrella. "In fact, I'm sure of it.
I mean, I was there at the time, right? Two words, Magpie. Ow-ee."

Her emotions dulled and battered by the brunt of the Engine's
power, Magdalena didn't find the reappearance of a dead person
especially shocking. What disturbed her was that Estrella was never
what you'd call the chatty type, yet, dead, she wouldn't shut up.

"You're going to say I asked you to shoot me. But that's what they
always say, isn't it? 'She was asking for it'?" Estrella's wry voice was
relentless, sometimes just barely a whisper, other times a bullying

shout. The words came faster and faster, tumbling over one another, mixing themselves up only to be somehow reassembled in Magdalena's mind. Estrella talked about the last seconds at the bottom of the crevasse, staring up at a sliver of scalded sky, at Magdalena's face looking back down. All she could think about was how the oval crevice resembled a closing eye, and that Magdalena's head was its pupil, like the Eye of God staring at her. That, and the pain.

"But it all worked out for you, didn't it, Magpie? You succeeded where I failed, and look what you finally have. The Engine of Creation."

"The Engine," echoed Magdalena.

"We both wanted it so badly. Of course we would want the Engine; there were a million reasons to want it. But you and I, we never really asked ourselves the important question: What would we do once we actually got our clever little hands on it? Are you going to study it? Put it in a museum? Be honest now—much as you respect the universe's antiquities, deep down the quest for the Engine is something entirely selfish. It's about completion. Validation. And that's a one-player game.

"Look at yourself. You've sacrificed everything for that relic. Love. Family. Motherhood. And for what? So you can hang it on a wall? You can't sell it; it's worth more than anybody in the universe could afford to pay. It's so valuable that it's all but worthless."

A dry cackle escaped Estrella's lips. "Funny about the cane. Ol' Ignatius had no idea there was a piece of the Runes attached."

Neither did I, thought Magdalena.

Estrella shrugged. "Can't blame you for that. One hardly expects one's husband to be so resourceful . . . especially not your husband."

Estrella paused. Magdalena glanced ahead at Beka and Rafe to see if they were hearing or seeing any of this. Apparently not, as both were single-mindedly trudging toward Hangar Deck Twelve.

"Aren't you curious about it?" Estrella asked, finally.

What about it? thought Magdalena. There seemed to be no need to speak it aloud.

Estrella laughed, pirouetting in circles around Magdalena. "About what the Engine does. Or more accurately, what it's already doing."

Estrella knew a great deal about the Engine of Creation, as it happened—more than Magdalena herself, which struck Magdalena as odd if Estrella was, as she assumed, a figment of her fevered imagination. Estrella kept up an extended commentary on the history of each piece, from the moment the Vedrans found them to the moment the pieces reached the *Andromeda*. She knew every hand they touched, where they'd been taken, and the places they'd rested secretly for hundreds of centuries. She assured Magdalena that the Engine wasn't as great as any of the legends portrayed it, nor was it as great as either of them had dreamed.

In fact, it was greater.

According to Estrella, the Great Sage Rochinda herself unearthed the ancient artifacts at a dig in the Tarn-Vedran wasteland of Uyteel. It was she who named the relics the Runes.

The Great Sage knew the Runes were not merely decorative; they were technology, a technology that predated the Vedrans. Rochinda is celebrated as the discoverer of Slipstream drive, but she no more discovered it than Tyr's fabled Columbus discovered America. It was already there when she found it. Its creators no longer existed—or, at least, they didn't exist in the normal definition of the term. They'd moved beyond anything so low tech as the physical plane. These entities had become part of the very fabric of the galaxies themselves.

"I think the Engine is what made their transition possible," said Estrella. "A sort of pass-go-and-collect-the-next-level-of-existence card. But then again, they knew how to use it."

Still, one doesn't get to be called the Great Sage for nothing. Rochinda was wise enough to see that the Runes were too powerful, too advanced even for the Vedrans. Given a few thousand centuries, perhaps her descendants would be able to take them on. Until then, Rochinda wanted the Runes far away and hard to find.

Rochinda approached her friend and associate, the Teacher Rovona. Rovona took a prototype Slipcraft and crisscrossed the galaxies for 260 years, scattering pieces of the Runes as she went. When she returned to Tarn-Vedra, Rochinda was long dead.

The *Avrexat Vingareth Ot* is Rovona's account of her travels. Problem was, by then few Vedrans remembered who Rovona was, and fewer still believed her story. Her tales were dismissed as fantasy; the Vedran Runes were lost and all but forgotten.

Until now.

Estrella pointed to the Engine. "Say a Silesian chimp wanders across a Slipfighter, keys in the ignition. Maybe the chimp gets it started, maybe she even gets it off the ground—but we all know a chimp can't fly. Eventually, there's gonna be one very bad crash. And, Magpie? In this instance, you would be that chimp."

Just as suddenly as she had appeared, Estrella was gone. And when Rommie materialized in her place, Magdalena thought her imagination was simply thinking up new tricks to play on her. But no, this apparition was solid. The avatar blocked the hallway ahead and effectively brought the procession's forward momentum to an abrupt end.

The repair conduit hadn't been built for humanoids; specifically designed repair 'bots called "skitters," cylindrical and able to move quickly to the top and bottom of the shafts with the aid of an anti-grav field, were far better suited for the environment. Only the legacy of Harper's childhood malnutrition made it possible for him to scoot around inside them, and for Rommie's human interface android, it was a very tight fit indeed.

Rommie summoned a skitter, grabbed on to the 'bot's lower stabilizer arms, and held on as it dropped her a hundred meters. The skitter slowed as it neared Hangar Deck Twelve, and Rommie swung her legs into a maintenance duct that traveled exactly above the corridor Beka was using to reach the hangar. She crawled the short distance to a grate that was mounted in the corridor's ceiling. Rommie would beat the warbot by a few minutes and she hoped that, by doing so, she would make its services redundant.

The Andromeda Ascendant really hated messing herself up, even a little. Scuffing her floor with one of her own boots was enough to immediately marshal the nearest maintenance 'droid. But this was no time for fastidiousness; Rommie brought both fists down on either side of the grate and punched it loose. The grate clattered on the floor below and Andromeda sent a quick message to Dylan: *I'm here.*

She lowered her legs through the opening, then dropped to the ground, several meters ahead of the Fabulous Flying Valentines. Rommie was startled by the approaching group's appearance. Beka's and Rafe's faces were flushed, a sheen of sweat glistening on their foreheads and cheeks. Their hair was matted, their clothing sweated through. They were beginning to show signs of dehydration, and their pulses were hammering on overdrive. There was a physical price to pay for standing so close to the Engine of Creation. The two stood protectively in front of Magdalena, who didn't look so hot either.

The avatar held up a hand. "Beka, stop!"

Beka thought she was seeing another of Rommie's holograms, which so far she'd been waltzing straight through. The last thing she expected was this hologram to reach out an arm and push her on her ass. She stumbled backward; Rafe barely caught her before she hit the deck.

"Listen to me," said Rommie. "That artifact is more dangerous than you realize. It's pulverizing Alpha Centauri, and that's just the beginning."

But Rommie's warning was only so much background noise. All Beka could hear was the overpowering orchestra noise of the Engine, like a fragment from a song she once owned. *"Oh, the power and the passion . . ."* The power and the passion. Power. Passion. The Engine returned Rafe and Magdalena to her life, and the Engine would continue to keep them together. This made it valuable. It was the power. It was the passion.

And right now, Rommie was threatening all of that.

"Beka, listen to me. You're not behaving rationally. Use your common sense," said Rommie. "The Engine is affecting you, all of you. It distorts matter and energy at a primal level."

"We're wasting time," croaked Magdalena, trying to bull her way past the avatar.

"It distorts time, too!" cried Rommie, but no one was listening to her.

Beka expressionlessly approached Rommie to push her out of the way. Rommie swatted her hands away, but Beka abruptly turned and chopped Rommie in the throat. It didn't hurt, as Rommie doesn't feel pain—Harper never could see the point in that particular alarm system beyond stopping children from putting their hand on the stove for a second time. After all, pain invariably happens when it's already too late. But Rommie did feel astonishment, a feeling she communicated to her captain. Dylan's subvocalized response was terse: *Just stop them.*

Beka was relentless. She got Rommie in a headlock, dragging the android's head down until Rommie was bent over double. Rommie picked up a heel and raked it along Beka's shin. Pain flared along Beka's leg but she didn't notice, nor did she release her grip. *Power. Passion.* Rommie grasped Beka's forearm and applied increasing pressure until she was close to snapping through the bone. She hesitated. Rommie was willing to hurt Beka, but only when everything else failed. When Beka didn't react to the mounting pain, Rommie tried another tactic. She encircled the backs of Beka's knees with an arm and, using a combination of leverage and brute strength, swept Beka off her feet.

Beka still wouldn't let go. Rommie toppled on top of her as she fell.

The weight of the android now had Beka pinned. *That wasn't too bad*, thought Rommie. She'd gotten the upper hand and didn't have to break Beka's arm. Then somebody grabbed her from behind, wrapping strong hands around her face and yanking it back. Rafe. He pulled Rommie off of Beka and punched the avatar in the face. He probably did more damage to his knuckles than he did to Rommie, but if he didn't succeed in breaking her nose, he at least succeeded in breaking her stride.

Magdalena only marginally noticed the fight and had only one concern about it: it wasn't ending fast enough. Estrella had been right, Magdalena realized. This was all about her. Everything was always all about her. Her single-minded quest for the Engine was purely personal—it had never involved her husband or her partner or her children, not even now.

Magdalena tried to collect her thoughts, but there were no thoughts. There was only the one thing that had propped her up all these years: naked, selfish ambition. Beka had led them to the hangar bay, and now Magdalena had no further use for her or Rafe. Well, maybe there was one thing Beka could do. . . .

Magdalena helped Beka struggle to her feet. As she did so, she brushed her hand along Beka's pockets. Then she sidestepped the Rommie/Rafe wrestling match and hurried down the corridor, tightly clutching the hangar door access key she had just snatched.

Pickpocketing is just one of those skills one acquires in the treasure-hunting game.

Rommie knew that Magdalena was walking away with the Engine. She also knew that, no matter what, the Engine was her first priority. She planted a foot in Rafe's solar plexus and pushed. *I said, no more Mister Nice Robot.* Rafe flew three-point-seven meters, and landed badly. Rommie was sure he did break something in the process, but

medical triage was a luxury she couldn't afford. First, she had to stop
Magdalena.

Rommie climbed to her feet and was about to go after Magdalena
when something hit her on the head, hard. *That was no fist*, she
thought, if not quite that coherently. Whatever it was, it momentarily stunned her processors. Rommie swiveled around—there was
Beka, breathing heavily, holding the hefty ceiling grate Rommie had
recently punched through. Beka swung it again, and this time Rommie deflected it only inches from her face.

Beka wound up for another swing. She lifted the grate high above
her head, then paused. *What the hell . . . ?*

A rumbling filled the corridor and the floor began to shiver. Metal
and machinery clattered down the hallway with the steady click-
click-click of fullerene treads. Rommie smiled.

The corridor darkened as something blocked the light. Something very big. First there appeared the twin barrel tips of two
heavy-caliber Gauss cannons, and right behind that came the sinister
hulk of Tweedledum. It pulled into the central corridor, then rotated
on its axis, turning to face them. The 'bot's square head stopped
within a few centimeters of the ceiling; it barely cleared the walls on
either side.

For the first time since Rommie had encountered them, Beka and
Rafe displayed an emotion. Fear.

The Andromeda Ascendant delighted in the effect her warbot self
had on people. Ten metric tons of offensive brawn with one sole
purpose: to blow stuff up. Sure, the 'bots had a stealth mode that
rendered them absolutely silent, but she preferred not to use it. The
juggernauts were so much more intimidating without it.

Tweedledum rattled to a stop behind Rommie. Two small tur-
rets mounted above the smoked visor that shielded its sensor array
swiveled in Beka's and Rafe's direction, ready to fire plasma beams
at Andromeda's command. (Since the Tweedles are themselves

Andromeda, it could be said that they fire at their own command, but this would shortchange Andromeda's ability to compartmental-ize. Andromeda prefers not to be shortchanged.)

With a painful squeal, a panel in the warbot's midsection folded down, revealing not another gun, but a comm screen bearing Dylan's face.

"Thanks, Rommie," said Dylan. "I can take it from here." Rommie nodded, squeezed past Tweedledum, and sprinted toward Magdalena and the hangar bay. Beka made a halfhearted attempted to follow, but the Gauss cannons turned on her. Noisily.

"Beka, don't make me shoot you," said Dylan.

Beka stopped. The farther away Magdalena got with the Engine, the more her mind returned. But the Engine's song still resonated, and her desire to maintain her family was still overpowering.

"You won't shoot me," she croaked. Using her voice was like try-ing to play a musical instrument from a lost alien civilization. She cleared her throat and tried again. "You don't have the guts."

"This isn't about guts," said Dylan. "It's about saving lives. An unimaginable number of lives."

"I don't believe you. You just want the Engine for yourself," said Beka. "You can't have it. It's ours. Mine, and Rafe's, and Magdalena's."

Dylan shook his head. "Have you been paying attention at all? If this thing isn't stopped, there will be no you, or Rafe, or Mag-dalena."

Beka's head cleared slowly, like morning fog burning away. She wasn't completely sure of the chain of events that had led her here. She looked at Rafe; he seemed just as lost as she was. What was Dylan talking about? Nobody was going to die.

"Don't be stupid, Dylan. It's the answer to everything. It's what we've been searching for."

"No, it's not," said Dylan. "It's lying to you, Beka. The Engine is controlling you—exaggerating your needs and desires. You have to trust me on this one. Do not go after Magdalena and the Engine. Let Rommie handle it."

Beka desperately pieced together random bits of events, trying to reconstruct what had happened today. She remembered hydroponics, remembered finding the Triangulum Eye. That nagged at her suddenly, the unlikelihood of finding a piece of the Engine of Creation in the rose garden. From there, she couldn't remember much. She knew the Engine had been completed—that was something she'd never be able to forget. She could still feel it, still feel the deep yearning inside. It was in there yet, but less and less overpowering.

Beka glanced at Rafe. *Looks kind of ill*, she thought. He cocked his head in her direction, giving her a silent signal. That barely noticeable smirk was a number thirty-four B, his do-we-make-a-run-for-it-or-what? smile. It was a classic, and it had gotten both of them in plenty of trouble. Beka sized up the warbot and counted the number of barrels pointed in her direction: she and Rafe were outnumbered four to two. Not to mention that the 'bot could probably squash them with a pinkie.

Lastly, Beka looked at Dylan's image on the comm screen. He seemed surprisingly resolute in his determination to vaporize his XO. She knew Dylan. Death threats weren't something he usually faked.

Beka took a deep breath. It felt good, like she hadn't taken one in a while.

Which will it be? she thought. *The Engine of Creation? My family? Or Captain Dylan Hunt?*

That's when Magdalena's little going away present hit zero and detonated, turning the corridor into an incandescence of white light and noise. Beka collapsed to the floor in a quivering mass of firing synapses, and the decision was no longer hers to make.

SEVENTEEN

Gravity sucks, but earthquakes swallow.

—GRAFFITI ON THE BATHROOM WALL
AT THE BROKEN HAMMER SALOON

Forty-six billion three hundred fifty-five million seven hundred twenty-two thousand four hundred nine to one. Those were the odds that Tyr would manage to surprise Trance. Go figure. Trance blamed the Engine; its waves crunched branches of probabilities outright, and had made it hard for her to see clearly. It probably even skewed the odds in Tyr's favor. Or maybe it was just one of those flukes, a forty-six-billion-to-one long shot whose time had come. Either way, it didn't bode well for Trance's plans. Things were dangerous enough without lethal Nietzscheans taking her out of the action.

Trance pushed the fuzzy bottom of her leotard against the

smooth bottom of the hydroponics vat and sat up. She wasn't sure how long she'd been unconscious. One by one she felt her extremities: *Yep, all there.* So the universe hadn't been squished yet. This was encouraging. Trance got to her feet, still a little woozy. Her spiky blond hair was stuck to her forehead, trickles of water fell off her body and dripped into the pond. Fortunately for Trance, a little breathable oxygen (or lack thereof) didn't spell the difference between life or death. Trance had a different relationship with living and dying than most. "Trance, you're still alive?" was an all-too-common refrain among *Andromeda*'s crew. No doubt she'd be hearing that again later, if anyone else lived through the day.

Trance took stock of the situation. Obviously the Engine was no longer in hydroponics, although she could tell it was still on the *Andromeda*. Nor was anyone else in hydroponics. Odds-wise this was a bad sign, although not too worrisome. What was greatly worrisome was the way Destiny was being compressed into a mere two outcomes, which Trance loosely identified as "is" or "isn't." Ideally, the options remain in perfect balance, but that had changed the moment the Engine was fully assembled. Now, the odds were building in favor of "is," in direct proportion to the amount of time remaining before the Engine achieved critical mass.

At the end of the countdown, the rug got pulled out from underneath the universe.

Trance could see that the paradoxically named Engine of Creation was living up to its reputation as a pain in the ass. She wished there had been another way—and had, in fact, considered them all, from hiding the pieces far beyond the reach of any curious Magdalenas to destroying them herself. But as many strings of probabilities as Trance followed, and as many possible futures and alternate histories as she considered, there was always one result: the Engine would be assembled.

Because there were those who wanted the Engine to come

together as badly as Trance wanted it not to. Entities as powerful as Trance and whom Trance would never be able to outsmart. Eventually, they would have gotten the pieces themselves and assembled them in their own image. And that would have been bad.

Of course, the Engine might simply be doing all the work on its own. It was extremely powerful, and the pieces longed for connection. Its yearning is incredibly infectious, and it never took long for the Engine's desire to become the desire of those who possessed it. Just look at Magdalena.

Okay, so it was unavoidable that the Engine would be reconstructed. And reconstruction means activation, and activation means the universe reverts back to one unbearably dense monomolecule of dark matter, ready to spring out all over again in the Great Cosmic Do Over. The chaos and flood of the universe are reined into an atom-sized prison and born anew.

Unless . . .

The alternative was Trance's personal responsibility. If the Engine got put together under her supervision, she might be in a position to affect the end result. She'd be able to encourage the right things at the right time so that the odds tilted toward the light. Away from the Other, from the not-Trance.

The Engine's assembly provided the very means necessary to destroy it.

The first thing Trance had done was get her hands on a piece of the Engine; that way, she would be assured a stake in the action. Before ever hooking up with Beka and the *Eureka Maru*, Trance "stumbled" upon a shipment of death masks freshly raided from the tomb of X U Ling. There she "found" the Triangulum Eye. She'd had it with her ever since, waiting for the pieces to come together, waiting for her chance to act. When Trance got to the *Andromeda Ascendant*, she hid the Eye with the only friends she knew who could keep a secret: the plants.

Then Trance began the task of wrangling the rest of the Engine. Beka and Rafe had been able to help with that. Trance liked having Beka involved—her presence improved the odds immensely. And so far everything had gone according to plan. Until, that is, she paid her unexpected visit to the rose pond.

Trance stepped out of the vat and tried to ascertain what had happened. She ran the possibilities forward; without the facts the results weren't completely reliable, but the leading contender was that Beka, Rafe, and Magdalena had the Engine.

Trance focused on the Valentine scenario, playing it out to its various conclusions. The results weren't exactly encouraging. She looked for opportunities to intervene and hopefully improve the odds. Again, snake eyes. Trance sighed; she'd been absent for too long. She wanted to just smack the stupid Engine with a hammer, but it was physically impossible for her to get within one-point-five meters of it—not that a hammer would accomplish anything anyway.

Trance considered a few Hail Mary scenarios, from the vaporization of whoever had the Engine to letting the Engine succeed and just doing the whole thing over from scratch. The results were predictably depressing.

Trance crossed the garden. She saw blood on the floor and made a quick calculation. It had to belong to Rev Bem or Tyr—probably Rev. She hated to dwell on the past, but that could have been avoided. She wished she could have done more, but now it was mostly up to the players themselves. She didn't kid herself; things didn't look good. But, as Tyr had so recently and so forcefully reminded her, people could surprise you.

Trance headed out of hydroponics, sopping wet, leaving behind a trail of wet footprints. She ran to Command Deck.

Magdalena lurched aboard the *Hypatia*. She leaned against a hanging E-suit to catch her breath. It was no use though; her breath was somewhere on holiday, sitting poolside and flicking cigarette butts at cabana boys. Her right arm was still pulled tight around the Engine. With her free hand she grabbed a handful of necklaces, lifted them over her head, and dropped them on the floor. That felt better; all those trinkets were getting too heavy to carry.

She stumbled into the cockpit and went to drop the Engine of Creation into the copilot's chair. On second thought, she wasn't sure she could do that. Her arm seemed to be frozen solid around the object. A chill radiated from it—most intense in her arm, although she now felt it throughout her whole body. But there was another reason she didn't toss the Engine into the chair: Estrella was sitting there, strapped in and ready to go.

"This is exciting," said Estrella. "Just like the good old days." Magdalena ignored her and plopped into her own seat, initiating the *Hypatia*'s warm-up procedures.

"Whoa, you must really be out of it," said Estrella, waving her thumb toward the airlock. "Or were you planning on making a run for it with the door open?" Magdalena's dull eyes looked at the *Hypatia*'s monitors: Estrella was right, and a warning light was vigorously agreeing with her. Magdalena absentmindedly punched in the appropriate commands, closing the door. This elicited a shout from the direction of the airlock. The monitor displayed a new problem: there was something stuck in the door.

"Magdalena!" cried Rommie. She forced her arms farther into the *Hypatia*, slowly pushing the door back open so she could squeeze inside. "Listen to me before you do anything. The hangar doors are locked, you can't get out."

Rommie squirmed inside and the door slammed shut behind her. She ran to the cockpit, her boots clanging hollowly on the metal floor. Magdalena was plotting a seemingly random course into the nav computer. Rommie leaned across her and tapped in some commands of her own.

The *Hypatia*'s viewscreen flared to life and Dylan appeared on it, the sweeping archways of Command Deck behind him. "Magdalena, I'm not letting you leave my ship with that artifact. I'll take it by force if I have to."

Magdalena was getting tired of all these visitors. It used to be that people didn't just conjure themselves up out of thin air. Used to be they had the decency of at least being visible from a distance before they started shouting at you. If Dylan had something to say, he was going to have to get in line; there were far too many voices clamoring for attention. There was the Engine, mainly—although that wasn't so much a voice as it was an overpowering desire to flee, to escape, to leave everything else behind. Then there was Estrella, and Magdalena far preferred her company to Rommie's or Dylan's. Magdalena would listen to her before she listened to anyone else.

"Oh, please," mocked Estrella. "You never were very good at listening. What did I used to tell you? 'It ain't worth squat if it don't breathe,' right? And how did you take my advice? You started a family and then ditched as soon as it got tough.

"Let me redefine, then. In the end, it ain't worth squat if you don't have love. Yeah, yeah, I know you loved them, once—once loved Ignatius, once loved your children, once loved lots of people. But it never lasts with you. Why is that?"

Magdalena was dimly aware of Rommie's hand on her wrist. The avatar was trying to pry her hand from the Engine.

Estrella had a whole speech prepared, and she wasn't going to be squelched. "You always have to run, don't you?" she asked. "Aren't you tired yet? Aren't you tired of looking out for you and only you? Maybe it's time you looked out for Rebecca, and Rafael. You don't have a lot of chances left, you know."

Estrella pointed to the Engine. "That thing's never going to love you back. And it's never going to make you feel any better about running. It's going to make you run forever. You don't want to run forever, do you?"

Rebecca and Rafael. Magdalena thought it was nice that Beka had Rafe. And it was nice that Beka had a place here on the *Andromeda*. It's good to belong. Magdalena thought Beka would have understood what Estrella was talking about. She would have been stubborn about it at first, but she would have gotten it eventually. Magdalena realized that maybe she, finally, was starting to get it. And she realized that no, she didn't want to run anymore.

Rommie was beginning to hurt her.

"I am tired," said Magdalena. And what was Dylan saying? The Engine was dangerous? Why was he talking about black holes and supernovas? Magdalena looked back toward the copilot's chair. Maybe Estrella could make herself useful and tell her what was going on. But the copilot's chair was empty.

Magdalena did see a face, reflected in the copilot's systems screen. Only, it wasn't Estrella's. It was the face of an attractive woman who looked like she'd caught some hell recently. She looked faded. Sad. Magdalena finally recognized the person. It was herself.

Magdalena sagged. She felt devastatingly lonely. There was no Estrella. Estrella was still very dead; Magdalena had only dreamed her. Maybe it was her mind's way of getting her to pay attention to something she'd neglected: her heart.

And it was right. She didn't want this to be about just her anymore. She didn't want to run.

"You can let go, Rommie," said Magdalena, sounding quite lucid. "Dylan, I understand what you're saying." Slowly, Rommie released her. Magdalena turned to her and said, clearly, "I'll give you the Engine."

Magdalena stood up and looked down at the Engine of Creation. It didn't seem so incredible anymore. It was just another object, one more lifeless thing in a universe of lifeless things. It would never breathe. It would never love.

She followed Rommie toward the airlock and opened the door for her. Rommie stepped out, got one foot onto the deck. Magdalena moved quickly. She pushed Rommie from behind, sending the avatar sprawling, then immediately closed the door. Rommie was fast, but not fast enough. Magdalena could hear her fists pounding on the *Hypatia*'s exterior, just as the door finally settled home.

Magdalena returned to the cockpit. She fed Beka's access key into the computer, and engaged the *Hypatia*'s engines.

Rommie was broadcasting what she was seeing onto the Command Deck viewscreen. Right now, that was a bouncing view of Hangar Deck Twelve as Rommie raced toward the *Hypatia*.

Harper watched the scene with one eye while monitoring the black hole and soon-to-be supernovas with the other. To his chagrin, the black hole and its sidekick quasar had doubled in size, while the system's suns had become ridiculously unstable. "Guys? This is not looking good."

"There's got to be some way to reverse the Engine's effects," said Dylan.

"Ever the optimist," said Harper. "I know I'm a genius and all, but even a genius needs more than five minutes to think up a plan to counteract the single most powerful object in the universe."

"Where's Tyr Anasazi when you need him?" joked Dylan, grimly. He knew perfectly well that Tyr was immobilized by Magog paralytic poison, and that the Nietzschean was surely feeling twice as frustrated and impotent right now as Dylan was himself. He looked at Rev Bem, Tyr's inadvertent assailant. Already the gashes in the monk's face were less obvious, thanks to a bevy of nanobots stitching the skin back together from the inside.

Rev knew what the captain was going to say next. "I'm sorry, Dylan. I'm afraid I have no suggestions. Only prayers."

These were not the responses Dylan had been hoping for. He needed Plan B, in case Rommie didn't get to the Engine in time. He *always* had a Plan B. Except now. Now, he didn't even have a Plan A. *It's not like you come across the reset button for the universe every day.*

"We have to destroy that damn Engine," said Dylan. "I'm taking suggestions." Assuming they get their hands on it in the first place. *Scratch that*, thought Dylan. *We will get it.*

"We could try tossing it into the AP reactor," mused Harper. "Or I could strap it to a Nova bomb. I mean, I could think up a million big explosions, but they're gonna take time."

"I can help."

The sound of Trance's voice startled Dylan. He turned to find her entering Command—still dripping, her leotard soaked through.

"What happened to you?" asked Harper.

"I got wet," said Trance. Her voice sounded stronger and more assured than usual. She pointed to the black hole Harper was studying and said definitively, "That doesn't look good. We have to stop it."

All heads turned to look at her. She wasn't bothering covering up what she knew anymore. She couldn't afford to.

Trance studied the beings on Command Deck. She could see the visible cords of connection between them: Dylan's affection for Harper, Rev Bem's respect for Dylan, Harper's growing awe of Rev. She'd spent so long thinking of them as pets; now, she was going to have to think of them as colleagues. She noticed the cuts on Rev's face and her eyes widened in understanding. Following the backward tangents of probabilities, she could replay what had happened in hydroponics. It made her face ache.

Rev Bem now knew his suspicions about Trance Gemini had been valid, but it no longer made a difference. She was more than she seemed, but he still had no idea who or what she was. All he could do was go with what he felt. And he felt that Trance was a good person, and that her motives were good ones.

Dylan didn't hesitate for a moment. "Tell me how to stop the Engine." He couldn't worry now about why Trance knew what she did; she was helping, and that was all that mattered.

"Well, I can't get all sciency about it, but if you threw the Engine into the black hole, that would probably work."

"Probably?" asked Dylan.

"*Very* probably," said Trance, coming to stand next to him.

Harper interrupted. "I was going to suggest that next. Honest."

Dylan ignored him and spoke aloud to the ship. "Andromeda? Did you hear that?"

"Yes," said the AI, appearing on the viewscreen. "My calculations support the likelihood that once the Engine's gone, there will be no power to sustain the environmental effects. But predicting how the Engine will respond to the black hole is impossible. I can't guarantee that it would in fact be destroyed."

An Andromeda hologram appeared on deck and announced: "Report from the hangar bay. Magdalena's beginning launch procedures. I'm almost there."

Dylan watched the avatar's progress on the viewscreen. She'd reached the *Hypatia* just as the doors were closing. He was relieved to see that Rommie was able to bull her way through. *Not a minute too soon.*

"I need to talk to Magdalena," said Dylan. "Activate her communications console as soon as you get in."

Dylan hoped he could somehow convince Magdalena to cooperate. But after feeling the Engine's effects firsthand, he doubted that a simple argument would do the trick. He turned to Trance.

"Is there any way to make her listen?" he asked. "Any way to negate the Engine's pull on her mind?"

Trance shook her head. "Besides moving her away from it, no. But it can't hurt to talk. The engine is powerful, but . . ." Trance looked at Rev. "But it can be resisted." Rev almost blushed; Trance was *proud* of him.

"There is one thing," she continued. "Once it reaches maximum power, the alternate probabilities will collapse and we'll no longer have a choice. We don't have much time."

The trio watched intently as Rommie hurried through the cramped corridors of the *Hypatia*. She entered the cockpit and came up alongside Magdalena, who didn't even register her appearance, much less stop her from activating the *Hypatia*'s comm module.

Magdalena appeared on the Command screen. She looked like she'd aged twenty years; her face was puffy and flushed. Rev was shocked by her appearance, but Trance seemed to expect it.

Subvocally, Dylan ordered Rommie to take the Engine if Magdalena didn't come around. By force, if necessary. Then, aloud, he addressed Magdalena, laying out what he hoped was a powerful argument for giving up the Engine. *As if "it's destroying the universe" isn't enough*, he sighed. Dylan explained that the Engine was not only destroying Alpha Centauri, it was killing her as well. Even if she escaped the *Andromeda Ascendant*—which was impossible because the hangar doors were not going to open for her—she wouldn't get very far, since the Engine would inevitably destroy all of creation.

"We only have one chance, Magdalena. The Engine has to be destroyed, and the only way to do that is to launch it into the black hole." *Does she hear what I'm saying? Can't she see that Alpha Centauri is tearing itself apart?* And Alpha Centauri, Dylan knew, was just the appetizer, a footnote to what would eventually unfold.

"Do you even care?" asked Dylan. "About Beka, about Rafe? About anyone?"

That seemed to do it. Magdalena finally responded. She told

Dylan that she understood him. He watched her undo herself from the pilot's chair and stand up.

"Awright!" cheered Harper, who'd been sweating smart bullets.

"It's not over yet," said Dylan. "How are we going to get the Engine into the black hole?"

"I'll take a Slipfighter," offered Rommie's avatar. "I'm right here on Hangar Deck."

"No bendin' way!" shouted Harper, spontaneously.

"I have to agree with Harper," said Dylan. "I can't let you destroy yourself."

Two *Andromeda* holograms, a maria and the AI, spoke up in unison: "That's not me. That's just my avatar. Harper can make me another."

"No, uh-uh, no way," said Harper. "You are my finest creation. Galatea to my Pygmalion, Eliza Doolittle to my Professor Higgins."

"Harper, this is no time to play Earth Trivia."

Harper looked lovingly at his perfect, petite Rommie. His eyes misted. Then the devil on his left shoulder whispered, "*Two words, Seamus: 'D cup.'*" And he told Dylan that whatever he decided was fine with him.

Dylan got an approving nod from Trance and then said, "I wish there were another way."

"It's a small price to pay," said Rommie. She was getting out of the *Hypatia* with Magdalena in step right behind. Dylan wasn't sure exactly what he had said to make Magdalena come to her senses, but he was glad he said it.

As Dylan watched, the image on the viewscreen suddenly spun as Rommie landed face first on the deck. Dylan felt a cold sweat break as Rommie turned to see the *Hypatia*'s door closing on the pale, blank figure of Magdalena.

Rommie was on her feet within seconds, but it was too late. There was absolute silence on Command; the only sound was the *Hypatia*'s engines being activated. Trance was quivering with panic. Finally, Dylan spoke.

"Send the warbot. Bring down her ship."

Andromeda's voice echoed hollowly: "Too late. She had an access key for the hangar door."

Déjà vu, thought Dylan. *Like daughter, like mother . . . unfortunately.* He scrabbled for a viable option. "What if we hit her with a missile once she gets out?"

"That won't work," said Trance, with conviction. She seemed genuinely scared. Dylan looked at the rest of his crew. Rev was quietly chanting a prayer. The color was draining from Harper's face. *Andromeda's* hologram looked at her captain hopefully; she was out of ideas, too.

So this is it, thought Dylan. *This is the end of life as we know it.* Dylan felt sick to his stomach. Worse still, he felt hopeless and helpless; there was nothing more he could do. And then—

"She's hailing us," said Rommie.

Magdalena was smiling, but it was obvious it was under intense effort. "Hey! Why the long face, Captain?"

Dylan simply stared. What do you say to that?

"I know what you're thinking," said Magdalena. "And you're wrong. I'm not making off with the Engine. I'm destroying it."

"She's telling the truth," whispered the hologram, dumbfounded. "She's heading for the black hole."

Magdalena grimaced; she was obviously in pain. But her words were precise. "Suddenly, everything made sense. Call it a moment of clarity. And I got it. You were right: the Engine needs to be destroyed. I'm the one who has to do it."

It took Dylan a moment to absorb what she was saying. Unbelievably, Magdalena Valentine was sacrificing herself. "You don't have to do this, you know," he said. "There are other ways." Although he knew that at this point, there probably weren't.

"No, I do have to do this," said Magdalena. "This piece of junk has consumed my whole life. I'm bound to it. This is the only way this can end. Besides, it's high time I did something for someone aside from my own sorry self."

Dylan could see that Magdalena was struggling against the pull of the Engine, and he could see the toll it was taking.

"I've run away from everyone and everything that matters for so long and so far that I can never come back. I'll never be the mother my children deserve, but maybe I can undo some of the damage I've done. I can at least give them their lives."

Trance watched the display track the *Hypatia* as it plummeted toward the black hole. *Andromeda*'s sensors didn't show it, but Trance knew that as Magdalena approached the event horizon, the Engine's twin potentialities were reversing themselves. The "isn't" was rapidly asserting irrevocable control. She realized she had been tightly gripping Dylan's arm, and slowly removed her sore fingers.

Trance had known pretty much from the beginning that this could cost Magdalena her life, but she frankly never thought the woman capable of outwilling the Engine. She was surprised, for the second time in one day, and she was impressed. And even though this death wasn't a surprise, Trance Gemini mourned for Beka's brave mother.

Magdalena opened her mouth to say something else, but the message froze somewhere between "tell" and "my children."

"She's nearing the event horizon," announced Andromeda. "The gravitational pull is affecting the transmission."

In fits and starts, the rest of Magdalena's message came through. "Tell Rebecca and Rafael they're the best kids a mother could ever have hoped to abandon. Tell them it was the best I could do with what I had. Tell them . . . tell them I'm sorry.

"And Captain Hunt? Tell them I love them."

The message sputtered and flickered out. That was it. The black hole had gobbled her up.

Dylan watched the blip representing Magdalena's ship head for the middle of the yawning singularity. He hoped that Trance was right and that this was all going to work. Considering that Trance wasn't running for cover, he figured it probably would. Magdalena was one tough old broad; you couldn't rear a handful like Beka and not be.

"Any idea what's going to happen when the Engine hits the event horizon?" asked Dylan.

Harper shrugged. "Fireworks?"

"I suspect that's an understatement," said Dylan. "Andromeda, would you move us as far from the singularity as you can, as soon as you can?"

"Done, Captain." The ship launched a drone to keep visual contact and steered toward Natal. They'd get a signal lag of a few seconds and a cushion of a few hundred thousand kilometers. Anything was better than nothing.

"It seems to me," offered Rev Bem, "that when balance is restored, there will still be a great deal of excess energy that has to go somewhere."

"Like I said, fireworks," said Harper.

Andromeda's AI appeared on the viewscreen. "She'll be there in three—"

"I want everyone to take up crash positions," said Dylan, tightening his grip on the command console.

"Two—"

Rev shuffled to the nav station and held on. Harper and Trance braced themselves against the monitors.

"One—"

Good luck, Magdalena, thought Dylan.

"Impact."

Nothing happened. Dylan was just deciding that it hadn't worked when Command Deck was bathed in brilliant light. Space surrounding the singularity had ignited, sending waves of purple and green undulating in a corona extended hundreds of thousands of kilometers.

Rev squinted against the glorious incandescence. The colors contained the same shifting spectrum as the orb Trance had hidden in hydroponics—so long ago, it seemed. The black singularity sat unflinchingly in the midst of this chaotic bubble as bolts of energy rocketed across it, disintegrating as they reached its outer edges. The baby quasar was reversing itself, spewing back the gases that had been swirling at its center. It looked like a glowing, billowing anemone. As the fluctuating sphere of dark matter continued to build, the nuclear forces became visible as long writhing strands that reached all the way to the *Andromeda*, ghostly fingers that flailed and thrashed, funneling energy to their tips, where it seared off into space.

It was hideous and powerful and wild and beautiful.

Dylan thought it would swallow everything in its wake but soon it destabilized and blinked out of existence, leaving behind only a glowing residue that quickly dissolved. The corona shuddered and collapsed on itself.

"What did I tell you?" said Harper, smiling. "Firewor—"

Harper spoke too soon. He was cut off by another flash, brighter than the first, a searing white light that preceded a visible, roiling shock wave that exploded from the singularity like thunder. Harper shouted something, but Dylan couldn't hear him over the relentless barrage. Command Deck shuddered as the shock wave passed through it; the console under Dylan's hands felt as if it were going to shake off its moorings. Rev Bem covered his eyes with both arms.

Harper's head and neck whipped back painfully. Trance steadied herself with two fingers, prepared to make a bigger effort the moment anyone noticed her . . .

Either the black hole is destroying itself, thought Dylan, *or it didn't work, and I'm watching the universe die.*

It was almost intolerable, like standing at the bottom of a mountain while an avalanche rained down on him. Dylan clenched his eyes shut to blot out some of the sensation, but even with his eyes closed it was like staring directly at a sun. Sparks exploded from the viewscreen. Dylan felt them burn his hands and face, heard them sizzle and pop in his ears. Acrid smoke filled the air.

Tyr, laid out on an exam table on Med Deck, watched impotently as anything that wasn't nailed down toppled and fell to the floor. He came dangerously close to toppling himself, as waves of turbulence shifted his weight halfway over the edge of the table. Whatever Rev Bem had given him to counteract his paralysis was taking its sweet time; Tyr was about as flexible as a plank of ebony, unable to call on either his intellect or his brawn to save himself.

He hated it. He was afraid. He was convinced that he was going to die, and that he was going to die on his back, helpless.

And then the shock wave passed. The noise and the tremors receded, and the *Andromeda Ascendant* regained her bearings. On Command Deck, Dylan cautiously pried open an eye. The image of the singularity was gone; all that remained was a large, smoking hole in the viewscreen that shot the occasional spark. Around the edges were faint images of distant, blurred stars.

"Like I was saying," said Harper, in a register an octave or three higher than normal, "fireworks."

Dylan unhinged his hands from the console. The crew appeared shell-shocked, but alive. "Status report," he ordered softly.

Andromeda's hologram appeared, looking as cool and calm as

always. She had the distinct advantage of not needing to tremble uncontrollably or hyperventilate, like some crew members who shall remain nameless.

"Solar activity is rapidly returning to normal," she announced. "The shock wave did hit Natal, and it jolted the HIA and the Drago-Kazov pretty well, but there are no casualties. EM and nuclear forces are back to normal levels."

Harper began to laugh, and then to whoop, and then to loudly applaud. His enthusiasm was infectious and soon Trance had joined in, giggling uncontrollably. The two made a beeline for Dylan in an attempt at a group hug, and promptly knocked him over. And in spite of himself, Dylan cracked a smile.

Reverend Behemial Far Traveler grinned. And for once, the Magog's sinister grimace didn't look remotely sinister. He gazed upward. "Thank you," he mouthed.

Dylan looked up from the pileup on the floor and asked his ship, "What about you? Have you sustained any damage?"

"Well, you perhaps noticed my main viewscreen," said the air, restored to full snark. "Some of my sensors overloaded, there's a little stress damage. But Harper can fix me."

It had been a rough ride, and they had gotten through it. Still, Dylan knew, the cost had been high. Arca. Magdalena. And there was the toll the Engine had taken on their psyches and spirits. They had suffered wounds no healing needle could cure.

But they'd make it. Dylan was sure of that.

EIGHTEEN

I hollowed me out
Where my heart lies
To make room for your dreams
My intentions speak true
Where my heart lies

—"LOVE AND SALVATION,"
ULATEMPA POETESS, CY 9824

It must have been some kind of record; Beka had now been to the *Andromeda*'s hydroponics garden twice in one week. She didn't think she'd been there twice since the *Eureka Maru* hauled the thing out from behind the event horizon two years ago.

Since the Engine of Creation had been destroyed, Beka had kept a pretty low profile. There was a visit to Med Deck, both to check her corpus and to gawk at Tyr's, and some hey-how's-it-going chats with Dylan. But mostly she just holed up on the *Maru*, wrestling with the way Magdalena had come in and out of her life. That's why she was in hydroponics now. She had questions about her mother that only Trance Gemini could answer.

Beka crossed through the atrium—long strides, head high. She didn't feel the sense of dread some of the others felt when approaching the rose garden. But then, Beka had a tendency to live each day like it was her last anyway. Anguished hand-wringing was never her long suit.

Minus the tsunami presence of the Engine, the garden had returned pretty much to normal dull. Trance knelt over the vat with her back to Beka. She was reseeding.

Beka coughed theatrically to get Trance's attention. "Hi, Beka," said Trance, without looking up. She had, of course, been expecting this. She got up and sat on the nearby bench, motioned for Beka to sit next to her. "Sit. Take a loaf off."

"It's not . . . never mind." Beka shook her head. Was there ever a point in correcting Trance's malapropisms? "We've known each other a long time, right?" continued Beka, sitting down. "We're shipmates."

"Of course."

Beka cast around for the proper words. "If I promise not to get into what's-the-meaning-of-life and who-are-you-really, can I ask you one question about this whole Engine of Creation thing?" Trance looked at her squarely, and bobbed her head. Beka took a deep breath, then asked: "Did you know Magdalena was going to die?"

Because if Beka and Trance were ever going to work together again, ever going to be friends again, Beka Valentine had to know that her mother's death wasn't just part of a scheme to benefit Trance's highly personal, entirely mysterious goals. She needed to know that Magdalena's death had been *necessary*.

Trance knew that now wasn't the time for a confused-and-innocent act. Her tail curled and uncurled; she was fidgeting. "I knew someone could die," she said carefully. "*Would* die. But . . . I didn't know who it would be. Not for certain."

"Were you in a position to . . . affect who it was?" asked Beka. Beka was suddenly uncomfortable with the image of a godlike Trance, deciding who lives and who dies.

"No. Definitely not. It's hard to make you see. But you have to believe me, things could have been much worse. You know what the Engine was capable of. If Magdalena hadn't found it, you would have. You know that, right? Or maybe Rafe would have . . . and imagine if there had been no one there to stop it. The thing is . . ." Trance's words trailed off as she followed various possibilities into the future. In fact, meeting her mother was a good thing for Beka, and it boded well for the future—both Beka's, and the *Andromeda's*. Unfortunate as Magdalena's death was, it had a positive effect.

"The thing is," said Trance, cryptically, "everything has to come apart, before it can come together."

Even though Beka didn't exactly know what Trance meant, on a gut level that she couldn't quite articulate it did make sense. Beka felt like she was starting over, somehow, like a lot of old family muck had been washed away and her spirit was cleaner. It felt like a lot of things that had been holding her back weren't there anymore.

Beka watched Trance's twitching tail. The two of them had been through a lot together; hell, Trance had saved her ass on more than a few occasions. Beka wished the mysterious purple girl—if she was really purple, and if she was really a girl—could be a little more forthcoming, but then, we all had our flaws. Trance hadn't steered her wrong yet, and it didn't feel to Beka like she was doing so now.

Yes, she lost a mother. But it was a mother she never had to begin with, right? Magdalena had a choice, and she made it. Beka could respect that, even if she didn't agree with it. *How many yard apes have you raised your own self, Miss Fear-of-Commitment Valentine?* she chided herself. Sure, she would have loved to have memories of a pie-baking, apron-wearing, forehead-kissing mommy. Who wouldn't?

But she was finding it hard to grieve over a person she never knew, and a family that never was. More than anything, she mourned a relationship that had never been.

Finally, Beka said, "Maybe you're right. Maybe old connections have to be broken, so that we can form new, better ones."

Trance put a comforting hand on her shoulder. Trance really did care for the *Andromeda*'s crew—Beka, especially. They were silly at times, and particularly adept at getting themselves into trouble, but she found this endearing more than anything else. She liked to think of it as a two-win street, to use her own phrase. She looked out for them, and they helped her.

They just didn't always know it.

"You should be proud of her," said Trance. "What she did was incredibly difficult."

"I am," said Beka. And she meant it.

Dylan leaned casually against the arched entryway of Command Deck. The collar of his uniform was unbuttoned, his sleeves were rolled up, and he had recently told Rommie to, in effect, hold his calls. He needed some time to relax, and any imminent catastrophes were just going to have to reschedule themselves to occur at a date more convenient to his calendar.

It had been two days since the Engine of Creation—or Engine of Destruction, as he called it—cascaded into a black hole, and Dylan was keeping the *Andromeda* in an easy orbit around Alpha Centauri in case there were any Engine aftereffects, and to monitor the Drago-Kazov exodus. Harper and a posse of skitters would need time to fix a toasted viewscreen and some overloaded sensors, and then—vacation. Dylan and the crew were due for some well-deserved R&R. Maybe he'd bring his guitar. . . .

Rev Bem followed Tyr onto Command, apologizing profusely, for perhaps the hundredth time, for having paralyzed him. Tyr kept walking, mutely refusing the monk's amends. The whole incident was an embarrassment to the Nietzschean. It was one thing to be bested by an enemy, another entirely to be felled by friendly fire and then put on display. The crew continually failed to remember that while he couldn't move, Tyr could still see and hear. And while he could tolerate their "friendly" visits to Med Deck, he could *not* tolerate Trance's giggles, Beka's pointing fingers, and Harper's clownish pantomimes.

Even Dylan was teasing Tyr about the experience; such golden opportunities to needle the *ubermensch* Weapons Officer came along so rarely. But, being Dylan, he went about it with a studied veil of sincere curiosity. "What if you needed to sneeze?" he would ask. "What if you had an itch?"

Tyr clenched his jaw and snarled, "Why don't you ask Rev Bem to help you find out?"

Dylan let it go when he saw that the discussion was making Rev uncomfortable. By now the cuts on Rev's face were healed, but light brown scars still ran along both of his cheeks. Those would disappear eventually, and Rev didn't seem to mind them. If anything, he wore them like a badge. He had proved to himself that biology was *not* destiny, and that a Magog could determine his own path—even a path as demanding as the Way.

Because as forcefully as the Reverend Behemial had made his argument to Lord Parchman that your fate was not predetermined by your DNA, the truth was that in moments of weakness, Rev himself feared it wasn't true. But he had been tested, and he had passed, and for that he was grateful.

Rev Bem had, of course, confronted Trance about the Engine of Creation. But the moment the Vedran artifact was destroyed, Trance reverted to her usual happy-go-lucky self, and all the events surrounding the Engine seemed forgotten. She always managed to wriggle out of his questions like a Than grub out of a redbird's beak.

Rev wasn't fooled, but it was never his style to force people. He would just continue to do what he always did—watch and listen. Magog live a very long time, and Rev Bem was very, very patient.

"Chutak, the slave, has been returned to Natal," said Rev, changing the subject. "He was reunited with his family."

Tyr snorted. "The human victory on Natal smells like bad meat on a hot day. The Drago-Kazov allowed themselves to be beaten, and that's not Nietzschean behavior."

Personally, Dylan didn't care how the Dragans were beaten; they had packed up and left, and that was all that concerned him. That, and the fact he had a new addition to the Commonwealth: the Freedmen System of Alpha Centauri.

Dylan shrugged. "The HIA have reports of Dragans sabotaging their own bases. I imagine Rasputin worked up a plan to save his hide and his career at the expense of his troops." Dylan smiled at Tyr. "*That's* Nietzschean behavior."

Tyr smiled. His report detailing Rasputin Genovese's visit to the *Andromeda Ascendant* and his conduct in the Rebellion of Alpha Centauri was speeding on its way to the Drago-Kazov High Council. Admiral Rasputin will not be an admiral much longer. Indeed, he will probably not be alive much longer.

Revenge from a distance. That's Nietzschean behavior, too.

Currently, the human settlements of Alpha Centauri were taking part in a system-wide bacchanal of celebration. Dylan had been repeatedly invited as a guest of honor but repeatedly declined; he was just too exhausted. All he wanted was to lie down someplace dark and not move for a week. Even Harper, usually a big fan of bacchanalia, bowed out. Even when Pac Peterson radioed to invite him to an installation ceremony where they'd be erecting a statue of Seamus Zelazny Harper, he declined. At first Dylan thought it was the after-effects of the Engine on Harper's brain, but from the way Harper quietly deflected his questions, he realized the young man was still in mourning for Arca. He left him to his thoughts.

It looked like a bomb had recently exploded in the machine shop. That wasn't unusual, though, partly because Harper felt comfortable in a mess and partly because, well, things did explode here. Not all of Harper's inventions are winners; just ask Tyr. Rommie sat patiently as Harper addressed the damage a face-plant on the Hangar Deck had done to the avatar's optical sensors.

"Is it soup yet? I'm not getting any younger, you know," Rommie said loudly. Okay, maybe "patient" isn't exactly the right word.

"You're not getting any older, either, Rom Doll," said Harper, examining a circuit in her left eyeball. He pulled the eyelid up as far as it would go: "One more adjustment, then we're done. I'll need a micro driver, though."

Harper moved to his workbench, a clutter of disused parts, half-drawn schematics, empty cans of Sparky Cola, and other assorted flotsam. Most observers assumed everything was scattered around randomly, but this wasn't really the case. Harper knew the terrain upside-down and blindfolded; everything was where it needed to be for him to find it. This controlled confusion was something he'd learned back on Earth. The best way to stash his parts, he found, was out in the open, where the Dragan overseers would just assume it was a bunch of junk.

Harper reached for the micro driver, but the first thing his hand touched was a chain with a circle of metal hanging from it. Arca's dog tag. He ran his fingers over her name, felt the indentation of each letter. He turned the medallion over and his eyes began to sting. There was the small area where he had laser-etched the couplet "Z + A" and, underneath it, a new carving: "R.I.P."

"Bored! Very bored," called Rommie. Harper tucked the dog tag

into his pocket, and patted his eyes with the back of his hand to make
sure they weren't wet.

"I knew it," said Beka. There was no sign of Rafe on the *Andromeda*,
so Beka crept aboard the *Maru*. Rafe was there, rifling through her
ancient music collection. What was left of it that he hadn't already
stolen, that is. She caught him by surprise, as she had intended, and
for an awkward moment he tried to make it look like the Clash CD
in his hand had landed there by accident.

Secretly, Beka's heart sank. If Rafe was stocking up on her music,
it meant he was about to make an unannounced and hasty exit. She
had hoped . . . well, she wasn't sure what she hoped. Maybe it was the
aftereffects of the Engine of Creation and its rather intense idea of
family, or maybe it was the fun they had together on the *Eureka
Maru*. Either way, her brother was suddenly terribly important to
Beka. "Going somewhere with those?" she asked.

Rafe's features morphed into a hurt pout. "Why are you always
accusing me of stealing your discs?" said Rafe.

"Because you always *are* stealing my discs."

"Huh. I do, don't I?" said Rafe, as if realizing it for the first time.
"I suppose I should come clean. I was going to take off."

Yup, Rafe was getting that familiar itch. He needed to be where
the action was. And right now, despite a good run, life on the
Andromeda had turned practically bucolic. Bucolic gave him hives.

Beka's spirits took a nosedive. Some things never change.

"The Pyrian Compass. Ring any bells, Booster Rocket?"

Beka crossed her arms, noncommittal. "I've heard some things."

"I *know* some things," said Rafe. "I met this Nightsider, see, a
made man with the Krrendar Tong, and he knew this guy who knew
another guy . . ."

Beka cut him off with a dismissive wave. "I get the picture." She
turned and started to walk away. "Good luck, yadda yadda, whatever."

Rafe ran after her. "You don't understand. I want you to come with me. Partners."

Beka stopped and stared. Rafe had a wide smile on his face—a new smile, one she didn't recognize.

She mentally ran through the list, trying to put a number to it, but she couldn't identify it. Unlike his other smiles, this one seemed . . . genuine.

"I don't do partners," she said.

"First time for everything." He shrugged.

Beka looked at her brother. Her unreliable, cocksure, infuriating only living relative. Her flesh and blood. "Are we gonna get any money out of it this time?"

Rafe laughed. She was hooked. "We can't *not* make money. The only problem is how to split it. See, if we were partners, I'd say fifty-fifty. But if we're not partners . . ."

Beka placed a hand on her hip and shifted her weight. "If we're not partners, you can pay for my piloting skills just like everyone else."

"Fifty-fifty's good."

Beka brushed by Rafe and patted him on the cheek. She sauntered toward the cockpit, paused, and looked back over her shoulder: "So, partner. Are we leaving, or what?"

A baritone voice boomed through the airlock: "Do I have a vote?"

It was Dylan. Beka looked up at the towering High Guard officer filling her airlock door and flinched. "Hey, Captain. I was just about to report to you. Sir."

"Don't try to butter me up with military talk. It doesn't suit you."

"No, it doesn't, does it?"

Beka looked from Rafe to Dylan, from Dylan to Rafe. Is this what it came down to? Choosing between adventure and duty, between spontaneity and responsibility? Beka *hated* structure, and hierarchy, and answering to anyone other than herself. But at the same time,

Dylan had become important to her. His mission to restore the Commonwealth mattered. And if she was going to be on his team, she was going to have to play by his rules. *Suck it up, Rebecca. You know what you have to do.*

"I was going to ask your permission to take off for a while—officially, like I sort of forgot to do before. But I changed my mind. I think I'll stay here. After all, we've got worlds to save and stuff, and you rely on your XO. As well as, um, trust and depend on her."

She just looked at him, her expression earnest. Dylan knew how it tore chunks out of Beka's hide to apologize, or to back down, or to ask anyone for anything. Coming from her, "I changed my mind" was an abject surrender. He felt an unexpected surge of warmth for this strong, independent, and deeply wounded woman. He saw the childlike way she looked at her rediscovered sibling, and he saw the disappointment that Rafe was doing such a manful (if not entirely successful) job of covering. And then he grinned.

"We just saved the universe," declared Dylan Hunt. "I think you deserve some shore leave. Both of you."

Beka stammered a refusal, but Dylan cut her off. "That's an order, Captain Valentine. Get out of here— just, try not to get into too much trouble, okay?"

Beka and Rafe glanced at each other and broke into matching renditions of number fifty-two, the yeah-right-like-that'll-happen grin. They laughed spontaneously and in harmony, and then Dylan joined in, and Beka knew that she was finally with her family. An untraditional, unbiological, and highly unexpected family, for sure. But it was hers.

EPILOGUE · DYLAN

From a million sovereign planets
Scattered through the endless night
Bound by blood and High Guard honor
Hold the line against the night

—"THE MARCH OF THE HIGH GUARD"

Dylan Hunt was thinking about baseball. He loved sports; it was something he got from his father. Basketball was his favorite. But right now, he was thinking about baseball. He remembered when he first saw an actual ball from Earth in the Imperial Museum's collection of Games and Toys. It wasn't solid, as he had thought. It was a tangle of string wound tightly around a nugget of cork. One hundred and twenty-one yards of four-ply blue-gray wool yarn, forty-five yards of three-ply white wool yarn, and fifty-three more yards of three-ply wool yarn—this time blue-gray. That's what it said on the plaque, at any rate, and that's what he went with when he tried to make his own baseball and instruct his schoolmates in the fine art of the hanging curve and the stolen base.

Dylan thought about those threads wound so tightly into that dense globe, and he thought of the threads that held the galaxies together. Strings of gravitational force, strings of electromagnetic force, strings of strong nuclear attraction and weak nuclear force. The Engine of Creation, it seemed to him, was trying to collect all these strings back into itself, back into one great singularity. Dense and compact like a regulation baseball, so that it could, at the time of its choosing, send them back out into the universe in a new Big Bang.

They had stopped the process, for now. But that's not what made Dylan think about the baseball. When he was a boy, he had not only wound himself a baseball, but because he was a boy, he had also torn one apart. The tightly wound yarn exploded out in a tangle that covered half the floor of his bedroom.

So Dylan wondered. If the Vedrans—or the race that came before them, whoever or whatever that might have been—built a machine to pull the strings holding the universe back together . . . did they also build a machine that would tear them apart?

ABOUT THE AUTHORS

ETHLIE ANN VARE was the first writer hired on the television series *Andromeda*. She helped develop the show's characters and universe, penning episodes such as the Gemini Award–nominated "The Pearls That Were His Eyes," and the Prism-honored "It Makes a Lovely Light." She has written for several other shows, including *Earth: Final Conflict*, and is the author of a dozen books, including the award-winning *Mothers of Invention*. She lives in Southern California.

DANIEL MORRIS was born in California. He is currently living in New York as a freelance writer.